D1242003

Payne & Misery

A Christine Sterling Mystery

Catherine Leggitt

Ellechor Publishing House, LLC

Ellechor Publishing House
2431 NW Wessex Terrace, Hillsboro, OR 97124

2011 Ellechor Publishing House Paperback Edition
Payne & Misery / Catherine Leggitt.

ISBN: 9780982624296

Ellechor Publishing House
2431 NW Wessex Terrace
Hillsboro, OR 97124
info@ellechor.org

Printed in the United States of America.

Ellechor
PUBLISHING HOUSE

www.ellechorpublishing.com

Books by Catherine Leggitt

Hurray God! (Compilation)

CHRISTINE STERLING MYSTERY TRILOGY

Payne & Misery

The Dunn Deal

Parrish the Thought

To my three mothers:

Deloris "Pill" Rogers, the mother of my birth, for accepting and believing.

Dessie Williams, the mother of my childhood, my mentor and example.

Zora Jane Harman, my mother-in-law, for keeping the excitement alive.

How blessed am I to stand on such shoulders as I reach for the sky.

Author's Note:

Although I used many actual street names and landmarks from scenic Nevada County, I took frequent liberties with their locations. Mixed with the real names, I also used names birthed solely in my imagination. I ask the readers' kind indulgence and understanding. PAYNE & MISERY is a work of fiction and in no way depicts any actual events or people living or dead. I found my Grass Valley neighbors to be considerate, helpful individuals, and my memories of living there are sweet.

"Why is light given to those in misery, and life to the bitter of soul, to those who long for death that does not come, who search for it more than for hidden treasure, who are filled with gladness and rejoice when they reach the grave? Why is life given to a man whose way is hidden, whom God has hedged in? For sighing comes to me instead of food; my groans pour out like water. What I feared has come upon me; what I dreaded has happened to me. I have no peace, no quietness; I have no rest, but only turmoil."
Job 3:20–26 NIV

"When I pray, coincidences happen, and
when I don't pray, they don't."
William Temple

"We look upon prayer as a means of getting
something for ourselves; the Bible idea of prayer
is that we may get to know God Himself."
Oswald Chambers

"Pain is inevitable but misery is a choice."

1

Chapter One

Dark—the word fit him like a bad guy's black hat—complexion, glasses, expression, knit cap pulled low over his ears, tufts of curls poking out underneath. I concentrated on memorizing his suspicious features as I observed him through the plate glass window of the Humpty-Dumpty Restaurant where my husband Jesse and I often ate brunch after Sunday morning church. The man's lurking worried me.

"Maybe he's an Arab." Not that I'd know an Arab if I bumped into one on the streets. Except for Hispanics, Grass Valley, California, maintained a mostly snow-white population, much like most small towns in the foothills of the Sierra Nevada Mountains.

Around us, flatware scraped stoneware, glasses clinked, voices swelled and ebbed interspersed with occasional laughter swirling through the appetizing breakfast smells, but I couldn't pry my eyes off the shady man in the parking lot. Nevertheless, I would guess Jesse didn't so much as look up from his breakfast when he answered. "Who?"

"Out there." I jabbed a finger toward the culprit.

"Where?"

I let out the anxious breath I'd been holding in and pointed again. "See the man hiding behind that forest green car?"

Jesse frowned as he chewed a few more bites of chili bean omelet. "Honestly, Christine. If he's behind a car, how can I see him?"

"He keeps popping up. There he is! Look, look. Now."

Jesse dutifully followed my pointer and then sustained a long stare before turning his attention back to his food. "Okay, I see him. So?"

"He staked out that car. He's been waiting the whole time we've been here. He paces behind it, trying to stay out of sight. When the driver comes back, he'll jump out and mug her—take her cash and jewelry and who knows what else. Bet he has a gun or a knife in that pocket where his hand is. Watch him."

Jesse rolled his eyes. "Give it up, will you? You're jumping to conclusions again. How do you know a woman drives that car? Even if there is a man driver, maybe he's in a hurry to get home and his wife is taking too long in the restroom."

"Then why doesn't he unlock the car and get in?"

Jesse stopped chewing and blinked. *Ha! I got him there.* I went back to studying the perpetrator, in case I got called on to identify him in a line-up.

Jesse's delayed answer mumbled out between chews. "Maybe his wife has the car keys."

After being married to this man for thirty-five years, I should expect Jesse's reaction to my gift of observation. He never took it seriously. "You're going to be sorry when you read in tomorrow's paper that some poor woman got murdered in the Humpty-Dumpty parking lot while you gobbled down a chili omelet."

Jesse didn't look up, just harrumphed and kept on eating.

I returned to surveillance, thankful for last year's laser surgery, which had given my vision razor-edge clarity. The man stood in the shadow of an overhanging oak, but from the direction of his head, I could tell his eyes remained fixed on the front door of the restaurant. My stomach knotted into a pretzel. Danger! I narrowed my eyes. Would Jesse run out to save the woman when the man attacked her? Jesse, my hero, the love of my life. I'd be right behind him, swinging my heavy purse.

Just then, a woman in a leopard-print Spandex dress exited the restaurant and minced across the parking lot toward the man. I held my breath and then whispered, "Jesse!"

Neither of us moved while the woman's rectangular bag flopped from side to side on its thin strap in rhythm with her swaying hips. Like a lamb to the slaughter, she sauntered closer to her fate without a trace of fear in her walk.

A gasp escaped my lips when the dark-complexioned man popped from the shadows directly in front of his victim. After a short verbal exchange, the woman opened the door of the green sedan and slid in. The mysterious villain hurried to the other side and settled in the passenger seat. Back-up lights flickered. The automobile reversed out of the parking space and sped away.

Without so much as a punch or a yell. He didn't even grab her bag.

I leveled my gaze at Jesse and blinked.

He opened his mouth.

I held up one hand. "Don't say it."

Instead, he shook his head and grunted again before returning to his omelet.

I gulped coffee and fidgeted with my napkin. "He *did* look suspicious. You can't deny that."

Jesse buttered his biscuit, took a big bite, and chewed. I felt the lecture building in his brain like a sudden summer thunderstorm. He stared at me with a curious expression—as if I'd grown a second head—swiped his mouth with his napkin and sighed. "You never give up, do you? There's something sinister happening everywhere we go. Face it, Chris. This is an ordinary small town in northern California. Good people live here. Bad things don't happen. That's why we retired here. Remember? Extremely low crime rate. But you insist on seeing evil everywhere we go. You won't stop snooping into other people's affairs. Looking for ..." His shoulders sagged and he waggled his head once more. "If it wasn't so sad, it would be funny."

"Funny? What would?" *Do I dare ask?*

"Your imagination." He leaned forward and pointed his fork in my face. "Someday, that wild imagination of yours is going to get you into real trouble."

2

Chapter Two

"Singin' joy to the world …"

Even as I listened to the nonsensical bullfrog song, I felt its inability to lighten my brooding thoughts. With a sigh, I scrubbed the guest room tub with more gusto. I never got that song anyway. What does a bullfrog know about making wine?

Using the back of my hand, I pushed a clump of hair off my sweaty forehead before reaching for the Bose system to click off the oldies station. Then I stood and stretched.

Joy? I sure wasn't feeling it. Instead, I entertained a particularly bad mood—one I'd nurtured layer by layer since Sunday brunch at the Humpty-Dumpty. By midweek, it had taken on a life of its own, like a giant out-of-control snowball careening down a steep hill. Fed by festering resentment over Jesse's new hobby, our short disagreement about the woman who might have gotten mugged in the parking lot lengthened into days of silence. I felt unappreciated and unloved. Jesse ignored me, spending his time riding Ranger, his jet-black Morgan stallion, and preparing his gear for the upcoming weekend shooting match. His preoccupation irritated me like a burr poking in my sock.

I found no comfort in the fact that up to now my life had been relatively blessed. What did I know about real suffering—the physical kind—living fifty-five years with relatively good health and prosperity? Never had a major illness or operation, always had enough money to do what we wanted. But heartache, relationship stuff—I'd had enough of that. No more. No, thank you. I glanced heavenward. Deliver me from trying to understand men—my husband in particular. I clenched my jaw. *How could Jesse go away again?* He'd already been gone two out of four weekends this month. He'd been so excited he hardly slept last night. He wouldn't even miss me. Probably never did.

Hunching over the tub had produced a back kink. I pressed it hard with the tips of my fingers while I stretched. Oh, great! Now I had chronic back pain too, just like those biddies at church meetings who try to outdo each other with complaints about their health. On the positive side, I'd now have something to commiserate with them about.

Just then, a flicker of movement caught my eye as the back door of the house down the hill swung open with enough force to bounce it against the doorframe. I blinked out the window, feeling my forehead wrinkle.

Directly down our hill, a gray house squatted on the landscape like a homeless person on a city street. An empty house, so far as I knew. I'd seen lights in the windows at night, which I assumed must be on a timer. But during the two years we'd lived here, I'd never seen any kind of movement there.

Until now.

I climbed into the tub where I'd previously discovered the best observation post for spying on the offensive house. To achieve maximum viewing, I stood on tiptoes in the middle, hands braced on the windowsill above the tub, straining for a sight or a sound—assuming I could hear anything that far away through double-pane windows.

From the open doorway, a man in a dark ball cap and barn-red jacket edged out. When he stood and scanned the backyard, the man looked thin as a snake, his shoulders curved over a concave chest.

Who is that? And what's he up to? I pressed my face into the glass to watch the man bend over something he attempted to wrestle free. When he stepped back to appraise his progress, I saw a box wedged in the doorway. A box that size would never fit through the doorframe, but he didn't give up, jerking one side before tugging on the other. Several repetitions gained him little, but he persevered until he liberated it at last.

He tugged off his red jacket and flung it onto the porch, and then peered around once more before rolling up his shirtsleeves and tackling the box again. I imagined him grunting as he pushed and dragged it along the stoop to the edge. Next, he shuffled around the corner, disappearing from view.

I stared at the box. If only I could conjure up laser power to bore through the cardboard. *What's in there? Drugs? Stolen booty?* What would be so heavy he couldn't lift that box? Given his level of secrecy, it must be something illegal.

But why had he left it unprotected on the porch in full view of nosy neighbors? *Could I be wrong?* Probably a perfectly ordinary explanation would present itself if I watched a little longer.

Before I could shift to a more comfortable position, the man returned, bouncing on a tractor seat. When he reached the stoop, he scooped up the box with the tractor bucket and jounced away. I stretched my neck until it popped, straining for another sight of him. Nothing.

Maybe if I hoisted a roll of aluminum foil in one hand I'd get better reception.

Now that I'd actually seen a living person at that house, I didn't dare move lest I miss something important. My imagination clicked into high gear. Questions battered my brain. What could he be up to? Why hadn't I ever seen him before? What if he was hiding from the law? I shivered. Criminal activity right under my window? What kind of place had Jesse moved me to? Maybe we'd been wrong about the purported low crime rate. What if the Realtor lied? I suspected that possibility, when I read the front-page newspaper article crediting this part of the state with more lawbreakers per capita than any other area in California. Apparently, criminals found the dense tree cover helpful when hiding from the law. Suppose my skinny neighbor turned out to be a convicted child molester? Or an escaped rapist? Or—*shudder*—a murderer? I clicked my tongue. A person should be warned about such things.

Soon Mr. Ball Cap reappeared, bobbing on his tractor seat. Another hefty box rode in the bucket. Chalky instead of cardboard-brown, the shape also distinguished it from the first. I watched until the deck blocked my view.

I maintained my position in the tub until the pain in my toes became unbearable. At my age, a cramp in the foot didn't take long. Maybe it would help if I flexed like a ballerina. Up, down, up, down. But in the down position, the railings on the deck outside blocked my view. That wouldn't do. Standing on a chair might help. Couldn't use my office chair; that one had wheels. Maybe a dining chair.

When I turned to go after one, I heard a faint sound—a grinding like a tired engine sputtering to life. Up on tiptoes, I spied the truck heading down the sloping driveway and out to the street.

Captivated once again, I pressed my face into the window. *What could be in those boxes?* A chill shimmied down my spine as the answer materialized in my imagination: *a body. He's getting rid of a body.* But whose? Someone who hid in that house with him. His wife … or at least his woman. She complained about everything—a real shrew. Wanted out, but he couldn't let her go. She'd run straight to the authorities. This morning, for the millionth time, she yammered about leaving him. Something inside him snapped and he reached for a gun. I cringed, hearing her shrill, mocking laughter. *"What do you think you're doing? Put that thing away before you hurt yourself."*

She grabbed his arm. The struggle escalated; the gun exploded. When the smoke cleared, she lay dead on the floor. He only meant to protect himself, to make her leave him alone. But no one would believe him. Not with his record. He had to get rid of the evidence. All of it. So he cut up the body and packed the pieces in those boxes to be buried in the woods. He'd gone … to town, of course. For bleach to clean away the evidence.

Enveloped in my imagination-cocoon, I didn't notice Molly, my border collie, until she whimpered. When I jerked in her direction, Molly tilted her black-and-white head to one side, chocolate eyes frightened. I patted her silky fur. "Sorry. You're right, of course.

That's a bit far-fetched." Jesse had it right. That stuff only happened in mystery novels. Who did I think I was anyway, Miss Marple? I shook my head. I had too much time to read. Just because I couldn't guess the "perfectly ordinary explanation" for what I'd seen didn't mean there couldn't be one.

I collected my rags and returned to cleaning but kept coming back to peer out the window, the fear in my chest multiplying with each visit. *Maybe I'm having a premonition of coming danger.* I pressed one hand over my palpitating heart. If I were in real danger, would Jesse rescue me? He'd have to. I smiled. That would be nice.

At length, I abandoned all pretense of cleaning and concentrated on surveillance. If only I possessed X-ray vision to penetrate those walls in search of the secrets lurking inside. Maybe I'd even see a female occupant—if she still lived.

The longer I watched the neighbor's house, the more the puzzle gnawed at me. A couple more hours passed without another sign of the white truck. I paced without aim, biting my thumbnails while uneasiness grew.

He must be up to no good.

Blame it on my wild imagination if you must. Obsessive curiosity overtook my better judgment, insisting on immediate action. I would never rest again until I knew if a woman lived inside that house. And if she did, I needed concrete evidence that she was doing just fine, thank you very much, and not at all in need of my assistance.

Only one thing would allay my concern: I must see Mrs. Ball Cap with my own eyes.

3

Chapter Three

"I'm not intruding. Not at all. I'm just a neighbor bearing gifts," I said to Molly as I packed a get-acquainted basket with a few of my best homemade fruit jams nestled in a pile of raffia. I tied a red gingham bow on the handle to complete the appeal. Between the jars, I placed a card with my name and phone number.

"See?" I tipped the basket so Molly could look in. "A lovely gift that would delight anyone." It made a perfect excuse for a visit. After months of watching that house for signs of life, I don't know why I hadn't thought of this before. Of course, I only put the basket together to excuse my snooping, but that didn't bother me a bit.

Well … hardly a bit.

I opened the door for my happy dog. "Come on, Molly. You need a walk."

I swung the basket as I strode toward the gate. "Nothing sneaky in this. I'm just walking my dog and taking a gift to my neighbor's front door."

Why, I practically qualified for sainthood!

By the time I got to the street, I'd changed my mind about going all the way to the front door. Maybe I'd just peek in a few windows. If spotted, I'd say I got lost hunting for the front entrance.

Tramping down the hill onto Percheron Drive, the street connecting mine to his, I changed my mind again.

Oh, for heaven's sake. Make a decision, already. I drew a deep breath. Had I actually sunk to the level of a cowering snoop sneaking through the bushes, peeking in windows to find out what her neighbors were up to?

I shifted the basket from my right arm to the left. *The front door then.*

Dust puffed from beneath my feet as each step drew me closer. I rehearsed what I'd say in case someone answered the door—how to work in questions about the mysterious boxes.

I hesitated where the tar from Percheron Drive jutted into Mustang Hill Road. Did I really need to disturb these outlanders? I didn't want to end up in a box of my own, being transported to the woods in that bucket. Perhaps I should scope out the place first after all.

Usually, I didn't need to put Molly on a leash, even in the city. She obeyed so well, she'd come right back when I called. She trotted ahead, paying no attention to my stops and starts. At the entrance to the neighbor's driveway, she paused, looking back. I understood her signal to me and quickened my step to catch up. Soon we stood together, surveying the neighbor's property.

A steep, curved gravel road made an elbow turn at the bottom into a partially wooded lot. At the side, someone had planted iris bulbs, which had multiplied over time into hundreds of plants. Although splendid during spring, the flowers had long since dried and crumbled. Traces of crinkly leaves and headless stalks remained, towering above the brittle tangle of dry weeds.

Molly's innate need for movement allowed only short inactivity. She expressed her impatience with a whine and trotted ahead, stopping again a few paces past the driveway to look back over one shoulder.

I threw her an apologetic glance before focusing on the house.

A grizzled atmosphere hovered over the property like a funereal tent. Thick curtains covered the windows on the inside, holding in the secrets. Part of the exterior grayness might be due to lack of paint, stripped away by the elements. The remaining gunmetal paint curled in freeform stripes on the fascia board and siding. Shingles dangled off the roof in places. From the street, the house appeared larger, perhaps once grander, than I'd noticed from the back—a tattered old lion stretched in the gloom, waiting to die.

Two disparate garages, like unmatched bookends, anchored the building to the landscape on either side. On the left, the attached garage gaped open, allowing a view of stacked firewood. A paneled door with windows along the top blocked the contents of the detached garage. The secondary building crouched against the hillside, away from the house, as if attempting to hide from nosy neighbors.

Nothing moved. Even the trees possessed a lifeless aspect, more ghosts of trees than real ones. Although the temperature registered in the normal autumn zone, the atmosphere made me shiver.

I whispered, "Let's go, Molly," but my feet didn't move.

Several minutes passed. Molly returned halfway and whined. The tug on my heart intensified. Why did this house conjure thoughts of pain? Chronic, debilitating suffering seeped through the cracks and filled the air like choking smoke. I could almost smell it. Where did that come from? I simply must find out.

Calling Molly, I plunged down the driveway to investigate.

Silence hovered low like a dark storm cloud. When I topped each step, I paused to listen. Not a single bird twittered, even though just up the hill in my yard, flocks chirped autumn songs and gorged seed from my bird feeders. The air hung deadly still. I tensed. Shouldn't there be a dog? Almost everyone out here had a dog.

My feet felt stuck in cement shoes. I gulped, trying to dislodge the large pebble stuck in my throat while I stoked gumption. Molly's yelp jerked me from temporary paralysis. I flattened both hands over my ears to block the piercing sound. "Easy girl. I'm thinking."

Bony fingers yanked open the curtain nearest the door. While I stood transfixed by the sight, a pale gaunt face flashed into view. Before I had time to determine the gender, the heavy curtains sagged back in place and the apparition disappeared.

I definitely didn't imagine that.

With my insides quivering like a Jell-O mold, I raised a shaky finger to the doorbell. The rusted apparatus looked questionable, so I knocked instead. While I counted to a hundred, I shook tremors out of my knees. The door still hadn't budged, so I pounded louder.

A tiny tinge of relief threaded through my tense shoulders. Maybe my intervention would not be required after all.

Then, creaking like a horror movie set piece, the door inched open.

The expanding gap revealed a withered woman of indeterminate age. Haunting eyes peered from dark hollows above sunken cheeks and colorless lips. Her skin reflected a dispirited grayish pallor, similar to the house. Stringy silver-blond hair fell limply from her shoulders to the back.

I forgot my rehearsed opening and stared.

Jesse teased that everyone looked tall to me, but at five feet one and a half inches, I had to look down to gaze into those pallid, gray-blue eyes. She must be shorter than my twelve-year-old granddaughter.

The woman didn't speak, but tilted her head and frowned.

Disheveled hair made me wonder if I'd caught her napping. She didn't attempt to rearrange it, and I couldn't tell if she didn't know or didn't care about her physical state. She held the door with one dirt-smudged hand, revealing unkempt fingernails. An oversized tan sweater and faded black sweatpants draped her skeletal frame. Around her body, an overripe smell hung like an offensive aura.

I swallowed the shock that rose in my throat like an undulating swell of nausea. "Hi. I was out walking the dog today, and when I came to your drive, I thought, um, that I've never met you. I live just up the hill in the log house. We've seen lights on—my husband Jesse and I have. But I've never seen you before. So … I thought I'd stop in to say howdy." I presented my friendliest smile.

The part of the entryway I could see beyond the lady appeared drab and dim. She blinked, her enlarged pupils contracting in the sunlight. To be polite, I paused for her answer, feeling my smile go stale.

After several seconds, the burgeoning silence became unbearable and unplanned words erupted from my lips. "You know, sometimes it's good to know your neighbors … in case you have an emergency.

We live so far out in the country, if something happened and we needed help, someone coming from town would take at least half an hour to get here."

Was she deaf? Maybe she had a mental problem or didn't speak English. Could she be mute? I'd never met a mute person before. Maybe she never went outside because she couldn't speak and didn't want to draw attention to her disability.

When nerves overtake me, babbling flows from my mouth whether I want it to or not. "Or you might call me if you get lonely sometime. I'm lonely often, actually. We're retired and there's not much to do anymore. What I'm trying to say is, you can call anytime."

Still no sound from the lady. *Maybe it's a processing problem. I should wait longer.* I clapped a mental hand over my mouth.

Seconds ticked by before her lips twitched open. I leaned forward. *Wait for it.*

Words breathed out on a whisper. "Which house?"

I pointed. "The log one … on the hill … just up that way from here. You can see it from the back of your house."

Air leaked out in a sad sigh, with words tumbling through. "Up the hill? The big house?"

"Big, did you say? I guess it's big … probably too big for the two of us, anyway. Sure seems that way when I clean. We bought it from the McCarthys. They built the house themselves—did all the labor and everything. Do you know the McCarthys?"

She offered a single nod. "Dogs … lots of dogs." Her voice reminded me of the rustle of leaves in a gentle breeze.

"That's right. The McCarthys bred golden retrievers. That's probably what sold us on their house, actually. Those six silky dogs greeted us every time we visited. Not barking like watchdogs. So graceful. I think they staged it. I always heard music in my head … you know, like in the movies." I stopped short of breaking into song, praying the woman would take no notice of my babbling.

"I had a dog … Baby."

Did she say *Baby*? Did she mean she named her dog *Baby*?

Good thing I didn't have a hearing problem like Jesse or I might not have heard her at all. I stared harder at her face so I wouldn't miss anything that might lend insight. "My name's Christine Sterling." I smiled to encourage her. "What's yours?"

The pale blue eyes narrowed to tiny slits. "Lila … my name is … Lila … Payne." She pronounced it as if hearing her name spoken aloud surprised her.

Lila *Payne*. How fitting.

"Hello." I extended my hand. She didn't move, so I let my hand drop. "It's nice to meet you. I have a dog too. That's Molly." I pointed.

Molly finished smelling the front yard and advanced toward the detached garage with her nose to the ground. In Lila's protracted silence, I called Molly in case Lila wanted to pet her, but she only watched the dog with a strange longing expression. At last, a smidgen of interest.

My faithful sidekick returned to sit at my feet, waiting for direction. "Molly's a good dog. Smart too. The best dog we ever owned." Molly's brown eyes locked on mine. I could almost swear she smiled, so I returned the smile. When I glanced back at Lila, the grin still covered my face. "Maybe you could come to my house one day—to play with her. She'd enjoy that. So would I."

It looked as if the corners of Lila's lips tried to turn up but couldn't. Probably hadn't used those muscles for a long time. Maybe her head would crack open if she achieved an actual smile.

Lila lowered her head and melted into the darkness as if shrinking. Afraid she intended to shut me out, I pushed the door. "Lila—Mrs. Payne—I brought you a gift."

Without comment, she lifted her eyes to the basket.

I thrust my offering toward her. "I made extra jam last summer so I'd have plenty to give away. These are for you. I wrote my name and phone number on the card."

She frowned into the basket. A skirmish seemed to rage inside her head about whether or not to take it, and I guess *not* won. I held the jam out anyway, ignoring the blooming ache in my arm as my muscles fatigued.

Lila's gaze moved from the basket to the dog sitting at attention on the porch.

"You can pet her. She loves that." I demonstrated by reaching for the collar of ivory fur between Molly's ebony head and body. Then I ran my fingers all the way to her soft chest, where she loved to be scratched. To finish off, I gave her several pats between the ears.

At first, I thought Lila would pet the dog. Her bony hand moved off the door and paused. The stretched-out sweater sleeve dropped from her forearm. Four plum bruises about the size of dimes stood out garishly against her alabaster skin. They appeared to be imprints of fingertips, running upward on her arm from the wrist. Beside each, a faded blue-black bruise discolored her arm.

Alarmed, I searched her face. But she appeared as heedless of the exposure as of her overall appearance. She focused her entire attention on the dog. A solitary tear slipped from one eye and slithered down her cheek.

I stepped closer. "It's really okay. She's gentle. She'd never hurt you."

Molly sat beside me, ears poised for instruction.

Lila's anemic blue eyes moved back to the basket and then slowly to my face.

The jars clinked companionably as I lifted the basket toward her. "I want you to have these. I made them myself. There's a peach, a plum, a raspberry, and a blueberry." I fingered each as I mentioned it hoping to lure her to the jewel-like hues sparkling within the jars.

A glower flushed her countenance. "Red."

I didn't know what that meant, but made one final pitch anyway, refreshing my smile to enhance the appeal. "The fruits and vegetables in Nevada County are incredible, don't you think? Much better than we had in southern California. That's where I grew up. I bought the fruit at the farmer's market in Grass Valley—the one they have every Friday night in the summer. Do you ever go to that?"

No response.

"Please take them. You do eat jam, don't you? On toast or biscuits in the morning?"

The glower intensified.

"I know you'll like them. Try them with peanut butter. Jesse eats peanut butter with almost everything." I shrugged. "It's weird, but that's Jesse. Anyway, I brought this jam as a get-acquainted gift. Maybe you'll come eat lunch with me sometime."

Those last words scarcely left my lips when something snapped in her face, almost as if I'd slapped her. She took a giant step backward.

"Just a minute! Mrs. Payne … are you all right? What about your arm? Did you hurt yourself?" I moved to follow her inside, but the door started closing. "Do you need anything? There must be some way I can help you." I craned my neck in an attempt to see inside, standing on tiptoes for a better view. "Are you here all alone?"

The closing halted.

Lila thrust her head into the remaining slit of open doorway. Her terrified eyes darted beyond me. Words burst from her lips in a scream without the volume. "Don't come again! It's not safe!" Then she disappeared and the door banged shut.

Lips tight, I turned and trudged up the driveway, gravel crunching under my feet. At the top, I lingered, squinting back at the house while Molly lagged to sniff clumps of iris stalks.

It's not safe. What does that mean? Not safe for whom? From whom?

The sound of tires on loose rock yanked me from my thoughts, and I spun to see the rickety white pickup veering into the driveway. A spray of pebbles fell at my feet, and an old man's wrinkled face glared through the windshield. Mr. Ball Cap. I offered a greeting smile, but something about his expression checked that before it fully emerged.

Angular features in his face combined with a firm mouth to render his countenance cold and unyielding. Small, steely eyes hid behind thick-rimmed glasses, but I felt the power behind their stare. Reflex sent my hand to cover my mouth, holding in a cry that welled from my chest.

As the driver's side window dropped open, I retreated one hasty step away.

His gravelly voice asked, "You lost?"

I shook my head harder than necessary. "No, no. That is ..." Clapping my hands, I pretended to summon Molly. "We're just ... taking a walk." Molly trotted to my side. I grabbed her and pulled her close.

He scowled at my basket. "We don't need nothin' from you."

In his elevated position, maybe he couldn't hear my knees clapping together like cymbals. I hoped so.

Revving his engine, Mr. Ball Cap slammed the truck into gear and rumbled down the driveway. His macho display of dominance left me coughing his dust.

I waved away the flying dirt cloud and narrowed my eyes to slits. Rather than the deterrent effect he obviously hoped for, that moment a firm commitment to rescue Lila Payne bloomed in my heart.

4

Chapter Four

Lit by the nearly full moon, the pond below our deck rippled under a slight breeze. Lights glowed through the curtains of the gray house beyond the pond, but as far as I could see, not a creature stirred.

What terrible abuse might be happening? Both inhabitants had to be home. I imagined Lila's shrieks as the man with the ball cap beat her; the sickening thud of her frail body hitting the floor, her cries of anguish disregarded. Then he'd drag her to the bedroom and lock the door from the outside so he could gorge himself with double portions of dinner.

I had to help before he killed her. But what could I do? I'd never encountered anything like this situation before. I needed an ally—someone with experience being neighborly. Someone like Zora Jane.

In the world-class-good-neighbor category, Zora Jane Callahan would rank number one. On first-name basis with most of the community, she managed a drop-by visit with each of us from time to time, always on the pretense of delivering a plateful of homemade cookies. The woman must bake every day.

I punched Zora Jane's number into the portable phone and paced while waiting for her answer.

About one and a half laps around the kitchen island, she picked up. "God loves you."

I never knew how to respond to that. "This is Christine Sterling."

"Christine! What a slice of heaven!"

"Listen." I peeked out the window. "I've been watching that gray house across from you ever since we moved here. I always meant to ask you who lives there. I know it sounds hard to believe, but I've never seen anyone go in or out of that house until today."

"The house down the hill?"

"Right. Today I saw a man there and I went down to introduce myself. Do you know them?"

"Well, that's the Paynes' house—Lila and Will Payne—with a 'y' instead of 'i'. I met Lila shortly after they moved in. Took a plate of cookies down. Lila answered. I opened my mouth to welcome her to the neighborhood, but she snatched the cookies out of my hands and closed the door. Didn't get a single word out."

So even the Paynes had been recipients of Zora Jane's cookie ministry. "What did you make of that?"

"Must've been the wrong day for a visit. She has a sweet tooth, though, the poor little thing, 'cause she sure wanted those cookies."

Typical of Zora Jane to spin rudeness in positive terms. "Humph."

"They moved into the neighborhood the year my youngest grandson was born. Todd. That would be … about ten years ago."

"Okay."

"Oh, my word! How could I forget that day? I made those cookies just after I came home from visiting my daughter at the hospital. So ten years ago last spring. Ten and a half years, since it's fall now."

And I thought *I* babbled! I started pacing again. So far I hadn't come close to anything that might help Lila. "Do you know where they came from?"

"The Midwest, I think. A small town in Iowa. Elk something—Elk Field, Elk Farm, Elk Grove. That's it. Elk Grove, Iowa. Just off Interstate 80, west of Des Moines."

"Why did they move all the way out here?"

"I don't know. They don't get visitors often. Least I haven't seen many. Don't think they have family nearby. They do get outside, though. I can't imagine why you've never seen them before."

"Well, I never have."

"You only see the back of their house and from a distance. Our house faces theirs. Maybe that's why."

"Maybe."

"We start conversations whenever we catch them working outside. Ed managed to get a bit out of Will once or twice. They're quite … reticent might be a good word for them."

"Reticent? They're downright reclusive!"

"I'm sure there's a reason for that."

I pressed my back against the wall, afraid the reason wouldn't be a happy one. "Uh-huh."

"Let's see. What else do I know? They used to have a boat. Think they said they took it to Lake Tahoe sometimes. When they got back, we'd see them cleaning it. Don't know what happened to the boat. All of a sudden, it just disappeared."

"How long has it been gone?"

"I don't know, at least a year now."

"Huh." *What possible help could any of this be?*

"Now and then, Lila putters outside. She put in all those irises along the driveway—gloriosa daisies at the front, a small rose garden on the side, Iceland poppies and perennials in the flower boxes—a nice colorful garden. I always wave at her, but she never waves back. Now that I think of it, the flowers have been gone a long time. And I guess I haven't seen her either … maybe for as long as a year."

I straightened. "A year? Same time they got rid of the boat?" Now we were making progress—but what did it mean?

She paused before answering. "Could be."

I hadn't the foggiest notion what to make of the connection.

Light extinguished in one window of the gray house just before another lit up. I smushed my face into the glass but couldn't see figures behind the drapes. I sighed in frustration.

"Whatever made you stop in today, dear?"

I told her what I'd seen from the deck, about the puzzling transportation of the boxes on the tractor. "But the bruises, that's what worries me."

At first, she didn't answer. When she spoke, her voice assumed a tender quality, as if reassuring a frightened child. "You know, dear, sometimes you imagine things are worse than they actually turn out to be. I'm sure there's a simple explanation for what you saw."

I shifted from one foot to the other and expelled a breath. *Why does everyone blame my imagination?* I composed my answer with care, speaking slowly. "She told me not to come anymore. Said it wasn't safe. Why would she say that?"

"I don't know. Maybe she's afraid of strangers. She might be a bit eccentric. You know, some people would rather be left alone."

Did *I* ever understand *that*! It would be so much easier not to suffer relationships. My frequent daydream of the idyllic life in a hilltop monastery with a locked gate wound like wisps of smoke around my head. I closed my eyes. Wish I could shut out the pain of dealing with people as easily as blocking the daylight.

Her question pulled me back to the present. "You still there, Christine?"

Right. Where were we?

I fought the strong urge to isolate. My odd little neighbor needed our help. Despite the possibility that what I saw might not have a sinister cause, a nagging gut feeling demanded me to keep probing. "There's something wrong in that house. I just know it." Of course, I didn't *know* it, but when I staked this claim, some inner authority confirmed it as fact. The vision of Lila's battered arms sent cold shivers skittering down my spine. "Those bruises. Someone restrained her—held her with enough pressure to leave bruises. Or they made her do something she didn't want to. If you turned her forearm over, I'm sure you'd find a thumb mark on the other side."

"Christine—"

Her tone alerted me the imagination lecture would launch next. I hurried on, hoping to persuade her with logic. "Don't bruises usually change color after a few days?"

"I guess so, but—"

"Purple means they're fresh, then. And apparently she's been injured before, because there are black bruises underneath the purple ones."

"But really, Christine. Who would abuse her?"

Inwardly, I stomped my foot. "If only two of them live there, then the husband is the obvious suspect."

"That's a serious accusation. We've never noticed anything to point to that. Not in all these years. Are you sure you're not just … embellishing what you saw?"

If only Zora Jane had been with me today. I expelled a calming breath and changed the subject slightly. "He left this morning in a white pickup. Does he leave every day? Maybe he has a job."

"I haven't paid attention to that. Don't know about a job, though. Back in Iowa, he did something farm-related … something with machinery, I think. But they're retired now. At least, he is. She's much younger, of course."

I tried to justify using the word *younger* on the woman I'd seen, but could imagine nothing short of *less old.* "How much younger, do you think?"

"Wasn't that obvious when you saw them? Must be at least twenty or thirty years between those two."

"So you're saying she might be as young as forty?"

"I guess so."

"Huh!" I never would have pegged her as young as that. I let the word sit in the air until the idea sank in deeper. "Could you come with me tomorrow morning if he goes out? Just to be sure she's okay."

"I'm sure everything's fine—"

"Please!"

"Well, okay." Then, in typical Zora Jane fashion, she added, "Why don't we pray for her too?"

I frowned at the phone, face flushed at the implied reprimand. "Certainly we should pray for her."

Syrup dripped from her tone. "I know you believe in the power of prayer, Christine."

"Of course I do." Sure, I believed in a God out there somewhere. I just wasn't convinced that he cared about the niggling details of my unexceptional life.

"God longs to hear our prayers. He delights in answering his children."

Who's she kidding? "It's just … he never answers me."

"Oh, Christine. He answers. He doesn't always give us what we ask for, because sometimes that would be bad for us."

"Hmm." Memories of unanswered prayers dropped into mind like an oppressive bundle of soggy newspapers. I figured God had better ways to spend his energy than fixing things at our house. Must have been busy helping powerful, important people.

Zora Jane continued. "God knows everything—past, present, and future. He sees the big picture. He knows how things will turn out if we do them our own way. We can trust him, Christine. His way is always best."

Despite the patronizing tone, I knew her heart ached with compassion. But prayer hadn't held a high priority for me in many years. I hadn't been communicating well with anyone, worst of all God. I gritted my teeth. "Pray for her, Zora Jane, please."

Her voice sang through the phone. "Heavenly Father, thank you for laying the Paynes on Christine's heart. You love them far more than we ever could. Help us love them with your love. Please protect them and keep us from doing harm. We pray this in the blessed name of Jesus. Amen." To me she said, "God will make a way."

I thanked her with half my heart, and we arranged that whoever spied Will's pickup leaving first should call the other. I didn't want to encounter that snarling face again unless I absolutely had to. I even felt resistance to praying for God's protection over him. I didn't like Will Payne. Not one bit.

Part of me argued that we shouldn't intervene. After all, Lila Payne never asked for help. In fact, she warned me to stay away. Maybe we should just mind our own business.

A faded, lilac-colored apparition invaded my dreams that night. She floated ahead, hidden by fluid drapes. I raced to catch her. An eerie melody penetrated the night silence like movie background music. She whispered in a singsong voice like quietly rustling leaves. Although I strained to hear, I couldn't catch the words. Who was she? The distance between us precluded definite recognition.

I slogged ahead in that frustrating slow-motion gait of dreams. My mind commanded speed, but my legs wouldn't cooperate. The putt-putt of a motor sounded close. When I glanced back, a dilapidated white pickup followed. I hurried on.

A withered vine blocked my path. I clawed at the brittle plant until I made just enough space to crawl through, then raced on, dodging in and out among huge headless iris stalks as tall as trees. An aged oak materialized; a tree with low, clinging branches that tore at my hair. I pushed through a thicket of bushes with long thorns that cut into my flesh like sharp claws, shredding my shirt. Blood seeped from the scratches, but I didn't stop. The white truck closed in, and the lilac lady sprinted far ahead.

The urgency to catch up soon gave way to an even greater terror that billowed around me like my mother's sheets pinned to a clothesline on a windy day. The gossamer lady disappeared through a dark hole. I squeezed in after her and found myself in an expansive black tunnel—so dark I feared I might never see light at the end. "It's not safe! Not safe! Not safe!" echoed through the air. I couldn't see where the words came from.

The pickup's engine grew louder.

A heavy feeling of evil engulfed the darkness. Spiders and snakes, maybe. I squinted into darkness as thick as chocolate pudding. Patting along the walls, I stumbled at last through the end of the tunnel, only to hear the pickup's groaning engine even closer.

An enormous gray portal with layers of peeling paint appeared in the distance. The tiny lady tore through cobwebs shrouding the door and vanished inside. By the time I arrived, the cobwebs had closed ranks again as though no one had passed through.

The engine droned on. *Hurry, hurry!*

In the middle of the huge door, a fine layer of dust covered a gigantic brass knob. I fumbled and tugged, but the knob wouldn't turn. The pickup gathered speed. Fear's arrow pierced the target of my heart.

"Help!" I coughed on the swirling dust. "Someone please help me!"

The truck bore down on the door. Closer and closer until the engine's heat blistered the skin on my neck. The volume rose to a deafening crescendo. With no way of escape, I turned and squared my shoulders, resigned to face my destiny.

I bolted upright in bed, gasping for air. My heart pounded like a judge's gavel. Then, through the open window, I heard the roar of a diesel engine.

5

Chapter Five

The strong scent of tuna awakened me next morning. I opened my eyes to four almond-shaped orbs fixed on my face. The cats, Roy Rogers and Hopalong Cassidy, meowed in unison. Why did they always have tuna breath when they only ate dry cat food made from chicken and turkey?

Yawning and stretching, I upended my two black-and-white buddies. They alighted on their feet and then settled on the carpet, maybe waiting to see whether I required further assistance. Jesse never allowed them in our bedroom at night, for fear they might pounce on him while he slept. Needing all my furry friends around me whenever he departed, I left the door open so they came in and out at will, taking full advantage of my generosity.

The digital clock on my bedside table announced eight forty-five in bright, red numbers. I did a double take, thinking I'd misread the time. "You boys must be hungry."

Molly's brown eyes peeped through the wire door of her sleeping crate in the corner of our room. She licked her lips with her big red tongue.

"Okay, okay. I'm up already."

First thing, I checked the house. In the morning light, all the rooms appeared intact and unmolested. I had stayed awake a long time after my dream, listening for the truck to crash through the gate. It never did, of course. However, assorted evil creatures paraded out of the darkness while I lay on my back, staring at the log ceiling. Maybe that's why my mother wouldn't let me watch scary movies as a child, although enough other monsters had populated my years for a lifetime of nightmares. Those images ever hovered in my brain, waiting to terrorize me.

Unable to return to sleep, I made a thorough house search, turning on every light and double-checking every lock and window. I pushed dining chairs against the outside doors and piled them high with stacks of pots and pans. Only after fully convincing myself that no one could sneak into my bedroom without making a great deal of noise could I venture back to bed. Judging by my stiff neck and aching muscles, I must have slept soundly until the cats came.

The morning sun glowed in the autumn air as I descended to the exercise room via the spiral staircase Jesse put in for easy basement access. Heaven forbid it should be work to get to the workout area! Formerly a storage room, we painted this space raspberry and sage, coordinated to the colors of the vivacious oak-leaf-and-berry pattern swirling on the carpet. Jesse and I intended to frequent this room every day in pursuit of good health in middle age and hoped the vibrant colors would energize us. After the newness wore off, I went down alone most of the time and not as often as I should. Jesse occasionally reminded me of my need for strenuous exercise, but he didn't usually follow his own advice. However, on the chance the window in the exercise room might afford a first-rate station for spying on the gray house, I hopped on the treadmill and commenced surveillance.

Unfortunately, no action appeared. A slight breeze teased the weaker leaves off the oak trees outside the window. They drifted lazily to the ground. I watched a woodpecker drilling holes in one of the blue oaks in the backyard. At least he wasn't attacking the house. Thank goodness for that. Having an all-wooden house tainted our enjoyment of the redheaded creatures.

I picked a piece of straw off my sweatshirt as I trotted along—a reminder of Jesse's orders to feed the two horses he left in my care. Let me be clear here: I am fully aware that ownership of animals necessitates a certain amount of labor. However, the pleasure derived from their company far outweighs the inconvenience, so I don't mind tending the horses when Jesse is gone. The problem was that Jesse never asked for my help; he issued orders. Did he ever appreciate anything I did? Or just assume he had the right to command his slave to obey his every whim?

When I finished power walking, I hefted the barbells for a few minutes, hoping to tone up that persistent fish-belly flesh under my upper arms. Still nothing stirred across the pasture, so I stood at the window a few minutes longer, studying the back of the Payne house.

From this lower vantage point, I saw most of the weed infested back yard and a small patio connected to the house through sliding glass doors. On the patio rested one chair, deserted and lonely. Who put that there? And why? I'd never seen anyone sitting in it.

My eyes scanned the back door and stoop without stopping. Continuing past the propane tank beside the house, my scrutiny stalled on a stack of boxes. They appeared to be cardboard, an irregular mound of many sizes and shapes, some white, some brown. Could that be where he deposited the boxes I saw him carrying on the tractor?

In this part of the county, we dismantled discarded boxes and disposed of them at a common location so the trash collector had only one stop to make in our neighborhood. The trash company assigned specific days during the month to flatten cardboard boxes and leave them along with other recyclable materials.

Why was he hoarding boxes instead of getting rid of them?

An image of burning dropped into mind. Perhaps this pile of boxes rested on the ashes of the huge fire I watched last year. I shuddered, remembering tall flames that shot into the sky for days. Since apparently no one monitored the inferno to make sure it didn't burn out of control, I'd been at my window nearly the whole time. Fires always terrified me, ever since the corner of our kitchen caught fire the year I turned six.

Just then, something moved in the periphery of my vision, but when I jerked to look, only the motionless gray house appeared. Hairs on my neck prickled. Someone was watching me. But who? I scanned the pasture and house again. No one. Must be my imagination.

More than a mite paranoid, I fled from the window. Upstairs I showered and dressed, this time in a bright blue sweater and my favorite black jeans. Then I peeked out again.

Still nothing to see.

I returned to the bathroom, where I busied myself arranging my unruly hair and applying a dash of make-up. My face stared from the mirror. Intentional blond highlights enlivened my brown hair. Once thick, it had thinned but hadn't grayed yet. Only puffy bags under my eyes suggested age. Maybe the laugh crinkles at the corners of my eyes were more numerous than in my youth, and maybe the smile lines had deepened, but I didn't believe I looked as old as my driver's license proclaimed. I certainly didn't feel old inside.

Jaclyn Smith still looked stunning at about my age. No bags under *her* eyes. Whenever I mentioned that, Jesse pointed out that I could achieve her look if I spent as much money as she probably had for plastic surgery. Of course, no amount of plastic surgery could transplant Jaclyn Smith's sculptured beauty to my plain round face.

I piled my hair in a big clip and stepped back to survey the results.

Roy and Hoppy watched from the edge of the bathtub with inscrutable cat expressions. I faced them and smiled, but their visages remained unchanged. "Well, I'm afraid that's as good as it gets."

After pouring a cup of decaf, I settled on the back deck with a book and the portable phone. The cats followed. Molly trailed behind and flopped at my feet, stretching out in the sun. Roy continued to the yard to explore, but Hoppy rubbed against my calves, demanding attention. I picked him up and curled him into my lap so I could stroke his soft black-and-white head and scratch his ears.

Every now and then, I glanced across the pasture at the Paynes' house. Did Zora Jane stand at her window watching too? I'd grown most fond of Zora Jane. Dependable and full of compassion, she quickly endeared herself despite her straight talk and pushiness. When I first met her, I hadn't been sure I'd be able to handle that.

As the self-appointed representative for the welcome wagon in our neighborhood, Zora Jane had arrived at my doorstep a few days after we moved in, before we hooked up the automatic gate to keep uninvited strangers out. When I opened the door, I blinked at the blast of color. Tall and svelte, Zora Jane's reddish-brown hair curled around a heart-shaped face. Her tunic-length blouse exploded with bright red, orange, and yellow flowers amid lime green leaves. Skin-hugging lime capri pants drew the eye down well-shaped legs to matching lime green sandals with red-painted toenails peeking out.

She pointed to a small brass plaque engraved with the words, *Welcome in the name of Christ.* "Did you put this on the door?"

A sob caught in my throat. "Oh … yes. That's a going-away gift from a dear friend." I never wanted to retire to Grass Valley. Leaving our son, two daughters, and four grandchildren in southern California ripped an irreparable hole in my heart. Not to mention the pain of being so far from my friends. The move had been entirely Jesse's idea. He decided, and as usual when he makes up his mind, no argument could dissuade him. He wanted to get away from traffic. He wanted room for his horses. He didn't care how much I suffered, leaving everyone dear to me. But I didn't need to share all that with this flashy person, whoever she might be.

The woman clasped her hands. "Praise the Lord! I've been praying for Christians to buy this house ever since the McCarthys said they were selling."

Oh no. A Jesus freak. "Really?"

"Welcome! I'm your neighbor, Zora Jane Callahan." She smiled, extending a plateful of chocolate-chip oatmeal cookies. The appetizing aroma told me the cookies weren't long from the oven.

Chocolate should never be denied. "Thank you."

She paused, looking past me through the open door.

Is she waiting for an invitation to come in? I suppose I must. She brought cookies. "Won't you come in?"

When she drifted through the entry hall, a cloud of flowery perfume enveloped me, mixing with the cookie smell in a way that reminded me of my mother. Still, how chummy did I want to get with someone who peppered her conversations with *praise the Lord?*

She seemed to know how to navigate around our house already, marching straight through the living room. I followed, an uneasy feeling rumbling in my stomach as if a runaway bus barreled toward my kitchen. She stood a moment beside the island, staring at the piles of still-unopened moving boxes.

I summoned my manners. "Would you like coffee? I can make a new pot. Decaf if you prefer."

With the grace of a princess, she settled at the kitchen table. "That would be a slice of heaven."

Who asked her to sit? I frowned and bit my lip. I shouldn't have offered coffee. Now she'd just stay longer.

However, by the time we were both seated at the table, chatting about our children and grandchildren, I relaxed about her ulterior agenda. I missed my family a great deal. Southern California might as well be halfway around the world for as often as I got to see them. She even blessed me by exclaiming over pictures of my extraordinarily beautiful grandchildren, demonstrating exquisite taste.

Looking into her sparkly green eyes, I saw that Zora Jane loved people almost as much as she loved God. Warmth crackled around her like fireworks. She wanted everyone to love Jesus just as much as she did.

She had leaned toward me, laying a hand on my arm. "Tell me, my dear, have you found a church home yet?"

6

Chapter Six

A cat-snore from Hoppy interrupted my musing. I glanced up to see the white pickup backing out. Lumpish as a slug, the engine coughed and sputtered objections. A peek at my watch made me think of what TV's Detective Columbo says, "People don't usually forget to do that which they usually do."

Just before eleven. Yep. He followed his usual pattern, all right.

Zora Jane answered the phone after the first ring. "I've been watching out the window."

An exuberant giggle tried to escape, but I squashed it. "I've been sitting on the deck all morning, worried that today of all days he might decide to stay home."

"Well … let's get going then. I'll meet you at the street."

I dashed to the Jeep.

When I pulled into her driveway, Zora Jane jumped into the car dressed in a metallic gold jogging suit with a neon-green-and-gold striped shell sparkling underneath the jacket. She looked as appetizing as the peanut butter chocolate-chip cookies in her lap.

Grinning like conspirators out to play a prank on schoolmates, we drove the short distance to the Paynes' house. We stood together on the leaf-strewn porch, me in newly laundered sneakers and Zora Jane in gold flats with pointy toes. Quick, firm raps on the door announced my impatience. When the door creaked open this time, a tiny smile of recognition surfaced in Lila's blue eyes, although it seemed unable to continue all the way to her lips.

Lila wore the same dirty, mismatched outfit as on my previous visit. If possible, her stringy gray-blond hair seemed even more disheveled. She blinked several times as she took in her visitors.

"Good morning!" I said. "I brought Zora Jane along today. Do you know her? She lives on the other side of the street in the big yellow Victorian house with the sheep and donkeys grazing on the hill."

Two mournful eyes dropped to the plate Zora Jane carried. I almost saw her mouth water. I guess Zora Jane noticed that too, because she lifted the plate where Lila could reach it. "These are for you. I hope you enjoy them."

In one fluid motion, Lila grabbed the plate and ripped off the plastic wrap. In a flash, she'd stuffed a whole cookie into her mouth. She closed her eyes and tilted back her head. Her expression brightened while she chewed, as if she'd never tasted anything so scrumptious before. Then, without warning, she shoved the plate back at Zora Jane and the dark cloud overtook her again. "Can't! Must not bring them into the house!" Terror sparked from her eyes. "Go … now." She reached for the door.

"Now just a minute, young lady." Zora Jane stepped into the doorway and pushed on the door from our side. "We've come for a short visit. Won't take much of your time. You seem hungry. We'd be glad to make you a proper lunch."

Lila's brow crinkled and she hesitated as if internally translating the words from a foreign language. Perhaps hunger overwhelmed her, because she let go of the door. The opening widened as Zora Jane pushed harder. "You are hungry, aren't you, dear?"

In answer, Lila managed a stiff, uncertain nod. Without hesitation, Zora Jane marched into the house. "Where's your kitchen?"

I followed, leaving the door ajar.

The interior air reeked of rotting food and another foulness I couldn't immediately identify. I paused to allow my sniffer to distinguish the odors. Definitely not urine. More musty, as if the house had been closed to air circulation too long. Maybe mildew, as well.

The empty entryway opened to the house on either side. Zora Jane turned right through a large, bare room perhaps originally built as a living room and headed through another smaller room into the kitchen. I lingered, tentatively examining the spaces. Lila loitered with me, monitoring my movements like a mother dog protecting her newborn puppies.

Lila's house appeared as neglected as she did. Old orange shag carpet blanketed the floors, the long shag from the late 1970s or early 1980s. The rug needed cleaning and raking badly. Why would anyone choose this carpet on purpose, even in those bizarre days? At the windows, minimal outside light filtered through shrouds of faded yellow burlap drapery. A large stone fireplace dominated the far end of the room. Several inches of fine dark ash obscured the bottom, indicating how long the fireplace had waited for a proper cleaning.

After a minute, Lila gave up escorting me to pursue Zora Jane into the kitchen. I trailed after her through the smaller room that once might have been the dining room. Lacking furniture, the room now served no function. With nothing on walls or floors, how did they go about their daily lives? What did they sit on? I didn't see a television either. Hard to imagine a house without television these days.

A dull substance covered the kitchen counters, making the yellow tiles appear as drab and dated as the geometric vinyl on the floor. Daisy-strewn wallpaper peeled off the plaster in great hanging pieces. Judging from the open doors in the kitchen, I surmised that Zora Jane had already rooted through the medium oak cabinets without discovering food. Next, she stuck her head in the harvest gold refrigerator but pulled it right out with a groan. She frowned over the top of the door. "There's no food in this kitchen. Where is your food, child?"

Lila stood trancelike.

Zora Jane heaved a deep sigh. "Well, goodness, I have a pot of soup on at my house. Won't take me a minute to run home and get it."

Without input from either of us, Zora Jane grabbed my car keys and rushed out.

I moved to follow her until I glanced at Lila. Wilted into a tiny wisp in the corner, it appeared that she had retreated into another world. I didn't want to leave her like that.

After a brief pause that felt lengthy, I wandered around the small space, exploring what wasn't there. "Have you lived here long?"

Lila didn't answer, but her head jerked to attention as if she'd just discovered my presence. I continued trying to engage her. "The irises along the driveway were beautiful this spring. Did you plant them?"

Her head bobbed as she followed my movements with her eyes.

I peeked into one of the empty cabinets. "I planted irises too, but a gopher or a mole ate them. I don't know which. Everything here in the country surprises us. Heard of a new creature … a vole. Do you know what that is?"

She averted her eyes. I closed the cabinet door and the latch snapped as the magnet grabbed hold. Lila jumped.

"Bryan, the landscape guy, told me if you plant bulbs in a wire cage, the critters can't get them. I'm so lazy I can't imagine going to all that trouble. I guess your irises grew without being eaten by varmints. I wish I could grow irises like yours."

Lila tilted her head, regarding me askance. She bit the side of her lip. Then words tumbled out. "Mrs. McCarthy—Maggie—she brought the iris bulbs. Right after we moved here. They make pretty flowers."

Leaning on the counter, I nodded.

Light flamed in her eyes for a second before the vacant stare returned. "Blue, yellow, and purple flowers." She chanted, repeating the words twice more.

I forced my tense shoulders down and rubbed my stiff neck. What's the best response for that? "How nice of her."

With a swipe of one open palm down my jeans, I attempted to remove the sticky stuff from the counter. "You remember Zora Jane, don't you? She has animals at her house. Have you seen her three-legged goat? She named it Eileen. Don't you just love that? A three-legged goat. Get it? *I lean.*" I demonstrated.

No reaction.

Did lack of a sense of humor indicate lack of intelligence? I read that somewhere. More likely, this woman was simply too depressed to find humor in anything—even a three-legged goat named Eileen.

Adopting a softer, gentler tone, I stepped closer. "I notice you have bruises on your arm."

She cradled her injured arm with the opposite hand.

I took another step. "How did you hurt yourself?"

She didn't answer, but her eyes widened and the pupils dilated.

"Did you hurt yourself, Mrs. Payne? Or did someone hurt you?"

Her voice sounded even smaller than before. "Not hurt. No. Not … hurt." She backed away, shielding her neck with both hands.

Did she think I would attack her? I reached out with one hand. "Don't be afraid. I mean you no harm. Please, can I see your arm? Let me check those bruises."

She dodged away, wild, stringy hair swinging from one side of her neck. Just above her sweater, an enflamed line stretched into her hair. I couldn't see the full extent of the injury, but surely swelling indicated serious trauma. I only caught a quick glimpse before the hair covered it again.

I baby-stepped toward her. "Your neck. What happened? Please. I want to help you. Mrs. Payne—Lila—I won't hurt you, I promise." I kept my voice as even as possible, trembling inside at the horror of discovering more wounds.

She retreated, maintaining distance between us.

Following with slow steps, I whispered, "Who hurt you?"

She appeared to shrink, becoming so small I feared she might disappear altogether.

Let it go. You've frightened her. I never intended to add to her fear. I heaved a heavy sigh. How could I help her if she wouldn't let me close?

I backed off increasing her personal space by several feet. "Someday soon you can come up to visit Molly. She's a wonderful dog. I know you'll love her. She's so gentle and …"

I continued babbling for what seemed like an hour until Zora Jane returned bearing hot soup and crusty bread, which she set on the counter. She removed the lid from the tureen with a flourish and faced Lila. "Where are your bowls?"

Another blank look crossed Lila's face, but when her eyes swept the room this time, they came to rest on the steaming food. Lunging toward the counter, she crammed the serving ladle into the tureen and then right into her bird-like mouth.

Homemade chunky vegetable beef soup sloshed onto the counter. Broth dripped off her petite chin and ran like a brown river down her neck to the dingy sweater. A few drops even ended up on her worn gray slippers. Her ravenous eating reminded me of Molly—always starving, even right after a feeding.

With a twinge of conscience, I recalled the sparkling jars of jam still resting in my raffia-lined basket. How could I have waved them under her nose and then snatched them away while she starved for food? Why hadn't I left them here?

Lila finished the soup and several pieces of bread as we watched in amazement. In a flash, she collected the empty containers and shoved them toward us. "Go! You must go!"

She delivered the words in a volume I would never have thought possible. We had to comply.

As she ushered us through the empty entryway, I looked back over one shoulder. "We'll be back tomorrow."

"No. Don't come back. Never again … never!"

Even after the door banged shut with a crash louder than nearby thunder, her plaintive cry echoed through my brain. Zora Jane and I stood on the stoop, exchanging expressions of shock. *What in heaven's name had we gotten into?*

7

Chapter Seven

Zora Jane launched a commentary as we snapped into our seatbelts. "Well, there's definitely something strange going on here. Did you notice how bare that house is? There's no food in the kitchen or hardly anything else. Where do you suppose the furniture went? What do they sit on? Goodness, what do they sleep on? I'm sure the house hasn't always been empty. I remember them unloading furniture from a big moving van. That poor woman hasn't eaten or bathed in days, maybe weeks on the bathing. Must be ill." She wrinkled her nose. "She has that smell."

I bobbed my head in agreement, overwhelmed by an unfamiliar sense of impotence at what we'd just witnessed. When I stopped the Jeep in front of the Callahans' house, Zora Jane invited me inside for muffins.

My eyes soaked up the comfort of Zora Jane's house as I settled at her round breakfast table. A large lump formed in my throat at the stark contrast between the Callahan kitchen and the one we'd just visited. Scrubbed clean, cheery warm, stylish, and inviting, Zora Jane's kitchen mirrored its owner. I stared at the fresh muffins and comforting pot of tea as a wave of urgency washed over me. "Did you see the bruises?"

Zora Jane nodded.

"There's something on her neck, too. She wouldn't let me close, but a red line runs right along the side." I demonstrated. "Like someone tried to strangle her."

Her teacup clinked as she returned it to the saucer. "Poor lamb."

"I asked what happened but she wouldn't say. She's frightened. Classic abuse symptoms. I've read about them before. Right down to protecting her abuser. Maybe she's sick too, like you said. She looks awfully frail. You can almost see through her skin. And did you notice how thin she is? He must be starving her."

With tears glistening in her eyes, Zora Jane nodded again.

A shrill alarm screamed through me. Someone must intervene soon. I picked up my teacup and took a sip, then cupped both hands around it, relishing the comforting warmth. "What're we going to do?"

She finished off a piece of muffin and gave her fingers a dainty swipe on her napkin. "God is still in control. Our job is to trust him. We must keep praying."

Not waiting for my agreement, Zora Jane prayed. "God, you see everything in this world, no matter how hidden. Your word tells us you care about those who are hurting, those who are sick and sad. You love Lila with a love beyond our understanding. Please show us how to help her. We will trust you and wait for your time and your way. In Jesus' blessed name, amen."

As she poured another cup, I studied her face. Did she seriously believe God cared about someone as insignificant as that frail woman?

Zora Jane dropped a lump of sugar into her tea and stirred. "We need to talk to someone about what we've seen. An authority."

I nodded. If we had discovered a child suffering such injuries, we'd already be on the phone summoning the law.

"Our son-in-law's a deputy here in Nevada County. Have I ever mentioned him? Baxter Dunn. He's a wonderful Christian man. Maybe we should run this by him."

"That's a good idea."

She lifted the handset of the old-fashioned telephone hanging on her kitchen wall and paused a moment. "I hate to bother him just now, though. He only returned to work yesterday after an injury and he hasn't fully regained his strength. I think he should have waited another few days before going back. He'll be swamped with paper work. Besides, do we actually have any facts? We don't want to make an unfounded accusation. These are our neighbors. That's a horrible stigma to lay on someone if we're wrong."

"Maybe. But what if we're right?" I felt the ticking of Zora Jane's kitchen clock. Time mattered here. Lila's safety was at stake. Perhaps even her life. If Zora Jane deemed this matter urgent enough to bring before God, how much more information did we need to summon the authorities?

She replaced the phone. "Why don't I ask Ed? He handled plenty of abuse and neglect cases. He'll know what to look for, as well as the legal aspects."

That made sense. Ed retired from the San Francisco police force after twenty-five years of service. "I guess I could talk to Jesse too. He's good at pointing out the obvious." At least he always noticed everything I did wrong.

Her eyes smiled understanding into mine.

But how *could* she understand our conflicted marriage? Did she know how much I wanted to run home and tell Jesse everything with confidence that he'd care enough to listen? "I'll tell Jesse when he gets home."

Zora Jane broke off a chunk of muffin. "Where *is* Jesse?"

"He's at a shoot. In Fresno."

She cocked one eyebrow. "A *shoot?*"

"Cowboy-mounted shooting—his new pastime. They race horses around a course marked by balloons attached to orange highway cones."

"Oh, that's what he's been practicing in the arena."

I nodded. "It's timed like barrel racing, with the added challenge of shooting balloons in order and the added fun of dressing in period costumes. These are grown men, mind you."

Zora Jane tilted her head and gave a slow nod. The questions in her eyes told me she wasn't sure whether I intended to be facetious or not. "Boys will be boys, I suppose."

Talking about Jesse made me feel empty and sad. Before he retired, I thought I was the most important person in the world to him. Now … well, I didn't know exactly where I stood, but I probably wouldn't place in the top ten. It might be easier to get a divorce and never see his face again than to put up with his sporadic attention.

I'd never mentioned my marital problems to anyone before. Zora Jane stared at me, tenderness radiating from her eyes to my heart.

"Retirement has been a challenge for both of us, I've got to admit. Since I finished remodeling and redecorating, I haven't found anything interesting to fill my time. Oh, there's always gardening, but I can't garden all the time, you know?"

Zora Jane poured the remaining tea into my cup. "No, I guess not."

"When Jesse first retired, he moped around. Said he felt as useless as a four-card flush. So he tried art lessons, joined a woodcarving group, and then he discovered mounted shooting. It's a perfect fit for him. He's always loved horses, and best of all, he gets to dress in cowboy costumes." I sighed. "I should be thankful, I know."

Zora Jane shrugged. "He could've chosen worse ways to fill his time. Maybe you're feeling left out because he's having fun without you. Are you sure you're not jealous?"

I rejected that idea without considering whether it might be true or not. "You don't understand. He's consumed with this stuff. When he leaves, he's gone for four or five days at a time. Even when he's home, he's not really there. He devours Western magazines and books, cleans his guns, gets his gear together, or practices with his horse. It's like nothing else on the planet matters anymore. Frankly, I can't share it with him because it's all so … frivolous. I can't find anything more meaningful, though. Sometimes I wonder what my purpose for living is when I'm not doing anything useful."

Where did that come from? I don't usually share such intimate stuff.

"Oh, my dear!" Zora Jane patted my hand, eyes sparkling. "God has something wonderful for you. Ask him to reveal it."

For Zora Jane, the answer always started with prayer. If only I felt so confident that God cared about my life. He'd never sent me a message before. Why should he start talking to me now?

She leaned toward me. "Meanwhile, why don't you try mounted shooting? You'd look so cute in a cowgirl outfit."

I threw my napkin at her.

We each finished another delicious orange-walnut muffin lathered with generous globs of homemade peach preserves. Then I headed home, wondering what God could possibly have for *me* to do in retirement.

❧

The phone rang as I entered the house. I hustled to beat the answering machine. "Hello?"

"Hey." Jesse's voice boomed over the line. "How's everything?" My heart somersaulted as it always did whenever I heard his voice. A foggy memory of Jesse's hushed pre-dawn departure the previous Thursday morning surfaced in my mind. He tried not to wake me when he left early. But that meant I never got the chance to say good-bye.

The initial delight of hearing his voice faded when I remembered that once again he'd been gone when I needed him. Since I hated explaining anything over the phone, I gritted my teeth and fibbed. "Everything's fine here."

"Think I'm coming home tonight." His original plan had been to return Sunday, still more than a day away. "Ranger's limping. Can't figure what's wrong with his leg."

Another injury? Ranger slipped and fell in the mud once, right after they finished running a course. Jesse's elbow didn't heal for a couple of months. When would my husband understand he'd grown too old to play cowboy? "Did he fall again?"

"No. That's why I can't figure it out. I haven't seen him do anything to cause the limp. But it's the same foot he had trouble with before. Maybe it's arthritis. Old Ranger's not as young as he used to be. But hey, who is? Anyway, there are storm clouds gathering here. Looks like we may get rain tonight. I don't want to ride him through the mud. If I leave now, I'll get home before dark."

"Okay. That's good actually." I'd been dreading another sleepless night listening for Will's truck to break through the gate.

"You'll have to get rid of your boyfriend early."

Boyfriend? I shook my head. Strange sense of humor. "Sure. I'll tell him he has to go."

As I hung up the phone, conflicting feelings churned in my stomach like toxic chemicals. I was grateful he'd be home before another night. I was. But resentment at being left unprotected overpowered the positive emotions. He *never* considered my need for safety.

I occupied myself vacuuming and doing laundry, trying to fill up the afternoon. Busyness kept me from worrying about Lila's plight. Then I made a batch of my mother's chicken lasagna—yummy, but labor-intensive. Nutmeg and green onions give it a unique and delicious flavor. Jesse better appreciate that I spent all afternoon preparing his favorite dish.

I stayed so occupied I forgot to watch for the return of Will's white pickup. About four thirty, I put on a peppy Shania Twain CD and set to work cleaning up the lasagna mess, bopping to "Man! I Feel Like a Woman." The phone jangled in the middle of the second chorus and I jumped.

"Hello?"

No response.

I clicked off the Bose music system. "Helloo?"

Still nothing. *Must be a telemarketer.* As slowly as possible, I drifted back to the dry sink to hang up the phone, praying for a computer to kick in with a sales pitch.

Curiosity reared its tempting head. I lingered just another moment, hoping for a clue to the caller's identity.

Then—heavy breathing, a grunted profanity, and a loud click as the line disconnected.

I didn't imagine that! I dropped the phone in the general vicinity of its cradle but misjudged the distance. The phone landed on the dry sink with a loud whack.

My gaze flew out the windows toward the gray house just in time to see the back door fly open again. Will stood on his stoop, one hand on his hip, the other shielding his eyes to stare at our house.

Oddly enough, in my panic, I thought of the animals first. Hoppy snored in a little black-and-white heap on Jesse's white leather cowboy chair in the living room. Roy and Molly were somewhere outside. I hadn't seen them for hours. I raced to the front door on the other side of the house as fear's icy fingers clutched my soul. No sign of either one of them. My voice trembled like an old woman's. "Molly! Here, Roy! Here, kitty-kitty."

Roy's head popped up from behind a clump of rosemary near the fence. He'd been foraging for lizards, field mice, blowing leaves—anything that moved. Tail up, he bounded toward me. When he got to the dry stack stone wall holding back the upper part of the hill, he balanced in perfect form just long enough for me to admire him. Then he jumped onto the driveway with a kerplunk. In great relief, I gathered his bulky body into my arms and dumped him through the front door.

"Good boy! I'll be right back." I secured the door so neither cat could escape and faced the late afternoon landscape. *Now, where could Molly be?*

I rushed up the driveway toward the front gate. A slight wind rustled the tops of the trees, but no sign of Molly there. I turned to search the other way. When had I seen her last? At the corner where the driveway curved up the hill to the exit gate, I started to sprint. Before long, my panting forced me to stop. When had I gotten so old and out of shape? *Admit it, Christine. You've reached the age when jogging uphill ceases to be a good idea.*

I limped back to the corner to lean against our huge rock, huffing and puffing. I hunched over with both hands on my knees to rest. Rats! I'd trampled the Boston ivy we planted last summer. Straightening, I pressed my back into the boulder until my heavy breathing subsided. "Cornerstone Rock," as we called the boulder, consisted of a mammoth chunk of granite taller than me. Unearthed during the construction of our house, the rock had been placed in a prominent position at the corner of the driveway. It added a stunning focal point to the landscape. The sight of it usually evoked feelings of continuity and security. Just then, however, the enormous hard surface heightened awareness of my own insignificance and weakness.

Where could Molly be? Think, Christine. Watching for birds? The pond. I retraced my path along the front of the house and veered left. Straining to see, I nearly tripped down the stone steps.

My eyes scanned the terrain. "Molly!"

Out of the corner of one eye, I caught a glimpse of the white tip of her wagging tail. She stood to my left at the fence between the yard and the pasture. Arms crossed, Will faced her from his stoop. A spasm of fear shivered through me, paralyzing me for an instant.

"Molly." My voice quivered. She jerked her head in my direction and charged toward me. I crouched to caress her soft fur without bothering to wipe her slimy licks off. "I'm glad to see you too, old girl."

I drew her into the safety of the house as quickly as possible. Why had Molly been down there? Did he lure her? Could this be connected to my visits with Lila? Did Will make the obscene phone call? If so, how did he get our unlisted phone number?

Trembling, I raced to the kitchen window.

Will Payne had disappeared inside the gray house again.

8

Chapter Eight

As the sun dropped in the sky, I watched Jesse pull in and unload Ranger at the barn. I raced outside as he dragged his bags from the back of the pickup. Molly followed—tail wagging. She stopped a moment at Jesse's feet, then moseyed to the truck to sniff the tires.

Overwhelmed with joy at the sight of him, I threw my arms around his neck, resentment temporarily forgotten.

Jesse stiffened and drew back. "What's this about?"

I pressed my face into his chest to inhale the mixture of sweat, sexy aftershave, and horse that clung to him after a day of riding. "I'm glad to see you."

He set down his luggage and bent his six-foot frame to look squarely in my eyes. "Why? What's going on?"

Part of me wanted to savor the romance a moment longer. "Aren't you even a little bit glad to see me?"

"Yeah, I guess. So, what's going on?"

Why bother? We'd gotten too old for romance. Jesse didn't care about me that way anymore. "Well, come in first." I pulled him inside and closed the door. "It's probably not as bad as I think."

"You're scaring me, Christine."

With a toss of my head, I flounced toward the kitchen. "Are you hungry? Chicken lasagna will be ready soon."

He dropped his gear on the stairs and followed. "Come on, what's wrong?"

After I made him beg a little longer, I launched into a detailed account of the peculiar events of the last two days. I told him about my fears for Lila and of Will's bad behavior. I told him about the truck that tried to crash through our gates and how Will threatened Molly.

While I babbled, Jesse crossed his arms and leaned against the kitchen island. At length, he interrupted. "Sounds like one of your jaunts into the land of make-believe. How much of this really happened?"

"Why does everyone always say it's only my imagination? Honest, Jesse. All this happened."

"Maybe you're overanalyzing then."

I scrunched my face and squinted. "You know I hate to be accused of overanalyzing."

He held up both hands and chuckled slightly. "Okay. Where's Molly now?"

"Molly?" I laid aside irritation to remember. "She went outside when you came home."

But when I looked out the front door, Molly wasn't on the driveway. I hustled to the sliding glass doors but didn't find her in her usual spot on the back deck. She didn't return, though I called her name repeatedly.

Not again. Where could she be?

Standing outside, I listened for the jingle of dog tags on her blue collar, but only heard the gurgle of the waterfall splashing into the pond.

While I searched, darkness settled into the twilight sky. Jesse grabbed the big stainless steel flashlight that always sits on the granite counter in the kitchen. I turned off the oven and flipped on lights illuminating the yard near the house as we hunted for our truant dog.

For the next half hour, we scoured the property. We took turns pacing back and forth on the driveway, but that didn't bring her home. Using the flashlight, we hiked the entire perimeter inside the fenced portion of our yard. We called her name until our voices became nearly hoarse in the chilly air. She didn't come.

At length, Jesse stopped. The expression on his face read concerned but not panicked. Maybe he'd gotten too tired to panic. "I'm going to get the car. She might be out on the road somewhere. You know she's been squeezing through the gate to run down the hill lately."

Twice in the past few weeks, I'd called her back from one of her exploring trips. Cars often zoomed along our street as if propelled by jet fuel.

I shuddered involuntarily. "You don't think someone hit her, do you?"

"At dusk, she'd be hard to see."

More likely Will Payne took her. After all, he'd somehow lured her to the fence and held her spellbound while I yelled for her. When I followed Jesse to the Jeep, that fearsome possibility sunk into my stomach. Jesse backed out, then steered up the driveway and out the gate.

The bright Jeep lights lit a wide patch of ground in front of us. Our eyes swept back and forth, searching. We crawled to the top of the hill without finding her. I looked down past our house at forests and valleys in the distance. The enormity of our task throbbed in my mind. Once off our property, she'd be one small dog in a big, unfamiliar world. Where should we begin? I already knew the answer.

Memories flashed through my fear. "Do you remember when we first saw Molly? So tiny—the smallest one in the litter—but she wiggled over to introduce herself just like she chose us. Remember, Jesse? Such a sweet puppy with so much personality."

"We'll find her, Christine."

"And remember when we took her home to Chamois?" Chamois reigned over our house as top dog at that time—an elderly, often-crotchety, blonde cocker spaniel.

Jesse chuckled. "She herded Chamois down the garden path, nudging from one side to the other so Chamois couldn't stray onto the grass."

The memories brought a smile to my lips.

Jesse maneuvered into the driveway leading to the barn and horse corral at the bottom of our property. In the glow of the floodlight atop our green barn, we resumed our search in the horse area. Ranger whinnied softly when we disturbed his much-deserved rest. Dolly Desperado, the older brown quarter horse, followed us with her velvet eyes, but Vegas Dice, the feisty Appaloosa, snorted as Jesse flooded each stall with light. We didn't find Molly in the barn, the arena, or anywhere nearby.

"That was a long shot, I guess." Jesse climbed back into the Jeep. "Molly wouldn't come down here."

"No. Molly doesn't like horses."

Years ago, before Molly had fully grown, long before we moved to Grass Valley, Jesse introduced her to his horses in hopes of training her for trail rides. In the barn, Molly sat while Jesse saddled his steed. However, the instant he swung his leg over the saddle to mount, she rocketed into motion. Around and around she raced, circling the horse wildly. The startled horse tried to follow her crazed movements while Jesse shouted, "Molly! No! Molly! Stop!" After several uncertain seconds, the horse reared upward to flail at the intruder with his hooves. Off balance, Jesse had slumped to the ground.

Jesse slammed the Jeep door with unnecessary force. At this stage in his fatigue, I knew better than to comment, even in sympathy, so I returned to my reverie.

Although afraid of horses, Molly instinctively loved sheep. For a few months, Jesse accompanied her to herd dog training. A quick study, Molly immediately demonstrated aptitude for sheep work. Jesse, however, needed further training. Molly's vocabulary comprised an amazing variety of verbal commands, including "go find the cat," if on occasion I couldn't get a stubborn cat to come inside at night. Working with the sheep proved more play than work for her. I pictured Molly's ears flowing in the wind as she darted in and out, corralling the stubborn sheep, obeying the trainer's commands with amazing inborn skill.

Otherworldly luminescence hovered over the terrain on this night before the full moon. Nevertheless, our field of vision didn't extend far enough into the darkness to find a black-and-white animal in a black-and-gray-world where shadows blurred distinct features. After a mile or so, Jesse stopped the car and turned to face me. "We'll have to wait 'til daylight. Sorry, Christine."

Tears inundated my eyes. We hadn't seen an injured or dying dog by the side of the road. For that I should be grateful. But where could she be? Never before in all her twelve years with us had she gone off alone without coming back when we called. Someone or something must be restraining her. I knew just who that would be.

As we returned home, the gray house loomed before us in the headlights. The night shadows and eerie lighting made the house look even more malicious than in daylight. Could there be a legitimate reason why that strange man had watched Molly? I couldn't think of one.

A torrent of sadness cascaded over me. "We've got to find her, Jesse. And we'll have to go in that house to do it."

9

Chapter Nine

I didn't sleep much, tossing and turning for hours. Exhaustion overcame me at last, and I lay still in a puddle of wakeful memories and thoughts. Jesse enjoyed the contented slumber of those who get up early, exert themselves in the hot sunshine, and then drive for hours to get home.

Through the sleepless hours, I sorted and rearranged the odd cluster of events surrounding the disappearance of our dog. What did she see down by the fence? Maybe that man *did* hide a body in the boxes piled just below our pasture. Did he take our dog to warn me to stay away from Lila? Swirling around such musings, recollections of Molly wove in and out like colorful ribbons fluttering away in the wind.

I rolled to one side, pulling the comforter to my chin. Maybe Will Payne didn't take her. But if not, where could she be? I hoped she would stay warm and dry and find her way home in the morning.

At some point I must've fallen asleep, because Jesse's stirring awakened me. I squinted at the clock through puffy eye slits to see seven o'clock in red numbers.

Jesse hunched on the side of the bed. "Are we going to church this morning?"

"Oh, it's Sunday." I stared into Molly's sleeping crate. For the first time since we brought her home as a curly-haired puppy, I didn't see her brown eyes peeking back through the door. A huge knot lodged in my throat.

A groan escaped when I flopped onto my stomach. "Do we have to?" I had no desire to make the effort.

Jesse stood and stretched his arms over his head. "Church would be a good thing today. We need encouragement. We'll look for Molly as soon as we get home."

Turning over, I pulled the covers around my neck. "But I don't want to. How can I think about anything but Molly?"

He patted my leg and pretended not to hear. Men are good at selective hearing. Especially Jesse, whose escalating hearing loss gave him continual opportunities not to hear what I said. He just didn't want to hear me. Not anymore.

I rolled out of bed, mumbling these sentiments to myself.

Hoping for distraction while I dressed, I switched on the TV news after my shower.

A well-coiffed lady in a tidy blue suit maintained a respectful serious face. "And in local news, a fatal hit-and-run last evening claimed the life of a four-year-old Nevada City boy. Police are searching for anyone who saw or heard the accident. So far, they have no leads. In other developments …"

"What's that?" Jesse asked from the doorway.

"Just more bad news." I pressed the off button. So much pain in the world. "I don't know why I ever watch TV anymore."

We finished dressing in silence. Jesse didn't sing. Most mornings, he belted out snippets of tunes while he dressed. He wove songs into an amusing jumble, liberally mix-matching lyrics and melodies from his extensive repertoire.

Although I love to sing, I never sang with Jesse because he unpredictably moved to the next song whenever he ran out of words. Besides, I never knew what tune he would use. I often complained about his truncated crooning but missed it when he didn't sing.

Along the drive to town, we hunted for some sign of the dog. I tried not to blink as I scanned the shoulder and down the side of the roads, thinking if Molly had been hurt, she might've dragged herself out of the street and into a ditch somewhere. No matter how hard I looked, no dog appeared, hurt or otherwise.

"Where could she be?"

Jesse shook his head. "I don't know, Christine."

Tears bubbled into my eyes. "Well, *I* know. That man took her."

"You're jumping to conclusions again. The neighbor has no reason to take her." Jesse smiled weakly and patted my knee. "Don't worry. We'll find her."

If only I could be so sure.

While walking through the church parking lot, we caught up with the Callahans. For a change, Ed wore black slacks and a sports jacket. Church seemed to be the only place he wore anything besides plaid golf pants and a bright golf shirt. I greeted them and added, "Molly's missing."

Zora Jane gathered her gray wool coat tighter around her until the fake fur collar haloed her face. "Your dog? What do you mean *missing?*"

Jesse caught up with us. "*Missing* as in we can't find her. We hunted all over the property. Even drove the neighborhood last night, but not a sign of her."

Ed's frown made deep furrows that extended into where his hairline used to be before he shaved his head. "Has she ever gone out of bounds before?" Ed frequently salted his speech with golf terms. Maybe because he hadn't considered anything unrelated to golf since his retirement.

Tears filled my eyes again. "Never. It's just not like her."

Zora Jane laid her hand on my arm. "Oh, my dear. How long has she been gone?"

I blinked hard. "Since yesterday. Last night, actually."

They glanced at each other and grins broke out.

Next they'd say she hasn't been gone long and (pat, pat) don't worry, she'll probably be home by the time you get back. Didn't anyone ever take me seriously? I sniffed. "She never stayed away all night before."

Zora Jane threw one arm around me and, sure enough, she patted my shoulder. "I'm sure she'll come home soon. We'll keep our eyes open for her too."

I stiffened and bit my lip. At their urging, we resumed our amble toward the sanctuary until Ed hauled up, his expression a study in concern. "Have you looked in the woods behind your house? The trees and brush are real thick there. If she fell down one of those slopes, she might get stuck at the bottom."

I froze in mid-step. Another frightening possibility I'd never considered. Thick woods covered the north and rear of our lot, continuing behind the Paynes' property. Vines entwined the trees, dense and impenetrable. We didn't even know whether fences marked our property boundaries hidden in those woods. After we heard that the woods were full of wild creatures, we'd never been brave enough to hunt for fences. I shuddered as panic invaded my chest.

Jesse's expression brightened. "Good idea."

Ed slapped Jesse on the back. "Wear thick boots and long pants, Ace. And tuck your shirt in—your pants too. Snakes and ticks live in those woods."

Snakes and ticks! My hand covered my mouth as I winced.

Ed screwed up his face, imitating a lunatic. "And watch out for that old duffer who's been sleeping in the woods. They say he's crazy as a sandbagger."

At my horrified gasp, Zora Jane punched Ed in the arm. "Come on, Ed. We don't want to scare them away completely."

I glared at Ed for making jokes at my expense.

Ed leaned toward me, his voice thickly accented with a Boris Karloff quality. "Take care. They say a crazy tramp lives in those woods."

Jesse grinned. "Bring him on. We can take him. We'll do just about anything to find Molly."

Sure, laugh. But what *would* we have to do to find Molly? Queasiness in the pit of my stomach predicted that before this ordeal ended, I'd find myself in more than a few places beyond my comfort zone.

❧

I don't remember much about the sermon or any other part of the service, except one comforting song that promised God's love for all living creatures. Mostly, our upcoming foray into the woods consumed my thoughts.

The ten-mile road from Grass Valley back to our house snaked through lush trees and neighborhoods over a succession of hills and dales as the elevation declined. Jesse appeared deep in thought, so I stared out the window, praying for a successful search. But did God care what happened to Molly? Or would he dismiss Molly as being *only* a dog?

Although emotionally detached most of the time, now and then Jesse could be spot-on in tune with my thoughts—maybe because we'd spent so many years together. Just then, he read my mind. "I asked God to keep Molly safe. Do you think he answers prayers about animals?"

My immediate answer flew out as much to convince myself as to persuade Jesse. "He made them, didn't he?"

Jesse glanced my way, offering a tentative smile.

A childhood memory flashed to mind. I looked away. Should I share it? The wonder of it had not dimmed over the years. Maybe this would be beneficial just now, if he would listen.

I faced Jesse, laying my hand on his arm. "When I was a girl, our boxer, Rexanne, had a big litter of puppies. I picked out one with lots of personality and named him Wiggles."

Jesse jerked his head, frowning at me. "Wiggles?"

I nodded, searching his eyes. I could never tell whether he made fun of me or not.

He returned to watching the road. "Very imaginative name."

I shrugged. "I was just a kid. What do you want? My imagination hadn't developed yet."

He let out a tiny "Ha!"

"Anyway, one day I found a hard growth about the size of a walnut on his neck. He lay so still. Didn't want to eat. My mother said not to touch him because I might hurt him. She told me to leave him in his box. She didn't think he'd live."

Now for the wondrous part. I bent toward Jesse to see if he was listening.

"And?" he asked without looking my way. "Can't you tell this without the drama?"

I flopped back in my seat. Did I really want to share my wonderful story?

He sighed. "Go on. I'm listening."

I stared out the side window, knowing he'd have trouble hearing if I didn't face him. "That afternoon, I sat on the front steps holding Wiggles as tight as I could in my little girl arms and prayed for God to heal him. Next morning, the lump was gone."

Jesse slowed the car and leaned toward me. "What?"

I stared at him before the words rushed out. "The lump went away after I prayed."

He blinked before turning back to the road. "And you think God healed him?"

For a moment, a slight smile played on his lips and I feared he might break into laughter.

I looked out the window again. "That's what I thought at the time."

I guess I did have *one* answered childhood prayer after all—God answered my prayer for Wiggles.

When we rounded the next corner, Jesse grabbed the steering wheel with both hands.

Racing toward us, a weathered white pickup careened into our section of the road.

In a millisecond, Jesse yanked the wheel to the left. "Hang on!"

I screamed and grabbed the door handle to keep from falling.

Tree branches scraped the side of the Jeep. Dust swirled, mixing with exhaust fumes as spinning tires sought traction in the sandy shoulder. Taking sudden hold, the Jeep fishtailed back onto the pavement.

At the same time, a white blur whizzed by and continued its erratic rush out of sight around another bend. I twisted my head to look out the back window. "Did you see that guy? Was that the neighbor's truck?"

Jesse re-adjusted the rearview mirror as if the encounter threw the whole car out of alignment. "He came out of nowhere. Want me to turn around and follow?"

"Do you mind?" My heart still pounded from the near miss. "I guess he *does* go out every day after all. *That's* not my imagination."

Changing direction on the narrow roadway took more time than we anticipated. Jesse accelerated to decrease the gap between us. After a few minutes, we came to the stop sign at the end of the street. I looked both directions but didn't see a white pickup anywhere. Where had he gone? Did he go the same place every morning?

Questions about Will Payne just kept piling up. Why couldn't we find any answers?

10

Chapter Ten

"Which way?" Jesse pulled onto the shoulder, turning his head from one side to the other as he waited for direction. To the right, the street we usually took into town wound through the trees. Left led to Highway 49, bypassing Grass Valley.

A car behind us slowed before continuing around the Jeep. The occupants peered askance at us as they passed. I offered a weak smile and a shrug.

I fidgeted, expecting my instinctual direction finder to kick in. Sometimes I have a good sense of direction and have guessed correctly more often than not in our travels.

Patience had never been Jesse's strong suit. His fingers tapped the steering wheel while he monitored oncoming traffic in the rearview mirror. "Christine?"

No matter how hard I concentrated, I had no idea which way to turn. "I … don't know."

He pursed his lips.

I didn't want him to lose his temper; not while I needed his help. "Maybe we could go after him another time. Anyway, if there are leftover clues to Molly's whereabouts, they're getting colder by the minute."

Jesse agreed, so we returned home to change clothes.

Mindful of Ed Callahan's warning, we outfitted ourselves in pants tucked into hiking boots and long-sleeved shirts tucked into work gloves. We advanced along the fence around our yard—heads bowed to search for anything we might have missed in the dark—but found nothing out of the ordinary.

Hands planted on my hips, I scanned the yard. She couldn't have disappeared without leaving a single trace. I felt my blood pressure elevate a few degrees.

Jesse linked his arm with mine. "Not time to worry, Christine. We haven't scouted the woods yet."

When I didn't move, he tugged me toward him. Arm in arm, we marched to the gate on the wooded end of our yard. From there, we had to continue single file along the narrow dirt footpath meandering into the trees. I followed Jesse, treading as if on cat paws. The deeper we tramped into the woods, the more vegetation blocked our way. Soon, we lost the path altogether.

Jesse stopped and cupped his hands around his mouth. "Molly. Molly."

A tree branch crashed to the ground. We stood still to listen.

No Molly.

Jesse pivoted 180 degrees and called in the opposite direction. "Molly." After maybe half a minute of silence, we returned to thrashing through the undergrowth.

Ahead, something scurried in the leaves.

I froze. "What was that?"

"Squirrels. Or birds, maybe. Something small."

"Sure it wasn't a snake?"

Jesse smirked. "Couldn't be a snake. Moved too fast."

I picked my way through the brush, arms bent and pinned to my chest. By affecting various intricate contortions, I managed minimal contact with tree branches and plants. Jesse disappeared ahead, intruding on the forest like a bulldozer.

After a few minutes, he backtracked, scowling when he found me. "What are you doing back here?"

"Trying not to touch anything."

"Why?"

"There might be ticks on these trees."

He waved his arms. "For Pete's sake, Christine! Of course, there are ticks. Ticks and all kinds of icky bugs. Don't be a whiny baby. You can't avoid them in these dense woods. Not with all the deer. Just push through. Think of it as … an adventure." He crashed forward into the brush.

I'd rather not have this kind of adventure, thank you, but soon I had to accept the impossibility of avoiding the trees. I took a deep breath, extended both arms in front, and closed my eyes for a moment before setting out again. Somehow, I managed to pull through the tangle, ducking under limbs and breaking branches as I forged ahead. I banished thoughts of ticks, but then I thought of Molly. *Where would Will hide her?*

Here and there, I sighted bare ground peeking through. Every now and then, I spied a footprint—deer and lots of smaller ones like raccoons or squirrels—but nothing I thought the right size or shape to be Molly's.

By plodding steadily, I soon caught up to where Jesse stopped to call again. Through my shirtsleeve, I scratched a spot that felt like a bug bite. "Are we still on our property?"

"Don't know." Jesse glanced back the way we'd come. "No telling where we are at this point." He turned, staring into the woods on all sides. "Wish I'd brought a compass."

"What kind of Boy Scout are you? You're never going to make Eagle Scout at this rate." *What a stupid idea.* Molly had more sense than to come into these woods. I scratched madly at another spot on my arm, taking out frustration on imaginary tick bites.

Jesse lumbered off again through the brush.

I called after him. "Wouldn't we have seen something by now if she came this way?"

He didn't break stride, yelling his answer over his shoulder. "Don't think she did. She couldn't get through. Plus, as you say, no prints or clumps of black-and-white fur on broken branches. Not a sign of her."

I nodded. Of course, the two of us would never be able to comb this entire area looking for fur on broken branches.

After another session of pushing through the brush, we stopped again. Stillness embraced us with not so much as a breeze moving in the treetops. It felt as if the thick woods had swallowed us whole. Newspaper headlines flashed into my brain: *Grass Valley Couple Found Dead in Woods Only Yards from Home.* "What if we get lost in here?"

Jesse shot an intolerant glare over one shoulder.

"Seriously, Jesse. Do you know how to get out of here?"

"We're going downhill. Just keep up, will you?"

But down what hill? I hurried to catch up again.

After another interval, I noticed shafts of light touching the ground between the trees. We quickened our pace and before long pushed through the brush into a small clearing.

Jesse stooped to examine a dark lump on the ground. "Someone camped here. Could be the tramp Ed mentioned."

I bent for a closer look. "Very funny. Why would someone camp way out here?"

Jesse found a stick to poke into the mass. The damp clump tore apart like clothing. It might have been a shirt or sweater rotting in the damp fall air. Beside the mound, blackened pieces of wood, cigarette butts, and a rusty tin can minus the paper label provided evidence of an intruder.

"What kind of fool makes a fire in these woods?" I asked from a safe distance. With as little rain as the Sierra Nevada Mountains had gotten lately, one small campfire threatened to consume the forest in seconds. "I'm surprised no one saw the fire and came to investigate."

Jesse pointed. "Look over there. Is that a building?" We trudged onward a few more feet before emerging at the back of the Paynes' detached garage.

"Well, look at that. Must be a sign we need to hunt for Molly down here." I brushed off my arms and legs in case of ticks. We should've come here in the first place. "Jesse, come with me to see Lila. We can ask her about Molly. Please."

He put his hand on his hip. "Why would Molly be here?"

"Just a gut feeling. That man took an unusual interest in our dog."

Jesse grabbed my shoulders and shook. "Stop with the feelings already—and the imaginary villains and jumping to silly conclusions. I want to find Molly as much as you do. I just think we should use our heads. And frankly, I'm tired." He let go of my shoulders and bent to stare in my eyes. "Let's take a break. Huh? We'll go home and call the Callahans. Maybe they've heard something by now." Jesse turned and plodded toward the hill leading to our house.

He didn't understand. I couldn't quit. Not yet.

I glanced toward the gray house but didn't see Will's truck. Drapes covered the windows at the back, with no faces peeking out. "I'll be there in a few minutes."

I turned to the stack of cardboard boxes.

Laying three and four deep in a heap almost shoulder high, the boxes took up more space than I'd guessed from my exercise room vantage point. These boxes must be significant. I skirted the outside of the mound and returned to my starting place. All appeared to be closed and taped.

Behind me, a shuffling broke my concentration and I looked up to find Jesse striding toward me. "I thought you were right behind."

I ignored his disapproving tone.

"Is this the same place they burned the branches and leaves last year?"

He frowned. "Looks like it. There's a layer of black ash underneath the boxes."

I crouched to stare closer at the pile.

"Christine."

I peered up at him.

"We're trespassing."

I shrugged, certain that any sensible sleuth would just open the boxes and look inside. Nancy Drew would. I removed my work gloves and stuffed them in the pocket of my jeans. I pushed at a box and heard the contents shift inside. "These boxes are not empty." I pointed to the tape. "Give me your knife?"

"Knife? Now hold on a minute—"

I leveled a *don't-mess-with-me-now* look.

With a sigh and quick glance toward the house, he grabbed my arm and steered me around to face him. "Look, Christine. I'm uncomfortable digging in the neighbors' boxes without permission. Don't make me drag you home by the hair."

He picked a fine time to try his macho humor. I planted both hands on my hips and glared. "Like you Tarzan, me Jane? Come on, Jesse, what could it hurt?"

He sighed. "Okay, Sherlock. Against my better judgment, let's ask Lila if she's seen the dog."

First we came to the detached garage. I tried the knob on the side door. Locked. I headed right, peeking in a dirt-streaked window. In the interior darkness, shadowy furniture appeared to be stacked high against the walls, leaving the center empty—a space roughly big enough for one car.

"Is that a dresser?" I pointed. "Why would the furniture be in the garage and not in the house?"

Jesse stood beside me, shielding his eyes for a better view. "That *is* weird."

After calling Molly's name as we circled the garage again, we satisfied ourselves that she wasn't inside. Then we wandered to the front door via a small wood-plank patio connected to the front porch and walkway. I knocked, paused, and knocked again. Jesse pounded. No one came.

"She's not here." How could that be? According to Zora Jane, Lila never went anywhere. "Could there have been someone besides Will in that truck that almost hit us?"

Jesse hunched his shoulders. "I barely even saw the truck."

Maybe she was hiding from us or sleeping so soundly she couldn't hear knocking. Either way, no one would stop us. "All righty, then. Let's see what's in those boxes."

I spun on my heel and strode toward the pile. Jesse followed.

When he caught up, I opened my palm like a doctor in an operating room. "Knife, please."

Jesse hesitated, but I didn't withdraw my hand, so he pulled his silver autographed Chuck Buck knife out of his pocket and sliced open the nearest box.

Sucking in a deep steadying breath, I steeled my emotions and peered inside. A jumble of fabric peeked back. From the clothing, I tugged out a dirty, aqua blouse about Lila's size. Poking and pushing, I dug inside to find the box filled with ladies' clothing—sweaters, pants, skirts, and blouses—stuffed together without care. "I don't get this. Why pack the boxes with clothing and dump them outside?"

Jesse shrugged and glanced toward the house again. "I really think we should go. Now, Christine."

A bolt of energy charged through me. Partaking of forbidden fruit ignited an unfamiliar thrill. I indicated another box while I replaced the shirt and tucked the box flaps together so they would stay shut. "Open this one."

Jesse applied his blade to the tape and popped open the second box. A wad of yellowed newsprint tumbled out as he tilted the box toward me. Voracious as though starving, I pawed through paper wrapped around various knick-knacks: a couple of milk glass vases, bookends, a few chipped ironstone bowls and small plates, assorted china animals—mostly dogs—and several mismatched salt and pepper shakers with salt and pepper still inside.

I blinked at Jesse. "Why are they getting rid of all this?" Not waiting for his answer, I bent to study the ashes underneath the boxes. "And why take the time to wrap the stuff and box it like they're moving if they plan to burn it?"

He shook his head, eyebrows pulled closely together.

My groping fingers closed on a flat, padded piece and I drew out a business envelope with several photos inside. The subjects in the pictures looked strangely familiar—a younger, healthier version of Lila and Will. In a couple of photos, Lila might have been forty or fifty pounds heavier—hard to tell because a long, loose caftan covered her body. She still had that lost waif expression, but her face appeared rounder. Neither of them smiled. One picture showed Lila holding a puppy. "These must be Will and Lila, don't you think?" I held the pictures out to Jesse.

"Probably. They weren't taken here, though. That's not this house." He pointed to a farmhouse, featured as the backdrop in several pictures, and then checked the Payne house again. "We need to go … now."

While I filed through the pictures once more, Jesse bent to retrieve the wad of newspaper that fell out, flattening its wrinkles between his palms. "This is a newspaper from Iowa."

Most of *The Des Moines Herald Examiner* heading showed at the top but only part of the date. "Zora Jane said they came from a small town in Iowa. I think that last number in the date is a five, but it could also be a two."

Jesse studied the heading. Since he wore glasses with lineless bifocals, he could read close-up without any problem. I needed magnifiers, since only my nearsightedness had been corrected by the laser surgery.

"That's a two, February 2." He stuffed the paper into the pocket of his jacket. "Okay. Come on, Christine."

Jesse took the newspaper, why not one of the pictures too? I palmed the photo of Lila and the puppy as I slid the others back into the envelope, managing it unobtrusively. With a flourish, I placed the envelope back among the wadded newspaper in case an audience watched my performance. Then I folded the flaps together and piled the two boxes on the mound so the tucked-in sides rested underneath to hide their violated openings.

"No one's home," I said, doing a mental hand rub. "Let's check out the house."

11

Chapter Eleven

I pounded on the front door. "For sure she's not home. She couldn't sleep through all this racket. Not unless she's unconscious or drugged." I punched the rusted doorbell once more for good measure.

Jesse fidgeted at the bottom of the porch. "Right. Let's go!"

The white truck had not reappeared, and no sign of life presented itself. Despite the sunshine at our house, the sinister cloud of silence hanging over the property seemed to grow darker and thicker by the minute. I didn't budge. "Something is wrong here."

Jesse threw me a disapproving frown. "How much real trespassing do you propose to do today?"

"Come on, Jesse. We need to be sure he's not hiding Molly inside. I know he took her. If you saw how that man glared—"

"We're *not* breaking into their house, Christine, no matter what you know."

"Okay. Okay." I stalled to think. "Let's just look around a bit." Off I went, looking. I didn't know exactly what I was looking for, but all the answers had to be hidden in this house.

Jesse followed a few paces behind as I inched along the wood-plank walkway. Narrow flowerbeds between the sidewalk and the house held hard-packed dirt and a few straggling dried stalks. Firewood filled the detached garage.

He stared at the wood. "Looks like they've been storing wood a long time."

Stacks of wood had been piled so tightly together that even a small person like Lila would have trouble squeezing through the gaps. "There's not even a path to walk between. How do they get to the back of the garage?" And why hadn't we ever heard them chopping or splitting wood?

The little garage contained other things besides wood. At the side closest to the house, an old-fashioned rounded refrigerator like from my childhood crouched in a dark space with just enough room to open the door. Concealed by the short front wall on the side of the opening, I'd never noticed it before.

A thick metal chain circled it, fastened by a heavy-duty lock.

I leaned closer. "Why put a padlock on the refrigerator? Are they afraid someone might steal their food?" I peered behind the refrigerator into darkness to determine whether it was plugged in or not. Motor chugging answered back.

In the rear of the garage, a row of storage cabinets stood like weathered sentinels guarding the wood. Stacks of firewood blocked the cabinet doors. Along the side near the refrigerator, an assortment of mason jars with old-looking liquids perched on spacers between the exposed wood studs. "What's that?"

Jesse peeked in. "Judging from the way the liquid separated, I'd guess paint."

Below the jars, a worn red gas can leaned against the wall. On nails on the other side of the jars hung an assortment of garden tools, their wood handles aged to gray and their rusty metal crusted with hard clods of red Nevada County dirt. At the far end, metal chains and ropes looped on hooks. A couple of aluminum folding chairs rested underneath. In the rafters, fishing poles teetered. An old brown leather suitcase and a well-used fishing creel crammed a narrow ledge. Two dovetailed wooden crates like the ones my father stored ammunition in held down an unsteady pile of flattened cardboard boxes. A thin layer of dust blurred everything.

I finished my examination of the rafters just as Jesse stood from a crouch, frowning at an object in his open palm.

"What—?" I didn't finish the question as the significance of what he held registered in my brain.

Dog tags. Molly's dog tags. The O-ring that once connected them to her blue collar had been twisted open as if ripped apart in a struggle.

My heart raced as I met his eyes. A wave of dizziness roared over me. I grabbed Jesse's shirtsleeve to steady myself. "I told you that man took Molly. Where were they?"

Jesse pointed to a weedy patch just outside the opening to the garage. His eyes held a mystified quality, as if processing this development required slow deliberate concentration. I bent to pat the area, but only found an abandoned spigot. The round faucet handle had partially broken off and the threads had rusted red. Dry hard-packed dirt precluded footprints.

Jesse swiped his forehead and gazed toward the house. "This might be more than we should tackle alone." He nodded toward the Callahans' house on the other side of the street. "I think we need to call in reinforcements."

My eyes followed his gaze. I shook my head, unready to leave. "Maybe she's inside. We could try all the doors and windows in case one is unlocked." I knew Jesse wouldn't approve, so I threw that last bit in evenly, hoping to make it sound reasonable.

The stiff set of Jesse's jaw revealed his desire to protest. I took off before he could do so. Striding manically from window to window, I tugged and pushed. The screens in the front didn't move. I proceeded to the side, mindless of whether Jesse followed or not. All the windows fit snugly in their tracks. I continued to the door on the back stoop, which I found locked just like the sliding door on the concrete patio. I kept going until at last one of the back windows moved a bit as I pushed it through the screen.

Jesse stood on the patio with his arms crossed.

"It opened!" I threw him a pleading look. "Come here. Jesse, please. Help me. If I can just make this opening a tiny bit bigger, I can peek inside."

His expression said he wanted to say no, but he inched closer anyway. By then, I'd already commenced pushing and wiggling the screen.

"If you find something, how will you explain your actions to the authorities?" Jesse always plans before he acts. I usually act first and then realize I'd have fewer mistakes and better results if I had planned.

This time, though, I trusted my instinct. I needed to get into this house. Answers waited. Molly waited. I applied greater pressure, breaking a fingernail in the process. I stopped a moment to inspect the damage and then attacked the screen with renewed vigor to punish it for ruining my manicure. As if in contrition, the screen slid up and popped out. So I yanked the offending barrier from the window.

Ha! Score one for acting first.

I opened the window enough to stick my head through and peeked into the dark interior.

A typical bedroom greeted me. A mid-century maple bed rested close to the window. The tousled bedclothes exposed one corner of striped ticking. My nose puckered at the odor of sweat and dirty socks. *Washing machine must be broken.*

Beside the bed, an old-fashioned black dial telephone perched on the carpet atop a pile of wadded clothing. The enormity of the space dwarfed the bed, which sat alone in the center of the room.

Jesse's shout sounded far away. "Does the phrase, 'breaking and entering' mean anything to you?" The voice of conscience.

I pretended not to hear.

Jesse whispered, "What do you see in there?"

Turning my head to his side, I stage-whispered. "It's just a bedroom. Can you boost me up so I can get in?"

He stepped behind me and put his hands on my hips as if he could hold me back. "Get in? Are you crazy? You're not living in a movie mystery, you know. This is reality. Come on, Christine. Let's get out of here. Do you hear me?"

I heard him, but it didn't matter. I'd come this far and couldn't turn back. Opening the window as wide as I could, I gripped the side and jumped a couple of times. Somehow, I managed to boost myself upward far enough so my middle cleared the ledge. Leaning forward, the momentum propelled me off balance so I toppled into the room. I landed on my head and one shoulder with a muffled thud that surprised me and knocked the air out of my lungs for a moment. Pain throbbed where my waist scraped the windowsill. A stabbing headache pulsated inside my brain.

"Christine Sterling!" Jesse stuck his head through the window. "I can't believe you did that. Do you know how old you are?"

This from a man who dressed in cowboy costumes. I closed my eyes and ears, but I could still hear him blabbering.

"You could break something. Come out right now!"

By then, I'd righted myself and begun to investigate the room. Rubbing the welt that throbbed across my midsection, I ignored both Jesse and the bass drum beating inside my brain.

A closet door stood ajar just enough to detect outlines of clothing. I stuck my throbbing head in and saw a walk-in closet, about medium-size. A wave of nausea washed over me as I inhaled pungent shoe odor. Piles of work boots littered the floor. Rows of men's clothes hung along the back. On a hook at the left dangled a red plaid wool jacket. A small cutout door in the ceiling indicated attic access.

Not a feminine sign in the entire room. *Where is Lila?*

I tiptoed toward the doorway. "I'm going to look around," I said over my departing shoulder. "Meet me at the front door."

12

Chapter Twelve

Jesse mumbled something in which the words *snoop* and *brain-dead* featured prominently. I tiptoed into the hall, as preoccupied as a cow at milking time. To my right, I first came upon a closed door. Opening it with caution, I peeked into a second smaller bedroom. Stale air and body odor filled my nostrils and I almost gagged. Air circulation in this room had been restricted far too long. The room's only furnishings included a mahogany nightstand and a single bed in much the same condition as the first bed I'd seen. Checking the closet, I found it empty, except for a couple of hangers that fell to dwell among the dust bunnies.

I couldn't deduce the identity or gender of the room's occupant from the furnishings or lack thereof. Just like the larger bedroom, the color and design of the décor gave no hint. The red plaid wool jacket and men's clothing in the first closet belonged to Will. That seemed logical. But I hadn't yet seen anything that looked as if it might belong to Lila.

"Molly?" I called aloud, hoping to fill the emptiness. "Are you here?"

Silence answered.

Turning my attention to the nightstand, I encountered stacks of old paperbacks, sections of yellowed newspaper, assorted magazines, and wads of used Kleenexes—an untidy mess. I grimaced. *Dirty*

Kleenexes? Why save them? I pulled the gardening gloves out of my pocket. Bulky and clumsy, they would at least protect my hands from germs. They wouldn't leave fingerprints either. I moved the pile to the bed, examining each item.

At the bottom, I came to a writing tablet, the kind held together with a metal coil on the left side. I removed one glove so I could flip from the beginning and discovered several pages of writing in a small, cramped, but painstakingly neat hand, devoid of punctuation and capitalization. Doodles embellished several pages. Being a former librarian, the lack of proper mechanics grated my sensibilities.

Stuck between two of the pages I discovered a black-and-white photograph, crumpled and bent as if someone handled it too often-a young girl and a smaller boy. The pair held hands and stared directly into the camera. Wide eyes, no smiles, hopeless and helpless. The girl looked like a young Lila.

I returned the picture to the middle of the tablet and flipped to the beginning. There I read a melancholy verse, which I assumed to be a poem, although the ends of the lines didn't rhyme. I wrinkled my nose, much preferring poetry that rhymes. The writer—Lila, I assumed—overused exaggerated images of blood, murder, and punishment to the point of seeming contrived and intentionally gory. "Dark avenging angels—piles of maggots—punishing fire—screeching ravens—Oh, ick!" I turned the page.

The words of the second poem painted an even darker picture of impending doom. Surreal images of babies with wicked-looking grown-up faces heightened the distasteful mood. Drawn in pencil on all four borders of the page, the ghoulish babies stood out luridly against the paper. The hair on the back of my neck prickled.

Leafing through with tentative fingers, I counted thirteen poems, some illustrated, some not. The drawings looked so creepy, I hurried past them. A newspaper article had been scotch-taped inside the back cover. Both newsprint and tape had yellowed and become brittle with age, like the crumpled newspaper in the boxes on the fire pile. This article must have been cut from the middle of a page because it didn't include the date or a heading.

The body of a baby boy was discovered outside Harvard on Saturday morning by a group of local children. Wrapped in a blue receiving blanket, the newborn had apparently been interred in a shallow grave for some time. Authorities did not know the identity of the child, nor how it came to be abandoned in the town of fewer than 400. The Iowa Division of Criminal Investigation and the Guthrie County Sheriff's Office are investigating near the water tower where the body was found. An autopsy will be scheduled to determine cause of death.

As I flipped back to the beginning to reexamine the first "poem," I heard Jesse pounding on the front door. Startled by the thunderous racket he made, I inadvertently tore the page.

"Oh, dear!" I hesitated, unsure what to do about the tear. "Might as well pull it all the way out, I guess." I tore out the page and stuffed it into my pocket. Jesse's loud commotion continued. Soon he would rouse the neighborhood. I replaced the notebook on the night table and tugged my glove back on.

I reassembled the untidy stack with great care, puzzling over the article. *Whose baby was that? Lila and Will's?* Someone killed him. What if it was Lila? She cut out the article and kept it in her poem book. Clearly, the article interested her or was important for some reason. Why keep it if she wasn't involved? But how could the frail creature I met be involved in something as hideous as infanticide?

I moved toward the knocking.

Down the hall—the one Zora Jane and I hadn't taken from the entrance the other day—I came to a gap in the wall where stairs descended to the lower level of the house. Under normal circumstances, a black hole leading to who-knows-what would scare the soup out of me, but this didn't qualify as a normal circumstance, and the stairs beckoned. I peered into the inky stairwell.

Jesse's knocking persisted as I raced downward. Were his knuckles getting sore? I rounded the corner, and a large room opened before me.

In the dim light filtering down the stairwell, what might once have been a game room became visible. Two closed doors faced each other on either side. I picked one and pushed it open tentatively, my heart thundering so loudly that for a moment I couldn't hear Jesse.

The small room lacked a window, being only marginally larger than a good-sized walk-in closet. Stacks of cardboard boxes lined one wall, as if placed there by someone in the act of moving out or moving in. Must be a storage chamber built into the cool slope as an afterthought.

I went to the next door and opened it with less anxiety. Again, unsteady stacks of cardboard boxes were piled in the middle of the space, but the room held nothing else.

Tiptoeing to the darker side across the dim subterranean hall, I pulled on the knob of the third closed door.

At first, I saw only thick blackness. But as my eyes adjusted to the lack of light, a shrine appeared, spread along the far wall. Dozens of half-used white candles covered the floor in front of a low altar. In the center of the room, a large, irregularly shaped stain spread across the concrete floor like a dark rug. A thick roll of something leaned against the wall in one corner. I couldn't identify the material, but an image of crumpled wrapping paper discarded after a birthday party came to mind.

A strange, acrid stench overpowered my senses. The air hung thick with naked evil.

Why did it remind me of snakes and spiders?

My heart raced, roaring in my ears like a jackhammer about to blow a gasket. My airways constricted, repulsed by the air I sucked into my lungs.

Go to the light! Hurry!

I jumped back as if I'd touched a red-hot stovetop. Operating on pure survival instinct, I staggered out and up the stairs the way I'd come.

My heart pounded as if it might explode as I rushed to the front entryway. When I opened the door to daylight, I abruptly encountered Jesse, inflamed with aggravation.

He yanked my arm, dragging me out. His face flared red. Anger seethed from his usually emotionless voice. "What were you doing in there?"

"We've got to get out of here! Quick!" I tugged his arm, but he didn't listen, as if he hadn't noticed my rapid breathing or the terror in my voice.

"Were you born in a barn?" He reached inside to lock the door before banging it shut. His eyes flashed when he spoke. "This is completely unacceptable—"

"Okay, okay, lecture me later. Right now we need—"

"I replaced the window screen for you. You probably forgot all about *that*. Even wiped it down in case you left fingerprints. Do you know you can go to jail for breaking into—?"

"There's no time now, Jesse. We have to go." I ran, turning back at the corner to beckon him.

Jesse glared after me, arms akimbo. His fury had shut out reason. Had he heard anything I said?

I motioned him to hurry.

Mouth set in a thin rigid line, his eyes narrowed before he marched toward me. He nearly knocked me over as he rushed by. At our property boundary, Jesse high-stepped over the fence, but didn't stop a second to assist me. With short legs like mine, getting over the fence proved challenging, but he didn't glance back to see how I fared. Nor did he help me negotiate the hard, lumpy sod of the weed-infested pasture. How could I love someone who behaved in such a thoughtless, unkind manner?

I brushed away tears as I struggled to keep up. He had no right to be upset, not after what I'd just experienced. Once again, when I needed his support, his own agenda came first. I felt my face redden and I steamed, hot with vexation. Maybe I just wouldn't tell him what I saw. Maybe I'd never speak to him again.

We had never used our back gate before. It opened to the pasture in the corner where our property lay closest to the gray house. When Jesse got to the gate, he yanked it open without breaking stride, using such force I looked to see if he'd ripped it off it's hinges. I stomped after him.

He was angry, for sure.

But so was I.

13

Chapter Thirteen

Even after we returned to the sanctity of our house, Jesse continued the punishing silence. Instead of speaking to me, he called the Callahans to share the latest news. "Ed, this is Jesse Sterling. Listen, our dog Molly is still missing. You haven't seen her, have you?"

I paced across the kitchen while Jesse listened to Ed's answer.

Without looking my way, Jesse shook his head. "I don't think she went into the woods. We followed the path you suggested but didn't see any sign of her." He turned his back and lowered his voice. "We ended up at the Paynes' and found Molly's dog tags beside that first garage."

I crept closer. Not too close, though, since I didn't know whether Jesse might explode or not.

Molly's dog tags at the Paynes' must have interested Ed, because Jesse repeated that information twice, adding additional details the second time. I returned to pacing, debating with myself about sharing my discoveries with Jesse. He certainly didn't deserve it.

Jesse listened a short time. "Well, if you hear anything or happen to see Molly, we'd appreciate a call. Thanks, Ed."

The phone crashed into its cradle on the dry sink. Placing both hands on the slate surface, he lowered his head and sucked in several deep breaths, letting the air out slowly. I stepped back, keeping the kitchen island between us in case a shield became necessary.

When he faced me, his eyes crackled, but the evenness of his voice almost masked the intense feeling mirrored in his eyes. "Did you hit your head and get brain damage? What were you thinking? You can't go around jumping in people's windows without being invited. Have you completely lost your mind?"

"Just a minute, Jesse." My voice quivered. "I have to tell you … about the room downstairs." I shivered, aware of coldness deep inside that I feared might never get warm again. "Bad things are happening in that house."

To justify my actions, I told him about the poem book, although I didn't show him the page I tore out. That secret plunder burned a quiet hole in the safety of my pocket. Rather than feed him the whole sordid story at once, I'd give him a little and see how he reacted.

He crossed his arms.

Words flew out faster. "There's a newspaper clipping taped inside the back cover, like the papers we found in the boxes—from Iowa. The clipping is about a dead baby."

A scowl spread over Jesse's handsome face. He shifted weight, showing his usual impatience with holding off judgment while I elongated my story.

I paused, studying his expression.

His fingers drummed one arm, intolerance growing as seconds ticked by. "What's your point? They subscribed to the *Des Moines Herald Examiner.* That would be normal for someone living in Iowa." From his pocket, he extracted the crumpled piece of newsprint and held it in his hand. "Are you suggesting this baby connects to the Paynes?"

"Certainly to Lila. Maybe it's Lila and Will's baby."

"Because you found a newspaper article?"

"Not just that." How could I make him understand? "The back page with the clipping … it's covered with splotches. Like she cried on it … more than once. And the poems mention babies dying and the pain going on and on. I definitely think they're connected."

His lip curled into a sneer.

My insides burned like salt in a cut. "Don't laugh at me, Jesse. That woman is wounded, and her pain has something to do with a baby."

Jesse leaned against the kitchen island and recomposed his face. He wasn't smiling, but his features were no longer tight either. "What you've got is an overactive imagination. You always do this. You take some little observation that may or may not be fact and make up a story to explain it. Pure guesswork. In this case, there could be any number of other explanations."

I cocked my head. "Such as?"

"Such as, Lila clipped the article out of morbid curiosity like when people gather around accident sites. Maybe she can't have babies, so she's fixated on other people's babies. Did you ever consider that your sweet little Lila might be a psycho?"

My shoulders drooped. I hated to be talked down to. Why couldn't he ever accept what I said? After all these years, why didn't he remember how good my hunches usually proved to be? At least half the time, anyway.

He dropped his arms and re-crossed them the opposite way. "Most likely there's no connection at all."

I lowered my eyes, staring at the kitchen tiles.

"Did Lila sign the poems? Was her name anywhere in the book?"

I shook my head without looking up.

"So you don't even know if she wrote them. This kind of thing is not real evidence, you know. You'd need a handwriting expert to prove Lila wrote it."

Oh, sure, use logic against me. "There was also a photo in the book. A boy and a girl. I'm sure the girl was Lila."

"Because Lila's name was on the picture?"

He had no clue what I'd seen and felt. A brief flashback of that dark hole skulked across my memory. "That's not even the worst part. In the basement, down the stairs …" Just the thought disturbed the regular beating of my heart.

With faltering words, I told him about the shrine room with the dark stain that looked like dried blood. "You can say what you want. I know something awful happened there. I can't explain it, but I felt it. I'm sure it's all connected to Lila." I shook my head. "You should've seen her eyes. Pain, intense pain. And bruises on her arm and neck … I don't know how that connects either, but it adds up to evil things in that house. We've got to help Lila. Plus, that awful man took Molly, and who knows what he's done with *her*. Don't forget he threatened me."

Jesse arched one eyebrow.

I started to cry. Maybe from that vile hormone fluctuation that comes at this season of a woman's life. Or simply from discomfiture. I didn't do it on purpose, but a crying female always elicits a reaction in men. Jesse softened as he drew me toward him. When I felt his strong arms around me, I let go and bawled like an orphan calf. After I'd cried it all out, I allowed him to comfort me.

The overcast autumn afternoon brought a chill that invaded the house like a foreign army, magnifying my disappointment about our failure to find Molly. The frosty air sent icy fingers curling around us, cutting off circulation to arms and legs. Jesse built a cheery fire in the river rock fireplace. The crackling comforted me, and soon the air warmed enough to thaw my appendages. While I soaked in the warmth, the sense of looming depravity dissipated into distant memory.

I collapsed onto the sage green sectional in the living room, tucking in with the beige afghan my mother crocheted at over eighty years of age. The cats came to console me.

Roy and Hoppy taunted and wrestled like rivals, and then groomed each other before entwining into one furry mass to sleep on my legs. I caressed the similar white markings on their black fur. Sometimes they were hard to tell apart. Sleeping together, they looked like a two-headed zebra.

Jesse stood near the fire, warming his hands like a stranger.

The first rain of the season fell outside, starting softly, then pouring down. Watching the cats sleep, I remembered poor Molly. Would God answer our prayers for her safety?

After a while, my growling stomach reminded me that we hadn't eaten all day, so I pulled out from under the sleeping cats. I guided

Jesse to the sectional and piled a fluffy green lap robe over him. Then I prepared a platter of his favorite Sunday night snack: cheese, crackers, and fruit.

When I returned with the food, Jesse sat staring into the fire as if mesmerized. I roused him so we could eat in the glow of scented candles while the fire warmed the room.

In the glittery light, I watched Jesse's face. Memories of better times left me wishing for more. His hazel eyes sometimes seemed mostly blue and other times mostly green. I never knew how to read them. His chiseled features and sharp wit always kept me guessing about his degree of seriousness. I called his sense of humor *edgy*. Some people called it *peculiar*. Too bad we couldn't turn back time to when I laughed in delight at everything he said.

Stomachs satisfied, we spent most of the next hour in thoughtful discussion of Molly's disappearance and Lila's unfortunate plight. Leaning on Jesse's strength and methodical problem-solving skills gave me hope. Although he couldn't immediately solve this particular puzzle with all its abnormal pieces, his attempts to organize it reassured me.

After we'd exhausted all angles we could think of, silence engulfed us. The fire crackled and popped. Jesse stared into the flames, holding a steaming cup of hot chocolate with both hands. "You know I love you, don't you?"

I wished he'd gazed into my eyes when he said that. "I guess you do. You're still here."

The fire commanded his attention. "I do. I'm sorry about this morning."

"What about this morning?"

"Yelling at you, calling you names, not helping you, accusing you of imagining. You know. All that stuff. That was selfish. I didn't mean it."

"You meant it. You were mad at me."

"I should've been more supportive, though."

I would've liked a wordier apology—at least fifteen minutes of groveling and pleading for forgiveness. But I'd gotten more than I expected. Jesse didn't apologize easily. Besides, I had to concede that I might have been a bit foolhardy in breaking into the Paynes' house. It must have frightened him. I moved closer and pried the mug from his fingers. Then I pulled him back onto the sectional where I burrowed into his strong shoulder and sniffed his familiar scent. "I'm sorry for scaring you." I reached up to touch his face. "I love you, Jesse."

The remainder of the evening blended into a hazy, contented blur, following the natural order of romantic interludes. Long-overdue lovemaking was tender and sweet. Afterward we lay in our bed, listening to the steady rainfall on the roof. Jesse drew me toward him to rest my head on his chest. His arm enfolded me securely. I snuggled. We lay without speaking, drifting to sleep, which for Jesse took only a few seconds, as usual.

Many moons passed since I last felt this close to my husband. I didn't want the evening to end. To keep myself from falling asleep, I replayed the entire interval in my mind and marveled at the easy way we'd conversed. So often, when I wanted to talk, Jesse did not, or vice versa. Whoever instigated the conversation ended up hurt and added another brick to the wall that separated us. More and more, we spiraled into parallel isolation, reinforcing my imagined inability to communicate.

With all my heart, I ached for healing in our relationship. Not merely a respite, like we'd just experienced, but a genuine cure. Clueless how to find it, I needed someone with power great enough to change us. Zora Jane always pointed me to God when I mentioned a problem. Maybe he had that kind of power. I would give him another try.

I slipped out of bed and padded barefoot to my office. Kneeling beside the ottoman, I prayed. *God, are you listening? I need help. How did this wall between Jesse and me get so immense and impregnable? Where did our friendship go?*

During the busy years of parenting and career building, the bond between us seemed strong, sustained by common goals. We shared interests and priorities for many years—more, it seemed, than most couples we knew. Before we retired, we always had someone or something else to focus on. Perhaps we allowed our relationship to become stunted by our busy lives. However it happened, at some point we ceased to encourage intimacy and the wall between us grew.

I stood to gaze through my office window. The roof jutted out, preventing a clear view of the Paynes' house. The Paynes—they were dysfunctional with a capital *D*. What caused the misery at that house?

Little hurts multiplied over time. Unattended, they could never heal.

A quiet voice in my head repeated the thought I had earlier—men are such poor communicators.

No, another soft voice argued. I must claim my fault too. I withheld communication for many reasons. Mostly stubborn resentment. Our relationship never matured enough to make resolution of hurts natural. A tower of unresolved injuries stacked up until it became so tall I could no longer see Jesse over the top.

I tiptoed back to our bedroom and peeked inside. Jesse lay on his back, snoring rhythmically. Did he have a stack of injuries on his side of the wall that kept him from actually seeing me?

Watching him, I remembered times it appeared that he tried to tear down barriers between us. Usually, I'd take the opportunity of his attention to attack him. Why did I do that? Was that a control issue? Regardless of the reason, instead of leaning toward him, I always bent toward my own inner despair.

I grabbed my heavy chenille robe from the closet, wrapped it close, and then wandered downstairs to the kitchen window.

Like most women my age, I bought the romantic notion that only one special someone would make me truly happy—my own perfect Prince Charming. I needed a man to make me complete.

Lights flickered in the windows at the Payne house. Did Lila think she wouldn't be complete without a man too? I couldn't explain what would have attracted her to Will otherwise.

In return for the sacrifices of dutiful wifehood, the perfect man would cherish and adore me no matter what, 'til death do us part.

Sitcoms of my era always ended happily after half an hour, proving a quick solution existed for every problem. In TV Land, instantaneous intimacy occurred immediately after "I do."

The reality of marriage had long ago shattered such romantic notions. Not counting occasional thoughtful gestures such as remembering birthdays and anniversaries, Jesse refused to fit the "Prince Charming" mold.

Along with that thought, Jesse's attempts to please me rose in my mind as if pleading their own case—stacking higher and higher over the years—plainly Jesse *did* possess a romantic side, albeit not exactly what I expected. With sudden clarity, I saw how I'd concluded that Jesse must have caused our marital problems. I plopped onto a kitchen chair with a thud as my own words rained on me from the darkness.

Jesse doesn't understand me.

Jesse criticizes everything I do.

He is never satisfied.

I can never please him.

He never notices my needs.

Complain, complain, complain. No matter what he did or didn't do, my expectations couldn't be satisfied. My own lack of acceptance had sabotaged hopes for intimacy.

I bowed my head into my hands. "God, if you're there, help me let go of this baggage I've packed my hurts in over the years. I want to accept Jesse just as he is, warts and all. I don't know how to get there, but I want to stop complaining and be thankful instead. Make us love each other like we did at the beginning."

Did God have power to transform me in that way? Marriage self-help books I'd read flooded to mind. I had tried to put various methods into practice. Not one had worked. I must be getting desperate to think God could change us. Yet, with my prayer, an unfamiliar peace descended, giving me a small glimmer of hope.

When I snuggled back into bed, thoughts of Lila still floated above my head like troublesome sugarplums. That same inability to make the puzzle pieces connect diffused my musing like a washing of watercolor paint.

I rolled to one side and shifted attention to Will, the perpetrator of the evil in that house. Okay, so I lacked concrete evidence. I knew what I knew.

Before I drifted to sleep, one errant thought rattled my brain with such force that my eyes flew open and I bolted upright in bed. "Jesse!" I shook him gently. "The gate. It wasn't latched when you opened it … when we came from the Paynes' today. You pulled the gate open instead of unlatching it. That must be how he got Molly out!"

14

Chapter Fourteen

I opened my eyes and indulged in one of my favorite perks of the retirement lifestyle: lagging in bed a few extra minutes before hurrying to begin my day. I kicked off the covers and then lay still to appreciate every minuscule thing in my world, from my bed-head hair to my pearl-pink painted toenails. A childhood hymn of gratitude surprised me when it floated from mind to lips. I hadn't remembered it for years. While I realized anew how truly blessed I'd been, I sang, "Praise God from whom all blessings flow."

The buttery yellow bedroom walls glowed in morning light. Last night's rain cleaned the fall air so it smelled like spring. Outside the window, a freshly laundered world awaited. Colors appeared brighter, bird songs sounded sweeter.

Soon, Jesse's singing echoed as he scrubbed in the shower.

Oh, I love a rainy night. Such a beautiful sight.
I love to feel the rain on my face.
Monday, Monday, so good to me.
Monday, Monday was all I hoped it would be.
I say, Lord have mercy, Lord have mercy on me.
You know I'm crazy 'bout my baby.
Lord, please send her back home to me.

I giggled. *Where did he pick up that combination?* Sometimes I accused him of making lyrics up to fill in his tune. Everything seemed right until my eyes settled on Molly's empty box at the corner of our room. Then sadness trickled in again.

Jesse exited the house singing, probably to continue all the way to the barn. I rolled out of bed and tied on my chenille robe. In the kitchen, I peered out the window at my favorite view. I saw Jesse's white Dodge dualie parked beside the barn. He didn't come right home after feeding the horses. That might mean he found an interesting neighbor to talk to, or more likely, that he decided on an early morning trail ride. He always said bouncing on a horse sifted out the extraneous details of a problem, making the solution easier to recognize.

The rich aroma of french vanilla wafted through the kitchen. Jesse had thoughtfully brewed coffee before he left. I poured a cup and turned to soak in the Grandma Moses landscape.

The Japanese maple beside the pond miraculously recolored to a spectacular coral red since I last noticed it. A flock of birds screeched by, hurried by the slight mist blowing from the left. My eyes followed their flight away from the haziness and then returned to the mist. It didn't exactly look like mist. Too dark. I cocked my head.

That wasn't mist. It was smoke!

I hurried to the deck to investigate. Tall tongues of fire snapped and popped above the hillside.

The Paynes' mountain of cardboard boxes full of household items and cast-off clothing burned under jagged orange flames and plumes of black soot. Tiny cinders swirled through the air above, while heat waves radiated toward our house.

Tractor chugging announced Will Payne seconds before his appearance from the front of the house. He rounded the corner bearing another large box in the bucket. This he dumped onto the pyre before heading back to the house. While I stood frozen by fear, he made four more trips to add boxes to the blaze.

Red-hot flames erupted like a volcano as he deposited each box into the debris. Flashes of light exploded in the blackened pile. Fueled by new supplies of whatever combustible material filled the boxes, the bonfire became a raging inferno. A hazy cloud floated above the neighborhood as a periodic breeze attacked and retreated. Thick clouds of black smoke billowed toward my kitchen.

Will climbed off the tractor and disappeared into the house.

I couldn't tear my eyes away.

The ringing phone demanded attention. I managed to reach inside and pull it to my ear without taking my eyes off the fire.

Ed Callahan's voice boomed. "What's he burning?"

A familiar voice! How comforting. "He made a huge pile of boxes. They're full of house stuff. I can't imagine where he's getting all of it. Do you think I should call the fire department?"

"Well, the rain last night broke our dry spell, so maybe the fire department won't consider this a potential fire hazard. Burn days start as soon as the first rain, I think."

Some morbid fascination with the fire kept my eyes glued to the sight. I almost forgot about Ed until I heard his voice again. "That fire's been burning for hours. I got up for dawn patrol and saw it then."

"What time was that?"

"Before six thirty."

Boxes in the middle of the fire imploded with a crash.

"That smoke is blacker than a hustler's heart," Ed said.

"It's a lot bigger than last year's fire."

"But last year, I think he just burned branches and brush."

The black plume puffed higher into the sky.

I remembered what we found in the boxes. "Why do you think he's burning clothes? Why not give them away if you don't want them?"

He chuckled. "Clothes? He's got clothes in there? He really is off-center." In the pause that followed, I imagined Ed studying the flames. "Listen, the reason I called—remember the Coopers? They live on the other side of the Paynes' off Mustang Hill Road."

"Sure. We met them at your house."

"Right. Well, they were here for dinner last night and mentioned the Paynes."

For a moment I'd felt hope, expecting him to say they'd seen Molly, but no such luck. "Oh."

"They were heading home about dusk Saturday. A vehicle spun out of the Paynes' driveway and almost hit them. Brown or some dark color. Older model sedan like a Buick LeSabre or about that size. Probably from the '80s. He called it a 'lead sled.' The way it jerked all over the road, starting and stopping, Mike thought the driver must be tipsy."

"Dusk? That's when he took Molly." Ed didn't respond, so I added, "I don't remember seeing a car like that at the Paynes'."

"Can't say I do either. I didn't know what to make of it, but I thought I should tell you anyway. Did I mention the woman at the wheel?"

"The woman?"

"Yeah, he said, 'The crazy woman almost hit me.'"

Why would Lila leave in a brown car? "Did he see anyone else in the car?"

"Said they didn't notice anyone else, but it all happened in seconds. Had to hit his brakes to keep from crashing into her. Then the car whipped by."

"What did she look like?"

"Longish hair pulled back at the neck. Didn't see much more. She took off toward town." He paused as if waiting for comment, but I didn't know what else to say. After a short silence, he said, "Well, hope your dog heads home soon."

I stared at the blazing fire. Was Molly in the brown car with Lila? Why would she take Molly? The puddle of blood in the downstairs room surfaced in my memory. Maybe I should give the Coopers a call.

However, the small matter of groceries required my attention first. Bare spots in our pantry cried for filling, and I'd run out of creative ways to recycle leftovers. Although not my favorite chore, people have to eat—even broken-hearted people with missing dogs.

I checked on the fire again when I finished showering and dressing. Monstrous blazing ribbons continued to dance in fiendish delight over the charred embers. Maybe Will added those boxes I saw in the basement storage rooms.

Sights, sounds, and smells from long term memory swirled through my mind—being awakened in the middle of our kitchen fire, my father's frightened shouts, the smoke, hurriedly gathering my few most prized possessions—heightened my terror about the possibility of this fire spreading. Nothing but a pasture lay between our house and the burning pile. If that fire blazed out of control, we could lose everything.

If the fire stayed put, it wouldn't invade the adjoining trees or bushes. With the clearing around it, not enough combustible material lay between the boxes and our property. Only a slight breeze blew, and everything should be soaked from the rain. Besides, last year's fire at the Paynes' flamed for days without advancing to our property.

I repeated those comforting facts several times until I felt convinced enough to abandon my fire-monitoring post.

Jesse hadn't returned by the time I tore myself away, although his Dodge pickup still rested next to the barn. I wrote him a note about my whereabouts and stuck it to the refrigerator with a shell magnet. On my way out, I stopped at the barn to look for him, but didn't find either Jesse or Ranger.

While I headed toward town, I pleaded with God. "If you care about little things in our lives, please protect our house today."

If only he would send some small assurance that he was listening. If only he would show me where to find Molly.

15

Chapter Fifteen

I switched on the radio as I drove along the winding road into town, channel surfing for a news report just in case someone had reported finding Molly wandering miles from home.

Instead, I caught this: "Authorities still search for information concerning the tragic hit-and-run accident, which occurred Saturday night in Nevada City, claiming the life of a four-year-old boy. The victim has been identified as Marcus Whitney, who lived in the vicinity of the accident."

When we bought a house in this beautiful location, we thought we were moving to heaven on earth. What kind of community had we chosen? Abused women, stolen dogs, fires. Now this. Children should be safe to grow to adulthood. I shook my head, wishing for the world of my childhood—back when we left our doors unlocked at night. Why can't the world be like that today? I reached for the button to change stations. I'd have to make myself think about something else.

I cast through my mental files as I drove across the overpass toward the grocery store. With only two large markets in Grass Valley, chances of bumping into someone familiar were greater than in larger cities. Maybe I'd see someone I knew today. I checked my lipstick in the rearview mirror.

As I passed Kmart, a quick glimpse of a green Explorer entering the parking lot made me slam on the brakes to read the license plate. The McCarthys—who drove a green Explorer—displayed their primary priority on a distinctive personalized license. Lila mentioned visiting the McCarthys before they sold us their house so they could build a new one on the other side of town beside a tranquil lake. Maybe they would remember something significant about the Paynes.

The car behind me almost rammed my bumper, but I managed to read LUVDOGS on the Explorer's plate. What a happy coincidence to find the McCarthys in town. I needed a few staples from Kmart anyway.

After minimal searching, I located them in the pharmacy section. Petite and peppy as a cheerleader, Maggie McCarthy frowned at displays in the middle of the aisle. Husband Don, a retired fire chief from Los Angeles, hunched over the shopping cart. He fidgeted as if impatient. Maybe shopping had taken him from needed work.

I wheeled my cart toward them. "Are you tired of looking at that beautiful scenery yet?"

As usual, Don let Maggie do the talking. "Still loving it. Always will." Her dimple appeared with her grin. "How about you?"

I returned her smile. "We love our view too."

She nodded. "We have puppies again. You remember Goldie? She gave us a litter of eight this time. All healthy and beautiful." To say that Maggie loved animals would be axiomatic. Just as plain as the nose on your face.

I raised my eyebrows. Eight! "How many dogs is that altogether?"

Maggie's lively brown eyes sparkled. "Sixteen in all. But the puppies are already spoken for, so we won't get to keep them long."

Trying to imagine caring for so many animals at once, I shook my head. "I went to visit Lila Payne this week. She said you gave her the irises she planted down the driveway. Do you know the Paynes well?"

Maggie and Don glanced at each other. Don opened his mouth, but Maggie spoke first. "Not well, no. They're kind of … different, you might say. Hard to get to know."

Don shifted and looked away.

What did Lila mention about the McCarthys? "She came to see you."

Maggie's dimple flared into view again. "She came to see the dogs. Lila is passionate about dogs. I'd let her help me feed. Or just take them running in the yard. A couple times I invited her for dinner, but she never came. I always thought she might be anorexic. She always acted funny about food."

"Funny? In what way?"

"Weird little things that always connected to food. Like once, I'd just baked a chocolate cake when she came, so I offered her a piece. She got so nervous, she cried. If I even tried to give her a cold drink on a hot day …" Maggie shook her head. The corners of her mouth turned down. "Once she came up while we were eating lunch. We had plenty, so I said, 'Why don't you join us?' But she wouldn't set foot inside the house. Didn't stay to play with the dogs either. Ran home right away, like a scared rabbit. The first Christmas after they moved in, I gave her cranberry bread, but she wouldn't accept it. Said she couldn't take anything red into the house."

I remembered the glower. "Red?"

"Yeah." Maggie waggled her cropped hair. "She said *he* wouldn't allow it. Like *he* would strike her dead for mentioning it. She definitely has issues about food. And she's unusually thin too."

"I assume by *he* she meant Will."

She nodded, screwing her lips tight.

Surely the McCarthys could tell me more. If only I knew the right questions. I stared into my cart, wondering how to get what I needed to know. "Did Lila ever say anything about a baby? About children?"

Maggie's pixie-cut hair cascaded to one side as she tilted her head. "You know, it's funny, now that you ask. She named her dog 'Baby,' but sometimes when she talked about him, I got confused because it sounded like she meant a person … you know, a real baby."

"But she never mentioned having a real baby?"

They both shook their heads.

"Did you ever suspect abuse?"

They leaned toward me.

"What kind of abuse?" Maggie repeated.

"Like maybe he's beating her or starving her?"

"Oh, now," Don said. "We didn't see them enough to know things like that."

Maggie shook her head. "Never saw abuse. But she's a sad woman, no question about it. Unpredictable." She brightened. "Remember that time she got so agitated?" She patted Don's arm. He raised his eyebrows. "You know, her face got all red and puffy. I asked what's wrong and she mumbled something about the boat and Baby … that she didn't want it to go. I didn't know if she meant the boat or the dog, so I asked which one. She sobbed like her heart was broken. I could hardly understand her. But I think she said, 'She did it … just like before.' Have no clue what she meant. Haven't thought about that in a long time."

Don nodded. "She seemed upset that day."

The story didn't mean anything to me either. "What about Will? Did you have better luck talking to him?"

Don looked at his watch and then glanced away. "I figure folks tell you what they want you to know."

"I mustn't keep you," I said. "I know how busy you are. But I see Will leave the house every morning. Do you remember him going to work?"

They leaned toward me as if they hadn't expected the question.

Don shook his head. "Didn't have a job that I know of." He glanced at his watch again.

I said goodbye and nice to see you and turned to walk away when another question popped into mind. I hurried back to where they'd just rounded the aisle of headache remedies. "Say, did the Paynes have two cars when you lived there or just the white pickup?"

"A pickup and a big car," Don answered.

"Do you remember what kind of car?"

He scratched his head. "A sedan, older model. Kept it in that little garage at the side."

"What color?"

"Brown," they said in unison before returning to browse the aisle.

"Did Lila drive it?" I held my breath.

Maggie peered through reading glasses at the bottle of pain reliever in her hand. "I don't think so. She said she couldn't drive." She lowered the container and removed her glasses. "Actually, she said she never learned to drive because speed kills."

Don cleared his throat. Maggie glanced at him. "That's what she said. And she didn't go anywhere, anyway. Not that we ever saw. He went out, but she rarely did."

Don directed a frown at me. "Why do you ask?"

"Just nosy." I smiled and continued on my way.

I finished at Kmart and then gathered groceries. While I descended from town on the curvy roads, I glanced at the digital clock on my dash. Eleven forty-six. A little later than Will's daily trip, but he might go later if he got busy tending the fire. With luck, I'd pass him when he came into town. After all, people usually do what they usually do. I'd never tailed anyone before, but I'd seen it done on detective shows and read about it plenty in mysteries, so I thought I understood the technique. Why not give tailing a try?

I parked the car just inside a driveway near the intersection where we lost the truck the day before. Leaving the engine running, I hunkered down. While I tarried, I half-listened to the local radio, sorting through the new revelations I'd gathered that morning.

Another radio plea for information on the hit-and-run grabbed my attention. "Police have interviewed everyone in the vicinity of the accident at the corner of Broad Street and Elm Avenue."

I pictured the location. Narrow streets followed the contour of the hillside. Trees overhung the street, impairing visibility. Once I almost hit someone in that spot myself.

"A reward of fifty thousand dollars has been offered by the family for evidence leading to conviction of the person responsible."

I released a sad sigh. If only I knew how to find the guilty party. Not because of the reward. What a despicable thing, to run from a fatal accident. What kind of person would do that? *God, if you care about little boys, please bring the person who did this to justice.* The newscaster droned on to another story, and I returned to musing about the mystery at hand.

Several cars passed along the road while I cogitated, some turning toward our house and some continuing straight both from the right and the left. Twelve fifteen just clicked off my dashboard clock when a red sports car approached from the direction of our house. Directly behind, the old white pickup accelerated up the hill.

I straightened to watch him pass.

Both cars veered toward town. I put the Jeep in gear and pulled out, keeping a turn or two behind. Sure enough, the white pickup continued along the curvilinear streets the same way I'd come. At the gas station, the pickup sped onto Highway 49 that runs through the middle of Grass Valley connecting to the neighboring community of Nevada City.

Letting him get ahead by several car lengths, I kept a close eye on the truck. He exited the freeway at Star Mine Road and turned right. By the time I maneuvered the right turn, he'd gotten so far ahead that I could barely see him. Then he disappeared altogether. I picked up speed, ignoring the posted thirty-five-mile-per-hour speed limit.

Without warning, a black van pulled in front of me. I slammed on my brakes to keep from hitting it. My purse fell off the passenger seat, contents spilling onto the floor. I bent on one side to retrieve the tube of lipstick that rolled between my feet. The car swerved, and I jerked the steering wheel, coming to a screeching stop at the side of the road.

Heart racing, I took a deep breath to steady myself. "Enough playing detective." I concentrated on re-entering traffic.

At the first stop sign, I glimpsed Will's truck straight ahead, disappearing from sight around another corner. Maybe I'd continue tailing a little longer.

Soon, businesses dwindled to a few spaced farther and farther apart and then no more. Trees and farms lay ahead. The stop sign at Brunswick allowed a slight rest. To the left, the historic Loma Rica Ranch occupied many scenic acres. On a small hill above the main house, the antique barn peeked between thick cedar trees. No time for sightseeing, though. A gap in cross traffic allowed me to squeeze through.

More twisting roads ahead wound up one side of Banner Mountain in a slow but steady upward grade. Fall dappled the hillsides with color. Imagine God's exuberance in creating this season. The slight difference in elevation from my house to here made a noticeable difference in the color palette. In my neighborhood, leaf colors only hinted of future glory. Here they sang in symphonic harmony of the artistic handiwork of the Creator. The many hues of russet, gold, burgundy, and brown stirred thankfulness in my soul. Maybe God cared about us after all. He had filled our world with an amazing supply of renewable beauty.

I slowed to gawk. Around the next curve, the road opened to another straightaway. Jerking attention back to my driving, I discovered with chagrin that I'd completely lost sight of the pickup.

16

Chapter Sixteen

Maybe I could decrease the gap between us. I accelerated, blurring the fall colors. Before long, I passed four side streets without the slightest sighting of the white pickup.

I slammed on the brakes—stopping right in the middle of the road—and craned my neck to look around. Luckily, no one followed too closely behind. Where had he gone? Surely he hadn't noticed my tailing and hidden from me. Did he turn onto one of the streets along the main roadway?

In this area, each side street accessed a residential micro-society with a communally maintained roadway and four to six homes set amid thick trees and bushes. Grass Valley didn't have any "good" neighborhoods or "bad" neighborhoods. Typical of the foothills, each area comprised a wide variety of homes. Buildings of different ages, styles, and sizes, from new and expensive to old and run-down, resided in dissonant harmony on one street, the only thing in common being location.

"Where is that natural direction-finder instinct when I need it?"

I raced to the next side street and stopped.

"Okay. Where are you?" I waited, hoping an answer would drop into my pea brain.

None came.

"Well, then let's backtrack." I reversed direction with care, thankful for no traffic. "Good job, Christine." Now I wasn't just talking out loud, I was carrying on a full conversation with myself. That must be a bad thing.

As I steered down the first street, I slowed to navigate speed bumps. A few houses lined the blacktop, spaced discreetly apart, but I didn't see the white pickup in front of any of them. At the end of the road, I circled the cul-de-sac and started back. Out at Star Mine Road again, I sampled the parallel street. Still no white pickup.

My luck didn't improve on the third street.

I willed myself onward, veering onto another narrow street while discouragement nipped my heels. But just when I decided to give up, I spotted the top of the white pickup tucked in the driveway of the second house on the left.

The small, mid-century clapboard house had been painted white with green trim. Nestled amid thick, overgrown pine and cedar trees, nature enveloped the structure. I passed the narrow asphalt driveway, searching for an inconspicuous parking spot. Not finding one, I parked along the road just out of sight. Then I settled in my seat, anticipating another long wait.

"What am I waiting for?" I asked after a few minutes. "He might be here for hours. I have frozen food in back. I can't wait for hours."

If I left the car and found a place where he couldn't see me, I might be able to spy on him; find out what he was doing here.

I didn't lock the car door in case I needed to hustle back for a speedy getaway.

Was I thinking like a crook? No. Just planning so I'd be prepared for … whatever.

As I approached the building, I picked with care through dense thickets and trees that camouflaged the front of the property. Arriving at the small two-car garage, I skirted well around it—mindful of the truck in front—until I found myself at the side of the house.

Three windows peeked out. I sneaked up on the first one, rising slowly from underneath to see a rectangular dining table with six empty padded chairs. Through an archway, I spied the living room beyond the dining room. No people there, either.

A closed door to the right might lead to the kitchen. That would be logical.

At the next window, faint voices sounded through double windowpanes—a man and a woman. I couldn't make out their words.

I crouched below, waiting while my ears adjusted to the volume, but still couldn't understand them. I studied the window, trying to gauge how best to peek in without being observed. From the muffled voices, I gathered they weren't standing close. Nevertheless, if they faced my direction, they might notice movement outside.

A row of sheer café curtains hung down from the middle of the window to the sill. After considering for a moment, I decided these might provide enough shield to hide behind while I peeked in from the side. To test my theory, I faced the wall beside the window. I placed one hand on the protruding wooden sill to steady myself while bracing against the wall with the other. In slow motion, I eased sideways until I could see in with one eye.

Just as I'd guessed, the kitchen adjoined the dining room. Will sat with his back toward me at a round oak table in the center of the room. A woman hovered over him, preparing lunch from the looks of the table contents. Judging by her shape and the wrinkles on her face and neck, she must have been about Will's age. She might have been as tall as he; hard to tell with him sitting. Angular features made her look rigid and uncompromising. At the same time, gray streaks in a brown ponytail tied low on her head gave her a mousy quality. Not a particularly appealing person, but there's no accounting for taste. Her face looked oddly familiar.

The two discussed something that must have been serious as she stirred the contents of a yellow-ware bowl. A loaf of bread, still in its baking tin, rested beside the bowl. Every so often, she paused and frowned at Will. Her face congealed in a sour expression that made her look like a habitual complainer.

I held my breath, standing as still as concrete, straining to catch the gist of what they said. Not being able to understand reminded me of Jesse's brother, whose hearing failed ten years ago. How often I'd seen him strain at conversations until overcome by frustration. Being too stubborn or unwilling to forego communication altogether, he learned to read lips. Maybe I could do that too.

I concentrated on the woman's mouth first, but that didn't work.

Jesse's brother had explained to me how to take posture and context into consideration, because they provided clues about the words. By broadening my focus, I soon concluded that Will imparted information the woman didn't enjoy hearing, but not much more.

Some words were easier to decipher than others, maybe because they were delivered slower or with more involvement of the lips. I squinted to see if that would make it easier, but it didn't seem to help. I thought she said "why," then several words I couldn't make out, then "no," some other words, and "cannot find her."

I raised my eyebrows at my supposed success. I couldn't understand the whole conversation, no matter what I did, but the longer I tried, the more headway I made.

She said something about "clean." Will responded. She said more words I didn't get until "have to use bleach." She dried her hands on her apron and rested them on Will's shoulders. Her face contorted into an ugly grimace. "Make sure there's nothing left."

She paused. The movement of Will's head indicated that he answered. Then she shook her head and spat out several words like a rapid-fire machine gun. I didn't get any of that. Next she said something about "fire."

A look of sheer rage crossed her face as she listened, and I feared she might slap him. Then she yelled loud enough for me to hear through the window. "It was an accident. Do you understand? Don't ever speak of it again." She shook his shoulders with both hands, lowering her face to an inch from his. "And keep your big mouth shut!"

Just then, a fluffy, yellow-striped tabby cat wandered around the corner of the house. When he spied me beside the window, he padded toward me and meowed with an annoying nasality. I kicked gently in his direction, hoping to discourage him, but at the unexpected movement, the cat jumped backward with a screech. The woman abruptly snapped her head toward the window. Will's head jerked in my direction, following her startled glance.

Without stopping to see what they would do next, I broke into a run. I tore around the garage, racing through thick underbrush toward the car. Tree branches tore at my hair, and thorns on the manzanita bushes sliced one of my shirtsleeves. I grabbed the car door, panting and out of breath. How fortunate that I left it unlocked! My hands felt thick and clumsy as I fumbled with my keys, but at last I managed to insert the right one into the ignition and retreat. I passed the driveway in time to see Will standing near the back of his pickup, hands on hips, staring toward the street.

As I reached Star Mine Road once again, I made a mental note of the name on the street sign—Sierra Vista.

No one followed. What a relief! My hand shook as I wiped my brow. When did I cross that invisible boundary from law-abiding citizen into this dangerous, unfamiliar territory? And why? A trickle of blood soaked through my shirt and dripped down my arm. I reached into my glove compartment and tugged out a container of Wet Wipes. The antiseptic liquid stung. With my hand shaking, I could hardly wipe off the blood.

I needed help. Now. Who could I go to? Would God be interested? Though not completely certain, I gave it a shot. "God, are you listening? Give me a sign or something if you are. The thing is, I don't know what I've gotten myself into, but I'm sure I haven't handled this correctly. I shouldn't have broken into the Paynes' house or spied on Will and his lady friend. Please forgive me. If there's a way to help Lila and find Molly, please show me what to do next. In the meantime, I ask for your protection, even though I don't deserve it."

Plump tears rolled down my cheeks. I waited. The situation remained unchanged but my shaking stopped. The tight feeling of helplessness relaxed as if massaged by a giant invisible hand. In its place, I felt a surprising calm—a sense that I wasn't alone. Although not a concrete answer, in my experience, sudden calmness didn't usually follow a panic attack. Maybe God heard me after all.

On the drive home, I pondered my sheltered, conservative life. Though impulsive by nature, I'd never ventured into anything truly risky before—never pressed outside my comfort zone where my need for safety bound me tight. Mostly, I let life happen, rolling with whatever came rather than pursuing a calculated plan—certainly not God's plan. I only called on him when life spiraled out of control. Like now.

So how had I come to intervene in someone else's problems—someone who never once asked for my help? Who was *I* to help Lila? Her life choices had spun her far outside my own personal boundaries. I had no experience, no resources. No power to change anything in her life. Did God grant power for such things? I knew he wouldn't approve of breaking into houses and spying on strangers. My motives might be righteous, but my methods hardly were. Definitely, I had acted wrongly.

One thing I knew for sure: I would never do anything this stupid again.

17

Chapter Seventeen

When I drove into the sanctuary of our driveway at last, Jesse's one-ton Dodge dualie greeted me from its usual place in front of the garage. I dashed into the house calling him, but he didn't answer. I found him in the backyard, hunched over the gate, studying the still-burning mound below. Outfitted in a hunter green wool Pendleton with brown suede patches on the elbows, he looked handsome and serene—a salve on my wounded spirit.

Jesse acknowledged my arrival with a brief nod, gazing away under his white Stetson. "That rain last night washed out any footprints we might've seen by the gate. I called the fire department. They said there's probably no danger of the fire burning out of control, since everything's still wet, but they'll send someone out anyway. Will must've started burning sometime in the middle of the night. It's been blazing since before I went to feed the horses."

He focused full attention on me then, taking in my tattered sleeve and the dried blood. "Christine! What happened?"

Not that I expected him to understand—why would today be any different from any other day—but in a rush of words and emotions, I told him about Ed's call, the "coincidental" meeting with the McCarthys at Kmart, and finally about following Will to see The Other Woman.

True to form, he got hung up on one part and interrupted. "Wait a minute. You followed him and then went up to the house to peek in the windows?"

I laid a hand on his arm. "That was stupid. I won't do it again, honest. It scared me but good."

He frowned. "And your arm?"

"When I raced back to the car, I caught it on some stickery branches. It looks worse than it is."

"You could've been seriously injured. What if he caught you? You should never have followed him."

"I know. I'm done playing detective. Really! I'm glad you called the fire department. We'll let the authorities handle this from now on."

I could see Jesse didn't believe me and wanted to reprimand me further, but before he could continue, a red pickup slowed out on Mustang Hill Road. The pickup sported an official emblem affixed to the door, probably the Nevada County Fire District logo. Sure enough, the vehicle rolled down Will's sloping driveway and parked in front of the detached garage.

Jesse opened our gate and ambled toward the fire mound, so I followed through the weedy pasture. The fireman moved toward the front of the house. I picked my way down the hillside, heading for the fire. Jesse reached the blaze about the same time the fireman did, with me arriving just afterward.

The fireman might've been in his late twenties, although age of anyone under forty had become harder to decipher as the years rolled by. He wore blue work pants and a nylon windbreaker with a fire station patch sewn on the left side. On his clean-shaven face, he also wore an expression of boredom.

The young man introduced himself as Fire Prevention Officer Jason McCullough. Jesse shook his hand and nodded toward our house while he returned the introduction, indicating where we lived and identifying himself as the one who called in the fire.

Officer McCullough studied the gray house. "Is anyone home?"

"Don't think so. The truck is gone," Jesse said.

Officer McCullough assessed the burning pile of almost-consumed boxes. Most only smoldered. Little flames shot up periodically here and there. Heat still radiated from the mound. A slight breeze continued to swirl the smoke. "Well … he had a big fire here. How long has it been burning?"

"Our neighbor saw it fully blazing at six thirty this morning," Jesse said. "So he must have started it before that."

I feared Jesse hadn't supplied enough information, so I added, "He's burning boxes filled with clothes and stuff from his house."

The fireman faced me.

I continued. "The woman who used to be here lived virtually as a prisoner, but now she's gone. We don't know what happened to her, but it's probably not good. Our dog's also missing. We found her dog tags beside that garage, so we know they took her." I pointed.

The officer raised his eyebrows. Jesse frowned.

I couldn't stop babbling. "We never saw these people before. No one knows them, even though they've lived here for over ten years. They don't have furniture in their house, but they have furniture stacked in the garage. There's no food in the kitchen, but there's a locked refrigerator near the woodpile."

I paused and glanced from the fireman to Jesse and back again. Now the officer frowned too.

Jesse looked at the ground before speaking. "My, uh, wife's been visiting here the last few days to help this woman. Actually, there are a few irregularities."

Officer McCullough cleared his throat. "The fire seems contained enough so it won't spread, although someone should be in attendance as long as it's still burning. The burn ban won't officially be lifted until mid-October, so technically he should've gotten a permit."

Jesse's eyebrows shot up. "Oh?"

I remembered my earlier conversation with Ed. "Our neighbor thought the ban was over with the first rain."

Officer McCullough looked away and shook his head. "We got a lot of rain last night." After a moment's pause, he glanced back at me. "There's little actual danger."

My lower lip dropped open and I blinked at him. How could he be so casual? Beside the smoke, the fire discharged a heavy, unctuous odor. *That* must be cause for concern. "How about that awful oily smell?"

But he shrugged that off too. "Probably used diesel as an accelerant. That accounts for this black smoke." He shifted feet and divided his look between Jesse and me. "It's not a legal fire. We'll have to take that up with the owner. About the rest …" While he paused, he shifted again and glanced toward the house. "I'm not sure you're talking to the right person. Have you contacted the sheriff's department?"

I wanted to stomp my foot. *Doesn't that just figure?* We had finally connected with an authority, but he didn't want to get involved.

The unhelpful fireman circled the fire once again. It looked as if he studied the burning mass as he walked, perhaps gathering facts with which to make his final evaluation.

The fire burned smaller now than in the morning. Just the center flamed constantly. Random embers glowed throughout the rest of the mound, occasionally spawning baby fires that flared a few moments before dying down again.

Officer McCullough returned to where we stood. "Nothing here requires my attention. Looks like he's just burning trash."

"But—"

Jesse stopped me with a glare. He turned to thank the fireman without enthusiasm, and we watched as he wandered back to the red truck, hands stuck in his pockets. He waved out the open window as he reversed and drove up the sloping driveway.

I faced my husband. "So much for Jason McCullough, Junior Fire Officer. Now what?"

But Jesse's attention had shifted to something in the debris, which he stooped to examine. "What does that look like?" He picked up a blackened stick to poke into the ashy pile. "Part of a mattress?"

He dug around another few seconds, and sure enough, a small piece of mattress ticking emerged, a tiny chunk with charred edges. He gazed up at me. "Whose bed do you think this would be? If it's

Lila's, why is he getting rid of her mattress without waiting to see if she comes home?" He stood. "I think it's time to call the sheriff, don't you?"

I agreed with my whole heart. Surely *they* would pay attention.

We climbed home through the pasture in silence, latching the gate behind us.

Jesse dialed the Nevada County Sheriff's Office. "I'm not sure who to talk to about this. There seems to be a problem at my neighbors' house." He listened. "My name is Jesse Sterling. I live on Paso Fino Place." He gave our address. "They live on Mustang Hill Road. Their name is Payne, Will and Lila."

He outlined our concerns, beginning with my visits to the tiny woman and ending in today's bonfire and Jason McCullough's visit. He mentioned the bruises on Lila's arm and neck, as well as her apparent terror. He left out the part about me breaking into the Paynes' house and what I found there. Neither did he mention me following Will to his girlfriend's.

Then he paused to listen. ... "Yes."

He stared at the floor. ... "Okay." He hung up and faced me. "The dispatcher will refer the call to a deputy who'll come out to investigate. Probably in a day or two."

I drooped, crestfallen.

Jesse draped an arm around my shoulders. "I know. She said they only have two detectives and they're both working on another case. Don't forget, we have moved to the country. But it's best for this to be handled properly, in case there was an actual crime. For now, let's forget about Lila."

I rolled my eyes. What about Molly? How could we forget?

As if reading my mind again, Jesse said, "We need something to do. How about the groceries? I'll help you bring them in."

By then, the frozen stuff had melted and soaked the boxes and bags, leaving lumps and puddles in the back of the Jeep. The groceries had become a room-temperature mess, much of them unsalvageable. I gritted my teeth as I flung the wreckage directly into the garbage can.

This is the thanks I get for trying to help someone in need. Lila's plight had trashed my life, in more ways than one. And where, oh where, was Molly?

18

Chapter Eighteen

Monday night and Tuesday morning dragged on while we waited for a deputy to investigate. I hiked the neighborhood, searching and calling Molly's name without finding a single clue. I knocked at every door within a one-mile radius. None of the neighbors had seen Molly. I called the newspaper to place an ad describing her, with a plea for anyone who'd seen her to call. It wouldn't be printed until Friday.

A deputy still hadn't shown up by late Tuesday afternoon, so Jesse called again. The dispatcher reassured him an investigator would come, and would we please be patient, as they were severely understaffed. Jesse strongly advised the dispatcher about Will's habit of disappearing by afternoon, so they should send a deputy in the morning. I couldn't believe no one took this situation more seriously, but I didn't know what to do about that.

Will left as usual late Wednesday morning. Still no sign of the brown Buick. The fire continued to smolder, but Will had apparently finished purging the house.

Foreboding hung like a lead necklace around my neck. I struggled to occupy my mind with other things but only enjoyed minimal success.

In frustration, I called Zora Jane and explained that Jesse had called for a sheriff's deputy to investigate the two disappearances.

"I'm so tired of doing nothing, Zora Jane. I just hate to wait. I've always hated it."

"Everybody does, Christine."

Disgustingly cheerful as always.

"I can't get my mind off this. I'm way past anxious, rounding the bend toward panic. I just know something awful has happened to Lila and Molly."

"You need a project to occupy your mind. Better yet, get out your Bible and read what God has to say. You'll find help and comfort there, I'm sure of it."

I didn't tell her that my former attempts to read the Bible had been even less successful than my childhood prayers. My mother's King James Bible confused me. How did people understand such archaic language? When I got off the phone, I roamed into my office and knelt beside the footstool of my rose-print chair. "God, I'm sure you know how much I hate waiting. Are you punishing me by making me wait? Or have you even heard my prayers in the first place? Zora Jane says you did. So help me think of things to do while I wait for your answer. You *are* working, aren't you?" If he knew everything as Zora Jane said, surely he wouldn't forget.

Now for a project to fill my time and my mind.

With no small amount of trepidation, I approached the computer, intending to produce a few flyers advertising our missing dog. The computer scowled back, face dark and menacing. I sighed and punched the power button. At least I remembered how to turn the thing on. I watched it run through booting-up, remembering the pain of quitting the job I loved at the library.

Technology had turned my familiar world upside down in a matter of weeks. I couldn't keep up. They bought a monstrous new computer—the latest and best—and hired a kid, a girl half my age, who knew everything about it. She was supposed to teach me, but instead she mocked my hesitance and lack of expertise. Laughed at me. How did I get to be a librarian without knowing anything, she wanted to know. I had given up rather than admit my incompetence.

But now, I must learn—just this one poster program. I set my mouth in a firm line and got to work.

After struggling for half an hour, I gave up. Computer language baffled me. Why couldn't they just write these stupid manuals in English? If only I could find a good computer class—something for someone who knew nothing and understood even less. Except for retrieving and sending e-mail and playing games, my efforts to conquer my PC frustrated me.

Instead of a polished computer poster, I'd make one the old-fashioned way. I collected several pictures of Molly and glued them onto light blue construction paper. With my markers, I added contact information. I posted one under our cluster of mailboxes and one each under the next-closest mailboxes on either side. I stepped back to survey the results. Not professional looking, but serviceable.

As I passed the Paynes' driveway, I didn't see Will's truck. So I made a detour to the gray house, just in case Lila had come home without our noticing. No one answered the door. The house remained as muted as before—maybe even more neglected looking, if possible. The air smelled of smoke. I didn't hear a sound except an occasional crackle from the fire.

An urge to do something for Lila overwhelmed me. Not knowing what else to do, I prayed. "Please, God, please protect her. She has no one else to help her."

When I ambled past the attached garage, I couldn't resist the urge to peek inside. To the right, the old-fashioned refrigerator hummed as usual, padlock snapped firmly in place on its door. But something was missing along the side.

What is it?

Mentally, I ticked off items I'd seen before: mason jars on wall crosspieces; the same garden tools; chains and ropes on hooks; aluminum folding chairs.

My gaze stopped at an empty spot. A gas can with worn red paint occupied that space the first time I snooped inside the garage. The gas can. Well, sure. Will used it to hold accelerant for the fire. My eyes roamed onward. The row of storage cabinets at the rear looked undisturbed. I gazed upward. The rafters held the usual assortment of fishing poles, crates, and boxes. Layers of dust muted everything.

I hesitated. Something else *was* missing.

The suitcase.

I stepped into the cool garage for a better look.

Just underneath where the brown suitcase rested before, the pile of wood showed signs of disturbance. Someone had climbed up to pull something down. I scrambled onto the unstable wood. Several pieces clattered to the floor. Even on tiptoes atop the pile, I couldn't reach the shelf with the tips of my fingers. Whoever retrieved the suitcase had to be tall, like Will.

Once I made that determination, getting down proved more of a challenge than I anticipated. At my age, I feared I wouldn't be able to jump that far without breaking bones. I resorted to sitting at the edge, dangling my short legs over the side. With sudden resolve, I pushed off, landing on hands and knees. Several pieces of wood thumped down with me.

I rubbed my scraped hands while my eyes inventoried once more. Not finding anything else out of place, I hobbled home.

While I cooked dinner, I relayed my latest discoveries to Jesse, but he seemed more concerned about the uninvited venture to the gray house than what I'd found. "Don't go down there anymore. What if Will came home while you were there?"

I let out a loud *tsk*.

He removed a Diet Pepsi from the refrigerator. "Besides, if Lila left in the brown car on Saturday night, she'd need a suitcase to pack her stuff in. Nothing odd about that."

"Even if she couldn't reach it without help?"

He shrugged.

When would someone take this seriously?

❧

After dinner, Jesse brought the entertainment section of the Grass Valley newspaper to the kitchen for my perusal. "What do you say to a movie? That'd be a great way to kill time."

I closed the dishwasher door. "There's nothing I want to see."

"How do you know? You haven't even looked."

"There's never anything I want to see. Movies aren't what they used to be—now they're all car chases and explosions. I don't even understand the jokes. Half the time, the plot is so choppy I get completely lost. And I never recognize any of the actors." Faces of my old heroes and heroines paraded across the catwalk of my memory—Loretta Young, Katherine Hepburn, and Clark Gable — *those* were movie stars.

Jesse imitated his hero. "I'd walk the desert barefoot to see John Wayne on the big screen again."

"John Wayne! You can see him any time of the day or night on TV."

Jesse threw me a pretend glare and swaggered into his John Wayne walk. "Watch it, little lady. You know how I feel about the Duke."

"Well, I must admit, you never need to tolerate bloody violence, profanity, or explicit sex in a John Wayne movie."

Jesse cocked his eyebrows. "Never."

In the end, feeling ancient and outmoded, we watched Jesse's favorite John Wayne movie, *The Quiet Man,* on the classic movies channel.

Midway through the movie, restlessness overtook me. During the middle of the town fight scene, I slipped out to call Zora Jane again. "You haven't seen Molly today, have you?"

"I would call you right away if I did, Christine. I know how concerned you've been."

I knew she would. In reality, I needed a distraction. "I've run out of places to look for her. I'm sure Will knows where she is, but I don't know how to get it out of him."

"I'm sorry. I know this is hard. I've been praying for you."

"Also, we're still waiting for the investigator from the sheriff's office. Waiting, waiting, waiting. Why doesn't God fix this problem? Doesn't he care what's happening in that house?"

"The Bible tells us to be anxious for nothing, but in everything by prayer and supplication, with thanksgiving, let your requests be made known to God. And—"

I interrupted. "Hold on, where can I find that? I'll look it up the minute we get off the phone." I heard sarcasm in my voice. *Uh-oh. That won't help. Come on, Christine. Give it a chance.* I sucked in air and let it out slowly. "I'm sorry, Zora Jane. I can't stop worrying. Well, maybe for a little while I can, as long as I keep myself busy. But as soon as I stop, even for a second, worry comes back, stronger than before. I'm thinking of going back inside the Paynes' house. There must be more clues there."

"Hmm. That doesn't sound like a good idea. The apostle Paul certainly understood what you're going through. Remember when he told the Corinthian believers to take every thought captive?"

I considered that impossibility. "Paul probably could do that. He was a saint. But do you think anyone else has ever conquered this war of the mind?"

"Conquering would demand constant vigilance in the power of the Holy Spirit. But yes, with God's help, this battle could be won."

Her blind trust didn't convince me. "Why is God waiting so long to answer my prayers?"

She sighed. "Oh, Christine."

"Seriously. You think he's working. What's he doing?"

"Well, he might be working on someone else—someone we don't even know is involved. We're not God's *only* children, you know. Or the waiting might be for our protection. Maybe he's letting a potentially explosive situation defuse. Or maybe he just wants us to learn submission to his sovereign plan."

I didn't like any of those possibilities. Action. That's what I wanted.

Zora Jane continued. "There are enough examples in nature to guess God intentionally built waiting into his plan."

"Like … what examples?"

She paused.

My inner pessimist complained. *Can't think of any, can you?*

But she could. "Like it takes nine months to produce a baby. Crops germinate in the ground before they produce food. Flowers don't pop out until the frost and snow have gone. Things like that."

I never thought of those as examples of waiting before. Could she be right? I made no comment while I considered.

"The Bible has stories about waiting. Read those. While the saints, patriarchs, and disciples waited, God polished the rough edges of self-centeredness and sin off. He needed to do that to make them useful for his purpose. Jacob waited twenty years in Laban's employment; Moses waited forty years in exile from Egypt before he led the Israelites out; Paul waited three years after his conversion before starting to preach the gospel. Even Jesus waited in the wilderness while he practiced conquering Satan with the Word of God."

"I never thought of that."

"Trusting God while we tarry, that's the key. That and being joyful in the process. God is able to create good out of anything he allows in the lives of those called according to his purpose. He promised that."

As I hung up, conviction for doubting God's timing nudged me. I knelt beside my office chair and raised my eyes heavenward but only saw the sloping log ceiling. Was God listening or was I just talking to myself?

"Oh, God," I prayed. "If you care, I need some help here. Will I ever get my attitude right? Forgive me for my impatience. Please change my thinking so I truly understand that waiting is a special gift. Help me not to waste it."

19

Chapter Nineteen

I spent the next day trying to dwell only on good things, but kept finding Molly's dog toys around the house while I did chores. Fingering each one brought back floods of sadness. Not wanting to be depressed, I stashed the dog toys out of sight in a cabinet.

About dusk, Jesse went to feed horses. I put a meatloaf in the oven and took a bag of garbage to the big green trash container, only to find the can filled to the brim.

Oh, dear. Jesse forgot to take this with him. We would miss tomorrow's trash day.

I stuffed in my latest contribution and pressed hard. No matter how hard I pushed, the lid wouldn't close over the garbage—too full to leave until another week's trash got piled on top. Rather than nag, I'd take it to the drop-off place myself. That would give me something to do while dinner finished cooking.

I dragged the heavy green can to the driveway, popped the Jeep's rear door, and hefted the trash container into the back.

By the time I arrived at the garbage pickup near the neighborhood park, cans already lined most of the parking area. I pulled our container out of the car and shoved it into the queue with our stenciled house number facing the street.

As I turned to leave, I caught a glimpse of Will's house number painted on his aluminum trashcan, halfway down the row.

I froze.

No cars had passed on the street since my arrival. Circling in place, I surveyed the neighborhood. I couldn't see houses from that spot. Did that mean no one could see me? I stared into the woods, just in case the homeless guy spied on me. Nothing there either, except a line of thick trees.

Discarded garbage constituted public domain. Wasn't that a legitimate way to gather evidence?

I held my breath and lifted the lid ever so carefully—as if something might jump out. When I let out the big gulp of air, a rotten stench assaulted my nostrils. The lid slipped from my grasp and clanked on the blacktop.

That really stinks!

I glanced around again, doing a slower scrutiny, and then peered into the can. Why didn't I carry plastic gloves for emergencies?

"Okay, here goes."

A black garbage bag lay on top. Careful to allow minimal skin contact, I lugged the bag out and cradled it in the lid. After taking a deep breath, I unwound the tie and peeked inside. Partially eaten food spilled out of plastic containers: hamburgers green with mold, stringy Chinese noodles with shiny worms roaming through, french fries with mounds of black hair, globs of congealed gravy supporting a new generation of tiny black bugs. This garbage hadn't been generated from recent meals. It must be weeks old.

I recoiled from the stench, dropping the bag. "Ugh!"

How cruel that Will threw away all this food while poor Lila starved. He had plenty to share. Some of this mess had barely been touched.

The pungent odor bombarded my senses even from a foot away. I didn't want to dig around in that, not without gloves. Too bad I didn't bring a clothespin for my nose. I sealed the bag as tightly as possible and turned back to the can.

Empty bleach containers had been packed underneath. I leaned closer and counted six of them. That was a lot of bleach to use all at once.

Why put them in the trash container? Why not burn them with the rest of the stuff?

Using just my thumb and forefinger, I tugged them out one by one and set them on the ground. I remembered my initial fantasy about Will and his boxes. "For cleaning up blood, perhaps?"

But whose blood? Lila's? Or—no. It couldn't be Molly's.

I peeked inside the garbage can again.

Reaching as far as my short arms allowed, I hefted out a solid black bag. The weight worried me. What if it turned out to be full of body parts? I had to use both hands to extract it and nearly dropped it back into the can. Curiosity demanded that I drag it out, so I tightened my hold and pulled.

After extracting the bag, I gulped another mouthful of fresh air and unfastened the knot holding it shut. Strong chlorine fumes made my eyes water even though I held my breath. The towels in the bag had been soaked in bleach. I could think of just one reason for that. My stomach lurched and I dry-heaved.

Leave them or take them, what should I do? *God help me do the right thing.*

I hesitated, hoping for audible instructions. Since I didn't hear a sound, I scooped up the bag and hefted it to the Jeep.

When I made my next trip to town, I detoured to the county library in Nevada City for information on anorexia. Most people would just look it up on the Internet, but I didn't know how to Google, and even if I did, I suspected that Internet information couldn't be trusted. It might be loaded with subliminal Communist propaganda or some other kind of liberal brainwashing. How did stuff get on the Internet in the first place? What would motivate someone to spend hours downloading all that data? Best not to rely on the Internet for information. Besides, the Internet would never give me that same multisensory reward for successfully locating the object of my quest that I could get at a good library.

To be frank, I craved that book smell. I've always loved libraries. No wonder I chose the library for a career. During childhood, my sister and I spent many Saturday mornings at the knee of the grandmotherly children's librarian, listening to story hour. In high school, I hurried to the library to begin my term papers the same day the teacher assigned them, even though most of my friends considered that odd. Yes, the library had always been my friend.

Standing between the first set of bookshelves, I closed my eyes and breathed the delicious musty aroma. I had been away too long. I ran my finger along one shelf, scanning the creative titles. Wondrous worlds awaited inside those colorful covers. I wandered slowly down the aisle, browsing the leather bindings. At the end, I pivoted and strolled along the other side, basking in the silence. How safe and predictable this world seemed.

Time to get to work. In the medical reference section, I scanned titles until I located a couple of thick books about eating disorders. Carrying my prizes to a table, I settled down to research. Maggie McCarthy suggested Lila might suffer from anorexia. I wanted to know more about that, so that's where I started.

I flipped pages until I found *anorexia nervosa* described as a serious, often chronic disorder defined by refusal to maintain minimal body weight. Most often occurring in young women, a classic cycle of fasting, binging, and purging left the body out of balance and depleted of nutrients. Various related medical complications developed over time and could result in death.

During a long stare into quiet library air, I imagined the state of Lila's physical health. She probably hadn't stepped into a doctor's office in years. After just two short visits with her—not to mention that I didn't possess a medical degree—how could I accurately assess her medical complications?

Moving my finger down the page, I discovered the hallmark of anorexia nervosa: preoccupation with food. The person so afflicted often manifested strange eating habits such as aversion to certain foods or refusal to eat in the presence of others.

I nodded. That described Lila well.

The next book described causes for the disorder, including genetic predisposition to obsessive behavior, as well as a wide range of environmental influences. Stressful incidents could trigger the onset and served to increase the risk. Initially a psychological problem of distorted body perception, the progression to physical involvement often occurred rapidly. Personality traits common in persons with anorexia included low self-esteem, social isolation, and perfectionism. In advanced cases, hallucinations and other mental abnormalities could occur.

Who knows what demons might plague Lila's consciousness?

While pondering life in the Payne house, I skimmed the rest of the page. The secretive nature of this debilitating mental disorder would preclude close relationships. Not to mention how lack of nourishment might affect her body. How would it alter her ability to bear children? Maybe the baby by the water tower died a natural death because Lila couldn't produce enough nourishment to sustain it. And what about stamina? She disappeared who-knows-where in the brown car. How would she find enough food for her frail body? In her weakened condition, she wouldn't last long.

Oh, Lila, where have you gone?

20

Chapter Twenty

After another troubled night tossing and turning and trying to sleep, I got up early Saturday morning. Without Molly's sweet presence, the emptiness in the house felt weighted. Although Jesse and I stopped discussing my obsession, the two disappearances consumed my every waking thought. I'd run out of places to search. Everyone in the neighborhood had been alerted. Where could they be? Why couldn't we find them?

We finished our usual round of chores in detached silence before I made my way down the spiral staircase to exercise again, just for the view. Jesse wandered to the arena to practice riding around the highway cones with Ranger.

About midway through my hike on the treadmill, a green-and-white Nevada County Sheriff's vehicle, complete with colored light bar on top, parked in front of the gray detached garage. A uniformed deputy stepped out and disappeared, hidden by the house. Cold shivers raced up my neck.

At last.

I completed power walking—which seemed to take hours—without seeing the deputy exit. Afraid I might miss something, I raced upstairs and jumped in the shower. I made a swift swipe at all my major stinky parts, then jumped out without washing my hair. I hurried to the closet and yanked on clean clothing.

Please, God. Please help the deputy get to the bottom of this.

I blow-dried my sweaty hair and clipped it on top of my head. I'd just finished when someone buzzed from the gate. The deputy requested admittance. When I looked out the window, I saw Jesse striding from the barn. He must have spied the vehicle as well. I pressed the star key to open the gate and dashed out the front door.

A stocky but tidy deputy emerged from the green-and-white squad car. Perfectly straight creases shouted that his uniform must be fresh from the cleaners. A shiny sheriff star decorated his uniform just above his only pocket. Under his hat, gray-brown hair had been clipped military-close. Aviator frame glasses perched on his most distinguishing feature—a honker of a nose so disproportionate, I struggled not to stare.

I broke off pondering that schnoz when he spoke. His voice, high-pitched for a man his size, had an affected, robotic quality. "I am Deputy Sam Colter from the Nevada County Sheriff's Office." As if we couldn't see the car or his uniform. With an air of self-importance, he extended a business card. Jesse arrived in time to grab it.

"Are you Jesse Sterling?"

Jesse nodded.

"I have come about the complaint regarding your neighbor, William Payne."

An unfamiliar, formal atmosphere settled over us. Jesse gestured into the house. "Please come in and sit down."

I didn't know the proper protocol for entertaining a lawman, since we'd never had one investigating on our property before. Jesse and I filed into the house in silence and headed for the living room with the stiff backs of children who had been called to the principal's office. The deputy chose the white leather cowboy chair, so we sat across from him, near enough to each other so our knees rubbed for emotional support.

Deputy Colter turned close-set brown eyes to Jesse and then me. He made a revving sound when he cleared his throat, like a signal for talking to commence. "I have just interviewed Mr. Payne. The female who resided at his home has departed. He does not know where she has gone."

Jesse frowned. "The female? You mean his wife?"

"Mr. Payne indicated they were never legally married, and in fact, never cohabitated as a married couple. Her name is Lila Kliner. She packed her belongings and departed, as I said." He drummed his close-bitten fingernails on the chair. "Tell me why you called in the report."

Not married? My head spun wildly. Good thing I wasn't standing or I might have fallen down. My brain detached from my wide-open mouth and words tumbled out. "He cleaned out the house. Threw out boxes of stuff—clothing and household items. Piled them in a big mound. I met Lila twice a week ago. Once I went alone and once the neighbor went. Lila's unusually thin and has purple bruises on her arm right about here." I demonstrated on Jesse's arm. "Also, there's an injury on her neck." I pointed out the location on Jesse's neck. "A red wound like a rope line from when he tried to strangle her. He's also starving the poor woman. Has a padlock on the refrigerator outside and no food in the house."

On and on I blabbered. Even as the words tumbled out, I heard how crazy they sounded. Since it wasn't coming out as I hoped, I leaned forward and spoke louder, hoping at the least to convey the urgency of the situation. "Apparently, a homeless man lives in the woods behind their house. We don't know who he is or what he's doing there. Lila exists in deplorable conditions. Not with the homeless man. At the house, I mean. It's like a prison. No furniture, except beds. One night, Will shook his fist at me. Next thing we know, our dog's missing and guess where her dog tags turn up?" I nodded for emphasis. "Beside the Paynes' garage."

I glanced away from Deputy Colter's icy gaze to Jesse for support. Jesse just blinked. More blabbering poured out. "Lila left the same night in a brown car and hasn't come back. Will burned boxes in a big fire with diesel to get it going. We think he burned her bed, too, 'cause we found mattress ticking in the ashes. Did you see the fire? It's not burning anymore, but you can see how big it was."

When I paused again, Deputy Colter interjected. "You are speaking of multiple issues. Exactly when did each of these allegedly occur?" He took out a small blue notebook and scribbled in it, using several pages while Jesse provided dates and additional details to fill in the gaps.

When Jesse finished, Deputy Colter cocked his head as if analyzing. He tapped the pen against the spiral coil at the top of his notebook a few times. "Well, according to Mr. Payne, Miss Kliner moved in with him when he lived in Iowa. He does not know much about her history. He felt sorry for her because she had nowhere to go and no means of support. However, her unpredictability made her difficult. At this time, Mr. Payne is unconcerned about her whereabouts. In fact, he seems relieved."

More tapping. "He claims no knowledge of your dog, nor any culpability in its disappearance. Mr. Payne has not seen the homeless man in the woods, although he mentioned having his locked garage broken into and that he suspects a homeless person. There should not be anyone living in those woods. I may look into that. Otherwise … I see no evidence of illegal activity in this matter." With an air of finality, he snapped his notebook shut and stood.

Surely, he couldn't be uninterested in Lila's injuries. "What about the bruises?"

He studied me a moment, looking over his spectacles and down his considerable nose. "Miss Kliner is unavailable, so I cannot assess the injuries you reported. I did question Mr. Payne about them. He stated that Miss Kliner is high-strung and emotional. When she is uncontrollable, it occasionally becomes necessary to restrain her. For her own good."

"He could have *restrained* her, as you put it, on her arm, but what about her neck? He tried to choke her. That's more than restraining her. How about the state of her health? She's being starved as well as abused. Are you going to ignore that completely? You're … you're just going to let him get away with it?" Any competent lawman would have spent a minimum of three hours interrogating us. "Don't you need to investigate? Aren't you going to find her?"

He raised an eyebrow as if he'd just discovered a fly in his gazpacho. "Ma'am, there is no reason to locate her. She answered the door twice when you visited, so obviously her movements within the house were not restricted. She packed her clothes and left of her own volition, driving a car from her own household."

"She's been gone a week. No one knows where she is."

Jesse put his arm around me—to hold me back, I think. Apparently, he couldn't speak.

Deputy Colter crossed his amrs. "She has not been reported as missing, so officially, she is not a missing person. I will check the whereabouts of the Buick LeSabre sedan registered to Mr. Payne. I advised him he could report the vehicle stolen, but he has not decided whether to do so. Other than that, I am afraid I have nothing to investigate."

He strutted toward the front door like a bantam rooster. But just before he arrived, he stopped mid-stride. "Why did you say there was no furniture in the house? And how do you know the contents of the boxes Mr. Payne burned?"

Jesse and I eyeballed each other. Jesse found enough voice to speak at last. "My wife visited the house several times and didn't see furniture other than beds. Apparently, one of the mattresses has been burned in his fire. We saw pieces of mattress ticking. We peeked in the window of the detached garage, which had furniture piled around the walls. Also, we looked inside a couple of boxes—before he burned them."

Deputy Colter stared at me. Then he raised his eyebrows and sighed. "Well, there is furniture in the house now."

I felt my skin flush crimson. "Lila's hurt and starving and missing under suspicious circumstances. He took our dog. We know this for a fact. Will you at least look into it?"

"Look, madam. I said I would check on the car. I have inspected the house. Mr. Payne cooperated completely. I observed no irregularity there. I will file a field report of what I have seen and heard. That is all I can do." He strutted resolutely out the door, down the steps, and back to his car.

I trailed to the driveway in case he changed his mind, but he kept right on going.

A tsunami of emotion crashed over me. My blood pressure zoomed. My heart pounded a drum roll.

Jesse stood behind me, his hands resting on my shoulders. "Let it go, Christine. We've completed our neighborly obligation."

I sputtered objections and spun to hide in his arms, where he held me and stroked my hair until my shaking subsided. Then he led me back into the house and sat me on the sectional.

As he settled next to me, his face looked as sad as I felt, so I leaned against him and snuggled into his shoulder. "But we still don't know anything, Jesse. We don't know where Molly is, and we don't know what happened to Lila."

"Maybe he'll find the car. Maybe …" His voice trailed off.

We huddled there a long time, while our brains made the adjustment from buoyant expectation to cold, callous reality.

"Oh no, Jesse!" I straightened and grabbed his forearm for support. "Do you think the deputy told Will who turned him in?"

21

Chapter Twenty-One

Another lengthy wait unfolded. I sent dagger-stares down the hill whenever I passed a window facing Will's house. After a restless weekend and another Monday passing without a single message from the deputy, I concluded I must do more than that. On the theory that the squeaky wheel gets greased, I would call the sheriff's office twice a day to badger Deputy Sam Colter about his efforts to find Lila and our dog. Between calls, I prayed for help. I got out the Bible, as Zora Jane suggested, but didn't know where to start reading, so I rested both hands on the cover. *God, bring Lila home, please.*

Tuesday morning, the dispatch lady reported curtly that the deputy had departed, so I left a message asking if he'd found the car. *God, are you working on this?*

About lunchtime, Zora Jane called, as chipper as always. "I spoke with my son-in-law about Lila's injuries. You remember the one who's a deputy? He's concerned that no one has done anything yet. He promised to speak with Colter."

"Finally."

"Besides that, Ed says it looks like you've already done all you can, but if you want to talk the situation over, he's available anytime."

"Thanks, Zora Jane."

"Meanwhile, the annual church bazaar is Saturday. It's the major fundraiser of the year for the Christian school. I'll be selling hats and accessories, and I sure could use your help. You need an outing as well. Why don't you come with me?"

"Oh." Sitting in a used hat booth all day ranked way down on my list of desirable diversions. I cast about for a good excuse. "I ... think I'll clean house on Saturday."

She ignored my words. "You positively won't believe all the people who come to this bazaar. Thousands. Not just from our church, but all over Nevada County. Maybe you've seen our flyers around town. From the beginning, we've advertised well, and of course, that makes a big difference. But after ten years, we're so well established that people plan their whole month around this event."

"Yes, but—"

"You won't have to do much. The hats and accessories are already sorted. We arrange them on the table around six. People start coming at six thirty, even though it's not supposed to open 'til seven. I'll come over to pick you up about five thirty."

"Five thirty *AM*?" How could I go anywhere or think of anything as frivolous as a bazaar until we found Molly? I'd give her one more chance to understand that I'd rather have a root canal. "I don't think so. That's pretty early for me."

"You could come down about nine, if you prefer. Eat a good breakfast first. They'll bring us lunch, so don't worry about packing food."

"Well, if you don't mind me coming at nine ..." *What was I saying?*

"Oh, thank you, Christine. I know you'll have a wonderful time. And it's for such a worthy cause."

"Well, as long as we're making plans, I would like to talk with Ed about the situation at the Paynes'. Is he free this afternoon?"

"He just got home from golf. Let me ask." She set the phone down with a thud and I heard her heels click away. *Where has Jesse gone?* I carried the portable phone into the living room. The television blared from the library landing above. He must be in his green chair.

Zora Jane returned in a minute, saying Ed wanted us to come right over. I informed Jesse. Maybe the four of us could concoct a plan to find Lila and get Molly back.

Zora Jane met us at the door dressed in an orange-and-yellow paisley one-piece lounging outfit with matching orange pumps. Their Jack Russell terrier jumped and barked at her feet. "Harry! Stop that." The springing and yapping continued while Zora Jane shooed him outside, banging the screen door behind him.

Then she motioned us into the living room where Ed reclined in his overstuffed green La-Z-Boy, wearing his characteristic plaid golf pants. He unlocked his hands from behind his neck and pushed his chair upright with a thud. "Hey, you two." With the TV remote, he clicked off the golf tournament.

Zora Jane stood at the kitchen door, the aroma of coffee wafting around her. "Please, sit down. Can I get you something to drink? Decaf's freshly brewed."

Jesse sank onto the couch opposite Ed. "Okay. That would be great."

I sat on the edge of the sofa and nodded.

In a few minutes, Zora Jane returned carrying a tray with four steaming cups and a china plate full of warm cookies. She balanced the tray in front of us, placed a cup on the table beside Ed's chair, and took one for herself.

Only Jesse felt the need for cream and sugar. We waited while he spooned a mountain of sugar and creamer into his coffee, stirred, and gulped a big swig. "I called the fire department about the situation at the Paynes' without getting any help. So I called the sheriff's office and they sent out a deputy last Saturday. That yahoo didn't see any cause for concern either."

Ed shrugged.

Jesse slurped another drink of coffee. "A woman and a dog are missing. Things look more suspicious by the day. I thought it might help to discuss this with you. You've had a lot of experience, and anyway, four heads are better than two."

Ed inclined his head.

I took a cup of decaf and slid to the back of the sofa. Zora Jane sat in the recliner next to Ed, sipping her decaf while she listened.

Jesse shot me a *here goes* look and cleared his throat. Beginning with my first sight of the boxes, he told Ed about the peculiar events of the last week and a half. This time he included the part about me breaking into the Paynes' house and following Will to see his lady friend. Ed interrupted several times for additional clarification, but generally concentrated in silence, bent arms resting on the armrests, fingers steepled.

The amount of detail Jesse offered surprised me. Apparently he *does* listen when I talk.

At the end, Ed glanced at me over his glasses and lifted his eyebrows. "You've been a busy girl."

I gave a sheepish nod.

Ed cleared his throat. "Well, first about that brown Buick. After we thought about it, we realized we *have* seen it parked in the upper driveway before. Must be that senior moment thing." He glanced at Zora Jane.

With her hands folded in her lap, her expression reminded me of a mother listening to her child's confession.

Ed continued. "Also, another car's been there a few times. Don't know who that one belongs to, but it's similar, maybe a little newer. Blue, I think. Anyway, you've got a couple different angles of approach here. Finding the dog tags looks suspicious. The Paynes may know what happened to your dog. The problem is, you don't have facts. You don't know what's wrong with Lila. You don't know she's actually missing, just that she's gone out of bounds and no one's filed a missing-persons report yet. You saw bruises on her arm and maybe her neck, but those could've been self-inflicted. Bruising is possible without even feeling the injury, especially if you're elderly or ill. Certain medication makes a person prone to bruising. You saw Will leave in the late morning for several days, but you don't know if he ended up at the same house each time. Et cetera, et cetera.

No facts. Inferences. That's what you've got. Nothing concrete." He peered over his glasses like a stern schoolmarm. "Did you get the address of that house Will went to?"

"I know the street name," I said. "I could find it again in a flash."

"Hmm." He scratched his bald head.

Zora Jane shook her head. "I must say Lila did look awful. She's either sick or actually starving to death. Poor lost lamb. There must be some way to help her."

Ed stroked his chin. "I'm concerned that you actually found a campsite in the woods. I thought those stories about a vagrant were nothing but urban legends. I'll report that. Security's supposed to keep homeless people out of here. That's what we pay them for." Ed supervised contracted services as president of our homeowners association.

What about the bruises? Surely he couldn't discount them. "But don't you see the urgency with that injury on her neck? Even if she bruised herself on the arm—which I doubt—that other one is different. How would you mark your own neck like that? He tried to kill her."

When Ed inclined his head, a glint off the top made me wonder if he polished it. "Granted, that's harder to explain. But you didn't see it happen." He frowned at me. "You get what I'm saying? You don't have evidence a crime has been committed. Granted, it looks odd, but the world is full of strange circumstances. Usually there are explanations that don't involve criminal activity." He massaged his head. Behind Ed's wire-frame glasses, the sparkle in his sea blue eyes told me his curiosity had been aroused despite his negativity.

"Maybe we should call Baxter and see what he thinks," Zora Jane said.

I'd forgotten about the Callahans' son-in-law being a deputy.

Ed nodded. "I was thinking that too. That might be a good idea. But you already reported to the sheriff's office. Maybe we should wait and see if this deputy gets a detective involved. Anyway, aren't the kids on vacation this week?"

"Oh, that's right," Zora Jane said. "They've gone to the aquarium in Monterey."

Ed unfolded his lanky frame from the recliner. "I know one thing we could do. We could Google the *Des Moines Herald Examiner* and look for articles about a baby found dead in Harvard, Iowa."

Why didn't we think of that? To say that Jesse and I are technologically challenged would be an understatement. We'd no more know how to "Google" than to fly.

Ed marched down the hall. In his office, I admired plaques awarded during his law-enforcement career and the golf trophies lined on top of his bookshelves while Ed connected to the Web site for the *Des Moines Herald Examiner.*

"Here we are." He looked pleased.

We crowded around his black leather chair to watch while he clicked on "Search our Archives," which included articles from 1994 to present. He typed, "dead baby found in Harvard" in the "Search for" slot. In short order, a listing of twelve articles appeared. A synopsis of the article and the date of publication accompanied each one. Scrolling down the screen, he stopped at number two, titled, "Infant's Body Found in Harvard." Dated February 22, this article exactly matched the one in the back of Lila's notebook.

Funny how technology familiar to most people could excite us oldsters.

Ed regarded us with a triumphant expression. "Hole in one!"

"Praise the Lord!" Zora Jane said.

I couldn't contain my joy. "Wow!"

Jesse asked. "Are there follow-up articles?"

Ed continued down the list. The next article, dated a few days later, rehashed the tragic details of the baby's discovery, including the alarm the tiny body created among citizens of Harvard. Statistics about abandoned newborns made it sound like an epidemic. Quotes from residents repeated rumors about the baby's possible parentage.

Jesse asked, "Why were the people of Harvard alarmed?"

"It's a baby, for goodness' sakes," I answered. "People get excited when it comes to babies."

"Also, it's a small Midwestern town," Zora Jane said. "In small towns, everyone gets involved in other people's business. You know that."

The next articles, one written two days later and one the following week, detailed the exhaustive search for the baby's mother or anyone with knowledge of the abandonment. The next, written March 8, outlined plans by the town of Harvard for a funeral to memorialize the unidentified infant. The townspeople named him "Baby Blue."

Ed asked, "Where did they get *that* name?"

I guessed. "They found the baby wrapped in a blue blanket."

Next, five articles had been written over a period of several months. The last appeared in mid-July. A thorough local investigation with a plethora of false leads failed to end in arrest. Authorities widened the search area to include communities across the state on both sides of Interstate 80. Quotes from lead investigator, Guthrie County Deputy Sheriff Russell Silverthorne, pleaded for information. "This tragedy has severely impacted the entire state of Iowa." The mayor of Harvard pleaded for the mother to come forward. A priest from the local St. Bartholomew's Catholic Church urged people to prayer.

The next article contained information released from the autopsy. Cause of death: a broken neck. Advanced decomposition from being buried beside the water tower for over a year, made gathering evidence difficult.

Written on the first anniversary of the discovery of the body, the final article included a few lines to identify the case and then another quote from Deputy Silverthorne. "Despite concentrated efforts, no arrests have been made and all leads have been exhausted."

Zora Jane sniffed. "What a sad story!"

I shook my head. "The baby died of a broken neck. That's murder." My stomach churned. "How could Lila murder her own infant?"

They all looked at me.

"You're jumping to conclusions again, Slick." Jesse said.

"Well, there's definitely suspicion of foul play." Ed locked his hands behind his neck and tipped back in his chair. "They wouldn't keep the investigation going without reason to think *someone* murdered the baby."

I stared at the monitor, trying to extract facts. "They discovered the body just before the Paynes moved to California."

Zora Jane wiped a tear from her eye.

I glanced at Ed and Jesse. "The timeline works. This must be Lila's baby."

"Easy there!" Ed said. "Don't play ahead. We need proof to make accusations."

Proof or not, I knew it had to be true. A faint outline materialized from the random puzzle pieces we'd gathered so far, enough to know it wouldn't be a pretty picture.

In spite of growing evidence against her, I didn't want to believe Lila had been responsible for Baby Blue's death. Not the delicate Lila I met. Not even the troubled Lila who wrote those poems. Something completely out of her control happened to that little boy. And Lila never recovered.

22

Chapter Twenty-Two

I settled into a routine. Each morning and evening, I called the sheriff's office, hoping Deputy Colter would have something to report. Most of the time, he was unavailable. Thursday, I didn't call until late afternoon, thinking maybe it might be easier to find him later. The dispatch lady asked my name and requested that I hold. She returned in a few seconds to inquire whether I'd like his voicemail, since Deputy Colter had taken another call.

I sighed. "If I leave him another message, is he likely to call me back?"

She repeated in an impersonal tone, "Would you like his voicemail, ma'am?"

"Sure, why not?" I paced while the recording completed. "This is Christine Sterling again. I'm calling to see what you've found out about Lila Payne—Lila Kliner, rather. Have you found the car? Can I file a missing-persons report on her? And what about my dog? Please call me back." I left my phone number one more time and hung up feeling helpless. My blood pressure started to rise again.

In the last few days, the fall colors had blasted out in chromatic symphony over the trees at our elevation. I stared at the vision of tranquility framed by the bay windows in the kitchenette. After several minutes of concentrated scrutiny, I sensed the peace of God's creation and sovereignty.

The waterfall gurgled into the pond while horses grazed across the valley. Sunshine lit the horse pasture and the whole top of the hill, making the versicolor leaves stand out even more. The air felt chilly outside, but a glimpse of sun imparted a notion of warmth. Above the hillside, huge, puffy-soft clouds hovered in arching layers against a clear robin's egg blue sky. Life in its resplendent cycle continued despite the catastrophes that troubled me.

Will's white pickup had departed in customary fashion late in the morning, and I didn't think it had returned yet. Looking out the windows, I contemplated another discovery mission to the gray house and had just about talked myself into putting on my shoes when the phone rang.

"This is Deputy Sheriff Sam Colter of the Nevada County Sheriff's Office," the phlegmatic voice said. "I am returning a call from Christine Sterling."

What a surprise. "If you recall, I called about our neighbor who's been missing now for over a week. Lila Kliner. I want to know if you've found her or the car. Or our dog."

A rustling filled the pause. For a moment, I couldn't imagine what might make that sound. He must be shuffling through file papers. "The Truckee Sheriff's Office located Mr. Payne's abandoned 1985 brown Buick LeSabre this morning near Mantis Lake in Truckee at the Sierra Meadows Campground."

"Mantis Lake? Never heard of it. Where is that?"

"East of the Truckee-Tahoe Airport off State Highway 267—a relatively remote area. It is just a lakebed at this time of year. The campground is closed, but a hiker found the vehicle in the middle of an access road with the driver side door wide open and an empty gas tank. Apparently, that is why it stopped there." His tone softened. "And ma'am, there is one more thing."

"What?"

"The trunk had been lowered but not fastened due to a rusted latch. Inside, they found the remains of a black-and-white dog wrapped in a light blue baby's blanket."

"Remains?" My vision blurred for an instant and I went light-headed. In slow motion, I sank onto a chair at the kitchen table. "No! No!"

"I am sorry, ma'am. That is the report."

I couldn't speak.

"Ma'am?"

As soon as I could, I whispered, "What about Lila?"

"No sign of her."

I cleared my throat and took a deep breath. Even so, my voice wobbled when I spoke. "She's been gone for more than a week. She's missing. Officially."

"Yes. Well, the car will be towed to Grass Valley in a day or so and held in the impound lot, pending investigation. You must understand that this is not a high-priority case. Even though Miss Kliner has been missing for more than a week, there is no evidence of foul play. The crime lab will process the vehicle and report their findings. I notified Mr. Payne late this morning. He is convinced Miss Kliner merely ran off." I heard what must have been a pencil tapping against his desk. "Did she mention anyone who might be interested in her whereabouts? A relative, for example?"

"We didn't talk about relatives. I only met her those two times, as I told you. I don't know anything about her family."

"I see … well, my condolences … about your dog." He heaved a long sigh. "The public thinks all sheriff 's offices these days are equipped with high-tech gadgets like you see in TV crime shows. Truth is, Nevada County is small, without a big budget or adequate manpower. We do not have resources to check out every suspicious-looking situation. So far, I have found no evidence of a crime in this case, except a possible misdemeanor concerning your dog. I will turn my report over to the detective, but do not get your hopes up."

His loud disconnect severed the conversation with the finality of a guillotine slash. I sat dumbfounded holding the phone cradled to my ear. *Poor, poor Molly! How did this happen to you? How frightened you must have been.* None of this made any sense. If Lila took her, why would she kill her? Lila loved dogs.

Why?

Hot tears rained down my face and dropped onto my shirt. I slumped in the chair as waves of sorrow rolled over me. By the time I viewed myself in the bathroom mirror, my nose had reddened and my eyeliner smeared into dark smudges under my eyes.

I sniffed at my frightful appearance. Wasn't it Colter's job to protect the public? How could someone with so little concern for our welfare be on the government payroll? I'd have to find Lila myself and hold her accountable.

Aware of my impotence, I fell to my knees. If God had all power and cared about our problems, as Zora Jane promised, now would be a good time to intervene. Fast-falling tears dribbled down my chin. "I don't know what to do, God. Help me." While I prayed, a soothing presence settled over me, bringing a sense of hope. I knew this wasn't the end. Despite what Deputy Colter did or did not discover, there would soon be more for me to do.

Being a visual person and a list-maker, I committed this vexing mystery to paper. I sat at the kitchen table with a yellow note pad and wrote out every fact as I thought of it—kind of like free association. Before long, I ran out of actual facts and had to write guesses. When I had filled up one page, I reread it. Wasn't this where a new connection displayed itself?

I waited, but nothing new occurred to me. I slammed the pad on the table and leaned back in the chair, eyes closed. Maybe the solution would appear on my mental movie screen. Instead, I came to the realization that most of what I thought of as *fact* was actually inference. Just as Ed pointed out.

What now, God?

A sudden yearning to see Molly with my own eyes filled my soul.

By then, I had memorized the number to the Nevada County Sheriff's Office. Again, the dispassionate voice of the dispatcher answered. I repeated my request to speak with Deputy Colter.

"One moment, please." She put me on hold. I paced, waiting. "Deputy Colter is not at his desk. Would you like his voicemail?"

Energy had been sapped away and I could only sigh. "Sure." I mouthed the words of his recorded message while it completed.

"Hello. Christine Sterling again. I want to file a missing-persons report on Lila Kliner. I want to bury my dog and I want to see the car. Can you arrange that? I know none of this is important to you. It's probably not important to anyone else in the big scheme of things, but Molly is ... *was* a special dog." The words caught in my throat, making my voice crack. "It matters a lot to me. Please call and tell me when."

Jesse's footfall sounded at the door. What should I say? Words failed me. I collapsed into his arms as tears flowed.

That evening, time slowed to a crawl. Powerlessness suffused the house. Jesse and I gave each other grieving space as a cocoon of mourning enveloped us. I wandered aimlessly, watching but not comprehending bits of TV shows and playing mindless games on the computer. I knew I shouldn't waste God's precious gift of time, but couldn't muster the effort to do something productive. I even entertained doubts about God's ultimate goodness and sovereignty.

Mostly I tried not to think about Molly.

23

CHAPTER TWENTY-THREE

From the kitchen window, I watched Jesse lead Ranger out to the arena to practice maneuvering around the orange highway cones on an unusually sunny autumn morning. With a whole day to fill and nothing of interest to fill it with, I put in a call to our son. He could only talk a minute because clients sat in his office at his RV dealership. Our oldest daughter, the nurse, just finished working a twelve-hour night shift. I knew better than to call during her sleep time. A call to the middle daughter connected me with her answering machine at the university, where she worked as a science professor. She spent most of her time in the research lab. *So much for staying connected with the children.*

While I went through the motions of my morning routine—exercise, e-mail, gardening, and tidying up the house—I forced myself to meditate on my blessings rather than complain about my problems. By being deliberate with my thoughts, I managed to keep them in check. Soon, the morning passed.

When Jesse returned, he found me sitting in my dark green rocking chair in the library, stroking a lapful of cats. Roy and Hoppy snored in unison, enjoying a midday nap. I even remembered to thank God for these two fine companions.

Jesse stopped at the head of the stairs when he saw me. "What say we have lunch at Rosita's?"

I beamed a smile his way.

"And maybe we could file a missing-persons report and do a bit of sleuthing too."

Now he was talking.

Jesse sang as we drove into town.

Put your sweet lips a little closer to the phone.
I'll tell the man to turn the jukebox way down low.
Chug a lug, chug a lug! Grape wine in a mason jar,
Homemade and brought to school by a friend of mine after class
Ramblin' fever, ramblin' on.

Enjoying his medley, I realized how different our relationship had become since I asked for God's help with my unforgiving spirit. Another answered prayer? Maybe God did care about us insignificant mortals after all. *Thank you, God, for mending our relationship.*

Jesse winked at me when he pulled out my chair at Rosita's.

I settled on the cushioned wood chair. "Such chivalry."

He bent into my shoulder and nuzzled my hair. "Maybe you'll let me open your car door now too."

The car door thing happened just after I met Jesse. A newly liberated college woman, I resisted his "chauvinistic" gesture of opening the door for me on our first date. I hadn't been sweet about it, either. It was a wonder he ever asked me out again. It had been years since I thought about that incident.

I patted his cheek. "Let's not get carried away."

He grinned as he slid into the chair across the table.

I tried to look serious. "And you picked Rosita's because …"

He sandwiched my hand between his and gazed into my eyes. "It's your favorite."

"Sure it's not because it's only a block to the sheriff's office from here?"

The waitress placed a bowl of savory salsa and a basket of warm flour and corn tortilla chips on the table. Then she retrieved her order pad from her multicolor apron. I opened my mouth to order, but Jesse spoke first, reading from the menu. "The lady will have homemade pork tamales smothered in rich reddish-brown enchilada sauce with rice and whole pinto beans on the side." He glanced at me and wiggled his eyebrows.

I clapped in delight. Who said Jesse didn't have a romantic side?

Jesse ordered a chicken fajita salad with whole pinto beans, smiling as he returned the menus to the waitress with his favorite restaurant joke: "We'll wait here."

Her eyebrows scrunched together and she tilted her head to the side. She blinked as if she had missed something. Jesse said this same line to every waitress we encountered and we always got the same reaction.

"Don't forget the homemade tortillas," I reminded her as she dashed away.

At the appropriate time, the food arrived—mine smothered in melted cheese. I sniffed my order, relishing the spicy aroma of cornmeal and pork. We talked like lovers while we ate, eyes locked in attention, instead of gobbling in silence like married people.

Near the end of our meal, a round woman in my direct line of sight behind Jesse's left shoulder scooped the mostly untouched contents of her plate inside her oversized red purse.

I gasped. "Oh, my!"

"What?" Jesse asked, turning

his head.

I lifted one hand. "Don't look now, but the woman behind you just dumped a full plate of food into her purse." I covered my mouth so a giggle wouldn't escape.

Jesse gave a short hoot. "Why would she do that?"

"She has starving children at home?"

Jesse leveled a long look at me.

"She wants a snack later?"

He forked a chunk of lettuce. "Or she's a nut case."

Without looking up, the woman carefully positioned her purse on her lap. While I watched, she slid the chip bowl to the edge of the table and upended its contents into the purse. I whispered, "Now she's pilfered the chips."

Jesse laughed. "Not the chips too?"

Utensils tapped stoneware, glasses clinked, laughter and talking continued undisturbed all around me. I glanced at the other restaurant patrons. No one else seemed to notice.

Jesse leaned toward me. "If she dumps the salsa on top of it all, we'll get the food police after her."

I favored him with a tolerant smile.

But the woman dabbed her lips daintily with her napkin, pushed back her chair, and tottered off in the direction of the ladies' room, swinging her now-heavy red bag.

My eyes trailed after her. "Where's she going with all that food? You don't suppose she intends to eat it in the ladies' room, do you?"

I popped to a stand but Jesse's frown made me sit again.

"Let it go, Christine. It doesn't matter. Let's just enjoy our meal."

I kept an eye on the hall to the ladies' room but never caught another glimpse of her. I slowed my chewing, trying to clean every scrumptious morsel off my plate and give her plenty of time to come out, but eventually had to admit I couldn't eat another bite. I'd never know her secret. I sighed, pushed back my chair and pronounced the meal, "Most satisfactory."

Leaving the restaurant, I felt a bit unsettled—kind of like waiting for someone to finish a sentence but never hearing it. I would always wonder what that woman had been up to.

Next stop: the Nevada County Sheriff's Office. Deputy Colter was not at work. Nevertheless, the receptionist ushered us into a small cubicle with a desk crowded in so tightly, I wondered if they built the workspace around it. A monitor screen sat atop the desk alongside several stacks of official-looking papers and files and, of course, a telephone with lots of extra buttons. Two chairs faced the desk. We settled into those. Across from us, a woman in standard uniform worked, half-hidden by the computer monitor.

While maintaining her humorless demeanor, the woman introduced herself as Deputy Laura Elliott. Coarse blond split ends stuck out from the thick curtain of hair that dropped to her back.

Her ruddy complexion indicated an outdoorsy girl without time for make-up or fussing. "How can I help you?"

Jesse described the situation briefly, referencing Deputy Colter.

She picked up magnifying glasses—the skinny kind that allow for peeking over without lowering the head—and adjusted them on her nose. Retreating to her computer screen, she typed information. After a while, she paused to read what came up. "I see," she said, without so much as a glance our way.

She didn't appear to be paying attention. I cleared my throat. "We want to file a missing-persons report on Lila Kliner. She's been missing now for almost two weeks. No one is searching for her."

Deputy Elliott maintained her focus on the computer screen. "Please state the full name of the missing party." Her fingers pecked the keyboard as we told her everything we knew about Lila, which was precious little.

When she finished, with a flourish of authority she punched a button on the computer keyboard. A whirring sounded, and a paper emerged from a nearby printer. She retrieved the page and placed it on the desk in front of Jesse. "Please read and sign."

Jesse read and signed, although most of the form remained blank.

"This will go out immediately." She peered over the top of the magnifiers. "Thank you." Then she focused on her monitor again. Apparently, we'd been dismissed.

I wanted to complain about her lack of interest, but Jesse pressed my arm firmly and led me to the car without another word.

After he settled into the driver's seat of the Jeep and buckled his seatbelt, he faced me. "Okay. Let's find the address of that house where Will went. Off Star Mine Road, you said." He dazzled me with one of his radiant smiles, and off we sped.

Passing once again through the business section, we made a Hollywood stop at the first stop sign. I usually complain when Jesse only taps the brakes as he rolls through the intersection, but after my royal treatment at the restaurant, I let it slide. We continued to the busy crossing on Brunswick, again ignoring the posted thirty-five-mile-per-hour speed limit.

The Loma Rica barn still peeked through the trees to the left. We lingered patiently several minutes, waiting for a break in traffic. Rather, I maintained patience while Jesse whistled and thrummed the steering wheel with his fingers. I didn't complain about that either. Patient or not, an opening appeared and we zipped across. A mile or so farther through the countryside, we began the gradual incline up Banner Mountain and soon came to Sierra Vista Road.

I pointed to the second house on the left—the white clapboard with green trim—and we noted that Will's white pickup once again rested in the driveway. Since Jesse had been so considerate, I thought he might allow me to peek in the windows again. I tugged on his sleeve and opened my mouth to ask, but he communicated a stern *don't-even-think-about-it* look, so I didn't press it.

I recorded the address painted on the mailbox before we circled the end of the cul-de-sac and drove out without speaking, as if someone might hear us if we talked out loud.

After we returned to the main street, I asked, "So, where to now?"

Jesse didn't answer until he finished navigating the curved onramp toward Nevada City. "Well, since we're out for a drive anyway, why don't we look at where they found the Buick?"

Smiling my assent, I settled back for a pleasant drive.

State Route 20 between Nevada City and Interstate 80 tops my list of favorite roads to travel in any season. In the fall and spring, its colorful foliage and flowers make for spectacular viewing. The highway held a special place in our family history as the scenic detour we discovered on our first visit to Grass Valley going home from Lake Tahoe one fall. The magnificent scenery along that highway led us to search for property in the area.

The lush leafage along the cool, tree-lined corridor didn't disappoint. We chatted about the children and grandchildren—especially the news of a new baby on the way, which I learned when I called our son—our hopes and dreams, and plans for the future. We made our way at last to the overlook point just before the turnoff to the tiny town of Washington.

Jesse slowed the car to a crawl. "Look at that view!" Mountains and trees spread before us in awesome splendor. Dotted with autumn color, the sight birthed a flush of joy that spread from my chest. Satiated with the magnificent beauty of the scene, we didn't speak again until Jesse rolled to a semi-stop beside a large meadow.

He bent forward on the steering wheel and pointed. "Wish I could build a house just there near the trees." Vast and lush, this place always brought out our pioneering spirit. I imagined Jesse peeling logs for a cabin nestled in that spot while I cleared brush for my vegetable garden.

From Jesse's favorite meadow, we continued up the hill and soon arrived at the interstate. Climbing ever higher into the Sierras, we passed through Truckee after another half hour and exited onto State Highway 257 on the north side. First, we passed an area of sprawling commercial development, but when we got as far as the Truckee-Tahoe Airport, we left all trappings of civilization behind.

A large, flat space with trees around the fringes opened before us. A few houses huddled against the foot of the mountains, but mostly we saw only open spaces. About in the middle, a road veered to the left at a sign labeled Mantis Lake.

A wave of anticipation washed over me. I leaned forward, aware of my heart beating faster. "There it is. Turn left, Jesse."

We followed the narrow, paved roadway along the outer edges of a dry lakebed. At least a mile and a half farther, a dirt road cut left at a signboard that read Sierra Meadows Campground. This road wound through tall pines until we came to the entrance. A tin sign bearing the single word Closed dangled from a thick rusty chain, which stretched across the roadway. One side of the chain dragged the pavement, low and wide enough to drive over without effort.

Jesse parked the car and unbuckled his seat belt. "Let's see what we can find." From the back seat, he extracted his camera, zoom lens attached.

I pointed at tire tracks in the dried mud. "Those look recent. At least they've been here since the rain." Nearby, footprints clustered together, their individual characteristics blurred. "How many people have been here?"

"Well, a hiker found the car. Then the tow-truck guy and maybe someone from the sheriff's department, Lila—"

"I see a lot of men's shoeprints. But I don't see anything small enough to be Lila's."

"This must be where the Buick parked." Jesse bent closer to inspect the tracks. "Maybe they stepped on her footprints."

"Terrible police procedure." I tiptoed to a better observation spot, taking great care not to trample the prints. "Well, she got here way before anyone else. Maybe the tow guys messed up her prints before the officers came."

Sherlock Holmes would have approved of our deliberate examination of the area. The camera whirred and clicked as Jesse meticulously snapped pictures, adjusting the lens every few frames. He crouched for a closer view and then squinted up at me. "I see work boots in at least two sizes and another set that might be made by running shoes."

I followed in his steps and bent to look over his shoulder. "Must be the tow people. They aren't small enough to be Lila's. See the dry patch between the tires?"

He nodded. "That's where the car sat during the rain. A bigger set of tires parked in front of the regular ones. Probably the tow truck." Jesse took a few more pictures before he straightened.

Unsure whether the sheriff's department inspected this road before towing the car, we stepped lightly around the campground loop. I advanced with exaggerated caution inside Jesse's prints. Heavy rain had fallen on Sunday night after Molly disappeared. If the Buick arrived Saturday night, as we supposed, it sat in the same spot through the rainstorm until towed away days later.

As we ambled back to the Jeep, a piece of galvanized metal near the edge of the roadway caught my eye—a funnel discarded in a dense pile of pine needles.

I stooped to look. "Evidence?"

Jesse saw it too. "Don't touch that. It might be important." He snapped a couple more pictures. Then he used his Chuck Buck knife to cut a long branch from a nearby tree, strip off the twigs, and push one end into the funnel.

Good technique. He carried his prize to the car without touching it.

I didn't get the significance of a funnel, though. "How would that connect to Lila?"

"Don't know." Jesse bent to sniff the funnel before banging the back end of the Jeep shut. "But back in high school, we used to siphon gas out of a tank with a funnel and a hose."

"That would mean the car didn't run out of gas but she tried to make it look like it did. How would she know how to do that? I wouldn't. And why would she do that anyway?"

Jesse shrugged.

None of this made sense. "Then there's the matter of the gas can. What did she do with it? Supposing Lila left the Buick here, she had to walk out." I scanned miles of uninhabited meadows and mountains. "Where'd she go?"

Jesse shook his head. "I don't know."

These unanswered questions didn't seem to gnaw at Jesse the way they did me. While we drove home in the late afternoon light, Jesse sang.

> *Dream lover, where are youoo?*
> *I want a dream lover so I don't have to dream alone.*
> *Hey mama don't you treat me wrong.*
> *Come and love your daddy all night long ...*

Seeing the place where Molly's poor sweet body had lain inside that trunk brought the sadness rushing back. *Why, why, why?* A tear splashed onto my sweater. I sniffed back more, digging for Kleenexes in my purse. Why would Lila kill my wonderful dog?

Maybe my judgment about Lila's basic goodness and need for help had been swayed by my desire to rescue her. What kind of person would Lila turn out to be?

24

Chapter Twenty-four

When my eyes popped open, I remembered that Zora Jane had recruited me to help at the annual church bazaar. Despite the fact that I couldn't muster enough enthusiasm to fill a thimble, I managed to arrive a few minutes after nine.

Zora Jane did not exaggerate about the crowd. Parking lots overflowed. Scores of cars lined both sides of streets on every side of the church. After much searching, I squeezed into a parking space five blocks away.

Booths covered the blacktop in front of the church, the welcoming center, the children's center, and just about everywhere else on the campus. Hordes of shoppers milled about, many toting bags loaded with treasures already discovered. Displays held an amazing array of used appliances, furniture, bedding, sports equipment, and household items. I even saw an automotive section.

Everything but the …

I squelched that thought at the sight of a kitchen sink peeking from under a table.

First, I stopped at the sporting goods booth for directions. From there, I was pointed to the children's center for clothing and accessories and I headed off in search of Zora Jane.

Inside the building, I soon spied her reddish hair bobbing above the mass of people. It's good to be tall in a crowd. I headed straight for her, bumping into a lady carrying an armload of sweaters. "Sorry, didn't see you there." The lady didn't stop to acknowledge my presence.

Zora Jane scooted through the throng wearing a white, long-sleeved blouse with the collar turned up in the back. A wide purple bangle decorated her wrist. The blouse hung just the right length over the top of rolled-up jeans. A violet-checked apron protected her front. Purple flats with cork wedge heels snapped the floor as she hurried. Just like Garage Sale Barbie.

Zora Jane grinned when she saw me. "You made it. Here, take these." She dumped an armload of miscellaneous hats, scarves, mittens, and belts into my arms. "I'll get the rest." She pivoted and dashed away before I could react.

A teenage boy elbowed me as he hurried by.

"Wait!" I shouted above the hubbub, trying to rub my arm without dropping my load. "I don't know where the booth is."

Not breaking stride, Zora Jane swept one arm toward the corner of the room where a small computer-generated sign read Accessories. I zigzagged between eager shoppers and finally arrived at the corner.

A lady—older and less attractive than Zora Jane—stood behind the accessories table talking with a customer. Her pinched features reminded me of a squeezed lemon. Arms full, I waited for her to finish the transaction. When she concluded, she glanced at me and scrunched her face into a grimace.

I smiled. "Hi. I'm Christine Sterling, Zora Jane's friend. She said to bring these over here." I spilled my armload onto the table.

"Whatever." She rubbed circles on her temple. "I've got a headache the size of Mount Everest. Come back here where you can sort those."

It sounded like an order, so I hurried where she pointed.

Miss Lemon didn't smile. "People started arriving before six. Can you believe it? Zora Jane and I had barely gotten here. Haven't had free time since." Two ladies approached the booth and one made an inquiry, so she went back to selling.

Zora Jane returned with another armful of accessories, which she dumped atop mine. "What a madhouse! Didn't I tell you? We haven't had a chance to finish collecting all the stuff yet." Her eyes sparkled like a kid at Disneyland. She nodded toward the other lady. "Did you meet Grace Woodson?"

Grace? I suppressed a snicker. *What a misnomer. But who would name their child Sourpuss? Even if the name fit.*

Another clump of eager shoppers descended on us, so conversation ceased. About an hour later, a short lull gave me a few minutes to catch my breath.

While we sorted the pile of accessories, Zora Jane continued the introduction as if she hadn't been interrupted. "Christine's my neighbor. I prayed for a Christian to move into the neighborhood, and here she is." She beamed at me.

Grace grunted as she slipped off her shoe to rub one foot. "Don't know why you want to live so far out there anyway. This is a crazy world. What if you have trouble? No one will get there for hours."

I glanced at Zora Jane. Maybe she knew how best to deal with this woman.

"Oh, we have plenty of help. There's a sheriff's substation in Alta Sierra that's manned most of the time. Besides, God is always with us. And it didn't take long for the fire department to get there last week. Did it, Christine?"

"No." *Why hadn't I heard about the substation before?* "The fireman came right away. Can't say the same for the deputy, though."

Grace's face puckered. She looked about ready to squeeze out lemon juice in anticipation of fresh gossip. "Deputy? What did the deputy come out for?"

Zora Jane glanced at me. I waited to answer, unsure how much we wanted to stoke the rumor mill.

Zora Jane's eyes softened. "Our neighbor is missing."

My throat tightened and I blinked back tears. "And my dog … has been killed." I hadn't acknowledged that out loud since I told Jesse. Hadn't spoken of it to Zora Jane yet.

"Oh, my dear." Zora Jane touched my arm and gazed into my eyes as I brokenly explained Deputy Colter's news. Then she gave me a hug.

"Wait a second." Grace divided her gaze between us. "Are you by any chance neighbors of Will Payne?"

We nodded in unison.

"I heard about him at the beauty parlor." She patted her tightly curled coiffure. "Maxine does my hair …" She paused as if waiting for us to acknowledge the name drop.

Zora Jane blinked and I shook my head.

She tsked. "Maxine. She's only the absolute *top* beautician in the county. Takes months to get in to see her."

We stared blankly.

She rolled her eyes. "A Cut Above is simply the best beauty salon there is. Everyone around here knows that. Well, anyway, Maxine and the operator next to her chat while she cuts my hair. I think the other gal's name is Cybil. Or Sylvia. Something like that. Anyway, last week they had plenty to say about William Payne, let me tell you. Cybil, or Sylvia, or whatever, she does Helen's hair."

"Helen?" Zora Jane and I repeated in unison.

Grace frowned as if she couldn't believe we interrupted her in mid-gossip. "Yeah. Will's sister. The one that lives in Nevada City. Helen Sterne." She stopped to stare. "You don't know his sister?"

His sister! *Why do I always think the worst about people?* "Does she live on Sierra Vista at the top of Banner Mountain?"

Grace shrugged. "I guess. Anyway, she went on and on, *Will* this and *Will* that. So when Maxine put me under the dryer I asked, '*Will* who?' Maxine said, 'Will Payne out in Alta Sierra.'" Grace crossed her arms and nodded, smug as Camilla Bowles after snagging Prince Charles.

"What did they say about him?" I asked.

Grace lowered her voice to confidential volume. We bent toward her and cupped our ears to hear above the din of the bazaar.

"Well, apparently Will Payne is mega wealthy. And he finally got rid of the gold digger who freeloaded off him for years. That woman wouldn't clean house or cook. Hardly ate anything, refused to touch meat. Can't imagine why he'd be attracted to someone like that, but there's no accounting for some people's taste. Maybe she put a spell on him."

I remembered what I'd read in the library about anorexia.

Grace chuckled and licked her lips as if she had come to the juicy part. "Then—get this—she made Will throw out his furniture. Said it was possessed. Why, some of those pieces were family heirlooms!" Zora Jane's expression didn't change, so Grace turned to me as if expecting a reaction. "Can you believe it?"

I closed my eyes and shook my head. What unspeakable things had happened in that house?

Zora Jane asked, "Did Helen say how Will got rid of this crazy woman?"

"Do you think he killed her?" Grace emphasized each word for maximum effect, fairly quivering with expectation, as though a murder would be cause for celebration.

I shuddered inside, recalling my own callous attitude when I first spied on Will. All the same, I wished she had more to tell.

❧

After I completed my shift at the bazaar, I trotted into the sunshine, hunting for my car. A tall woman carrying a load of bazaar purchases hurried past. With her hair pulled back in a low ponytail, she reminded me of the woman Will went to see—his *sister*, Helen Sterne. I shook my head at my misguided assumption. Although I wanted to get home and call Deputy Colter again, seeing the woman made me think how close the church lay to Helen Sterne's house in the woods. Perhaps a short detour wouldn't hurt.

I left the car in park with the engine running in front of Helen's driveway. Why hadn't I planned how to get in the door? "Hello. I'm Samantha Brown from the Travel Channel. I'm doing a segment on life in the foothills. Do you mind if I ask a few questions?" I'd need a notebook or recorder. Of course, that wouldn't work anyway if she'd ever seen the much younger and prettier Samantha Brown. Maybe I could be Samantha Brown's assistant. I'd still need a notebook. I looked around the car but didn't see one.

How about if I pretended to be a prospective neighbor? "Hi, I'm thinking of buying the house down the street. Could I ask a few questions about the neighborhood?" But how personal could I get before she became suspicious of my true motive? And what if there wasn't a house for sale on the street?

Just then, the front door slammed and Helen scurried from her porch like a cockroach running from light. I jammed the car into gear and raced out of sight. When I returned, Helen had just backed her blue sedan out the driveway.

The timing seemed a gift from above. I didn't have to peek in windows or break into houses either. *Thank you, God. Now help me tail her without being too obvious.*

She maneuvered right on Star Mine Road. I let a car pass before I followed, so she drove ahead of me with one car in between.

Excellent! I must be getting the hang of this.

I followed along the front side of Banner Mountain, headed toward Grass Valley. I rolled my window down and sucked in a deep breath of the crisp fall air. *Lovely day for tailing.* It made me feel like singing.

Helen proceeded straight to the hardware store. I squeezed the Jeep into a parking space between a white van and a black Chevy truck one row away, got out, and locked the car.

"Accidentally" bumping into her at the hardware store might seem a bit contrived, but it could work. After all, I "ran into" the McCarthys at Kmart.

Once inside, Helen marched toward the tool section, head high and purposeful. I hurried behind her, racing for the opposite end of the aisle she entered.

Now if I could head her off at the pass.

In my rush, I almost collided with a hardware clerk. He zigzagged at the last second—being younger with faster reflexes—but I threw him off balance. The box he carried thunked to the floor.

"Oh, sorry," I said. "Didn't see you there."

Brushing off his red work vest as if the mishap had soiled it, he glared at me.

"Is anything broken?" I retrieved the box and shook it. "Don't hear anything rattling."

His frown deepened as he grabbed the box and dashed off. The day they taught good customer relations, he must've been home with a cold.

I paused to steady myself with a deep breath and shot an arrow prayer heavenward. *Help me, God!* Then I turned the corner. Sure enough, Helen moseyed toward me, scanning the displays along one side.

Taller than I realized, she towered at least a full head above me. She might be close to six feet tall. Along with the same low ponytail as before, she wore a blue-gray sweater and jeans with dirty tennis shoes. Seeing her signature hairdo made me wonder just what she went to the beauty parlor for. Maybe she needed a captive audience to complain to.

Got to catch her looking this way. Careful, not too obvious.

A few shoppers browsed the aisles near the tool section. Fortunately, no one interrupted us. I surveyed the displays nearest me, pretending to search for something.

Helen sidled closer. I swung over to her side of the aisle.

Now for the tricky part.

She reached for something, I couldn't tell *what* without being obvious. Something long.

I inched toward her. When our feet were parallel, I took another deep breath and swung to face her. Cold brown eyes swept me with suspicion.

I smiled and bared my teeth. "Oh, hi. Aren't you Will Payne's sister?"

She scowled. "Do I know you?"

"I'm Christine Sterling. I live up the hill from Will in Alta Sierra. You know the log house?"

"How do you know me?"

Ignore the questions you don't want to answer and ask something else instead.

"We've been so worried about Lila. Have you heard where she's gone?"

She shifted to her full imposing height and glared down at me, one eyebrow cocked in a high arch. "How do you know she's gone?"

I felt like a bug about to be squished. Shaking off the intimidation, I heard the rapid pounding of my heart. "She's such a delicate little thing, I worry about her. Where could she be? She doesn't have any relatives in the area, does she?"

"Relatives? I wouldn't know. How did you—?"

"Last time I saw Lila, she had bruises on her arms and neck. Did she show those to you?"

She stepped back as if the question startled her. "Bruises?" She stared at the floor. "Don't know nothing about those."

"When did you last see her?"

She shrugged. "A couple weeks ago maybe."

"And you haven't seen her since?"

She glared at me without answering.

I shifted weight from one foot to the other. "Well, where was she when you saw her?"

"Will's house I guess. Why are you—?"

"What were you doing there?"

Eyes that had been flat before now flashed with angry light.

Careful. You're making her mad. How far can I push her? "Was she acting crazy so you got in a fight?"

Her eyes crackled with electricity. "Crazy? You don't know the half of it. *Stupid* little beast. Wouldn't come out of her room, crying and carrying on. Will didn't know what to do."

"But you knew how to handle her."

"That girl was a monster. You'd think someone mistreated her. He did everything he could to help her. And what did he get for it? She hid in the closet and screamed like a lunatic."

An eerie emphasis on certain words made me stifle a shiver. "So … you pulled her out?"

She snorted. "Didn't hurt her."

"Did you … strangle her?"

She leaned toward me with a menacing expression. "Sometimes people don't know what's good for them."

I took a step backward. *Did she mean Lila or me?* "That's really sad." I shuffled and twirled a clump of my hair between my thumb and forefinger. "You, uh, you and Will must be worried about where she's gone—because she can't take care of herself."

"Look, I don't know who you are, but you're mighty nosy." She stepped closer and lowered her angular face until her eyes locked on mine. "You might find trouble if you keep snooping." Her breath stunk like last week's garbage and her narrowed eyes glinted with malevolence.

Losing all pretense of courage, I dropped my gaze. Only then did my brain identify the object she gripped with knuckles as white as a corpse. In her large, manly hands, she held a heavy-duty bolt cutter with long, sharp blades.

25

Chapter Twenty-Five

Jesse and I slept in on Sunday. Neither of us remembered to set the alarm. After the frightening confrontation with Helen, I had no energy. I just couldn't make myself carry on normally with Molly still missing. I made a face at Jesse when he asked if we were going to church. He didn't ask why not.

Late in the morning, the gate buzzer startled me. Peeking out the kitchen window, I recognized Zora Jane's red Mustang convertible waiting outside the gate. *Of all times for a visit.* I glanced down at my pajamas and groaned. "Maybe we could pretend we're not here."

Jesse bent to look out as the buzz sounded again. He shook his head. "Now, Christine, that wouldn't be nice. They're our friends. Let 'em in."

I stared at him in wonder. When did he start considering polite behavior?

Jesse pressed the star key on the phone to open the gate.

I grabbed my robe and fastened it around me as I followed him. Jesse flung the door open wide as if delighted to see them.

They climbed the porch steps smiling. Ed wore his Sunday pants, and Zora Jane carried a casserole dish. Her bright yellow pantsuit dazzled the eye. The prominent collar made her handsome head look like a bust set on a pedestal. Matching shoes peeked out below the perfect-length pants. How many different pairs of shoes cohabitated in Zora Jane's closet?

Ed grinned. "Missed you at church. Thought you might want company."

I searched my mental excuse files for a good reason to miss church but found none, since it must be obvious neither of us was being fitted for a coffin.

Zora Jane filled in the awkward silence, nodding at the casserole in her hands. "I brought over that chicken noodle thing you liked so much last time I made it."

Hard to turn away such accommodating folks. Still, I couldn't muster an enthusiastic tone. "Come in." *If you must.*

Roy wandered into the entryway to investigate the commotion. Last thing we needed was for the cats to disappear too. By accident, I slammed the door, trying to prevent Roy's escape. Jesse smiled. "Oops, guess that door got away from you." He broadened his smile to include Ed and Zora Jane, accepting the casserole with a princely nod as Zora Jane passed by.

I blinked in disbelief. He didn't criticize my clumsiness—didn't even mock me with his usual "jokes"—and displayed impeccable hospitality. *What have you done with my husband, sir?*

As he waltzed them to the kitchen, he lifted the lid and inclined his head to sniff. The homey aroma of company chicken wafted through the air. He deposited the dish on the kitchen island, murmuring, "This smells wonderful. What a great idea! You folks can come over anytime."

Puzzled, I excused myself for a few minutes to splash cold water on my face and throw on clothes. When I returned, I glanced at the clock. "It's close enough to lunchtime that we might as well dig into this right now. What do you say?"

Zora Jane nodded, so I threw lunch together. Lettuce for a salad, sourdough rolls and butter, dishes from the cabinet. Ed and Jesse sat at the kitchen table talking like old pals who hadn't seen each other in months.

When we were all seated, Jesse offered a blessing, thanking God for such kind friends.

I passed the rolls. "Actually, it's a good thing you dropped by today."

Jesse nodded. "We need to update you."

Between bites, we took turns summarizing the events of the past week.

Ed munched and nodded throughout the discourse. When Jesse finished, Ed scratched his head. "Have you gotten any hits from your flyers?"

The question confused me. Jesse just told him our dog had been found.

Jesse shook his head.

Ed spooned another helping of chicken. "It's good that you filed a missing-persons report on Lila. Maybe someone will report seeing her. It might give us something to start on." While we considered that, he forked a bite of casserole and chewed. "Also, I have an idea I want to run by you. Been thinking about it since your last visit. Someone needs to talk with the deputy back in Iowa about the dead baby angle, beginning from the past and working to the present to see if they connect. We need more information about Lila and Will. Sometimes the past explains the present. Motives, you know. Did you tell Deputy Colter about the *Des Moines Herald Examiner* articles?"

My water glass hit the table with a thud when I nearly dropped it. I couldn't see how that would help. "We'd never be able to find those people after all this time."

Ed put his fork down and leaned forward. "If it's okay with you, tomorrow I'll make a few phone calls … see if I can shake out anyone who remembers the case. Could be the lead investigator from the sheriff's office still works there—Silverthorne, I think his name was. If the case hasn't been solved, maybe he'd like a partner—unofficially, of course."

Jesse and I exchanged a hopeful glance.

"We'd be so grateful," I said.

As usual, prayer came first in Zora Jane's mind. "We ought to pray too."

We bowed our heads while she began. "Most Holy God, show us how to find Lila. Go before us and guide our feet. Give the law enforcement people special discernment and creativity."

I added, "And please, dear Lord, forgive my impatience. Help me trust you to work this out in your own good time and your own good way."

Ed prayed, "Help me find Deputy Silverthorne. Give me words to say so I can gain his confidence right away."

Jesse finished. "Comfort us over the loss of our dog. And protect us. Help us think before acting foolishly. May your name be glorified in all we do. In Jesus' name."

After the Callahans left, I checked the phone hoping to retrieve a message from Deputy Colter. I found none, so I phoned the sheriff's office. To my surprise, the weekend dispatcher connected my call.

Deputy Colter said, "This is—"

I would recognize that arrogant voice anywhere. "I know who you are. Did you get my message?"

"If you wish to come to the station, you may file a missing-persons report at any time."

"We did that already."

"Oh." Tapping on his end. "Well, as for the other things you mentioned, it is irregular for you to view the car, since you are not the owner. However, since you *are* the owner of the dog, I arranged for you to collect it. I will be off tomorrow and Tuesday. Let me see. They will not get to the car right away. Are you available to come on Wednesday after they have completed their inspection?"

"Is a ten-pound robin fat?"

"Sorry?"

"Yes, I'm available on Wednesday. What time?"

"About one PM Wednesday then." Tapping again. He gave me directions to the impound lot. "I hope you appreciate that I had to jump through hoops to accomplish this."

"Thank you, Deputy. I appreciate your help. That will be just perfect."

Of course, it wasn't really *just perfect.*

Waiting until Wednesday meant three more days of poor Molly rotting in the car if they left her in the trunk. By then, the smell would be enough to knock out an elephant. Why didn't the tow people take her body out? Surely leaving her there must be a public health issue.

Three more days.

The waiting loomed on the horizon like a hulking giant.

Before tossing my jeans into the laundry, I extracted the picture of Lila and her puppy from the back pocket and the crumpled poem from the front. A wave of sadness overwhelmed me. I got out my magnifying glass to examine the photo.

The picture had been snapped at a campsite. Stately lodge pole pines framed the edges of the photo. A medium-size boat sat in a cleared area behind Lila and the dog.

"That must be their boat … the one Zora Jane mentioned."

Even with the lens, I couldn't make out the name of the boat without more than a few letters visible. It might be two words. Maybe the first one begins with "M."

I studied the image for several minutes before turning it over. On the back, in the same cramped but neat handwriting I'd seen in the poem book, Lila wrote two lines:

baby
sierra meadows

Without capitalization or punctuation.

Jesse came into the kitchen and peered over my shoulder. "I see you couldn't resist taking souvenirs from the Paynes' house."

I frowned. "And it's a good thing, too. Otherwise, they'd all be ashes. I guess this means Lila knows her way around Sierra Meadows."

"Right, but so does Will. That doesn't tell us anything."

I glanced at Jesse. "Funny name for a dog, don't you think—*Baby*?"

As I perused the picture, indentations in the front caught my eye. I grabbed the flashlight and held the photo at different angles hoping to see them better. "Someone wrote on another paper on top of this and the pressure of the pen made indentations. Numbers. Is that what you see?"

Jesse squinted at the photograph. "Looks like a phone number."

Nevada County had a relatively small population. "I don't know of a 5-0-6 prefix around here, do you?" I headed for the phone book. "No. It's not a Nevada County prefix. Where would it be?"

The idea of calling every area code in America sounded daunting. Yet, I felt certain that this number had enough significance that we should pursue it.

After a short pause, we said "Iowa" in unison.

I searched the front section of the phone book. Iowa had five area codes. I scribbled them on a piece of paper. "Elk Grove is 7-1-2. Des Moines is the closest big city. Its area code is 5-1-5. Those are the most likely, don't you think?"

Jesse nodded. "I say we give it a try."

I couldn't think of another way to find the 5-0-6 prefix, so I concurred.

First, he dialed the number using the 7-1-2 area code. "Hello. I'm trying to find someone who knows Lila Kliner." He paused to listen. "Okay. Sorry to bother you."

He hunched his shoulders. "Not a helpful person."

"Well, then, try Des Moines."

Jesse took a deep breath and repeated the numbers aloud as he dialed again, using the Des Moines area code this time. His expression told me the phone on the other end was ringing.

"Hello? This is Jesse Sterling. We're trying to locate a relative or friend of our neighbor, Lila Kliner." … "Lila Kliner. Do you know her?" … "Her brother, you say? What's your name?" Jesse celebrated his success with a triumphant thumbs-up. "Alan Kliner. Where do you live, Alan?"

I quickly handed Jesse paper to write on.

He copied the address. "Well, your sister lives next door to us. She left here two weeks ago and hasn't returned. She's weak and possibly sick. Do you know where she is?" He shook his head while he listened. "When did you speak to her last? … That's a long time ago. Well, we're concerned about her. She's been gone too long. Will doesn't seem worried. … Will Payne, the man she lives with. … Yes, that's right. He says she just ran off. Do you know where she might go?" Jesse shook his head again. "How about other relatives? Friends, maybe? Can you think of anyone who might know where she went? … No, we're in California. Lila lives down the hill from us." He raised his eyebrows as his eyes met mine. "Well, could I leave my phone number? That way, if you hear from her, you can let us know." He recited the number, thanked the man, and hung up.

Jesse turned to face me. "He's lived almost twenty years in a suburb of Des Moines—Hamilton. Hasn't seen much of Lila in that time. He seems confused. Doesn't know where Lila is and hasn't talked with her for a long time—months, he thinks. And she gets a little *loco* when she calls."

I raised my eyebrows.

"That's what he said, Christine. 'A little *loco*.'"

I hugged my arms tighter across my chest. *Another* crazy person? Just what we needed. They seemed to be materializing from the closets. When would we find someone who could make sense of this insanity?

26

Chapter Twenty-six

A mixed feeling of apprehension and expectation churned in my stomach on Wednesday as I rode with Jesse into the impound lot used by the Nevada County Sheriff's Office.

Just before one o'clock, Deputy Colter met us inside the high-fenced area near the one-room office building. Jesse shook his hand, and Deputy Colter led the way around the side of the office to a lot storing perhaps fifty cars. An attendant stood at the entrance to the lot. The deputy handed him a card, and the attendant nodded and directed us to the location of the Buick. Deputy Colter's scowl made his nose look even bigger than ever. Jesse wasn't smiling either.

My heart skipped a beat when I spied the brown 1985 Buick LeSabre. I would've recognized the car even if it hadn't stuck out because of its age and size. We came upon the front end first, which seemed unusually long—a hideous brown monster with boxy rectangular headlight eyes and prominent chrome grill mouth.

Deputy Colter marched toward the back end. Jesse followed, with me lagging behind, gripped with dread. When I passed the windows, I stalled, pretending to inspect the burgundy interior and split-bench seats. Years of sliding in and out on the cloth upholstery had worn the driver's side to threads. I avoided looking toward the trunk, but when Jesse reached the back, he exclaimed something that sounded like, "What the—?"

I hastened toward him, grabbed his arm for support, and made myself look. A mass of black-and-white fur was curled in the trunk. Decaying bones and yellow teeth protruded from the shriveled, cracked body. A light blue receiving blanket with a pattern of nursery rhyme characters enfolded it. Most of the blanket had deteriorated, leaving only a few small patches intact. The animal, though, couldn't be recognized as a dog.

I gasped.

It was not Molly.

This dog died long enough ago that no odor clung to the carcass and the skin had dried to leather. Years ago, probably. No one with half a brain would ever mistake the short, coarse fur for Molly's soft, wavy border collie fur. I blinked away tears, staring hard to be certain.

"Thank you, God!" whispered out of my lips. I swayed slightly, and Jesse steadied me. "That is not Molly." I fixed my eyes on Deputy Colter. Tears blurred my vision. "This is not our dog. This dog has been dead much longer than days."

Colter looked surprised. "I only read the report. If I had seen this creature, I would have known it could not be yours." He shook his head. "It is crazy to leave a mummified animal in the trunk of a car."

I glanced at Jesse. "Why would she do that?"

Jesse shook his head. "I … don't know."

In a memory flash I recalled the look on Lila's face when she whispered, "I had a dog."

Wetness moistened my cheeks. I swiped it away and stepped back to refocus. A couple more puzzle pieces chunked into place. "The running-out-of-gas thing. It doesn't work either way. Why would she drive out there if she knew she didn't have much gas?" I divided a gaze between Jesse and Deputy Colter. "That road doesn't lead anywhere; it just loops back to the front entrance. The campground is closed. It's freezing out there at night, and the nearest house is miles away. Where was she going?"

My voice gathered strength as I continued my litany of observations. "The funnel is all wrong. Why siphon gas out? Where did she put the gas she removed? Also, what direction did the car face when they found it? Did they turn it around to hook it up to the tow truck?"

Colter shook his head slowly.

"That means Lila drove it in and turned it around before abandoning it in the middle of the road. Why would she do that?"

Something seemed odd about the front seats, as well. "Can I open the door?" Without waiting for his reply, I opened the front door.

Deputy Colter hurried next to me while I leaned in. His high-pitched voice squeaked, "Do not touch the car. The crime lab has not completed their examination yet."

"Did someone drive this car away from the campground?"

"No." At last, I commanded his complete attention. He stared into the interior. "Standard procedure for towing is to hook it to the tow bar. No one drives. Why?"

"Lila couldn't have driven this car." I straightened to my full five-feet-one-and-a-half-inch height so I could get as close as possible to meeting his beady eyes. "Lila is shorter than I am. I couldn't drive this car with the seat in this position. My legs wouldn't reach the pedals. Also, Lila doesn't drive, according to the McCarthys. Someone else drove to the campground and abandoned this car."

A strained silence accompanied us on the winding drive from town. Waves of relief washed over me, alternating with confusion over what finding another dog in the trunk might mean. Jesse didn't sing as he drove. I interpreted that as focused problem-solving activity and let him have time to ponder. I broke the silence first, but not until he parked in our driveway. "Does it strike you as strange that the more we learn about this whole thing, the more questions we have?"

When Jesse ruminates, he's a man of few words. "Seems that way."

I followed him into the house. "So, if Molly isn't in the trunk, where is she?" I asked that more to myself than to Jesse. Those words had been bouncing around in my brain throughout the drive home. When I voiced them, they seemed to reverberate through the quietness.

Jesse had no answer.

How did Colter get that dead dog confused with our Molly? Must be because they both had black-and-white fur. I pulled out the photo of Lila and her puppy. Sure enough, Lila's dog had short black-and-white fur, much shorter than Molly's wavy coat. Baby might have been some kind of beagle-terrier mix.

The ringing phone made us both jump. I picked up the kitchen extension.

"Hello," a young female voice said. "Um. I got your number from the flyer at the mailboxes. Um. Do you own a black-and-white dog?"

I motioned for Jesse. "Yes, we do. Have you seen her?"

"I think so. We picked up a black-and-white dog on our way out of town last week. I guess she wandered out to the road all by herself. She had no dog tags, and we didn't know what to do with her. We took her to my mom in, um, Auburn. Mom tried to feed her, but the dog wouldn't eat. So she took her up to the Humane Society shelter in Grass Valley. You know—the one out by the fairgrounds. We've, um, my boyfriend and I have been out of town, but when we got back, we saw your notice by the mailboxes."

"The Humane Society?" I forced back excitement, lest I squeal into the phone. "Jesse, they took Molly to the Humane Society. Thank you. Thank you so much!" I disconnected without further ado, not even asking for her name. I couldn't wait another second to check the Humane Society.

A quick call to the animal shelter confirmed that more than one border collie arrived during the past two weeks. In fact, there were three—all without tags.

"Well." Jesse drew out his response like warm candy at an old-fashioned taffy pull. "We've been assuming these two things are connected—Molly disappearing and Lila leaving. Maybe they're not."

"But we found her dog tags at the Paynes'."

"Then there must be another explanation." He picked an apple out of the fruit bowl. "Maybe she caught her collar on that rusty water faucet by the house and tore it off."

Did I feel stupid! How narrow-minded to assume there could be only one possible explanation for Molly's disappearance. Maybe God had heard my prayers after all.

The drive back to town seemed longer and more tedious than a presidential debate. I jumped out of the car and raced Jesse into the Humane Society shelter. I stood on tiptoes in front of the desk, waiting to see the dogs. A small, round lady, who reminded me of a chubby toy poodle—maybe because of her kinky hair—quizzed us before allowing us to see the dogs. "Does she have a locator chip embedded in her skin?"

"No." Jesse glanced at me. "We never had the vet put one in."

As I remembered the conversation at the veterinary clinic, the locator chip had seemed like just another useless bit of technology we didn't understand. And another expense.

Miss Poodle frowned.

Did she think we were unfit dog parents? "We considered a locator chip. But we thought she didn't need it. She always comes back. Until now."

Miss Poodle's disapproving expression did not soften. "You might want to rethink that."

I fidgeted, rolling a pencil across the counter and re-arranging a small stack of paper. Miss Poodle threw me another deprecating glance and scampered around the counter to direct us to the border collies.

We found the dogs in a large warehouse-like space behind the reception area. When we entered, canine ruckus echoed off the walls: low barks and howls, whining, yapping, and deep woofs from dogs large enough to be small horses. The rows of cells had concrete floors, which sloped toward the back for easy cleaning. Sidewalks cut paths through each row.

Miss Poodle stopped at cage fourteen about halfway down. "Here's the first one." The dog in question appraised us with fearful eyes. Mostly white with a few black spots, she seemed agitated, pacing aimlessly back and forth in her cage.

I shook my head. "Too young."

Miss Poodle led us down two cages to an old creature standing forlornly at his gate, wagging a scraggly black tail.

"Too old." Something about this exchange reminded me of Goldilocks and the porridge.

She consulted her clipboard and shook her kinky hair. "Also, he's male."

Jesse smiled. "We're getting closer, though." The markings on the second dog were more like Molly's. Plus, only one remained.

Miss Poodle pranced to the end of the row. We followed. I clutched my purse and held my breath.

In the corner of the last cage, a hairy black-and-white heap appeared as wrung out as a dirty rag mop. Brown eyes dull and listless, splotches of mud clung to her wondrous wavy fur.

Jesse and I called in unison, "Molly!" At the sound of our voices, her head perked up and she shuffled to her tired old feet. Big brown eyes glistened to life as her tail swung with an exaggerated wag that nearly knocked her off balance. Miss Poodle unlatched the gate and we were reunited. Tears of joy poured down my cheeks, and I didn't scold her when she licked them off—Molly, not the lady.

"There's no doubt whose dog this is." Miss Poodle sashayed back to the entry area. Molly trotted with us, jumping up once or twice. I didn't scold her for that, even though her muddy feet smudged my shirt.

Miss Poodle resumed her official stance as soon as she returned to her post behind the counter. She consulted the computer. "Someone found her on Mustang Hill Road, south of town—with no tags." She barked the last part in a disapproving tone.

Jesse said. "We live south of town. She had tags but they came off somehow."

"Name, please."

Jesse furnished it.

She typed the information. "On Paso Fino Place?"

We nodded.

"Her license runs out in April. Would you like another set of tags? We can renew now and save you a second trip."

We did that with smiles of gratitude, paying a small fee for the license and for boarding.

When we returned to the car, Molly snuggled close, head resting on the console, wide brown eyes shifting between Jesse and me. After the engine started, she heaved a sigh of relief.

I kept my hand on her the whole way home to keep her from disappearing again. She had more gray on either side of her nose than I remembered. This ordeal had been hard on her sensitive soul. "We have one answer to our prayers, Jesse."

He nodded, expression solemn. "Now we have to find Lila."

27

Chapter Twenty-seven

The phone rang in the middle of the night. Groggily, I swatted the nightstand. The ringing continued after I slapped the clock alarm.

I fumbled for the receiver, finally getting it to my ear. "Hello?"

The speaker slurred his words as if tipsy. "Thish is Alan … Alan Kliner. Are you my shista's neighbor?"

Jesse turned, pulling the covers over his head. "What time is it?"

He always asked that when the phone interrupted his sleep. *What difference does the time make? When the phone rings, someone has to answer it.*

I waved for silence. "Lila? Yes, we're Lila's neighbors."

"Got this number. Some guy said call if you know where she went."

"Right." I sat on the side of the bed, now fully awake. "Do you know where Lila is?"

"This guy Lila lives with, what's his name?"

"William Payne?"

"William Payne. Right. The rich dude."

"Rich? I … don't know about that. I guess he has enough to live on."

In the long silence, I thought I heard him crying before he said, "Lila … poor little Lila!"

"Did you call to tell us something?"

"Who *is* that?" Jesse lifted a corner of the covers to peek at the clock. "Who calls at 2:14 AM?"

I shushed him, but he switched on the lamp. Light didn't improve his mood. He growled indistinct words at the same time Alan slurred something into the phone. It sounded like, "Helen. She knows."

Did I hear correctly? "Did you say Helen? Will's sister, Helen?"

"Ask her what happened in the boat."

"The boat?" Noise at his end sounded like the phone dragging across the floor. He cursed. Maybe the phone fell somewhere and he couldn't find it. "Alan? Are you still there?"

The commotion subsided as the connection went dead.

While I replaced the receiver, I repeated the conversation to Jesse. "That was weird. What do you think he meant?"

Jesse yawned. "I guess he meant that boat they used to have. We'll have Colter look into what happened to the boat." He switched off the light. "Not right now, though."

I started to complain about Jesse's tirade over the time, but caught myself and let it go. He'd been so changed.

Of course, now fully awake, I couldn't go back to sleep again. I flopped from one side to the other, trying to find a comfortable spot as Alan's words replayed in my mind. He didn't say, "What happened *to* the boat," he said, "What happened *in* the boat." That must be significant. I just didn't know why.

I couldn't wait for morning.

At nine the next morning, I tried to reach Deputy Colter, but he wasn't at work. I stared at the gray house, seeking direction. How could I find Lila? *Please, God, show me where to look.* The answer didn't immediately fall from the sky. Frustrated, I busied myself with chores, hoping to occupy my mind elsewhere.

By early afternoon, however, I'd gotten nowhere. My eyes zeroed in on every phone in the house as I went from room to room. *Could that mean I should call someone? But who?* I went through a mental list of possibilities. Only one person emerged as a likely source of information: Alan Kliner.

Alan sounded less sloshed but grouchier this time. "Yeah?"

"Alan. This is Christine Sterling. I'm your sister's neighbor, remember?"

"Yeah. What?" He yawned and stirred as if just awakened. From the sounds, I imagined him lighting a cigarette and taking a big drag.

"I'm worried about Lila. She's still missing. You said ask Helen what happened in the boat. What does Helen Sterne know about the boat?"

"You're calling me at this hour to ask that?"

I wrinkled my nose. What's the deal about men and the time of phone calls? "It's not early any more. It's 1:30 in the afternoon here. And Iowa is two hours ahead of us. Please, Alan, it might be important. Tell me what you meant."

"Important for who?" Mumble, mumble. A spate of profanities preceded another drag on the cigarette.

"Maybe you know something to help find Lila."

"Okay, okay. If it'll get you off my back." He paused to exhale. "I get this call a couple years ago. Can't remember when. Lila's bawling so hard I can hardly understand her. Something about a baby. 'Baby's gone.' Then she says, 'It was too fast.' Then something about the boat. I ask what boat, what baby? She says, 'Helen. Just like last time.'"

"Helen? What did Helen do last time?"

His tone sounded as if he spoke to a stupid child. "Offed the baby."

"What do you mean, 'offed'?"

He made an exaggerated tsk. "*You* know!"

A sudden memory of my conversation with the McCarthys clunked into my brain. Maggie said Lila got agitated about Baby and said, "She did it." The *she* must be Helen! "You mean *killed?* Helen killed the baby?"

"Well, yeah. Sayonara, baby."

His cavalier attitude flooded sadness over me. "Did she tell you anything else?

"That's it. Sorry."

Maggie remembered Lila saying *just like before.* "She said, 'Just like last time'? What did she mean by that?"

"Look lady, I dunno. I only heard about one time she got knocked up. She never said what happened. I just thought she wouldn't keep it 'cause she couldn't take care of herself, much less a baby."

"Did she ever mention Baby again?"

"Can't remember."

"How often do you talk to her?"

"What are you, writing a book? I don't keep track. She only calls when she's down."

Then she should have been calling every day. Why did she quit? I needed to know more about Lila. "Tell me about her. Please. I want so much to help her."

"Yeah, whatever, lady. I know your kind—do-gooders. Where will you be when we really need you?"

How could I convince him? "Alan, we're talking about your sister. She's out there somewhere all alone. She's weak and frail. Please help me find her."

"Look, I dunno where she is. Got it?"

"Just tell me about her, then. Maybe something you say will help."

"Don't know how it could, but if it'll get you off my case." He filled his lungs with nicotine. "Grew up in Des Moines. Lila's my half-sister—four years older." Exhale. "She took care of me, 'cause Ma was never around. But she was just a kid, ya know? We fought like two cats in a sack when we was kids, but after a while, the fight left her. Like she couldn't do it no more."

"What kind of person is Lila?"

"Shy. Don't take care of herself 'cause she don't want to be like Ma. That's what I always thought. Don't care about clothes or makeup or girl stuff."

"How about friends?"

"None that I heard of. She's a loner type. Had a lot of trouble at school, mostly 'cause she didn't go. Dropped out in her senior year, I think."

"What did she do then?"

"You don't quit, do you?"

"Please?"

He sighed dramatically. "I dunno, really. Cleaned houses—odd jobs, I guess. Never made much dinero, that's for sure."

"How about your mother?"

"How's that gonna help?"

"I don't know. Just tell me about her, please."

He exhaled slowly. "Now *there* was a real piece of work. Always into herself. No time for Lila and me. Never made enough to pay rent, so we moved a lot. Some new crisis every day. 'Dads' coming and going. Mostly jerks. Don't know my old man. Just know he ain't Lila's. We're not talking *Brady Bunch*. You get what I'm saying? I got out as fast as I could."

"What happened to your mother?"

"Probably more of the same. Some guy came to find me when she died. Think it was her heart, if she had one. I showed up for the funeral. Thought Lila might need me. But she didn't want nothing from me." I heard a whoosh as he lit another cigarette. Drag, exhale.

"Do you know the father of Lila's baby?"

"I heard she got knocked up but it coulda been anybody."

"What about Lila's father? Ever hear anything more about him?"

"Lila always wanted to find him. Used to talk about it all the time. Like it would fix everything. Heard she tried real hard when she got pregnant. Don't know if she ever did, though. Find him, I mean. I hope so. I hope he ain't some kinda jerk."

Given Lila's bad luck, if she ever did find him he probably *was* a jerk. He certainly hadn't been around when she needed him.

28

Chapter Twenty-eight

What Grace Woodson overheard in the beauty parlor rattled around my head all week. Maxine and Cybil—or Sylvia—might know more than they told Grace. Since I just happened to need a haircut and my roots touched up, I called for an appointment with the illustrious Maxine. The receptionist stiffly informed me that Maxine didn't usually accept new clients. I expressed my extreme disappointment and mentioned how highly Grace Woodson had recommended her.

"Hold, please," the receptionist said.

When she returned, she had managed to find an appointment, provided I could come early the next day.

After Jesse retired, I never made early appointments, not for anyone. "How early?"

"Eight o'clock."

I groaned. That *was* early, especially since it took half an hour to get into town. *Maxine better be worth it.* "I'll be there."

Fortified by two cups of extra-strong coffee, I exited the 49 Freeway and turned right across the Broad Street Bridge, away from downtown Nevada City. Once I crossed Deer Creek, I started looking for the address. Several stone buildings that looked like genuine relics from the 1800s lined the street. Before long, I found A Cut Above nestled against the hillside. From the looks of the rectangular edifice, I'd guess it originally functioned as a carriage house or some type of storage facility for the winery-turned-restaurant next door.

At precisely eight o'clock, I parked the Jeep in the narrow lot beside the salon. Once inside, I stopped at the reception desk. "I'm here to see Maxine."

The mini-skirted receptionist looked up from her computer, fidgeting with the phone contraption in her ear. "She's not here yet. Have a seat." She nodded toward a seating area, which consisted of four cushioned wicker chairs arranged around a metal and glass coffee table strewn with magazines. I sat.

A tall, skinny woman with flaming dyed-red hair and wearing tight black leggings and sling-back heels dashed in and tied on a black vinyl apron. I glanced at the receptionist. Both of them ignored me. The skinny woman took her place at the first beauty station on the right. Bottles and jars clinked as she rummaged through the pile on top of her table.

I continued to sit.

A youngish woman with huge hoop earrings and a streaked blond ponytail arrived next. She smiled at me but said nothing. I partially rose from my seat, but she hurried to the end of the row, yanked out the band holding her ponytail, and got busy redoing her own hair.

Within the next half hour, four more beauticians and several patrons entered and rushed to their respective workstations. The receptionist never spoke to any of them but occasionally fiddled with her headset and computer. From time to time, she answered the phone and apparently made a few appointments. I sat and observed the busyness. The beauticians and their clients interacted as hairstyling commenced, and soon women's chatter and laughter, water splashing in hair-washing basins, and the whoosh of blow dryers filled the room with sound. The pleasant perfume of hair products swirled through the air. Thankfully, permanent solution doesn't stink like it used to. My eyes watered, remembering those bygone days.

By eight thirty-five, I wondered why I bothered coming so early. My stomach growled loudly, reminding me that I skipped breakfast.

I approached the reception desk. "Excuse me. I had an appointment with Maxine for eight o'clock. Has she been detained?"

The receptionist frowned. "Honey, Maxine is not a morning person."

I hoped the receptionist couldn't hear my rumbling stomach. "Does Maxine know we have an appointment?"

Just then, the door opened and in sashayed a dour-faced woman wearing zebra-striped pants, black pumps with heels at least four inches high, and a tight black bustier that revealed way too much cleavage. Not exactly a work outfit in my book.

The woman waved toward the reception desk. "Is there coffee?"

I raised my eyebrows. It looked like she snapped her fingers at Miss Mini-skirt.

The receptionist rose instantly and trotted away.

The Diva never broke stride, continuing her sashay to the most prominent workstation—the first one on the left opposite Miss Flaming Red Hair. There she adjusted a leopard-print vinyl apron over her ample bosom and meticulously tied a front bow so the ends came out exactly equal. This accomplished, she appraised her appearance in the mirror. A hair-tuck here, a make-up touch there—judging by her expression, the face in the mirror didn't satisfy her.

Miss Mini-skirt scurried back with a steaming mug of fresh coffee, which she set on the vanity table. Only then did the receptionist speak. "Your eight o'clock is here." She nodded my way. "Mrs. Sterling."

The Diva, who was apparently Maxine, continued fussing in the mirror between sips of coffee as if she hadn't heard. After at least a full minute, she extended one arm toward me with a flourish. "Mrs. Sterling. I'm Maxine. Please sit here."

Not a single word about being forty minutes late for our appointment. Positively insulting! I fumed while I settled into her chair, almost forgetting my mission.

Maxine forced a smile that showed off gleaming white teeth. "And what are we about to create for you today?" Using the royal "we"—who did she think she was?

I cleared my throat, taking time to clear my mood as well. "I need a touch-up, don't you think? And a new hairdo would be great too."

Maxine scrunched my shoulder-length hair in one hand, as if examining the slight wave that had replaced the naturally curly hair I had as a child. "How short are you thinking?"

Short? I wasn't thinking short. "I—"

"I know the perfect cut for your face." Maxine's plastic smile never wavered. "You'll love it. But first, the color. Tiffany?" She snapped her fingers again.

What was with the finger snapping? I wouldn't respond to that, no matter who did it.

Miss Ponytail—Tiffany—appeared immediately, however, and Maxine issued directions about mixing color to fill in my dark roots. While waiting for Tiffany, Maxine studied herself in the mirror again.

Getting to the point of my visit, I said, "Grace Woodson highly recommended you."

While wiping stray lipstick off a corner of her mouth, Maxine favored me with a queen nod through the mirror.

"And Helen Sterne comes here, too, I think."

Maxine turned to stare at me. "How do you know Helen?"

"We, uh, bought the house next door to her brother."

Maxine removed a drape from a cubbyhole in the wall cabinet above her station, shook it open, and covered my shoulders, using a clip at the neck to hold it in place. "She's actually Cece's client." She nodded at the red-haired woman across the aisle. "Helen Sterne is a troubled woman."

Cece grimaced hearing Helen's name.

I spoke louder to include Cece (who apparently wasn't Cybil or Sylvia as Grace supposed) in the conversation above the buzz in the shop. "So I gather. I've been worried about Lila. Such a frail person. She's missing, you know. Apparently neither Will nor Helen are the slightest bit concerned."

Maxine's "Ha!" didn't seem as much a laugh as an exclamation.

I didn't know how to take that. I addressed my question to Cece. "Where do you think Lila has gone?"

Cece shrugged.

Maxine accepted two pots of hair-coloring paste from Tiffany and arranged them on her tray before speaking. "Helen's been trying to get rid of that girl for years."

Cece continued brushing out the back of her client's hair. "I thought after the dog incident, Lila would get the picture."

"The dog incident? You mean the little dog she named Baby?"

While we talked, layers of folded foil appeared on one side of my head as Maxine's quick fingers applied the coloring solution, folded and patted, and divided the next section with her rat-tail comb. "Helen drowned that dog, you know."

Chilled, I sucked in air. "What? Lila loved that little dog."

Cece shook her head. "Yeah, well. That's exactly why Helen got rid of it."

Maxine rolled her eyes. "Helen wants Lila out for good. That girl's just a gold-digger. She does absolutely nothing around the house. Then Will gets her this dog. Like she could take care of a dog when she can't even take care of herself. Please. Have you seen her?"

When I nodded, the foils swished. Maxine lifted both gloved hands into the air.

"Sorry. I was nodding. Yes, I've seen her."

Maxine frowned and went back to work. "Need I say more?"

Cece grinned.

It didn't make sense. "But dogs can swim. How did she drown the dog?"

Maxine swiveled the chair a quarter turn and pumped a couple times with her foot to raise the position before shifting to the other side of my head.

Cece continued. "Helen wheedled an invitation to Tahoe with them, then talked Will into letting her drive the boat."

Maxine raised her eyebrows. "*Pilot* the boat."

Cece shrugged. "Whatever. She threw that throttle into high gear and headed for the middle of the lake. That's where she 'accidentally' nudged the dog into the water. Can you imagine? Lila went berserk. You know how icy that water is? I guess Will had to hold Lila back to keep her from jumping in. Helen pretended to circle back to look for him, but for some reason they never found him until after he drowned. Wouldn't surprise me if Helen beat that dog down with an oar or something."

Maxine's lacy metal earrings jingled when she shook her head. "That's our Helen. Little dog never had a chance."

Shivers of shock trickled down my spine. An image of Helen's cold expression in the hardware store flickered to mind. What kind of person would intentionally drown a helpless dog? This woman must be even worse than I'd imagined—heartless and unspeakably cruel.

Maxine and Cece chattered on about another client whose cruelty to animals had bordered on criminal. Eventually the police prosecuted that woman. What would it take to convict Helen of the murder of this poor, defenseless dog?

After the foils were wrapped and I'd spent a few minutes under the dryer, Tiffany washed the color solution out of my hair. Apparently, in this salon, if you were a diva like Maxine, you had people wash hair for you. Tiffany escorted me back to Maxine's chair—a fluffy white towel wrapped around my wet hair.

"Now for the 'magic' part." Maxine's shears went snip, snip.

I wasn't sure I was ready for "magic."

While Maxine sectioned and cut, they continued the stories exactly where they'd left off before I went under the dryer. Maxine turned me away from the mirror while she cut the front. Feeling cold air at the base of my neck where I hadn't felt it for some time, I worried just how short this new "do" had become.

Cece continued talking while she adjusted her client's chair. "I heard they just found Lila's little dog in the back of Will's brown Buick."

I jerked my head her way, causing Maxine to lift her hands again. "Why didn't they just bury the poor little dog?"

An unladylike snort escaped the Diva's lips. "See how insane that whole bunch is? After the dog drowned, Lila insisted on fishing him out of those cold waters. Can't imagine how they ever found him. Must have taken hours. Then she took him home. Made a shrine in the basement with an altar and candles. Kept the dead dog there until Will couldn't stand the stench another minute." She turned the chair a quarter turn and lowered the seat a couple of pumps. "So he stuck the dog in the trunk of the car. I guess he intended to dump it somewhere."

Cece joined the guffaws. "But Lila sat behind the car with the trunk open for days and nights, mourning."

Maxine shook her thick black hair, making the earrings jingle again. "Unbelievable!"

When she finally stopped fussing with my hair, she stood back a moment to admire her creation. "You're going to love this!"

Cece nodded enthusiastically. "You've done it again, Max."

Maxine whipped the chair around so I faced the mirror.

In that instant, all words drained from my mind.

Short red, blond, and brown spikes stuck out all over my head. Short. Red. Blond. And brown. Spikes. In varying lengths, with the longest parts at my cheeks.

I blinked hard at my reflection, hoping to dislodge this image and make my old familiar hair materialize in its place.

Tears filled my eyes. "Oh … my!"

Maxine beamed. "I knew we'd love it."

I gulped over the lump in my throat. "It's … a bit shorter than I anticipated."

Maxine handed me a large round mirror and swiveled the chair so I could see my hair from every angle. It looked even more hideous from the sides, if possible—like an explosion at the clown factory. I felt numb.

"Wait until you see the colors outside in the sunshine," she was saying.

Yes, that's it. I needed to get outside. Fast. "How much do I owe you?"

She rattled off a figure that would have normally made me joke about taking out a loan to pay her. Instead, I wrote a check with a shaky hand, gathered my belongings, and fled, praying that no one I knew would be in town to recognize me.

When I gingerly entered the house, Jesse called from the kitchen, "You're finally home. Ed has some news. He wants us to come—" While he spoke, he'd been walking from the kitchen with a salami sandwich in one hand. When he saw me, he stopped cold, eyes wide. "Oh."

I grimaced, wishing I had hidden my hair under a paper bag.

Slowly, Jesse advanced, frown deepening. He circled without coming too close, staring at my hair from every angle. "Was … this the look you were after?"

"Not exactly."

He circled again. "It's … really … different."

I burst into tears.

Now he looked puzzled. "What?"

Sobbing, I tried to explain. "I just wanted to talk to Maxine. She knows Helen. I didn't know she would—"

Jesse backpedaled. "It's not so bad. Just, uh, really … different. I never saw you this way before. That's all."

I started crying again, louder, as I trudged up the stairs. Maybe I could comb it out. Make it lay flat. Maybe it wouldn't look so bad after I worked on it.

Half an hour later, the spikes were tamed—almost. I couldn't do anything about the streaks of color or the ragged cut. I kept repeating, "Hair grows. Hair grows. It'll be okay." Fortified by this mantra, I emerged and we made our way to the Callahans'.

Ed bounded from the house as soon as our car pulled into their driveway. Waving a yellow legal pad, he grinned as if he'd just won the lottery. Jesse climbed out the driver's side, and Ed rushed toward him. "I found him!"

Zora Jane appeared on the porch wearing a long orange turtleneck sweater atop orange-and-brown striped pants. "Oh, for goodness sakes, Ed. Let the folks come in before you start." But just then, she saw me. Her smile faded. "Your … hair."

I patted my head self-consciously. "I got a haircut. Tell you about it later."

She tried to refresh her smile but couldn't stop staring. It made the smile look forced. For a second, I feared she'd break out in prayer. "Well, come on in." She gestured for us to enter, scooping up Harry before he dashed onto the driveway.

Following into Ed's computer room, I admired Zora Jane's orange-and-brown striped cloth shoes with ribbons that tied around her well-proportioned ankles, and wished I'd never heard of Maxine or A Cut Above. I should have known better after I saw Grace's haircut.

Ed didn't even look at me until he turned to face us from the other side of his computer desk. He held up his yellow legal pad, displaying lines of crossed-out phone numbers and scribbled names covering one entire page. He started to speak but tilted his head instead. "Something's different."

I sniffed. "Bad hairdo. It'll grow out."

Ed and Zora Jane gave slow nods, looking as sympathetic as possible.

"Well, listen to this." Ed patted his legal pad. "I've been working for a couple of days, and I'm happy to report my persistence paid off. The murder of this one baby created enormous press in Iowa. Because of the case, state legislators drafted a new law to allow mothers to leave unwanted children at a safe place with no questions asked. Everyone I spoke to remembers it."

We murmured appreciation.

Zora Jane motioned us to sit, so we crowded onto the wrought-iron daybed while Ed sat at his computer desk. "Russell Silverthorne tried to keep this case active, but they exhausted all leads after a couple years without making any progress. Against his recommendation, his superior relegated the investigation to cold-case status. Silverthorne got so obsessed with finding the mother that he quit the sheriff's department over it." Ed shook his head. "Now he works as a private detective in Guthrie County but still searches whenever he can. Keeps boxes of information about the case in his office."

When Ed stopped for a breath, I said, "I can't believe you actually found him."

Ed beamed. "In Silverthorne's mind, this investigation will be open until the mother is apprehended. I told him about the poems and newspaper articles, as well as the blue baby blanket wrapping the black-and-white dog in the Buick. He got real excited. Called back twice to ask more questions. I told him we'd officially hire him if he'd come out to investigate. And …"

He paused, watching our faces. We leaned forward as a group.

"Yes?" Jesse asked.

"He said he would!"

Jesse's eyebrows arched, and the corners of his mouth twitched slightly before turning up in excitement. The Callahans probably didn't notice, but after thirty-five years of marriage, I knew what excitement looked like on my Jesse's face.

"When?" Jesse asked.

"Just as soon as he can. Maybe tomorrow." Ed slapped his yellow pad.

I clapped. "Hooray!"

Ed shifted in his chair. "Silverthorne remembers interviewing Will Payne all those years ago when he lived on a dead-end road about six miles north of Elk Grove. That was at the beginning, right after they found Baby Blue. Said Will had a small farm but operated a business in town repairing tractors and farm equipment. Town folks considered him strange because he withdrew after his wife died. Heard rumors that Will had wealth but lived like a pauper. Seems like the type who'd stash money under the mattress."

Jesse chuckled. "Wouldn't surprise me."

"What about Lila?" I asked. "Did he see Lila when he talked to Will?"

Ed shook his bald head. "No, Silverthorne thought Will lived alone. Specifically asked about seeing a pregnant woman around and remembers Will adamantly denying it. Never suspected Will Payne might be involved in any way."

Jesse said, "Surely he didn't talk to everyone in Guthrie County."

Ed tilted his head to one side. "Over several years of active investigation, I think maybe he did. Silverthorne said they covered the county thoroughly."

Jesse glanced my way. "Must be a rural area."

I could contain our discoveries no longer. I told them what I learned from Maxine and Cece. While I retold the story, I recalled Maggie telling me Lila didn't drive because "speed kills." Maybe she meant what happened to her dog.

"Besides that, we found a phone number on Lila's picture that turned out to be her brother's." I displayed it. "At last, we've found someone who actually knows her."

Ed looked as if he might burst. "And Russell Silverthorne is coming. I think we're finally getting out of the sand trap with this game."

"God is good!" Zora Jane said.

I wholeheartedly agreed.

29

Chapter Twenty-nine

Jesse got up before me on Sunday morning and let Molly out as he went to feed the horses. When I got downstairs to pour a cup of coffee, Molly poised in front of the sliding glass door on the back deck like a sphinx. In front of her paws lay a blackish object. I opened the door and bent to examine her scorched treasure.

Not completely awake, I didn't comprehend at first. "What's this you found?" When I realized what fire it must have come from, my head jerked toward the open gate.

"Molly! You must not go down there again."

Her eyes grew sad. She lowered her head, puzzled about my lack of appreciation for the trophy she offered. Tail between her legs, she retreated into the house.

When Jesse returned from the barn, I stood beside the desk lamp, examining the black piece with my magnifying glass. About the size of my palm, the artifact measured less than an eighth of an inch in thickness, with a texture like leather.

Jesse peered over my shoulder. "What's that?"

"Molly found it. I'm guessing in the fire pit at the Paynes' because the gate's open."

Jesse turned the charred piece to examine the other side. "What gate?"

He let out a short gasp when he realized. Molly stood next to the open gate.

Jesse scrambled out the back door. I jogged after Jesse, still wearing pajamas, robe, and slippers.

Molly took off ahead, as if playing a game of chase. She cleared the gate before we caught up and raced straight for the fire mound. Like a runaway parade, we dashed across the weedy pasture.

Very soon, I regretted my haste in leaving without dressing appropriately. I must have looked like the parade clown. Hoping to hide my pink pajamas, I tugged my robe tighter around my chest. My multicolored hair stuck out all over my head again. Sharp burrs and stickers poked into one heel where my fluffy flip-flop slippers left skin exposed. I couldn't stop to pull them out. Handicapped by both attire and size, I lagged far behind.

Will's pickup rested near the gray house, so we trooped as quietly as possible, hoping not to alert him. But just as Jesse reached the place where we had to climb over the fence, the back door flew open.

Will's tall frame filled the doorway. One arm dangled along the side of his body. In his hand, he gripped an imposing shotgun. He wasn't threatening us exactly, but the mere presence of a firearm spoke with its own voice.

Will growled a low but distinct snarl. "Git that varmint off my propity."

Hearing his voice chilled me. Perhaps his words made me shiver or the weapon dangling at his side. When I reached the place where Jesse halted, he stuck his arm out to gather me behind him like a mother hen protects her chicks. I peeked out around his shoulders to see.

Jesse's voice remained calm. "Sorry to bother you, Mr. Payne. Our dog seems to have gotten out the gate, and we just came down to take her home."

Oblivious to the drama swirling around her, Molly waded into the middle of the ashy mound and dug rapidly with both paws.

Will pointed his shotgun. "If you don't keep her offmy propity, I'll take care of it myself."

"No!" I pushed out from behind Jesse. "Molly! Come here."

Jesse grabbed at me but missed as I flew by.

Molly's head bobbed up at my call. She trotted back to our side of the fence, white paws now black with soot.

Still calm, Jesse said, "Not to worry, Mr. Payne. We'll keep her home."

I scrabbled up the hill with the errant dog in tow.

Over my shoulder, I watched Will monitor our retreat. The shotgun dangled at his side again. My heart pounded and my breath came in short gasps as I returned to the sanctity of our house.

At once, Jesse grabbed the phone to report the incident to the sheriff's office. "Also," he added after briefly describing what occurred. "Molly found a burned piece of something in the fire. We don't know what it is, but it looks mighty interesting." He listened. "Sure, I'll save it."

I tugged a brown fake-fur hat over my hair, not wanting to face the stares of people who wouldn't understand that sometimes you just get a bad haircut. We took Molly with us to church—not actually into the service, but in the car—because we were afraid to leave her outside at our house.

On the drive to church, the whole world seemed out of kilter. The cornerstone rock at the bend in our driveway appeared hard and unyielding. The bones of the trees showed without their leaves. Clouds obscured the sun, and a strange hush filled the air. Hideous secrets lurked in the shadows, ready to pounce on us as we drove by.

Passing the gray house, I considered Lila, who existed in a world of shadowy secrets every day. Poor Lila—that fragile shell of a woman—emaciated in body, mind, and spirit. How did she get to such a miserable state? Did she choose not to reach up to God or out to people? Or did that evil man foist those choices on her? Most important of all, where was she? I had heard statistics about the diminishing chance of her turning up alive after she'd been gone so long without a word or a sighting. It wasn't looking good. *God, please, protect Lila.*

Molly sat while we exited the Jeep. When I turned back to look at her as I followed Jesse through the parking lot, she had pressed her nose against the back window, making little crescents of steam where her warm breath met the cold glass.

Desperate for comfort in the storm raging around us, I scanned the bulletin for the sermon title: "Man's Search for Meaning." Would the pastor have real answers today and not the usual platitudes? How could he explain the insanity we'd been living through? I couldn't wait to hear.

"God created each of us with a God-shaped hole inside," Pastor Gregg said. "You've heard that before. We think we can fill it with earthly things—money, fame, hobbies, alcohol, drugs, promiscuity, even food sometimes; the lust of the eyes and the pride of life—but that hole can only be filled by God's Spirit. We find completion and purpose in God alone."

Surprised that he addressed my primary retirement dilemma, I straightened to listen. In the rows ahead, people nodded as Pastor Gregg expounded. But, having articulated the problem, he did little more than repeat the usual verses about keeping our eyes fixed on Jesus.

When he finished, a delicate older woman hobbled to the stage in response to an invitation by the pastor. Gleaming white hair circled her face like a halo. Pastor Gregg introduced her as Bessie Parrish. She told her simple story in a sweet, well-modulated voice. Her lifelong faith in God had sustained her through an often-arduous journey, which seemed to worsen after she retired from her career. "You've heard it said that pain is inevitable but misery is a choice. I determined early that I would not choose misery, no matter what life handed me. Instead, I thank God for whatever He allows into my life."

She had embraced retirement eagerly, she said, ready to be rewarded for perseverance in her duties as daughter, wife, mother, and career woman. "What I discovered, however, is that retirement is not the reward for a job well done. Heaven is. An intentional and continuous re-adjustment of thinking is required. You see there's no retirement in the kingdom of God. I thought retirement would be a time of leisure. It is not. There is work to be done. There are challenges to overcome, just as in any other time. Health issues become increasingly more serious and debilitating. Money is often tight or at least fixed, while expenses continue to increase."

Expectant silence in the sanctuary was broken only by Mrs. Parrish's reedy voice. I glanced at Jesse. He appeared to be absorbing every word.

A glow surrounded her venerable countenance. "Sometimes we wonder why we were put here on earth. Must we spend our lives discovering our own individual life purpose? It's simple. We were created to glorify God. That's our purpose. The specifics may change as life stages and circumstances change. But there's always only one purpose. When we strive to bring glory to God above all else, God provides whatever we need to complete the work he leads us to. That's why I keep doing what I can."

To that end, she explained her project taking food twice a week to the homeless teenagers living at Pioneer Park. "These young people are our future. They have so much to talk about, but so few adults will listen. Bringing food for their bodies allows me into their world to minister to their souls."

Jesse's eyes sparkled when he caught my eye. He inclined his head to whisper in my ear. "Sounds like she knows what she's talking about."

Could our purpose for existing be as straightforward as that? Glorify God. What did glorifying God look like? What would my retirement life look like if I made glorifying God the focus of everything I did?

❧

As we left church, Jesse said, "It's the weekend of the Draft Classic. What say we make a quick run through the art show?"

The Draft Horse Classic, presented annually by the local agricultural association, provided one of the most outstanding entertainment opportunities held at the Nevada County Fairgrounds.

The evening show featured Clydesdales, Percherons, Belgians and other draft horses prancing through various colorful exhibitions. In addition to the usually sold-out evening show, the chance to admire the magnificent animals in corrals and browse through art housed in one of the exhibition halls made the Classic an event not to be missed. Not to mention some truly great food. Almost everyone in the area attended one part or another of this autumn fair.

"Molly's with us." I reached back to pet her. She nuzzled my hand, tail thumping on the back seat. "We'll have to find a place to walk her. But sure. Why not?"

Jesse headed toward the fairgrounds.

I licked my lips in anticipation. Local charity organizations supplied the best junk food this side of Coney Island. Not necessarily healthy fare but delicious and mostly homemade.

When we entered the parking lot, I breathed in the tranquil setting. Tall Ponderosa pines shaded the fairgrounds, cooling the temperature even on hot summer days. The midway sported a long swath of lush grass. Flowerbeds had been groomed to perfection.

Jesse parked at the entrance near the art building and we got out.

I stretched. "What a beautiful place." Arguably the most scenic fairgrounds in the state.

Molly jumped happily out of the back and sniffed the grassy patch in front of the entrance. We gave her time to relieve herself and refilled her water bowl. She jumped back into the Jeep and settled down for a Sunday afternoon nap.

The art show displayed everything from quilts to photography, all crafted by local artists. Jesse's interest in sculpting and watercolor made him linger at those in particular. When we exited the building, the sweet aroma of fresh-baked cinnamon rolls beckoned us to Treat Street. I stopped and gazed that way.

Jesse asked, "Are you hungry?"

"Always hungry for food like this."

He smiled. "The problem is deciding which guilty pleasure to partake of."

I nodded, and we sauntered toward the cobblestone food court. "So what'll it be today?"

As we scanned the row of vendors, Jesse's eyes glazed over. "Might have to check them all out before we decide."

Choosing one often proved so challenging that we succumbed to the lure of more than one. The Job's Daughters' corn dogs were legendary. Steamy baked potatoes could be dressed with the most imaginative array of toppings I ever saw. Cornish pasties—made just like the meat pies Cornish miners ate while working in nineteenth-century gold mines—were a special treat. Of course, the gigantic cinnamon rolls ranked high on everyone's list. But my favorite of all—ice cream sandwiches sold from an old-fashioned ice cream cart—were made from scratch with a variety of flavors of homemade ice cream and thick homemade cookies at least five inches wide. Plenty to share with someone you love.

Mouths watering, we ambled up the street. When we'd gone about halfway, I stopped cold and tugged on Jesse's sleeve. On the sidewalk trudging toward us were Helen and Will.

"Well, lookie there." I dipped my head toward them without looking straight ahead. What should we do? *Lord, give me words if you want me to speak.*

Helen's long-legged stride led the two, with Will trying to keep up. They weren't talking. Seen side by side, the family resemblance was unmistakable—the same height and build, even the same scowling angular features.

We faced off in front of the Cornish pastie vendor. I caught Helen's eye first and smiled. She didn't return the greeting but lowered her head as if intent on pushing by without acknowledging our presence.

I stood solidly in her path. "Oh, Jesse, look who's here. Our neighbor, Will Payne, and his sister. Hi there."

Jesse extended his hand, as if Will hadn't pointed a shotgun at our dog that very morning. "Oh, hello."

Will appeared surprised, not pleasantly, managing a gruff, "Hello." He didn't grab Jesse's hand, but Jesse didn't seem to notice.

Without hesitating to plan my attack, words poured out of my mouth. "We've been so worried about Lila. Have you heard from her yet?"

A tall boy munching a corn dog dripping with mustard bumped Helen as he scurried by. She stared after him. When she looked back, her expression reflected nary a hint of a smile. "Oh, you're the meddling neighbor from the hardware store."

I glanced at Will. "We've been wondering why you burned Lila's mattresses so soon after she left." *Where did that come from?*

Jesse shot me a quizzical glance, eyebrows raised.

Will appeared bewildered too. "The mattresses?"

Helen narrowed her eyes. "How do you know he burned those?"

I couldn't think of an answer. How about another question? "Won't she need them when she comes back?"

Will frowned at Helen as if deferring to her for a suitable explanation.

Helen's eyes locked on mine. "Those mattresses were … soiled. Lila was a filthy creature … wet the bed."

A fleeting memory of odors in the Paynes' house rushed to mind—a mildew smell in the kitchen, stale air in Lila's bedroom. My smeller had definitely ruled out urine as one of the contributors. "But … but what will she sleep on when she comes back? She *is* coming back, isn't she?"

Helen's eyes continued drilling into mine, transmitting evil. In mere seconds, she defeated my feigned bravado with the power of her stare. "No, she is not. She packed her clothes and left. For good."

I lowered my head, focusing on the cobblestones. "She packed her clothes? In a suitcase?" That simply couldn't be. Lila's clothes had been packed in the burned cardboard boxes.

I peeked up to see them exchange another dark glance.

Helen leaned down to deliver her insolent threat directly to my face. "Snooping is not a healthy diversion. My advice is to mind your own business. You never know what might happen if you don't." She straightened and grabbed Will's arm. "Now, if you'll excuse us."

They shoved us aside in their rush to pass.

30

Chapter Thirty

I stood on the deck, wishing the gray house could talk. But of course, the house remained as quiet and closed as always, although a tiny part of Will's white pickup peeked from the front, so I knew he must be inside.

Ever since we brought her home, Molly had stayed close, but with the door open and me standing on the deck, she wandered into the backyard.

I planted my hands on my hips. What could she be up to?

Once she left the deck, she darted toward the back gate as if on a mission. Then she stood on her hind legs, front paws on the gate, rocking the top gently until she popped the latch open.

I gasped as the heavy gate swung away and bounced closed. Molly didn't go out into the pasture but sat beside the gate, looking up at me. Perhaps she expected a reward for such an outstanding trick.

Her ability to open the gate impressed me a great deal, but I scolded her anyway. "Molly, come back here!" She cocked her head and hesitated. When I persisted, she trotted up the stairs in obedience. To keep her from wandering off again, I dragged her inside the house by the collar. The sadness in her eyes reprimanded me, but I had to make sure she understood I wouldn't tolerate that behavior.

Well, at least I finally knew how she got out of that gate.

Next time I let Molly outside, I stood on the deck to watch her. She trotted straight to the gate and jiggled until it opened, just like before.

I yelled in frustration, "What is wrong with you, Molly? Come back right now. You can't go down there."

Will came out on his stoop, hands on his hips, assaulting us with his eyes. To be fair, I couldn't actually see his expression but guessed from his posture that he scowled at us. Clutched in fear's evil grip, I rushed to gather Molly back where I could guard her. For the rest of the day, I let her out the front door and directed her away from the fence to do her business.

~

Although I'd been sleeping soundly without any remembered dreams for more than a week, a strange vision disturbed my rest that night. The setting—a dark dungeon-like stage. I couldn't say where. I acted the part of the audience, rather than participating, viewing the scene through a gauzy veil, perhaps a curtain over a window.

Thumping on the stairs announced the approach of a man wearing the uniform of a fireman. He trotted into the large subterranean room and peered rapidly around, giving the room a quick once-over. His expression appeared bored and puerile. While he scanned the space, a spotlight illuminated a horizontal figure lying in a heap in one corner. It reminded me of wrapping paper, discarded after a birthday party. I pushed through the veil for a closer look.

In the half-darkness, the form of a man appeared. I strained to identify him but couldn't see him clearly enough. He lay on his side with his back toward me, facing into the corner.

The young fireman finished his cursory examination, turning not just his head but also his whole body in a circle. His gaze passed quickly over the man. Then he shrugged as if he had nothing to attend to and trotted up the stairs with his hands in his pockets.

While I pondered his actions, I heard footsteps on the stairs again. This time a crisp-uniformed deputy sheriff came partway into the room, tiptoeing on crepe-soled boots. He peered over aviator-frame glasses resting on an enormous cartoon nose. His gaze lingered in the corner. He cocked his head, deep in thought. Pulling a notebook from his pocket, he consulted it and tapped his pen on the coil a few times. Maybe that reminded him of an appointment, because he abruptly snapped the notebook shut and hurried out of sight.

I moved a step closer to the wounded man. He lay in a pool of thick, sticky blood, which spread out like a small receiving blanket under him. Slowly he turned his face toward me. Around him, a low sound rose from the depths of the earth, starting to crescendo until it became a roar. Pain, sorrow, and despair in one unyielding howl—the sound of human misery. I covered my ears but couldn't block out the agony.

After the noise died down, a light footfall on the stairs made me turn. A frail white-haired woman descended. She hobbled to the injured man and bent to her knees. With gentle hands, she dressed his wounds using bandages she carried in a bag slung over one shoulder. Then, cradling his head on her lap, she stroked his brow with tenderness.

I sobbed. She looked at me, extending one thin, wrinkled arm in my direction. Burdened as she seemed, she offered me comfort. "Pain is inevitable, but misery is a choice," she said in a sweet, well-modulated voice.

Filled with fear, I moved toward them until I saw the face on her lap. The once-steely eyes were closed and the angular features rested. In the stillness of his repose, William Payne didn't look like a monster at all.

Shaken deeply by possible interpretations of Monday night's vivid dream, on Tuesday morning I packed Molly in the car for company and set out for town, simply to get out of the house. I needed to buy groceries—I almost always needed to buy groceries—but by the time I arrived in town, my focus had shifted to Helen.

She most certainly withheld vital information, she and Will. How could I make them talk? While I mused over the possibilities, I drove past the grocery store turnoff toward Nevada City.

Helen's clapboard house reposed in its usual state, as if someone had duct-taped its mouth. Not a hint of action anywhere. Molly gazed out the window when I stopped the Jeep to study the house. I scratched her head. "Looks like nobody's home today, girl. Any suggestions about where to look now?"

Molly blinked and panted, tongue hanging to one side.

I put the Jeep in gear and headed back out Sierra Vista, turning left toward Grass Valley down the front of Banner Mountain. I didn't have a particular destination in mind, but maybe if I drove awhile, I'd think of something to do.

Before I reached Brunswick, I passed a one-story motel. I'd never paid much attention to it before. Common and unmemorable, it had a run-down quality, like those referred to as no-tell motels—the type someone might rent by the hour. I glanced quickly as I passed, and then turned back to the road. Belatedly, something familiar registered in my peripheral vision.

A blue sedan filled the parking space in front of room 115—the same kind of car Helen Sterne drove. I slammed on the brakes. Molly fell off the seat with a thud, but I hardly noticed.

How puzzling! This motel couldn't be more than two miles from Helen's house. Why would she rent a room here? "What do you know about that, Molly? I think we just found ourselves a surveillance job."

Molly climbed back on the seat from the floor. She watched as I maneuvered the Jeep into a parking space across the street from the motel, and then she curled up on the seat to sleep.

I roamed through radio channels, hoping to find music to pass the time. Instead, another news report informed me that there were still no suspects in the hit-and-run death of little Marcus Whitney. A month had passed. That poor family! I sighed and settled for an oldies station instead of news. I pushed the seat back and tilted my head against the headrest. An unusually sunny autumn day warmed the windshield, pressing onto me like a comfy blanket. Soon I felt as drowsy as Molly. A mushy love song soothed my nerves. I blinked my eyes, trying to focus on the motel across the street. But the harder I tried, the heavier my eyelids became. A little nap would be great.

I don't know how long I slept before Molly's shrill bark woke me. Molly doesn't bark often. The piercing noise sent my heart racing. I bolted upright. "What?"

An unsmiling uniformed policeman tapped on the driver's-side window. "What're you doing in there, sleeping?"

I stared at him, trying to make sense of his question.

He continued to frown, expression growing darker by the second.

I rolled down the window. "Sorry, officer. I didn't realize I fell asleep. Is there a problem?"

He leaned in as if trying to sniff my breath. When he straightened, he pointed to a No Parking sign right next to my front bumper. "Can't you read?"

I looked at the sign his finger pointed to. Where did that come from? It wasn't there when I parked. I gave a sheepish grin. "I … didn't see that."

"That sign is big enough to read from fifty feet. How long since you had your eyes checked?"

My smile weakened.

His expression communicated *what are you, an idiot?* "You're having car trouble then?"

I shook my head. *Of course not, you moron.*

"Have you been drinking or using drugs?"

I shook my head harder. Stupid question. *Who would admit that?*

He shrugged. "I give up. What's your excuse for parking here?"

I glanced over at the motel. "I … well, I know this is going to sound lame, but I think someone I know is in that motel, and I'm waiting for her to come out."

The officer raised his eyebrows as he withdrew his ticket pad from his pocket. I'm sure he thought this must be some kind of adultery thing. "Okay, lady. Let's see your license."

Not even a *please*? Apparently, they didn't teach manners in officer training. With a deep sigh, I collected the requested documents and handed them out the window. While he copied the pertinent information, I sagged in the driver seat and fumed. I glanced at the motel just in time to see the door of room 115 pop open. With a start, I straightened from my slumped position.

Helen Sterne exited the room, followed by a younger man wearing black. Slight of build, the man's expression looked haunted and hunted. Thick blond hair hung in his eyes. He needed a haircut badly. Silver chains dangled from his belt. His face reminded me of someone, but I couldn't think who it might be. Though not a large man, his attitude blocked the doorway. Standing feet apart with arms locked across his chest, he looked ready to defend his turf. Helen faced him. From the body language, I presumed she spoke. I couldn't see her face. He stared at her without expression.

The policeman completed writing the citation, followed by a lecture on reading street signs, and returned to his motorcycle parked behind my Jeep. By the time I looked back at the motel, Helen's blue car had disappeared and the door to room 115 had closed.

Who was that man in black? What was Helen doing in his room? Could it be the obvious? That just didn't fit with what I knew about this frigid woman.

I'd come to town intent on finding answers, but instead I returned home with another heap of questions.

31

Chapter Thirty-one

That night after dinner, I studied the forlorn gray house from my kitchen window. It reminded me of a discarded turtle shell.

Lila, oh Lila. Had she found a safe haven? *Please, God, help her.*

Burning with desire to connect with her, I rummaged through the drawer until I found the page torn from Lila's poetry book. The cramped but neat writing, without punctuation or capitalization, now had a familiarity that soothed my spirits. That is, until I scanned the contents.

sleepless nights erupt like daggers
heavy weigh my gaping eyes
dark perverts your flawless features
severing head and limbs asunder
piles of maggots consume the flesh
while ravens rip and screech
dark avenging angels circle
oh pain and loss that never die
why did i let her touch you
to burn forever in the punishing fire
is all thats left for me

A massive lump formed in my throat as I imagined her intense pain. She definitely lost her baby. Someone buried him in that shallow grave by the water tower. A feeling in my gut told me Lila couldn't have killed the baby herself.

I reread the poem word by word, stopping at "why did i let her touch you."

I studied that line, repeating it out loud twice. Who's *her?* Someone Lila had no power over. It had to be Helen. Both Maggie and Alan heard Lila say Helen did something just like before. Cece and Maxine confirmed that Helen killed the dog. A chill shivered down my spine as truth struck home. Helen killed Lila's dog, just like she murdered Lila's baby and buried him by the water tower.

The lump in my throat threatened to strangle me. I swallowed, trying to dislodge it. Although I still had no facts or motives, only inferences and hearsay, I knew what I knew. Would Maggie, Alan, Maxine, and Cece agree to testify?

How in the world could I prove this if they wouldn't?

❧

Wednesday morning, we sat in our living room with the Callahans and Russell Silverthorne. I covered my spiky hair with a visor that matched my shirt and hoped no one would wonder why I wore a sun visor indoors.

Zora Jane leaned forward extending her hand to Silverthorne from the bright blue mohair poncho she wore over tight black jeans. "Thank you for coming all this way out here on such short notice. We're so glad to meet you."

We all murmured agreement.

I sat on the edge of the sectional, hardly able to contain my excitement. "It's not even been a month since I first laid eyes on Lila Kliner and I only met her twice, but it feels like she's been part of my life forever. I'm so grateful you came to help us find her."

Jesse asked, "Should we call you Deputy?"

Silverthorne's eyes twinkled. "Oh, no. Russell suits me fine." Former Deputy Sheriff Russell Silverthorne's wavy white hair circled around a bald spot on top of his head like a glorious nimbus cloud. Well-placed wrinkles imparted a distinguished look—what some call "aging gracefully" when applied to men. Blue eyes sparkled from behind wire-rimmed bifocals—eyes that penetrated when he spoke. Perhaps he could see clear into our minds with such eyes. Bright and intuitive, he had none of the rudeness or lack of finesse I expected after my experience with the local sheriff's office.

We officially hired Silverthorne to investigate the possibility that Lila Kliner might be the mother of the water tower baby. He produced a contract, which the four of us signed before Zora Jane and I wrote checks to cover his usual retainer. Expenses would be billed separately. With paying clients, Silverthorne could legally work within the confines of California law. Ed Callahan would be his primary contact, since Ed had the law-enforcement background. Of course, Ed would share all reports.

Although the scope of his investigation didn't officially include locating Lila, in order to prove her connection to the baby, he'd have to find her. We took turns emptying our figurative puzzle box of clues, examining each in detail as we placed it on the table. The funnel Jesse so meticulously collected; Jesse's close-up photographs of Sierra Meadows; my black plastic bag of bleached towels—we surrendered our entire collection except the little charred chunk Molly found in the fire, because I couldn't find that. Silverthorne seemed mesmerized.

A wooden clipboard of papers and files lay atop Silverthorne's closed laptop, but he neither consulted them nor recorded anything while we talked. Maybe he had that kind of mind that retained things verbatim. Every now and then, he politely interrupted to ask a question. Mostly his sparkly eyes processed and assimilated like the lights that twinkle on the computer hard drive when it's working.

After a while, he asked for a description of Lila.

I jumped to my feet. "I have a picture of her." I retrieved it from the kitchen. "This must be an old one, because her dog looks like a puppy, but Lila's face shows up well." I pointed out the phone number indentations.

Silverthorne studied the photo as if trying to memorize her features. "Does Lila look the same now?"

"She's thinner and unusually frail." I pictured her in my mind. "Her hair is longer and grayer. She looks old, 'cause she's sick, I guess. But you could recognize her from this."

He nodded. "I'll check the phone number too. We might need someone in Iowa to interview this brother, Alan. Maybe he knows something he wouldn't say to a stranger over the phone. Could get lucky. You never know."

Ed uncrossed his legs and rearranged his trim frame in the white leather cowboy chair. With his high energy level, perhaps he disliked sitting so long. "Maybe the McCarthys know more than we do. Lila visited them now and then. They might remember something else she said."

I gave Silverthorne the McCarthys' phone number. He did write that down, along with the names and phone numbers of all the other people we mentioned, from the Coopers to Deputy Sam Colter. I also explained my latest deduction about Helen being the murderer of the baby and turned over the crumpled poem from Lila's tablet. Everyone found the possibility intriguing, and we spent almost an hour discussing just that one bit of news without anyone suggesting it might be my imagination. I considered that progress.

The only thing I didn't share concerned the man I saw with Helen at the motel. I don't know why exactly. I hadn't even told Jesse about that. Maybe because of the parking ticket. How could I be so stupid?

Altogether, almost three hours passed while we told, retold, and discussed the case. Silverthorne didn't seem hurried. His patience and generous gift of time encouraged us. When we'd clearly run out of information to offer him, he prepared to leave. "I'll be in touch as soon as I do a bit of research."

He faced us at the door. "You know, that little fellow in Harvard really impacted my life. My daughter's son drowned in the family pool right before. What a tragedy for our family! We'll never be the same. Then this baby." His blue eyes brightened with tears that didn't fall.

Zora Jane laid a comforting hand on his arm.

Silverthorne swallowed and shook his head. "I couldn't get him out of my mind. A random accident didn't take him like my grandson. Someone robbed him of the life he should've had. His death devastated our community too. Folks just couldn't believe it—to be broken and discarded like trash—so small and helpless."

Ed nodded. Jesse looked at the floor.

Silverthorne stared at the floor too. "I tell you, that little bundle haunts me every day. My wife calls it an obsession."

He looked up, a shaky smile playing on his lips. "On behalf of Guthrie County, God bless you for persevering. We may be the only people on earth who really care what happened. Thank you." He shook each of our hands. "I promise I'll do my best."

We thanked him back, grateful to have someone who believed in God take this investigation seriously at last.

Zora Jane said, "We'll pray for your success."

And we did.

Near noon on Thursday morning, Silverthorne called our house to report, since the Callahans hadn't answered their phone. His voice bubbled with excitement. "I've made a few interesting discoveries and I wanted you folks to know right away."

He paused just long enough for me to answer. "Oh?"

"I collected a swatch of the blue blanket from the car, which appears to be a match with the one wrapped around the baby. Age looks the same, as well as the same nursery rhyme pattern."

"Well, what do you know!" Receiving blankets were often packaged in threes. "That might mean they came from the same package."

"Right. I interviewed Deputy Colter. He relegated the case to an investigator, a Deputy Dunn in the Nevada County Sheriff's Department with the Crimes against Persons and Property Unit."

"Good," I said. "He's the Callahans' son-in-law."

"I'm on my way to meet with him now. Oh, and Colter reported several recent complaints of homeless men camping in the woods out your way. So far, no one's actually been apprehended. Whoever they are, they're gone by the time the investigator gets out there. But the sightings are on record."

"Really?" I didn't like the sound of that. "Are you saying there might be more than one homeless person in the woods?"

"He didn't say that exactly. He just said one's been spotted and there are multiple complaints."

"That's not comforting."

"No, I suppose not." He paused. "Also, the crime lab collected several hairs from the brown Buick, and they're not blonde."

I didn't expect that. "No kidding!" That sounded promising.

"I spoke with Mrs. Sterne, as well."

"Oh?"

"She seems delighted to have Lila gone. Had nothing complimentary to say about her. Evaded questions about the pregnancy, but eventually I got her to admit that Lila was already pregnant when they first met. Doesn't know the father or what happened to the baby."

"How'd she know about any of it?"

"Had a death in the family, one of their brothers. Helen went to Iowa for the funeral and found Lila living with Will. Actually, she said, 'sponging off' Will."

"How'd you get all this out of her?"

His chuckle had a lyrical quality. "Former deputy sheriffs have ways of getting people to talk."

"I'll just bet." Perhaps he inserted bamboo under Helen's fingernails. I rather liked that idea.

"I'm interested in Mrs. Sterne, actually. Something in her eyes when she talked about Lila—a coldness—just makes me wonder. Anyway, Deputy Dunn's been most accommodating over the phone. I think he'll include me in the loop whenever he can. I'm eager to interview Will too."

"You've been busy. Thanks for the update."

"I'll come by after the interview this afternoon so maybe you and Jesse can round up Ed and Zora Jane."

"I'll try." I heaved a hearty sigh. Would he come up with something concrete soon?

32

Chapter Thirty-two

I watched from the guest room bathtub while Silverthorne's rented white Taurus drove into Will's driveway. Silverthorne stepped out, waiting while another man climbed out the passenger side and joined him. Together they approached the front of the house. During their two-hour interview, I rounded up Zora Jane, Ed, and Jesse.

In our driveway, Zora Jane embraced Deputy Sheriff Baxter Dunn. Ed slapped him on the back and pumped his hand. With a grin, Ed introduced him as the father of four of their grandchildren. Deputy Dunn, a younger, brown-haired version of Silverthorne, stood at ease. I liked his broad shoulders, rosy cheeks, and sincere eyes.

"I've come as a courtesy to Mr. Silverthorne," Deputy Dunn said. "He says you folks hired him to look into an infanticide in Iowa. The Nevada County Sheriff's Office is conducting an investigation into the disappearance of Miss Kliner, so I'm not at liberty to share specific details of that case. However, in the absence of an official inquiry into the death of the infant, I'm going to hold off on that issue. I want to make sure you all understand that the time may come when I have to step out of these discussions." He glanced at each of us for understanding of his tenuous collaboration.

We murmured, each expressing our compliance.

"Meanwhile, I can consult with Mr. Silverthorne."

Silverthorne grinned at the young deputy. "These two cases intertwine, of course. But we'll try to keep from stepping on your toes."

Deputy Dunn's eyes sparkled with a sudden twinkle. "I understand you amateur sleuths have been helpful to Mr. Silverthorne."

Zora Jane took Deputy Dunn's arm and patted. "That's better, Baxter. Not so serious. Do try to relax. We have lots to talk about. It's a slice of heaven having you work with us."

Jesse led the way into the living room and seated our new friends. Ed and Zora Jane sat on one end of the sectional facing them, with Jesse and me taking the other.

Silverthorne began. "We heard an amazing story today. Will Payne is not much at communication, so we had to drag these few facts out little by little. He claims he doesn't remember my first interview with him, back in Iowa. Has no memory of that huge investigation we conducted to find the mother of 'Baby Blue.' I have trouble with that. Everyone in Iowa knew about that investigation." He shook his head in disbelief. "The media ran the story in all the papers and on TV for months."

I hadn't seen a TV at the Payne house. Maybe they'd never owned one.

Silverthorne cleared his throat. "Says he met Lila at a truck stop restaurant just west of Des Moines toward the end of the summer ten or eleven years ago. They struck up a conversation. He knows nothing about where she came from—has never heard of a brother named Alan. He didn't know about her pregnancy until she'd been living with him awhile." His voice went scratchy as he finished these last words. "Please go on, Deputy. I feel parched from all the talking."

Jumping up, I headed for the kitchen. "Where are my manners? I didn't even offer you a drink."

Zora Jane helped me provide drinks all around.

When we settled again, Silverthorne signaled Deputy Dunn to continue while he slugged down water.

"Mr. Payne and Miss Kliner made an agreement. If she kept house and cooked, he would provide food and shelter. Mr. Payne's wife had been dead more than two years then. He had difficulty coping with housework and cooking, as well as keeping his business going."

Silverthorne interrupted. "Did you notice he kept saying he never had any romantic notions toward Lila? Methinks he protests too much. Made me wonder about his original intentions."

Deputy Dunn nodded. "They kept separate bedrooms from the beginning. Mr. Payne felt it necessary to point that out three times."

Silverthorne lowered his glass. "Lila never kept her end of the bargain. She can't do housework or cook worth a toot. Has funny rules about food. Nothing red is allowed in the house. Requires each food to be eaten on a separate plate without touching anything else. Certain foods are taboo all together. Won't touch meat. Insists on wearing gloves if forced to. The list of acceptable foods keeps getting smaller. Got to a point she refused to cook at all."

I showed off my library gleaning. "Definitely anorexia nervosa—an advanced stage."

Silverthorne met my gaze. "That's my guess."

Deputy Dunn consulted his notebook. "One day, Mr. Payne came home to an empty house. Thought she'd gone for good, but she returned late that night no longer pregnant. He doesn't know how she went or came back either."

Silverthorne looked at me. "Apparently, she doesn't drive."

I nodded. "Speed kills."

Silverthorne continued. "Helen must have taken her, just as you surmised. She was visiting at the time. Will claims he left for work that day, same as always, and Lila never said anything more about it. But she sat in her room and cried for days. Will tried to make her stop. He thought a pet might help, because she'd always been fond of dogs. So eventually he got the dog."

The four of us had been sitting on the edges of our seats. When Silverthorne paused for another sip of water, we collectively turned to Deputy Dunn, in anticipation of another disclosure. But he only re-adjusted his position in the chair.

Silverthorne set his glass on the end table. "Helen had been in California for several years already. She begged Will to join her with stories of fine living and wonderful weather. He'd grown tired of the cold winters in Iowa. His business had slowed down, so he sold out and relocated. Thought a change of scenery might help Lila. They moved in the spring. Perhaps April or May."

I nodded. Zora Jane took the cookies to Lila around the middle of May that year.

Silverthorne gestured for Dunn to continue. Deputy Dunn shifted in his seat. "Mr. Payne recalled that just before moving, something set Miss Kliner off. She went into the crying mode again, 'crazy as a pig on ice,' he said, throwing fits and breaking dishes."

"That happened right before the move," Silverthorne said. "A year after she disappeared the first time. She wouldn't eat for days again."

Ed leaned forward, resting one elbow on the knee of his plaid golf pants. "Maybe that was when she read the article about the discovery of the dead baby in Harvard."

Silverthorne glanced at Ed. "Could be. Must have been right around the time I first interviewed Will. However, Will is adamant that he doesn't know what happened to the baby." He stared at the carpet. "Anyway, Lila perked up after they moved here, so Will thought she'd be okay."

Jesse shook his head. "Sounds like he cares a whole lot more than he admits."

"Good point." Silverthorne paused, drawing his lips together in a thin line. "Well, the irregular eating got worse. She goes for days refusing to eat and getting thinner. Then all of a sudden she'll gorge herself. He can't predict whether she'll eat or not, so he brings food every day. Most of it gets thrown away. She won't go anywhere anymore, not even outside, and sleeps a lot."

Memory of the disgusting garbage contents surfaced in my brain.

They'd answered some questions, but plenty of new ones rose to take their places. "Did he tell you about the padlock on the garage refrigerator?"

Deputy Dunn nodded affirmation while Silverthorne answered. "Lila put the padlock on the refrigerator. Got this idea food came from the devil and didn't want any more in the house. She hears voices telling her not to eat. Will eats at his sister's mostly, rather than try to make Lila cook."

Zora Jane's expression saddened. "She isn't getting enough nourishment, and it's making her crazy. The poor thing really is starving to death."

Someone who refused to leave the house had driven a car into the freezing wilderness. I pictured her frail body shivering. What made her go out there?

Silverthorne spoke again. "We asked about the rumors of wealth too. Will claims to be near poverty. Says living in California is expensive and he doesn't trust banks out here."

Many other questions clambered for attention in my brain. "What about the furniture? The house was bare when I saw it, except for beds. Is there furniture now?"

Deputy Dunn glanced at Silverthorne before answering. "When Miss Kliner left, Mr. Payne moved the furniture back into the house. Of course, the bed in Miss Kliner's room is gone, as you suspected."

I watched their faces for reactions. "His story is so full of holes. Is any of it true?"

Deputy Dunn leaned back in his chair. "I'd guess it's mostly lies."

Silverthorne shook his head. "It's partly true. He hopes the true parts will substantiate the lies."

Ed nodded. "An amateur. Did you notice some parts of his story had a lot more detail than others? When amateurs lie, they throw in extra details because they think that makes their story sound plausible. People don't actually remember many details of ordinary events."

Silverthorne acknowledged that with a single nod. "Some of it sounded a little canned, as if he rehearsed it. I'll compare today's interview with what he told Colter before. See where the answers contain the same phrases. We'll corroborate his story if we can." He cocked his head. "The thing that bothers me most is that he categorically denies knowledge of Lila's whereabouts. That's impossible. He was at the house that night. Lila left in his vehicle. I think the funnel means Will tried to throw us off by siphoning gas and ditching the Buick, so he was at Sierra Meadows with Lila."

I raised my eyebrows but didn't ask how he knew that. The others nodded. One thing for sure: Will definitely knew more than he'd told.

Jesse spoke next. "Did you look through the house? How about the stain on the basement floor?"

Deputy Dunn shook his head. "There's nothing on that floor now."

Jesse pressed, expressing my question. "Can you test for blood?"

Silverthorne stifled a small yawn. "Sorry. Haven't slept much lately. We might test the floor as you suggest—probably will, eventually."

Deputy Dunn appeared thoughtful. "We may need a search warrant."

Impatience overwhelmed me and I heaved a loud sigh.

Ed had questions too. "Hang on now. Why did he burn Lila's gear so soon after she left? Including her mattress. How does he know she won't be back like when she took off before? Same with the furniture. He moved that back right away. How did he move all that heavy stuff into the house without help? He's not a young man."

Deputy Dunn and Silverthorne shook their heads.

Ed continued. "There are problems with the Buick too. Will told Colter that Lila packed her clothes and drove the car out Saturday night. Now he admits she doesn't drive?"

I remembered the Coopers' account of Lila's erratic driving. "If Lila doesn't drive and Will siphoned the gas, what woman did the Coopers almost run into that Saturday night?" I looked from one face to another. "I know who gets my vote. She's not a blonde."

Silverthorne held up both hands. "Be patient. We're aware there are many problems with Will's statement. We'll have to keep digging."

They'd been laying down answers like tile setters, one little tile at a time. But they'd come to the end for the day. Once again, the more we learned, the less we knew. Fugitive pieces of the puzzle multiplied like fleas, the outer edges of the picture pushing farther out to include more disturbing possibilities. Where could we go next for answers?

33

Chapter Thirty-three

Fuzzy feelings about Jesse's new attentiveness coerced me into accompanying him on his next shoot. A weekend away would be healthy, although I had doubts about whether I could keep my mind off the investigation for a whole weekend. At any rate, I could wear a cowboy hat over my hair and no one would suspect that a disaster hid underneath.

So we loaded Ranger into the trailer, left the cats and other horses in Zora Jane's care, and set off with Molly for the cowboy mounted shooting event in Ceres. The four-hour journey proceeded pleasantly enough in the warm afternoon sun, but the quiet gave me too much time to think. While I jostled along in Jesse's Dodge dualie, I couldn't keep my mind off the investigation. Far too many unresolved details tangled the puzzle.

Jesse beamed at me. "This is awfully nice of you, Christine." I knew he could hardly contain his excitement about my proposed venture into his world. "These are nice people. You'll really like them."

I tried to reflect his enthusiasm. "At least the weather isn't too hot. I don't know how you can stand getting dressed up in all that leather with the temperature so high. Like in the summer." As soon as I spoke, I wished I could take the words back. I sighed. After the progress we'd made in our relationship, why couldn't I think of something positive to say?

He threw me a wistful glance. I'm sure he wished I understood how much he loved doing this. Deflated by my own lack of progress, I returned to my dark reverie.

A couple of hours later, we exited the freeway, pulling the horse trailer onto a frontage road. After a few more turns, Jesse slowed to pass under a lodge-pole entrance where a wooden sign announced our arrival at Willowbrook Ranch. In the back seat of the double cab, Molly perched beside the back window to watch.

Dust tornados swirled around us as we drove past the ranch house toward a weathered barn. A banner proclaimed the upcoming event: "Shootout at Willowbrook Ranch." A man in an old-time cowboy costume waved us to a stop with a clipboard. Jesse rolled down the window.

The cowboy asked, "You folks here for the mounted shoot?"

Jesse nodded. "We are. Where do you want me to park this rig?"

"What's the handle?"

Jesse provided his shooting name. "Buckaroo Bob."

The cowboy consulted his clipboard. "Stall ten for your ride. Keep going straight down the road. When you see the other trailers, pull in anywhere you find a space." He lifted his leather-cuffed arm to send us onward.

Farther down the dirt road, we passed the arena. Rough wooden bleachers overlooked the middle of the field, with oaks and cottonwoods providing shade. Next, we came to rows of stalls for the horses and then the camping area in a field across from the stalls.

All sizes and shapes of horse trailers and recreational vehicles lined the pasture—old, new, aluminum, and rusty steel—some with pop-outs extended and some with hardly any room for anything but the horse. Elaborate decals decorated a few, while the sides of others were bare. Around these trailers, contestants toiled to set up temporary housekeeping like a swarm of worker bees getting ready for the queen bee. Jesse deftly backed into a small space between two trailers he recognized, parked the pickup, and jumped out.

While he and Molly greeted friends, I stretched and began unloading.

Jesse's three-horse trailer contained a tiny apartment in the front, with a bed over the back of the pickup. Although it had barely enough room for two grown-ups to pass each other, somehow a minuscule kitchen and compact bathroom fit into the space as well. An undersized built-in couch provided the only furniture in the unit. Beside the couch, a plastic table attached to the floor to create a dinette or detached when company required seating.

Jesse unloaded Ranger and led him to pen number ten. Supplied with hay and water, Ranger settled in. His cohorts in the other stalls appeared just as grateful as he to be out of the confines of their small trailer spaces.

I rearranged several items that had shifted in transit. Jesse bustled in carrying a box of sodas and bent to start up the mini-refrigerator so I could unload the ice chest. While he worked, he sang:

I gotta woman, mean as she can be.
Why don't you love me, baby?
Like you used to do?
Tell me that you care,
Tell me that you'll always be there.
I spent a lifetime, looking for the right one
The one I'm dreamin' of…

I smiled, wondering how many songs completed his repertoire.

When we'd almost finished unloading, a loud rap-tap sounded at the door, followed by several cheery voices. Molly perked up.

"Anybody home?"…"Knock, knock."…"Hey, Buckaroo. You in there?"

Jesse opened the door and stepped out. He introduced the greeting party, using their riding pseudonyms. Express Man's crumpled black hat sported a rebel emblem. Dust covered his clothes as if he just rode in from carrying the mail on his pony. Cactus Kelly, a fit cowgirl attired in a split riding skirt, suspenders, and high riding boots, stood next to him. Her husband, Dirty Dan—a grizzled ranch hand—leaned against her. He extended a sweaty handshake. Calamity June chose jeans and a men's floppy shirt for her costume. Diamond Spike's clothes—creased black pants, a clean white shirt covered by a black satin vest, and a rounded bowler hat with a narrow brim—identified him as a card-playing dandy.

In great excitement, they all spoke at once. Molly added a cheerful greeting yelp, tail wagging. The clamor of voices overwhelmed me, but I appreciated the sincerity of the welcome. Jesse produced folding chairs from a side compartment of his trailer, and we set them out beside the front door of our miniature domicile.

The group had much to discuss: guns and ammunition, horses and their speed, upcoming events, new sources for period costumes, even a touch of club gossip. Mostly I listened.

Cactus Kelly tried to include me. "So, do you ride?"

"I did, when we lived down south. Owned a great horse too, but she died. Have you been competing long?"

She sent her husband a loving look. "It's not really my deal. Dan got us into this. He always loved horses. He rode fast … getting real good until his accident two years ago. Ended up with a broken pelvis and back pain so bad he can't ride anymore. Still loves coming out, though. Loves the camaraderie. Loves the camping. Now he's the official photographer and cook. You'll see. He rustles up a pretty mean barbeque."

"You still come, even though he doesn't compete? You do all this for him?"

"Well, at the beginning I just wanted to keep the family together. The kids were still young enough that they'd come with us. One of our daughters rode too. It used to be a fun family thing. We did it together."

"You're a better wife than I am, that's for sure."

She smiled. "We all get away from the routine. I'm not much good, but he loves teaching me." She winked. "That's a win-win."

Jesse rose at dawn, whistling and singing while he made coffee. He bathed with uncharacteristic speed in the tiny shower and got dressed. From our perch on the bed, Molly and I watched the transformation from Jesse to Buckaroo Bob.

First, he donned a striped western shirt and heavy western pants. Wide black suspenders snapped on next. He strapped his leather gun belt on his hips and pulled on long leather boots with jingling spurs attached. A fringed leather vest decorated with touches of red and blue Indian beading went on over the shirt. He tied a yellow scarf around his neck and secured it with a silver scarf slide. An extra-wide brimmed black hat completed the costume.

"I thought good guys only wore white hats," I mused.

"What about Hopalong Cassidy?"

He had me there.

With Ranger outfitted in fancy leather reins, halter, and red wool blanket under a vintage Visalia saddle, Buckaroo Bob swung onto his steed. The two of them could've come straight out of an Old West movie.

I settled on the splintery bleachers with a steamy cup of coffee, picking a spot in the shade of a spreading cottonwood tree. A colorful array of contestants warmed up in the arena—thirty-some riders. Men and women of various ages and sizes—men outnumbering women by about two to one—pranced and trotted. And the costumes! From the stands, spectators cheered and called out pseudonyms as the shooters rode by. A feathery saloon girl outfit clothed Belle Pepper, Tiger Lily wore a leather-fringed Indian-princess dress, and cavalry officer duds transformed Captain Crunch into a military man. In addition, assorted cowboys and cowgirls in colorful costumes sported imaginative names like Herr Trigger, Buck N. Wyld, and Robin Banks. The horses were varied as well—tall ones, ponies, and everything in between—black, brown, gray, white, some with manes and tails the same color as their bodies and some two-toned.

After about an hour, they completed their warm-up and gathered for a riders' meeting. Jesse assisted several other range officers setting up the first course in the center of the arena. They arranged four white balloons attached to orange highway cones in a V-shape with a barrel at the tip holding a fifth white balloon. A line of five blue balloons attached to orange highway cones intersected the V like an arrow shaft. After considerable conferring and rearranging by the cowboys in the field, everyone approved the spacing. The match would be composed of seven different configurations of balloons, or stages, over the next two days.

The head range officer spoke to the assembled riders. "Course number one is stage one today. Shoot all the white balloons first before rounding the barrel. Remember to stay on the outside of the white balloons. Then come back and shoot the rundown. Any questions?"

None were voiced, so the riders dispersed to the outside of the arena. A covered box above the far end housed timekeepers and announcers. A garbled welcome squawked from the loudspeaker, followed by the proposed lineup of the first five riders. The event kicked off with level one and continued through level five.

A cowboy on an Appaloosa stallion rode into the arena. The announcer introduced him as Ben Shot riding his horse, Freckles, and gave a short bio on the rider. She ended with a witty comment about Ben being on the lookout for a filly. Ben removed his beat-up black cowboy hat and waved it at the announcer. Replacing the hat, Ben led his horse in a couple short circles to gain momentum before tearing through the timer at maximum speed. He rode to the outside of the V formation, slowing to shoot the first four balloons without a miss, but rode too fast to hit the last one. Without pausing to express disappointment, he pivoted around the barrel and trotted toward the rundown, hooting while he kicked his horse in the belly. He shot all five of the blue balloons before spurring his horse back to his starting point.

The announcer proclaimed, "Time: 26.35 seconds. One missed balloon for a five-second penalty. That's a score of 31.35 for stage one. Good ride, Ben."

The small audience applauded.

Level ones entered the arena and ran the stage in turn, then level twos, and level threes. The times gradually decreased as the level of expertise increased.

Dirty Dan set up his camera at the far end of the arena. Barbeque and photography. He couldn't ride anymore, but his wife kept coming because he enjoyed the shoots. Maybe someday I'd become that kind of supportive wife.

Jesse's turn came at last. He entered the arena, sitting tall in his saddle. A surge of pride and excitement swept over me. Jesse did look good on a horse.

Ranger pranced and tossed his jet-black head, looking excited to begin. Jesse led him in warm-up loops. The announcer read their bio, but I couldn't hear it over the static. Jesse watched for the range officer's signal to begin.

Several riders sat nearby in the bleachers. One lady glanced my way. "Is that your husband?"

I nodded.

"He never misses," she told the lady next to her. They smiled.

Ranger galloped toward the V, long black tail trailing straight in the wind. Jesse shot the five white balloons in an exemplary manner, rounded the barrel like a pro, and commenced to the rundown without a moment's hesitation, shooting all five balloons in turn. He raced back through the timer. "Time: 19.5 seconds. No misses. Good job, Buckaroo! That's the time to beat, ladies and gentlemen: 19.5."

A lanky cowboy in a white Stetson and white shirt with extra puffy sleeves lowered his lean frame to sit beside me. I acknowledged his presence with a nod. He tipped his hat. "You must be Buckaroo's wife."

"Yes, I'm Christine."

"Around these parts I go by Nevada Slim. Pleased to meetcha."

We watched the next contestant begin his run. He rode fast but missed two blue balloons on the rundown.

Without looking at me, Nevada Slim asked, "This your first time?"

"Yes. Well, I've seen him practice at home, of course. I just haven't been to a shoot before."

"What do ya think?"

"It's interesting."

Jesse arrived just then, beaming like a boy who hit his first home run in Little League. He sat on the other side of me.

"That was great," I said, patting his leg. "You're ahead!"

"Well, it's early for a victory dance. We've got six more stages to run. Nevada hasn't shot yet. Wait 'til you see him."

Nevada grinned at Jesse. "I don't know, Buckaroo. You've been coming up every shoot. I gotta watch my back."

Jesse nodded toward Nevada. "I see you've already met one of Nevada County's finest. He works for the sheriff's department in Nevada City."

I glanced at Nevada. "Is that a fact?"

He inclined his head. "'Fraid so, ma'am."

Jesse leaned over to catch Nevada's eye. "Tell her what you told me earlier about the tramp in the woods."

"Oh, the vagrant. We got several complaints about someone illegally camping out your way. Thought they were just rumors. But last week we caught a guy building a fire in the woods. Had enough supplies to stay a week. We questioned him, let him sleep in the holding area one night, and released him. Told him he couldn't camp out there, but who knows if he'll listen. Seemed confused but harmless."

Jesse grinned. "Nothing to worry about. Just a confused pyromaniac."

I painted on a weak smile. "So you know about the investigation into Lila Kliner's disappearance."

"Sure. I'm not on the investigating team, but most everyone in the department has been involved on that one in some way."

Penelope Pink-Paynt, a tiny cowgirl, braids hanging long underneath her pink hat, rode a diminutive gray pony with a pink-painted tail into the arena. In a flash, she zipped across the timer. She rode like a cyclone toward the white balloons, braids and pink tail flying. Her guns looked too large for her little hands, but she didn't miss a single shot. She rounded the barrel in a tightly executed turn and headed for the run down.

I said, "She was our neighbor. Lila Kliner."

"Oh. Sorry." Nevada shook his head. "Can't seem to get a break on that one. Or the other one, either."

"What other one?"

"The hit-and-run in Nevada City. The little boy. They happened the same night." He watched Penelope speed to the rundown, shooting all five blue balloons as the spectators cheered. "I think they may be connected."

Connected? As in, whoever drove the Buick hit the little boy?

I opened my mouth to ask for more, but he spoke first. "Well, my turn's coming up. Been a pleasure, ma'am." He tipped his hat again as he stood. "Watch this, Buckaroo. I'll show ya how it's done."

34

Chapter Thirty-four

Our weekend away proved great marriage therapy, and we even stayed an extra night so we could participate in the group barbeque and bonfire, although I never got another opportunity to grill Nevada Slim about Lila. Jesse won his division, which seemed to please him.

Monday we took our time getting home. In the early afternoon, I rode next to Jesse, cuddled against his shoulder, but raised my head to stare at Will's house when we passed. I didn't see his white truck in its usual place, so chances were good he'd gone to town.

"We've got to fix that gate so Molly can't open it anymore," Jesse said. "She's obsessed with getting out."

"Curious, isn't it? Wonder what's calling her to that pile?"

Jesse jerked his head to look me in the eye. "No, Christine!"

"Come on, Jesse. Will's still gone and—"

"No more snooping. Do you hear me? Will has a gun, remember? We hired a professional. He can handle this from now on."

Jesse turned in at the barn and unloaded Ranger. Feeling disgruntled and deflated, I climbed the hill and marched petulantly into the house. Molly followed.

When I made laundry piles, I found the little burned chunk Molly retrieved from the fire pit. I had apparently tossed it into the pocket of the robe I threw on when I raced down the hill after Molly and Jesse. I turned it in my palm, trying to deduce its message.

It might be leather, part of a box. No. A suitcase. A brown suitcase sat above the rafters in the open garage the first time I looked in, but it wasn't there anymore. So Lila *didn't* pull that suitcase down to transport her clothes.

I picked up the phone and punched in Silverthorne's cell number. When he answered a moment later, I relayed my latest insight.

He sounded tired and decidedly underwhelmed. "We plan to speak to Will again. We'll ask about the suitcase. Dunn invited both Helen and Will to headquarters for questioning on Thursday. Voluntarily at this point. Would you like to come down for that?" He paused a few seconds as if giving me an opportunity to get to the real point of my call.

"I guess. But you need to look through those ashes. Molly smells something there."

"Uh-huh. Just like Lassie, eh?" He chuckled. "Well, thanks for your assistance, Christine. I'll talk with you tomorrow."

Lassie!

Molly sat in front of the sliding glass doors, staring outside. I completely understood her message. She wanted out. If only I could set her free to rummage through the remains of whatever Will had disposed of in the fire. She would no doubt find an important clue—something to blow the lid off this mystery right now.

I put my hand on the door and slid it open—one inch. Then I stopped.

Molly stood, wagging her tail, anticipation palpable.

Jesse would be angry.

Which was more important, solving the puzzle or keeping my husband happy? Tough decision. I teetered a moment, remembering our weekend. Then I closed the door. "Sorry, Molly. I've got to live with him. You understand."

She tilted her head and watched me with questions in her expressive brown eyes. I don't think she understood.

Wednesday's interview yielded a few additional clarifications, but progress seemed slower than the line at the DMV. This time we convened in the Callahans' living room to hear Silverthorne's report. Deputy Dunn remained standing, carrying his clipboard and maintaining a professional posture while the rest of us sat. Something about him seemed different.

Silverthorne didn't appear to notice. "The whereabouts of the suitcase confuses Will. First, he said Lila packed her clothes in it the night she left. He agreed it would've been difficult for her to get it out of the rafters. Now he doesn't know where the suitcase is."

Feeling frustrated, I said, "Well, it's gone. I saw that myself. I even climbed up on the wood to see if I could reach the ledge. Lila could never get it down. Did you see where the wood has been disturbed?"

Deputy Dunn frowned. "It wouldn't do much good to look now, since you already climbed up there."

Jesse threw me a glare.

Oops! Should have thought of that.

Silverthorne cleared his throat. "We'll have your chunk analyzed to see if we can verify that it's part of a leather suitcase."

Deputy Dunn bristled. The furrows in his brow deepened as he snapped on gloves before placing the small piece into an evidence bag. "These things you're collecting may be inadmissible in court. You realize that, don't you? This piece of suitcase, the towels, the funnel—because the chain of evidence has been compromised. Your own fingerprints will be all over them. In the future, please leave the investigating to us."

I wiggled in my seat fighting my budding annoyance. My voice came out louder than usual. "Molly found the leather. I'm just relaying evidence. Why wouldn't that be admissible in court?"

Silverthorne stared at the carpet.

In the awkward pause, words flew from my mouth without much forethought. "Also, the sheriff's department missed the funnel when they towed the brown car. I suppose we should have left it there. Then no one would know anything about it." I regretted the sarcasm even as I heard it pop out of my mouth.

"Possibly." Deputy Dunn's tense expression didn't soften. "But if we're accumulating evidence to prosecute, we must take great care. Call us before you touch anything else that might be evidence."

For an instant, the air between us crackled like high-voltage wire.

Then Ed asked, "Don't you have any good news for us?"

Silverthorne cleared his throat. "You may be interested to know a birth certificate in the name of Lila May Kliner turned up in the records search."

I held my breath, waiting for the good part.

"The birth certificate lists her mother as Naomi Lynn Kliner. Father's name unknown. Lila was born in Des Moines in 1961. In addition, I confirmed that Lila's mother is deceased. About Alan Kliner, the sheriff 's office in Des Moines hasn't connected with him yet. Neighbors say he's rather unstable—has a reputation involving abuse of alcohol and narcotics. He has a record, so I asked the sheriff 's office for a picture and prints. I'll get those out here as soon as they arrive."

It wasn't much to fill in the blanks about Lila's past.

Silverthorne paused. "As for the furniture, Will says he brought it back to the house with the tractor. Then he used a dolly."

Deputy Dunn shrugged. "That's possible. There's a furniture dolly in the closed garage."

Silverthorne consulted his notes. "The name of Will's boat—*Miss Misery*. That mean anything to anyone?"

Misery swirled around the Payne house like smoke from a wet fire. What a perfect name for their boat. I thought of the poor dog jettisoned into the icy waters. "Where's the boat now?"

"He said he stored it in Helen's garage," Silverthorne answered.

I got a mental image of skirting Helen's garage. "I wish I'd peeked inside.

Silverthorne said, "We've been discussing the inconsistencies in Will's testimony. It's plain he hasn't been forthcoming."

Understatement of the year! Inconsistencies, changed stories, strange circumstances, lies; when would we get to truth? Dunn and Silverthorne scurried away to continue investigating, leaving the four of us huddled together like baby birds waiting in the nest for food.

35

Chapter Thirty-five

Silverthorne invited Jesse and me along with Ed and Zora Jane to headquarters on Thursday during the questioning of Helen and Will. I covered my bad haircut with a pink sequined ball cap I'd purchased at the cowboy shoot, and we all piled into the Jeep.

Wearing a serious professional expression, Deputy Dunn cautioned us—including Silverthorne—at the sheriff's office. "First of all, this is not a formal interview. We are not ready to charge anyone. Don't even know if a crime has been committed yet. We're trying to determine what happened to Lila Kliner. You must realize your presence here is highly irregular. Mr. Silverthorne isn't part of the official investigation either. I'm allowing you to listen because of your history and insight in this case, hoping that you'll be able to verify their answers. If you think of anything important, please let me know." He frowned at each of us. "But I won't tolerate interference. Is that clear?"

We nodded, faces somber.

"Also, what you are about to hear is completely confidential. Breaking this confidence could make prosecution impossible. Assuming we get that far."

We each promised to maintain confidentiality.

As I trooped behind Zora Jane, her long, brown, front-buttoned skirt flapped against caramel-brown lacing boots. A charming coral turtleneck complemented her reddish-brown hair. I started to comment on yet another stunning outfit when they led our troop to a cubicle behind a wall of shiny one-way glass that looked like a mural of a moonless night. Silverthorne leaned against the doorframe while we four sat in stiff metal chairs without cushions.

On the other side of the glass, a deputy led Helen Payne Sterne into the room. In complete arrogance, she settled into a chair at a small metal table just like you might see in old black-and-white gangster movies. Deputy Dunn sat across from her, and another uniformed deputy stood at attention beside the door.

Wearing jeans and a sloppy gray wool sweater, Helen looked like the queen of Frumpyville. Her tangled hair probably hadn't been combed in several days. Angular features firmly set, she had that defiant expression that reminded me of Will.

Deputy Dunn clicked on a small tape recorder and set it on the table. He spoke the date and identified himself and the other uniformed officer. To Helen he said, "Are you aware this conversation is being recorded?"

She tossed her head like a rebellious stallion.

"State your answers verbally, please."

"I see the tape recorder. I'm not blind."

"State your name."

Tone sarcastic, she complied with his instructions.

"Are you the sister of William Payne of Grass Valley?"

Her lips curled in a sneer. "Yes."

"Are you acquainted with Lila Kliner?"

She snorted and called Lila an ugly name.

"For the record, Mrs. Sterne acknowledges acquaintance with Miss Kliner."

The first hour of examination continued in the same vein. When Dunn showed Helen pictures of the evidence, she lingered over the picture of the funnel with Will's fingerprints on it before turning to the brown hairs recovered from the Buick.

"What's your point?" she asked.

"Lila is a blonde."

She crossed her arms, scowling.

"I could get a court order—"

Helen held up one hand. "That won't be necessary." She puffed air out. "I drove the Buick to Sierra Meadows."

I gasped and slapped my leg. "Of course."

Jesse looked at me.

I whispered. "Everything makes sense now."

Zora Jane and Ed gave slow nods.

Jesse's eyebrows shot up. "Everything?"

Meanwhile, Helen had become less composed, although the stiffness in her angular features hadn't softened. I held up one hand so I could hear Dunn fire questions. "What time did you leave the house?"

"Before six. Six fifteen at the latest."

"Where was Lila when you left the house?"

Helen visibly squirmed. Staring into her lap, she clasped and unclasped her hands.

"Mrs. Sterne?"

She crossed her legs. "We had to get rid of the stinkin' dog."

"Lila's dog? The dog you drowned at Lake Tahoe?"

Helen fixed a withering stare on him—steely eyes, angry grimace. "Are you accusing me of murdering a stupid dog?"

"Did you?"

She pursed her lips into a fine line.

Dunn leaned toward the recorder. "Mrs. Sterne declines to answer."

She puffed out another exaggerated breath. "He was supposed to distract Lila while I drove the Buick to the campground. I would wait there until he came to get me. In the freezing cold. Then he would leave the Buick and the dog there."

"Didn't you think it odd to dispose of the vehicle just to be rid of a dead dog?"

She shrugged. "I'm not responsible for what he does anymore. He's a grown man."

Anymore? I glanced at the others, but no one else seemed surprised by Helen's word choice.

Dunn leaned forward. "So you left Lila and Will at the house?"

She dropped her head and mumbled.

Dunn leaned farther forward. "Please speak clearly for the recorder."

Helen lifted her eyes. "When he got there after midnight, he siphoned gas out of the tank."

"Why?"

She shook her head. "That's when he used the funnel. Ask him."

"Why did he siphon gas out?"

She huffed and puffed. "To make it look like the moron ran away."

Dunn raised the volume. "Where was Lila all this time?"

But Helen only shrugged again.

Dunn sat back and scanned his notes. "Your story doesn't make sense, Helen. You say Will left the dead dog in the car but siphoned gas out to make it appear that she ran away. Lila wouldn't let Will take that car away with Baby in the trunk. She adored that dog. How did you keep Lila from coming with you?"

I hadn't thought of that. Lila sat behind that car for a week after Will put the dog in the trunk. She would never abandon Baby without a fight.

Helen fidgeted and steamed, like a pressure cooker about to explode.

Silverthorne bent to scribble on a piece of paper. He folded it and disappeared out the door. Soon the uniformed officer ducked outside the interview room. Silverthorne handed the paper to the officer. The officer relayed it to Deputy Dunn with a whispered message.

Dunn nodded slowly as he read, and then refolded it. "Mrs. Sterne, what happened to Lila's baby? The one she had in Iowa?"

Helen made a show of surprise. "I guess she got rid of it."

"Do you mean 'got rid of' like you got rid of the dog?"

For a second, she looked ready to spring on Dunn like a tiger, but she spit words at him instead. "No one wanted that baby. Will didn't. *She* certainly couldn't take care of it."

"So how did she get rid of the baby?"

"There are places that perform abortions. Even in Iowa."

Dunn closed in. Hands flat on the table, he leaned across to within an inch of her face. "The baby was full term when they dug him up. Ten years ago, there were few places a doctor would perform a full-term abortion unless the mother's life was in danger. Mostly illegal places. But Lila never saw a doctor, did she?"

Helen pursed her lips and scooted her chair as far from Dunn as the small space allowed.

But Dunn didn't let up. "Where did Lila have the abortion?"

"I … don't remember the name."

"But you were there. You drove her. Didn't you, Mrs. Sterne? Because Lila doesn't drive. Isn't that correct?"

Helen writhed in her chair. "I heard about a place. I didn't ask if it was legal or not."

"But you didn't take her to get an abortion. She went into labor and you took her to the water tower."

"Now you're accusing me of murdering a baby?"

"Are you saying the baby was murdered at the water tower?"

Her breathing came out shallow and fast. She balled her fists, the belligerent façade wearing thin. "No. I … You just said the baby was murdered."

Dunn slammed his clipboard on the table. "Where is Lila Kliner?"

Curses spewed from her mouth like venom and her words screamed out. "How should I know? I drove the car to Sierra Meadows, remember?" She rose from her seat. "Look, I came here because you said you wanted to clear up a few loose ends. Nobody made me come. I came to help you. Are you charging me with something? What would you charge me with … helping? Is helping against the law?"

Detective Dunn opened his mouth, but Helen had already bolted for the door. "I'm done helping. I want a lawyer."

We stood for a breather before they interviewed Will.

Silverthorne scratched his head. "Well, I think that went just fine. Got her to commit to driving the Buick and what time she left the house. That's important. She contradicted herself a few times too. And she definitely nailed herself on the baby murder."

Ed nodded. "It'll be interesting to hear how Will tells the same story."

I didn't think it went well at all. "Why didn't he make her say where Lila is? We still have no clue."

Deputy Dunn brought strong sheriff's office coffee for each of us and passed it around. "They're bringing Will in now. Anything you want to tell me before I head back in?"

Silverthorne looked thoughtful. "See if he'll let you swab him for DNA testing."

We all faced Silverthorne and asked simultaneously. "Why?"

Silverthorne shrugged. "Just a hunch." That's all he would say.

Will Payne had aged at least ten years since I last saw him. They seated him in the metal chair behind the glass. He hunched, shoulders held tight over his concave chest. His face looked pale and drawn.

Deputy Dunn repeated the introductions and instructions.

Will nodded.

"Please state your answers verbally for the recorder."

Will breathed deeply before answering. "William Payne."

Dunn produced a swab and an evidence bag. "Would you mind giving us a sample from your cheek before we begin?"

"What for?"

"Routine part of the investigation. We're going to test your DNA. Do you object to that?"

Will shrugged. "Guess not."

"It'll only take a minute. Not intrusive. Open your mouth, please."

Will opened his mouth.

Dunn swiped and deposited the swab in the bag. Then he smiled. "That's all there is to it. Now tell me about the night Lila Kliner disappeared."

Will shook his head. "Told you a couple times already. Don't have nothing new to offer."

Dunn consulted his clipboard. "You told Deputy Colter that Miss Kliner packed a suitcase and drove away in the Buick on Saturday night."

"Yep."

"In fact, Mr. Payne, your sister drove the Buick out to Sierra Meadows that night. She said you wanted her to get rid of Lila's dead dog."

Except for widening his eyes, Will did not respond.

"Mr. Payne declines to answer." Dunn tapped his clipboard. "So, you were at the house with Miss Kliner after Mrs. Sterne left in the Buick."

Will stared at his rough hands. The color drained out of his face.

"What happened next?"

Will did not look up.

Dunn waited longer this time and then leaned toward the recorder. "Mr. Payne declines to answer."

"He looks like he's shrinking," Zora Jane whispered.

He did look smaller. Will's lanky body seemed to shrivel before our eyes. Was he falling off the chair?

Dunn leaned toward him. "Do you know where Miss Kliner is now?"

"He doesn't look well," I whispered to Jesse. "Somebody needs to get him out of there."

Just then, Will Payne crumpled to the floor.

I jumped out of my chair and rushed into the hall.

36

Chapter Thirty-six

Paramedics appeared quickly after Will's collapse. I watched them carry him away to the ER. Silverthorne accompanied the ambulance, promising to report back as soon as he heard Will's prognosis.

The four of us headed home, but I couldn't stay focused on anything. I divided my attention between the clock and the phone, waiting for Silverthorne's report. Meanwhile, I needed to hash over the latest developments with someone. Jesse had work to do but promised to keep his cell phone with him so he could relay Ed's message.

I invited Zora Jane to early afternoon lunch at a trendy restaurant in old downtown Nevada City. I covered my ugly hairdo with my pink sequined ball cap and applied extra make-up, hoping to distract from my hair.

Housed in a former bakery, the Bunnery touted California cuisine served in casual ambiance. *California cuisine* meant exotic fruits and vegetables, like sprouts, avocados, and butternut squash, used in imaginative ways to create an arty, pleasing presentation. *Casual ambiance* meant stained cement floors with rough barn siding on the walls.

Zora Jane had changed clothes. She met me outside the restaurant wearing a stylish pink and gray knit jacket over a hot pink shell. Charcoal gray stretch pants covered her lower parts, topping off hot pink mules with little black heels that clicked when we ambled to our booth. I wouldn't have guessed someone with Titian hair would look so gorgeous in hot pink, but there you are.

As I set my cell phone in a prominent position on the table where I'd be sure to get Silverthorne's call, I overheard a group of youngish women in the booth to our left. Glasses and silverware tinkled companionably. Their conversation drifted above the partition as we contemplated our menus.

A lady with a husky voice said, "The police still have no leads. Somebody out there must know something."

Another said, "It happened just after dark. When people are eating dinner instead of watching what's happening on the street."

A third said, "That poor little boy! It's such a terrible tragedy. Lucille says his mother is a mess. She'll never get over it."

Zora Jane scanned her menu. "They must be talking about that hit-and-run. Wasn't that the same night Lila disappeared?"

I'd been so preoccupied with Molly and now with Lila, I'd given little thought to the hit-and-run. What I wanted to talk about was the strange man I saw with Helen at the motel. I couldn't get him out of my mind. Who was he? "Terribly sad. Hope they find the person responsible."

"The newspaper says they're putting extra men on the investigation to cover all the leads they've received."

I slammed down my menu. "Oh, sure. They have extra men to investigate that little boy's death. But who's looking for Lila?"

Zora Jane patted my arm. "Now, Christine. It's been over a month with no answers. Imagine how those poor parents must feel. You wouldn't begrudge grieving parents a little peace of mind, would you?"

I started to say something I'd regret later but the waitress arrived to take our orders.

The young women in the next booth continued their discussion of the hit-and-run. When our food arrived, I took a bite of my bleu cheese walnut salad with apple chunks and sprouts tucked into sweet butter lettuce and chewed while eavesdropping.

The husky voice said, "The family's offered a big reward for information about the driver. I hope they nail him."

Zora Jane buttered a piece of crusty pumpernickel. "It happened just up the street from here. Beyond the old hotel."

Nevada Slim thought the hit-and-run and Lila's disappearance were connected. I told Zora Jane what he'd said.

"The timing does seem odd, doesn't it?" She smoothed her napkin thoughtfully. "But other than timing, there's nothing that connects."

I jiggled the ice cubes in my herbal iced tea. "Well, now we know Helen drove the Buick that night. That means Helen hit the little boy."

Zora Jane forked a bite of salad. "Right."

I set my glass on the table. "But there's no proof. Just hunches."

Zora Jane's eyes reflected sadness. "I'm afraid it's going to take more than hunches to get to the bottom of this."

"Also, I saw Helen and some guy at a motel in town." I described the sighting. "I need to talk to Helen again."

Zora Jane suggested we should pray for her instead.

I flopped back against the vinyl upholstery and frowned. "I know you're right. I just don't like it. Lila's still out there somewhere. I've got to do something to find her. No one else is working on that."

"Prayer is doing something." Zora Jane smiled sweetly. "God cares more about Lila than we do. We have to let go of our need to control this and let him work. That's what we do when we pray. We release our will and surrender to God's will. That's the 'Thy will be done' part."

I sighed. "But I don't see God doing anything."

"That's because we don't understand his timetable and we can't see everything like he can. God is never late. He's always on time."

We prayed for Lila right there at the table. And even for Helen and Will too.

After lunch, Zora Jane went to church for a ladies' ministry planning meeting, but I wanted to see the hit-and-run site. I hiked from the restaurant up the hill to the corner where it happened. Standing in the street, I prayed, *Please, God, lead me to truth.*

At the corner of Broad Street and Elm Avenue, the business district ended and the residential section began. To my right, the recently refurbished Union Hotel built in the 1890s dominated the street. To my left, a stately Victorian mansion with a large round tower and white picket fence lent a regal presence to the neighborhood. Across the avenue, another Queen Anne had been painted a garish pink. The gingerbread around its shingled front sported a rather disharmonious shade of pea green.

Color was desirable, but who chose that combination?

Around the front of the pink house, trees and shrubs hung like long, green bangs over the sidewalk, blocking visibility to Elm Avenue. That must be where the accident happened—a dangerous corner.

Why would a four-year-old be out after dark, anyway? Where was his mother? And why hadn't they cut back those trees and bushes?

I wandered closer, crossing the street. Could someone see the corner from inside any of these houses?

With no one around, I climbed the steps to the porch of the pink house, turned, and stared back at the street.

Good view from here.

I rang the doorbell.

Feet pattered toward the entryway. The woman who opened the door seemed frazzled. Her short-cropped hair stuck out like straw, and her makeup had faded and smeared. On one hip, she bounced a chubby baby. She spoke over children's laughter and squeals drifting from the interior. "Yes?"

"Hi. I'm investigating the hit-and-run on this corner several weeks ago. Did you see anything that night?"

"No. I was in the back, cleaning up. I already told the police that a couple times."

"Are you sure no one in your family saw anything? You can see the corner from here on the porch."

The baby expressed impatience with several loud cries.

The woman jiggled him on her hip. "Look … who did you say you are?" She shook her head and waved one hand dismissively. "Doesn't matter. I can't help you. Please excuse me." The gust of wind from the slamming door blew my bangs off my forehead.

One down. I marched to the imposing white Victorian and let myself through the gate in the white picket fence. A member of one of Nevada City's pioneering families still resided in this house—the older woman who spoke at church, Bessie Parrish. I climbed the blue stone steps to the covered porch and turned again to look at the corner. Here, too, a clear view of the accident site might be seen. Was Mrs. Parrish home that night?

I rang the bell. Big Ben chimes clanged "bing-bong-bing-bong-bing," appropriate for summoning an elderly Victorian lady, but no one answered—Victorian or otherwise. Maybe I could catch Mrs. Parrish at church sometime and question her about that night.

I rang the bell once more, just to hear the sound.

"Now what?" I wandered toward the old hotel. High on the second floor, side windows faced out at such an angle that a person couldn't see the street from them—unless the person happened to be a contortionist hanging out the window at just the right moment. Doubtful.

I circled to the last house on the intersection, kitty-corner to the Queen Anne—also a Victorian but considerably smaller. More Westlake, if I remembered my architectural styles correctly. Painted brown, it appeared to be in several stages of repair. Blue tarps covered a portion of the roof, and scaffolding trailed up one side. Matching bay windows on either end of the front entrance provided unobstructed views of the street corner. "Might as well try this one too."

I climbed the slate steps, rang the bell, and stepped back. A thirty-something woman opened the door, carrying a tea towel and glass bowl. I must have interrupted her washing the dishes.

She frowned slightly. "May I help you?"

"I hope so. I'm investigating the fatal hit-and-run on this corner a few weeks ago. Were you home that evening?"

"We were having a birthday party for my son. I've already spoken to the police. " She nodded toward the room at the right of the entryway. Through the arched opening, I saw part of a large mahogany dining table with chairs tucked around it.

"So, you were in there?" I stepped toward her, inclining my head toward the aforementioned dining room.

"Yes. Along with a dozen children eating birthday cake."

"Can you see the corner from that room?"

"Sure. But we weren't looking outside. Have you ever entertained a dozen ten-year-olds? They make a lot of noise. We didn't hear anything. We didn't even know something happened until the police showed up."

"Oh."

Now what?

A small inner voice urged me to pry a little deeper. I glanced back at the corner and bit my lip, thinking. The streetlight would have lit the corner at the time of the accident. "Did you take any pictures during the party?"

"I did. With my digital camera. Been too busy to look at them, though."

"Can I see them?" I didn't know what I'd find, but my heart fluttered as if I might be onto something.

She retreated into the house, returning with a silver pocket-size camera. She clicked it on and watched the photos whiz by on the tiny screen. "I'm sure there's nothing that will help you. I took all the pictures." She continued watching the monitor. "Nope. Can't see the street through the glass. Sorry."

She handed me the camera. In the foreground, a chunky boy with a pointy birthday hat attacked a large piece of chocolate cake with a plastic fork. Above his head, a burst of light flashed like fireworks in the window.

"Oh." I handed the camera back.

The woman clicked through a few more pictures. She paused at one, looking puzzled. "Well, I'll be darned! One of the kids must have taken the camera when I wasn't looking." She shook her head. "Those kids. But look. You *can* see the corner."

The picture was blurry, but clear enough to see a dark sedan stopped at the stop sign under the streetlight. The driver's-side door stood open, and a shadowy form hunched over a tiny lump lying in the street.

37

Chapter Thirty-seven

I'm sure I didn't open the door to let Molly out on Friday morning. Apparently, Jesse didn't notice when she sneaked out as he went down to feed the horses. That's my story and I'm sticking to it, unless we want to believe the cats let Molly out. However she did it, by the time I dressed and arrived in the kitchen, Molly had gone. I called her a couple of times, then I opened the sliding door and stepped onto the deck.

No Molly there either.

With a glance over the railing into the backyard, I called her again. Something dark caught my eye. In a pile of leaves under the blue oak lay a black object. I couldn't make out its identity, but the gate in the back fence stood wide open, so it must have come from the ashes. I hustled down the stairs to look.

Another gift—a fragment of jawbone with a few teeth still attached. Last year Molly dismantled a deer carcass she found beside the well in the pasture. For several weeks, she dragged up bones and left them in the yard. *Please let this be a deer.*

However, the black soot clinging to the bone meant it probably did *not* come from a decaying deer carcass.

What would a human jawbone look like? I shivered, cringing from touching it.

A flash of terror gripped me. "Molly. Molly! Come back here." I didn't see her at Will's rummaging through the fire mound, or anywhere along the back of the house. I scrambled toward the fence.

"Where has that dog gone now?" *Should I re-latch the gate?*

I didn't spy Will's pickup in its usual place in front of the house. He must be inside, though, given the hour. Silverthorne had reported that Will suffered a panic attack. They were concerned about his heart, which was beating abnormally. His blood pressure was too high as well. They scheduled a series of tests for the following week and sent Will home. Go figure. Someone sick enough to collapse like that and yet they didn't keep him at the hospital overnight. The quality of healthcare just kept declining.

Before pulling the gate closed, I hesitated, scanning the pasture.

A long, low howl rose to echo off the hills. Like no other sound I've ever heard except in my dream, its tone communicated loneliness and despair. I gasped in surprise, feeling the hairs on my neck prickle.

Barking followed soon after the howl died down. With a start, I recognized Molly's bark. Something must be wrong. I had to help.

This time I wasn't snooping. I was doing my neighborly duty. Yet, wasn't this where I started? Had I learned nothing from the predicaments my snoopiness caused?

I glanced toward my house and then at the barn, but didn't see a sign of Jesse.

"God, help me. What should I do?"

Urgency tugged my heart. I continued praying aloud as I picked my way down the slope. Foxtail spikes and burrs clawed at my legs. With difficulty, I climbed over the fence and hurried toward the back door of the gray house. "Stop me, God, if you don't want me to go."

The back door was locked, as was the sliding glass door on the small patio.

Déjà vu.

I circled to the front. The old truck snuggled close to the front door as if its driver hadn't been able to walk far. Dread shivered over me. Molly sat on the porch, whining like she wanted to do something but couldn't.

"Okay, Molly. I'll see what I can do."

Standing tall, I rapped on the door. Molly continued to whimper, so I gripped the knob. It turned in my hand. Without hesitating to wonder why the door wasn't locked, I pushed it open a slit and peered into the dimly lit entry. "Will? Mr. Payne, are you home?"

No answer. Then a muffled cry.

I called again. "Mr. Payne? It's me, Christine Sterling. Do you need help?" A louder moan made Molly commence whining again.

Although I knew I should go for help, I didn't want to leave him alone. "Dear God, what shall I do?"

On tiptoes, I moved toward the groans emanating from the stairwell.

So that I wouldn't surprise him, I kept talking in a loud voice. "Mr. Payne? Are you there? I'm coming to help you." I crept along the hallway. Standing in front of the stairway entrance, I hesitated before inching into a slow, deliberate descent with one hand supporting me along the wall. To my left, the door to the shrine room stood ajar.

Moans and sobs echoed off the cavernous walls.

"Mr. Payne? It's Christine Sterling."

An unrelenting recital of wrenching heartache greeted me. My brain said, *Run away!* but my feet didn't respond. I blinked to speed up adjustment to the darkness and forced myself forward until I stood in the open doorway.

Will Payne knelt in the center—precisely where the dark stain had been—rocking and sobbing in a deep, raspy voice.

Pale of skin, sweat dampening his shirt, he swung toward me when I entered. Intense pain radiated from his eyes. The right side of his face drooped. His left hand clutched his chest, knuckles and fingers drained of color to a ghostly white. The other also clenched into a fist, but the arm hung at his side.

I shivered in the chilly room.

Will didn't seem surprised to see me but reached out with the hand hanging at his side. The fist opened and a wad of paper fluttered to the floor. He whispered a slurred, "Lila."

"Mr. Payne." I toddled toward him. Just as I reached him, he toppled over, crumpling as if boneless. I wanted to run, but his look restrained me. I bent closer. "I … I need to find someone to help you."

His words were almost inaudible. "Please … don't go." Speaking seemed to require his total airflow. He sucked in another breath. "I … didn't … forget … what you wanted me … to do."

Eyes closed, he lay still as death.

I touched his chest. He was still breathing. "Hang on, Mr. Payne! I'll call someone to help you."

Heart racing out of control, I rushed upstairs to the back bedroom where I'd seen a rotary phone before. Dialing 9-1-1 seemed to take an eternity. Relief washed over me when a voice answered. The dispatcher requested information and then promised to send help immediately. I dropped the phone and watched it bounce on the carpet before it landed on a heap of clothes by the bed. Then I dashed downstairs to Mr. Payne's recumbent form.

The crumpled wad of paper lay undisturbed. My tidy-up reflex made me stoop to collect it without thinking—another page from Lila's poem book, written in a now-familiar hand, small, cramped, and obsessively neat, without punctuation or capitals.

baby waits he wont be denied
revenge is his at last
blaze in the fires of hell to atone
will my will its all there
dont forget you promised

Cradling his head in my lap, I reassured him help would arrive soon.

He opened his eyes, his gaze spearing through me. His black-rimmed glasses sat comically askew on his nose. I straightened them.

Although I had to concentrate to hear him, I think he said, "I … did … the best I could." Perhaps he wanted absolution. I didn't have that power. With exaggerated effort, he closed his eyes again.

"It's okay, Mr. Payne. They're coming to help you. Hang on. Someone will be here soon." With a fire station close by, I hoped they'd send paramedics from there instead of from town. I rocked slowly on my heels, unsure how to assist him.

When he opened his steely eyes a few minutes later, I saw renewed clarity. He seemed to understand who I was, or at least that I wasn't Lila. His words came out a bit clearer, though still slurred. "Head. Hurts. Bad." He blinked, chest heaving with forced breath. "Didn't mean her harm. That's … what she wanted."

In that moment, I knew Lila was dead, but I asked anyway. "Where is Lila?"

His lids quivered shut, but his voice continued—stronger as if he'd gained a slight second wind. "Had a cow once that lost her calf. Bawled all night long. Not just the first night, but the second and third. Next morning—" He pressed his hand on his head and closed his eyes. At least a minute passed before he spoke again. "Found the mama dead. Drowned in the river below the pasture."

My heart flip-flopped. "You mean Lila?"

He didn't seem able to hold his head straight. It flopped to the side and he gagged.

"Lila is dead. Is that what you're saying?"

He lifted thin eyelids with an effort that reminded me of prying open winter shutters. He gave a single nod, which seemed to require almost all his remaining energy. Icy fingers clutched my heart, and numbness set in.

The steeliness of his eyes softened to something more like lead. I cradled him in my arms, studying the face of this person I had so feared. With a jolt that jump-started my heart, I realized I wanted him to be okay. At that moment, he didn't seem sinister or scary. Just an old man in pain, a fellow creature with strengths and faults just like mine. That must be how God sees people when he looks at us.

I wished I could do more. I stroked his brow and prayed. "God be merciful to this man." All I knew was to recite the one Bible verse

I memorized as a child: John 3:16. "For God so loved the world, that he gave his one and only son, that whoever believes in him shall not perish, but have eternal life."

I repeated the verse twice, emphasizing different words each time. Gradually, the peace of God invaded the room. Will's body, once rigid and tense with pain, relaxed in my arms.

The piercing siren of an emergency vehicle wailed above us. The front door banged open and feet pounded down the stairs. Will's eyes opened one last time.

I asked, "Did you kill her, Mr. Payne? Did you kill Lila?"

He used all his breath to get out one word, "Fire." Then he sucked air with a loud, bronchial sound and whispered, "She made me do it."

38

Chapter Thirty-Eight

I waited by the phone until Zora Jane called with Silverthorne's report. William Payne had suffered a severe stroke. A CAT scan revealed hemorrhaging in his brain. Aphasia kept him from speaking. With a compromised airway, he had to be intubated in the ER. He slipped into a semi-comatose state, so they put him in ICU.

"Here's an odd thing," Zora Jane said. "Silverthorne got a full report on Alan Kliner from Des Moines police, including a picture and fingerprints."

Interesting. But not odd. "Uh-huh."

"Alan's neighbors told authorities he's been gone the last couple months. A search of his apartment turned up a flight itinerary for a trip to Sacramento in September. From the looks of his place, he hasn't been back since."

"Not possible. Jesse and I both spoke with Alan. Less than two weeks ago. He was in Iowa. At his house. There must be some mistake." From the way he talked, it sounded as if he'd never visited California. I tried to remember exactly what he said on the phone.

Zora Jane continued. "We don't know what to think about that. Silverthorne says he'll bring the picture when he comes this way next."

I didn't know what to think about that either.

Based on my conversation with Will prior to his stroke, detectives and forensic analysts swarmed the Payne property. Molly and I watched from the deck as they cordoned off the area with wide yellow ribbons of crime scene tape. We stayed away, though, and let the experts work. I knew what they would find. Silverthorne said the investigators used fluorescein and a UV scope to illuminate a large bloodstain in the middle of the floor in the former shrine room.

According to the newspaper article that appeared a few days later, a lengthy search of the ash mound uncovered parts of a skull, assorted bone fragments, and teeth belonging to a petite female in her forties. The blackened jawbone fragment matched the same person. What I'd seen leaning against the wall in the downstairs room had been Lila's tiny body wrapped in a roll of carpet instead of a casket. Will incinerated her on a funerary pyre along with all her possessions, just as Native Americans did in centuries past. What the article couldn't tell me was why. Will's last words echoed in my brain like a stuck record. "She made me do it."

Which "she?" Helen or Lila?

Sunday morning's newspaper featured a front-page spread about Lila's death. Apparently, crime scene investigators extracted a bullet from the forehead of the skull. Guns registered to Will Payne were confiscated for testing. No match could be made, however. A records search revealed no registered firearms in Helen's name, but detectives searched the 1995 Bayliner Capri—*Miss Misery*—found in Helen Sterne's garage to look for one anyway. Failing to find a gun, the issue of the murder weapon went unresolved.

I caught up with Silverthorne at the sheriff's office. He'd just come out of a meeting with Deputy Dunn. At the door connecting the waiting area with the inner offices, the two stood facing each other.

Silverthorne smiled when he saw me. "Hey! I was coming out your way pretty soon."

"I wanted to know if you've made any progress on the photograph from the hit-and-run scene." I'd gone directly to the sheriff's office after I found it.

They glanced at each other. Dunn answered. "Forensics magnified the license number and it matches the Buick's."

"Excellent. Did they identify the hunched-over person?"

Silverthorne spoke. "Couldn't make a positive ID. But it's definitely a female. Since Helen already admitted she drove the Buick that night, I'm sure that's enough to convince a jury."

Dunn nodded. "They're re-examining the vehicle at the impound lot."

Memories of Helen's scream that penetrated the double panes of her kitchen window flashed to mind. "When I heard her say *accident*, she meant the hit-and-run."

Silverthorne nodded. "Looks that way."

"So that means you can arrest her for killing that boy. At the minimum, she fled the scene of a fatal accident."

They flicked another glance at each other before Dunn said, "Already issued an APB."

Silverthorne's voice sounded weary. "Helen has disappeared."

Later that afternoon, I waited for a meeting with the Callahans and Silverthorne. I wandered to my office and got out my yellow legal pad of notes again. With a blue Sharpie, I drew a thick line through all the irrelevant data, then tried to reorganize the rest. Knowing several new facts, I hoped the solution would materialize. Now we knew that Helen killed Lila's baby and little Marcus Whitney. We knew Lila was dead. But how did she die?

Also, a couple details about the hit-and-run didn't make sense. The Buick's back license showed in the birthday party photo. So the car faced away from the house. That meant Helen was driving *toward* Highway 49 instead of *away*. She hadn't just made a detour when she hit the four-year-old. She was returning to the freeway from somewhere else. Where did she go first? What was she doing at that corner?

How about Alan Kliner? He couldn't be in California. We had talked to him in Iowa. I leaned back in my desk chair and closed my eyes. Unfortunately, a mental solution didn't materialize. Instead, I remembered Helen using past tense when we talked about Lila at the hardware store weeks before. Why hadn't I picked that up then? Some sleuth I turned out to be.

I stood and stared out the window at the gray house.

A shadowy silhouette darted across one of the windows—someone in Will's bedroom.

Who?

"I bet I know where Helen is."

I tore downstairs and raced for the arena where Jesse and Ranger practiced. We could catch her if we didn't create too much noise, so I didn't want to yell.

Jesse had just rounded a barrel when he saw me coming. He stopped and crossed his hands over the saddle horn. "To what do we owe the honor of this visit?"

Huffing from the run down the hill, I jabbed a finger toward Will's. "Someone's inside down there. Hurry!"

Jesse swung off Ranger—leaving him to wander the arena fully saddled—and led the way through the pasture. I followed closely, head down. Just before we got to the gate between our property and Will's, he stopped abruptly. I slammed into his back.

"What?" I whispered.

"Just saw her. She's in the kitchen." He plucked his cell phone from his shirt pocket.

I raised my eyebrows. Since when did Jesse start carrying that thing?

He punched in someone's number, waited, then whispered, "It's Jesse Sterling. We're watching someone at Will's. Think it's Helen." … "Meet you there." He snapped his flip phone shut.

By the time we arrived at the front door, Ed Callahan had gotten there too. They conferred in whispers before Ed crouched to hurry toward the back of the house. Then Jesse gestured toward the front door. We hunched like commandos and tiptoed, crouching behind bushes whenever possible.

The door creaked when Jesse pushed it open. We froze a second before entering cat-paw quiet and turning right toward the kitchen. Slamming cupboard doors informed us of the whereabouts of Helen's frantic search. Turning the corner with extreme stealth, we hauled up short at our first glimpse of the intruder.

It wasn't Helen.

Slight of build and rough, the black-clad man from the motel stood on a box, rummaging through a cabinet. He startled when he realized he had company. Catching himself before falling, he issued a profanity. "What are you doin' here?"

With a bold step, Jesse entered the room with me directly behind. "We might ask you the same question."

Just then, Ed jimmied the back door. It popped open and he pounced inside, weapon drawn. Ed looked shocked, straightened, and gave the man a quick once-over. "You're not Helen."

Footsteps from the front door made us all jump. In seconds, Zora Jane led Silverthorne into the room.

Silverthorne looked puzzled a moment before addressing the black-leathered man. "You must be Alan Kliner."

39

Chapter Thirty-Nine

According to Silverthorne's report, Alan Kliner wouldn't say much. Not why he came to California in September. Not how he knew Helen or what they were doing at the motel. Nothing about Lila's death. But he got real choked up when he talked about her. Silverthorne thought it was an act. After questioning Alan for hours at the sheriff's office, they let him go, advising him not to leave town until the loose ends got tied up.

"We seem to be stuck," Silverthorne said. "Alan's involved, but we don't know how. Will can't talk yet; still too sick." A weighty sigh tumbled out. "No one knows how Lila died. With the angle of the gunshot wound in the skull fragments they found, the coroner can't say for certain whether her death was suicide or murder. There's no way to establish the exact time of death." He shook his head. "We need more than bone fragments. We know the Coopers saw Helen leave between seven and seven thirty, instead of six to six fifteen like she says. According to Helen's statement, when she left, Lila was still alive. We have no way to confirm or exclude that statement. We've got Helen for the hit-and-run and the murder of Baby Blue, but we can't find her."

"Those are big problems," Ed said.

"We re-interviewed everyone, hoping they'd say something different. No such luck. I just wanted to ask you to pray."

"Good idea," Zora Jane said.

Silverthorne rubbed his eyes. He looked as if he needed a vacation or at the minimum, several nights of sound sleep. "You folks don't know anything about some treasure Will kept at his house, do you?"

We shook our heads.

"Why?" Jesse asked.

"Alan's been camping in the woods on Will's property, looking for something. He's the vagrant the sheriff's office arrested awhile back. Will mentioned someone breaking into his garage and rifling through his stuff. Maybe that's why Alan came out here a month ago."

Ed looked thoughtful. "It's a good thing they let him go, then. We'll watch for him. See if he tries again."

Jesse and I exchanged a glance. How could Alan have been here and in Iowa at the same time? What would Alan be searching for at Will's house?

I knew Jesse felt torn about going away for the weekend. But he'd been looking forward to this next shoot for a month, so I persuaded him to go and not worry about me. He needed to do something fun. What good would staying home do anyway? There'd been no sign of anyone at Will's since we found Alan. Helen must be hiding somewhere. Alan wouldn't be dumb enough to break in now that he knew we were watching.

So Jesse reluctantly left on Friday morning. He wasn't going far, only about an hour away, so he could get home quickly. I felt good about his decision.

Near dusk on Saturday, I went to fix my dinner. In the quiet kitchen, I piled leftover chicken enchiladas and rice from last night on a plate and slipped it into the microwave. This one modern technological innovation I deemed completely necessary. I had no idea why a person would ever need, say, an HDTV iPod with

Wi-Fi—I didn't even know what that was—but quick heating for leftovers made perfect sense.

Molly sat beside me when I placed my meal on the kitchen table.

"Thank you, God, for this food and for all your bountiful gifts," I prayed. "Please keep Jesse safe and help us get to the bottom of who killed Lila."

When I opened my eyes, a glimmer of light drew my attention down the hill. "Now, who do you suppose would be down there?" I cut into the enchilada and scooped the chunk into my mouth. Helen or Alan?

I chewed while light winked in Will's bedroom window. The light bobbed and swung, as if from a flashlight.

"What is she looking for? Or he?"

Molly batted her brown eyes adoringly. She licked her lips, anticipating a donation from my plate.

Jesse gave her table scraps. I never did.

She rested her chin on my leg. Her hot breath steamed through my jeans as she panted. Soft brown eyes blinked again. "You make it hard, don't you, old girl?" I rubbed her ears while I watched the lights a few minutes longer. Maybe it wasn't either of them. Ongoing news coverage alerted the community to the now-uninhabited state of the gray house. Plenty of bad guys watched TV. Could be a thief looting the place.

"I should call Deputy Dunn, don't you think?"

Molly just stared at me.

I went to the deck, hoping for a better view.

When I returned to the kitchen, I punched in the phone number for the Nevada County Sheriff's Office. The light flickered in and out of windows while I waited for someone to answer. "Deputy Dunn, please."

"Sorry," the dispatcher said. "Deputy Dunn is not available. Would you like his voicemail?"

"Sure. But maybe I should speak with whoever is there because if he doesn't get this soon, it'll be too late."

Apparently she didn't hear the last sentence because she'd already connected me to Dunn's answering message. I paced while the message completed. "This is Christine Sterling. I see lights on at Will's house. If you're looking for Helen Sterne, she's probably down there."

I hung up feeling dissatisfied so I dialed Silverthorne's cell phone. His answering message rolled. I sighed. What's the point of carrying a phone with you if you're not going to answer it when you're needed?

The lights continued to move.

Maybe I should have asked for the officer on duty. There must be others working this case with Dunn.

What if I just run down there and check it out myself?

I stood at the window, watching. After a minute or so, the light went out. I held my breath until a spark of light flickered in the kitchen window.

Not stopping to consider the consequences, I plodded down the hill as darkness settled over the hillside. I would just peek in the windows, go straight home, and call the sheriff's office again.

Previously, I had success peeking in windows. I braced against the side of the house and pulled myself up slowly until I could see into the kitchen with one eye.

In the eerie light cast by what appeared to be an industrial-size camping lantern, Helen rummaged furiously through the kitchen cabinets. Light from under her chin painted horror-film shadows on her face. Gaping cabinet doors marked the path she'd already searched. Boxes and trash cluttered her wake.

Fixed in amazement, I watched while she exited the room. Doors slammed and search noises commenced in another location. I crouched as still as possible until my muscles ached, before slinking around the house toward the bedrooms. With care, I stooped low to slide under each window—in case she might peek out.

I circled the back and then the side. When I arrived at the front of the attached garage, I slid between the outside wall and a tall shrub, where I fit snugly with a clear view of the front walkway and the garage. I'd stay put and see what she was up to.

The chilly air made me shiver. Why didn't I grab a jacket and maybe my cell phone? Also, why didn't I think of calling Jesse's cell phone? I never thought of cell phones. On the rare occasion I managed to carry the thing, I wouldn't have remembered to turn it on or charge it up. Useless technology.

The bang of the front door startled me. Perhaps Helen didn't realize how much noise she made. When the light grew brighter, I retreated deeper into my hidey-hole.

When she arrived at the garage, she paused to study the inside. Maybe she just noticed the wood stacked in her way. *How will she search through that?*

I inched out so I could peek around the corner.

Feet spread apart, a leather tool belt strapped around her hips, Helen's tall form draped the door of the rounded refrigerator. Gripped in her hands, she wielded some type of tool with long handles—perhaps the bolt cutter I'd seen her purchase at the hardware store. She suddenly compressed the tool and with a mighty snap, the lock popped open. She grunted a profanity. "What kind of lunatic padlocks a refrigerator?"

She jerked the door open and crouched to peer inside. Yanking out each item, she inspected it in the lantern light. I strained to see over her shoulder. The refrigerator appeared to be packed with leftover food containers.

She slung down a Chinese take-out box whose contents might have been growing hair. It smashed on the concrete driveway. "Disgusting! Why save this?" She opened several plastic containers and cursed in disapproval before turning to the rows of wood.

Stepping closer, Helen lifted the lantern higher until it lit the rafters. I leaned farther out to inspect the rusty fishing poles, woven fishing creel, and wooden dynamite crates with her. The wobbly pile of flattened cardboard boxes appeared as unstable as ever. The light moved to the ledge where the brown suitcase once rested.

Helen plopped the lantern onto the floor. I pulled back without a sound.

Helen stomped toward the house. When she returned, she dragged a ladder behind her. She propped it at the front of the wood and teetered slowly up the rungs. She could reach the box pile if she stood on tiptoe. After a moment, she dragged down a few boxes and threw them on top of the wood. These provided a smooth surface to crawl across.

She hesitated, testing the first box. Her footing held, so she proceeded farther. By re-adjusting the boxes as she came to them, she continued until she arrived under the wooden crates. Once there, she stood tall. She tugged gently, liberating the crate from its perch. It landed on the cardboard with a puff of displaced dust.

Following a quick glance inside the box, Helen flung it aside onto the rows of wood and turned her attention to the other box. When she pulled it down, she caught it like a circus acrobat and extracted a canvas bag. She peered inside, cursed, and tossed the second box onto the wood, producing another cloud of dust.

Arms akimbo, she inspected the line of cabinets at the back of the garage. "How'm I gonna get into those?"

Seemed like at least a minute passed while she pondered, looking like a colossus atop the wood. I shifted as another shiver passed over me.

I must have made noise without realizing. Helen jerked her head around. "Who's there?" She clambered off the woodpile and picked up the lantern. "Show yourself!"

While she slunk toward me, I shrunk farther inside my hiding place.

"Who's out there?"

My knees knocked.

From the tool belt, she produced a revolver. Lantern light glinted off the gun barrel. "Come out, now! Or I'll shoot."

The gun moved so close, I could almost grab it. With my luck, she'd shoot me anyway. Not knowing what else to do, I crept out of my lair.

She uttered another expletive. "Who is it?" She hefted the lantern higher. "What are you doing there?"

"It's me. Christine Sterling."

"Not the meddling neighbor again. I should shoot you right now."

If I chose my words with extreme caution, maybe I'd have a slight chance to keep her from shooting me. *Think like a negotiator.* "I saw lights, that's all, so I came to see what's going on."

"You got no right to be here." She gestured wildly with the gun, dark eyes gleaming like burning coal.

The hair on top of my head prickled as I stared down the barrel of that gun. Could this be the gun that killed Lila? The gun no one could find? With great resolve, I held myself calm on the outside and pretended not to see it. "You don't have any right to be here either. The sheriffs are looking for you."

She snorted. "Let 'em look. That's none of your affair. You need to go home before my finger gets itchy." She raised the gun higher, waving it in a threatening manner as if to make sure I could see it.

I retreated—inching backward so I wouldn't have to turn my back on a madwoman carrying a weapon—and kept my voice calm. "I just came to see who was here. Now I've seen and I'll be on my way."

She followed. "Hold on, Missy. You know I really can't let you go, don't you? You'll just go home and call the sheriff." She frowned. "This does complicate things. If I shoot you, they'll know I did it unless I can make it look accidental. Maybe like you were breaking into the house."

Dear God, what now? Give me the right words.

Could I keep her talking until I figured how to get away? I straightened to my full height and faced her, fighting off a wave of gun-induced nausea. "It looks like you're hunting for something." Many words were running through my brain just then, but not *those* words. *God, are you speaking from my lips?*

Helen leaned toward me, her glare spreading across her face. "How do you know that?"

I forced the tremor from my voice, ignoring the horrific thumping in my chest. "Do you have any idea what you're looking for?"

She scowled over the gun. "Who told you?"

"You don't, do you?"

The gun shook, but she didn't answer.

Nerves and guns—not a good combination. I sidestepped two paces. The gun shadowed me. My knees nearly buckled. The power to speak with a gun pointed in my direction must've come by divine intervention. "Let me help you."

"Help me? How?"

I backed away another step. "What do you think it is?"

She shrugged.

"Why do you think something's hidden?"

She waved the gun wildly. "Alan told me."

I stopped moving and blinked at her.

"Will hid something valuable. Lila watched. She told Alan." She used the gun as a pointer to emphasize her words.

I held up both hands to stall while I considered how to convince her she needed my help. Just keep babbling. "But you have no idea what it is."

"Right."

"Where have you looked?"

She cocked her head. "Alan looked through the garage. The one that's locked."

A drop of perspiration trickled down my back. I opened my mouth and babbled more. "My dad hid his stash in his bedroom. He wanted it close so he could get it fast." Inch by inch, shifting from one foot to another, I put more distance between us while I shuffled through memories of my father's intense paranoia over valuables.

The gun wobbled and lowered an inch. "I already looked everywhere."

"Are you sure?"

This time when she cocked her head to consider, she lowered the gun another notch.

Way to go, Christine. Distraction. It's your best weapon.

I continued my slow backward slide. "My dad didn't want to get trapped in the house with no defense in case the Communists attacked. So he kept cash in his bedroom—guns and ammunition too. I bet it's in his bedroom."

When I'd cleared the garage sufficiently, I spun on my heel, racing toward the front of the house.

Helen advanced faster than I would've believed a woman her size could move, waving her weapon like a Zulu warrior. "Oh, no, you don't!" Her long-legged strides closed the gap between us in a couple of seconds. She grabbed my hair roughly, knocking me off balance. "You want to help so bad? Fine. I could use an assistant." She dragged me toward the front door. "Come right in, Missy. I can always shoot you later."

I braced my feet, trying to skid to a stop. I couldn't go into that house. I might never get out again.

But she had height and strength on her side, not to mention a loaded weapon. She shoved me through the door. "Okay, genius, let's see what *you* can find."

40

Chapter Forty

The force of her thrust sent me slumping to the floor. She pressed the gun to my back, grabbing my arm to pull me upright. I moved sluggishly, almost paralyzed by fear. She handed me the lantern. I shuffled ahead through the darkened house, pausing in the doorway of Will's bedroom. Might as well start there. I found the light switch.

The maple dresser lay upturned on the carpet, its drawers scattered haphazardly. The small bedside table languished under a large rocking chair tipped on one side.

Helen pointed at the mess. "I already looked through here."

"You looked under the bed?"

"Of course."

"Between the mattresses?"

Sarcasm edged her tone. "Naturally."

I surveyed the room again. "How about the closet?"

She wiggled the gun at me. "You'll have to do better than that."

Shivering, I opened the closet door. The search tornado had already spun through there as well. Piles of clothing littered the floor.

Where would Will put something he didn't want anyone to find? *Dear Lord, help me.* With nowhere else to look, I gazed upward for divine inspiration.

Helen's eyes followed mine to the cutout attic door I'd noticed on my first visit. Like most houses of that era, a rope hung from the ceiling by which a folded ladder could be pulled down to gain access to the attic. She grabbed the rope and the ladder unfolded.

Helen motioned with the tip of the gun. Knees shaking as if afflicted with palsy, I climbed the unsteady ladder. At the top, I pushed on the trap door. It held tight. I pushed again, harder.

She snorted. "Put your weight into it."

Even in my terrified state, I stopped to stare at her. Was that a wisecrack about my weight? She waggled the gun at me with her skinny-minny arm.

I stomped up another rung, put my shoulder against the door, and shoved. The door popped open with a resounding *crack*.

Standing on tiptoes, I peered into the darkness.

Helen lifted the lantern. "Take this."

I could throw it. But if I missed, she'd shoot me right here.

Not willing to take the chance, I pushed the lantern through the opening, setting it on a nearby rafter. Then I hesitated. Helen climbed a few rungs and wiggled the gun at me again, so I pulled through the opening and sat on the ledge to rest, panting like a dog from the exertion.

It must be true, what Jesse said. I wasn't as young as I used to be.

The lantern illuminated a dusty space. The air smelled stale enough to be well past expiration date. Mouse droppings made my skin crawl, but I didn't hear skittering creatures. My eyes scanned the attic for windows or exits. No way out.

With my limited experience, I judged this attic as typical—except for a small rectangular platform about the size of half a card table just a few paces from the opening.

Helen bellowed from below. "What's up there?"

"Nothing really. It's just … I don't know why a platform would be here." I straddled the rafters with care. I didn't want to fall between them and get my leg stuck in the ceiling. She would leave me to die. Why didn't I send word to someone before coming down here?

After I reached the platform, I set the lantern on a rafter and crouched to inspect the boards.

Helen stuck her head through the opening. "What platform?"

Around the perimeter, the boards sat snugly, nailed in place like a frame. The center section wobbled when I stepped on it. "I think this part comes out."

She shifted the gun to her other hand and waved it. "Well, get it out."

I pushed my finger over the crack, but it wouldn't go in. "I need something to pry it out."

She produced a long screwdriver from her tool belt.

I jammed the screwdriver under the center section. Maybe I could jab her in the eye with the screwdriver. If I didn't do it just right, though, she'd shoot me. With gentle coaxing, I lifted the wood out in one piece. Beneath, three flat strongboxes had been wedged into the space, each secured by a heavy-duty padlock.

Helen leaned closer. "Pull them out."

I tugged. The boxes didn't budge. "They're stuck."

"Don't be such a lightweight." Helen grabbed the screwdriver from my hand and climbed all the way into the attic, positioning herself between the opening and me, careful to place the gun out of my reach.

Again, I contemplated using the lantern as a weapon but couldn't reach it without going around her. Instead, over the next couple of minutes, I assisted her.

Soon, the exertion had both of us panting.

Helen sat back on her haunches. "We'll just pop them open right where they sit."

She disappeared down the hole with the gun and the lantern, slamming the attic door shut. Sudden thick darkness filled the attic space—so dense, I couldn't tell where the access door had been. How would Jesse ever find me here? I imagined the headlines: *Remains of Grass Valley Woman Discovered in Attic Fifty Years after*

Disappearance. My groan echoed in the empty space. I'd have to jump between every rafter in this attic to find that little door. Surely, she wouldn't leave me forever. Not with these boxes unopened.

After a few minutes, she re-appeared carrying her heavy-duty bolt cutters. Strength renewed, she cut through one padlock with a loud *snap.* I imagined drool dripping from her mouth as she pulled back the lid. "Get the light."

I wanted to grab the bolt cutters out of her hand and bash her head for leaving me in the scary darkness, but I couldn't do it fast enough without her noticing. So, I moved to her other side and picked up the lantern as she directed.

Rows of tubes lined the box—tubes filled with gold coins.

The sight dazzled me. I'd never seen so much gold before. "That's a lot of gold."

She mumbled to herself. "*That's* why Will was always so interested in the price of gold."

"What did you think you would find?"

She settled on a rafter where she positioned the gun out of my reach. "Money, you know—bills. Will didn't trust banks." After opening a tube, she poured the contents into her lap. I'd guess the coins were one ounce each—the kind packaged ten to a tube. They jingled musically. She cupped them in her hands and let them slip through her fingers like water.

An inner voice commanded me to run, although I didn't know how I'd get around her and through the opening. The gun rested close to her right hand. No matter how fast I moved, I'd be dead before I got to the ladder. While the gold held her attention, maybe I could probe for answers, just in case I survived this ordeal.

My heart pounded wildly, but I kept the fear out of my voice. "This is Will's gold. Why did Lila tell Alan about it?"

She turned her head toward me as if she'd just noticed my presence. "What?"

"I don't get this whole thing."

She grunted and shook her head. "Lila thought someone wanted to kill Will for his treasure. That's what she told Alan. He offered to split it with me if we found it." After restacking the coins in the tube, she sat back in the small space. Rocking on her feet, she picked up tube after tube to examine it in the lantern light. Her eyes glimmered, reflecting the gold.

I slid toward the opening, pretending to shift weight to a more comfortable position. "Did Will know about this?"

Her voice remained as calm as the eye of a hurricane, and her eyes never left the pile of gold. "Of course not. He never met Alan. I never told him anything."

"So Alan hunted for the gold in the afternoon while Will went to your house?"

She continued to fondle the gold, dropping a few coins in her lap. "Of course, I never would have split it. Will isn't strong. I had to protect him. Same as I always have."

The chills returned. "But Lila was in the way. Alan couldn't search the house with her here. That's why you had to kill her, right?"

Helen's eyes were glued to the gold, but she expelled a long sigh. "She just wouldn't go away, no matter what I did."

I moved a little farther. "So … you shot her. And then you convinced Will to burn her body with the trash."

In the semi-darkness, I couldn't tell whether she nodded again. *Where is that gun?* Both hands held gold, so it seemed safe to keep moving. I maneuvered to a position directly behind her. She took no notice. "One thing has always bothered me. The first time I saw Will, he was throwing away Lila's clothes. Why did he throw out her clothes before she died?"

She laughed dryly. "That witch was crazy. He filled the garage with stuff she didn't want in the house. I cleaned out her belongings and packed them in boxes—told him it was trash and he should burn it."

I shook my head. "How clever. You made the plan, and Will carried it out."

"Will thought Lila was starving to death. I told him I'd get help for her. That's what he thought I meant to do that night—take her for help."

In slow motion, I reached out to brace my arms on the sides of the opening where I could lower myself onto the ladder below. "But you shot her instead."

"Stupid cow ran from me." Her voice became flat again. "Will believes she shot herself."

My stomach lurched. "One other thing. The hit-and-run. That four-year-old in Nevada City. You killed him too."

"That was an accident," she whispered.

I'd almost gotten my feet through the opening, but I leaned back to catch her words. "Right. But why were you in Nevada City that night?"

She snorted. "Stupid! That's why. I didn't use the main highway for fear of being seen. I went the long way around Grass Valley and Nevada City." She shook her head with vehemence. "I never get a break."

"Well, now you have. The other boxes must be full of gold too. You've got a lot of money here. Things are going to be great now."

In an instant, she exploded with rage. "No!" Her shriek echoed in the small space.

I froze.

As abruptly as Helen raised her voice, she lowered the volume but not the intensity. "You have spoiled everything. You meddling busybody. You will talk, won't you?" She picked up the black pistol and aimed it at my head. Evil flashed in her eyes as she hissed. "I can't let you do that."

The gun barrel kissed my temple.

My heart thundered in my ears, but I kept my voice calm and lied. "You don't need to be afraid of me, Helen. Why would I tell anyone? I understand what you've been through. Will's your brother. Lila was crazy. You did what you had to."

My searching feet found the highest ladder rung. I stood in the hole, hoping the height gave me a look of authority. "Put the gun away." I struggled to control the quiver of fear creeping into my voice. "I'll help you carry your gold down."

"I don't think so." Although her voice sounded even, unveiled rage pulsed the air.

She cocked the gun. The click echoed in the quiet attic.

Reflex took over. I slapped the gun out of her hand and knocked over the lantern. The gun clattered between the rafters. Tubes of gold bounced off Helen's lap and tinkled as they scattered when she grabbed the lantern and lunged for her pistol. I dove out of sight down the ladder before she regained control. By the time she made the opening, I'd nearly reached the floor.

She stuck her head through and aimed the gun.

Gripping one side of the ladder, I jumped, pulling sideways. I crashed to the floor. Pain exploded in my feet and ankles. I bolted from the bedroom like a crippled racehorse. Helen screamed curses. The doorjamb splintered as a bullet zinged into the wood beside my head.

She actually meant to kill me.

I hobbled down the hall.

How would I make it up that hill? *Dear God, give me strength.*

But when I threw open the front door, I collided with Ed and Silverthorne, pistols drawn.

41

Chapter Forty-one

The late afternoon sun diffused through sapphire, gold, and emerald stained-glass panes in the hospital chapel and sparkled on the opposite wall. Kneeling in front of the carpeted altar, I watched the dancing light through tears. For most of the last half hour, I'd pleaded with God to bring Lila's murderer swiftly to justice and heal William Payne. While I cried and prayed, stress loosed its steely grip on my soul, and in its place rested a firm certainty that God could still be trusted. Whether he healed William Payne so we could hear the complete story or not, God's ultimate goodness would not fail. Prayer might not change God's plan, but it changed me. The closer I got to having a real relationship with God, the more my thinking aligned with his.

I sensed someone in the small room and turned to see Jesse sitting quietly in the front row, head bowed. I hadn't seen him since he came home from his weekend that afternoon. I grabbed my Kleenex box and joined him, still sniffing.

He patted my thigh when I settled beside him. "How's the ankle?"

Sniffing again, I shrugged. The ankle I landed on when I jumped from the ladder had sustained nothing worse than a bad sprain. "It'll give me a good excuse for getting out of work for a week or so."

"I'm really sorry, Chris." He stared at the light shimmering through the window. His chin quivered. "I shouldn't have gone. I knew I should stick around."

I bit my lip and shook my head, laying a finger softly across his mouth. "It's okay. All of it."

"But she had a gun. She could have—" His voice broke. He reached for me, pulling me so close I thought my ribs might break. Jesse did care.

I let the sweet feeling wash over me a moment, holding my breath. Then I attempted a protest, but my head pressed to his shoulder muffled my voice.

He loosened his grip. "What?"

I gulped air. "Nothing really awful happened. God protected me. But what I discovered is that even if he hadn't, he knows what's right and he always does it."

His eyes bored into mine as if trying to see inside my soul. For once, I had his full attention. "Do you truly believe that?"

I nodded. "God's plan is good. I may not always like it, but I believe it will always turn out for the best."

After another pause to stare into my eyes, Jesse turned away to reach for the plastic bag he'd stuffed on his other side. "Here. I brought you a souvenir."

Jesse got me a gift? My heart overflowed. Jesse could barely remember to buy a birthday card. Oops! I almost lapsed into that old complaining spirit again. *Lord, help me.* "Jesse, how thoughtful." The shopping bag rustled in my fingers.

He nodded, looking almost shy. "I had them wrap it in your favorite paper too. Go ahead. Open it."

I tugged the bag open and pulled out something wrapped in pink tissue. Tearing through that, I reflected on this sweet gesture. Whatever got into him?

I unfolded the contents and shook out a robins egg blue T-shirt. On the front, an old lady bounced with glee on a pogo stick, wisps of gray hair flying loose from her lop-sided bun and a smile as wide as if she'd won the lottery.

Jesse assumed a Cheshire cat grin. "Turn it over."

On the back, in white block letters, the caption read:

> STAY OUT OF MY WAY!
> I JUMP TO CONCLUSIONS

When we finished laughing, Jesse sandwiched my small hand between his strong ones. "So did you ever figure out who killed Lila?"

"Can't prove she did, but I'm sure it was Helen. Alan must have come to California to search for Will's 'treasure' after Lila told him about it. Somehow, he connected with Helen and they decided to collaborate. I don't know if Alan was in on killing Lila or not. Don't know how to find that out." I shook my head. "But I still don't get how Alan could have been in Iowa and out here at the same time."

"Oh, that," Jesse smiled. "I think I know."

"How?"

"At the shoot, my friend Express Man called me. You met him, remember?"

"Pony Express rider. Sure."

"Well, he called from Colorado. But when I looked at my cell phone, it showed his Nevada County number."

I frowned. "How?"

Jesse's grin widened. "I said, 'Thought you went to Colorado.' He said, 'Yeah.' I said, 'How come your phone number shows up with the California area code?' Express Man says, 'I'm calling on my cell phone, dummy. It's the same number wherever I go.' See?"

It took me a moment. "We thought we called Alan's home phone in Iowa, but it was his cell phone."

Jesse nodded. "Right. Alan and his cell phone were in California. If we weren't such technology chuckleheads, we'd have thought of that sooner."

I never would have thought of it, but I didn't say so. At least I finally understood how Alan could have been in two places at once. He wasn't.

Molly darted eagerly in front of me as I re-latched the gate beside the front driveway. Gray clouds threatened rain in the chilly afternoon, but my ankle had nearly healed—although it was still wrapped for added strength—and Molly needed a walk. I carried the crutches just in case I couldn't hobble home. The fall colors were beautiful, although many leaves had already fallen to crunch beneath our feet. Jesse's leaf blower had been busy for most of the week, creating oak-leaf mountains in the pasture.

Molly and I moseyed down Paso Fino Place, admiring God's handiwork. We strolled down the hill past our barn and up again, turning left at Percheron Drive just as we did on our first visit to Will's house when I'd vacillated about going all the way to the front door. *Thank you, God, for keeping me going.*

God answered prayers for improvement of my marriage too, and supplied the picture of the hit-and-run. How amazing to retrace God's hand and see the way he'd been working all along. He *did* hear when I prayed after all. I'd just never stopped to think about the answers after they arrived or given him credit.

At Mustang Hill Road, Molly automatically veered left, leading the way. We passed the mailboxes where I'd put up the fliers. I thanked God for bringing her home. Then we came to Will's driveway and hesitated. Molly sat and I stood still at the top of the gravel roadway, saluting the property. This time, she didn't whine to urge me onward. She sat panting quietly and staring down at the house.

The gray house had truly been abandoned. A large For Sale sign stood at the entrance to the gravel driveway, dug in among the decaying iris stalks. Potential buyers weren't stopping in droves to view the house. Zora Jane said the Realtor priced it at a bargain and she supposed it hadn't been marketed properly.

A navy blue two-door Toyota hatchback rolled to a stop at the mailboxes and a young woman stepped out. The breeze tugged blond tendrils out of the ponytail at the top of her head and whipped them around her face. Her long legs and coltish movements reminded me of a fawn taking its first tentative steps.

She noticed Molly at the same time she reached the mailboxes. Stopping in mid-motion, one hand on the mailbox door, the girl smiled in our direction. Tail wagging, Molly raced toward her.

I called, "Molly." But she didn't stop.

Molly got to the girl before I did. She knelt to embrace Molly's soft black-and-white body. Would Lila look like this if she had lived a normal life?

As I neared, the girl lifted brown doe eyes to meet me. "Is this your dog?"

"Yes." I frowned, wondering how she became acquainted with my dog.

She flashed a beautiful smile. "Um. I'm the one who found your dog last month."

"Oh, my goodness! Hello." I extended my hand. "I can't thank you enough for picking her up. We're most grateful." I pumped her hand with vigor. "My name's Christine Sterling."

"I'm Amber. Um, Amber Cervine. Nice to meet you."

"Sorry I didn't get your name when you called that day. I got so excited about finding Molly, I didn't remember to thank you properly. Please forgive me."

"Oh, um, no problem. I'm just glad you got your dog back."

Her gaze settled on our clasped hands. Embarrassed that I still held onto her, I dropped her hand at once.

She reflected my feelings with a delicate blush.

"Could I get your name and address, Amber? I want to thank you for taking time to look after our dog. She means a great deal to us. She's been part of our family for a long time."

"That's so not necessary."

I laid a hand on her arm. "Please."

"Okay, um, sure. Here, let me write it down for you." She ducked into the car. When she popped out, she held a sheet of notebook paper on which she'd written her name and address in round juvenile writing.

"Your friend was with you, right?"

She nodded.

"Please write his name too."

She added the words "Tom Dale" underneath her address and handed the paper to me. Then she stared toward Will's house. Wind-whipped wisps of hair danced around her face. "It's awful what happened in that house, isn't it? That poor woman!" Details of the investigation still dominated local headlines and news stations.

"Dreadful. A horrible thing!"

She sighed wistfully. "I guess it happened the same night we found your dog."

Startled, I fixed my eyes hard on her. "What time did you find Molly?" My heart raced.

"What time? I'm not sure."

"Tell me exactly what happened."

Perhaps the urgency in my voice frightened her. Or my intensity made her nervous. She stepped backward as if re-establishing her personal space. With one hand, she flipped a clump of stray hair off her shoulder to her back. "That was weeks ago."

"Please, Amber. It might be important."

She fidgeted. "Well, um, Tommy picked me up at my dad's after he got off work. We were going to visit friends. In Modesto. The sun set just before we left the house, but it was still light out. You know, twilight. We stopped to see if I got any mail 'cause I expected something from college. This dog came running from that direction."

Amber pointed to her right. "We didn't see where she came from, but her ears were pinned down and she ran real hard like she was scared. She wouldn't come to us at first, but Tommy caught hold of her. That's when we saw she didn't have any dog tags." She looked down. "We were kind of in a hurry. Tommy said we should take her with us since we had no idea where she came from. I don't know if we did the right thing or not." She peeked at me through thick lashes.

"You took good care of her. Thank you."

A slight flush spread over her face when she smiled.

"Did you see anyone? Then or just afterward? On the street or in the Paynes' driveway? Anyone at all?"

She cocked her head. "No. Otherwise, we would've asked them about the dog."

"Did you notice anything unusual while you stood there that night? Did you hear anything? Think hard now."

"We did hear something. I don't know what, though. Just before we, um, got the dog into the car. Three pops—two close together and one later. Kind of faint and far away. *Pop*, then a couple seconds *pop* again. Tommy said, 'That sounded like a gun.' Then we heard one more pop. I don't know because I never heard a gun before, except on TV, of course."

"Amber, think about what you saw. Was there a vehicle at the Payne's that night?"

"You mean a car?"

I nodded.

She dropped her lids shut again. Seconds passed while she searched her memory. Her eyelids fluttered open. "Um. Actually, there were two. A white truck and a big brown car."

42

Chapter Forty-two

According to the article that appeared in the local newspaper, Amber Cervine and Thomas Dale individually and voluntarily gave statements at the sheriff's office the next day. Two crucial puzzle pieces dropped into place, gift-wrapped from above. Lila did not shoot herself. Three shots made a high probability that someone else shot her. More importantly, along with Helen's previous confession that she drove the Buick to Sierra Meadows, Amber's testimony about seeing two cars at roughly the same time she heard the gunshots provided sufficient proof that Helen and Will were both present when Lila died.

Newspapers continued to report on the daily minutia of the case. Jesse and I read the reports and discussed them each morning. Silverthorne stayed busy wrapping up loose ends with Deputy Dunn, and we didn't see him for a week.

At first, Helen blamed Lila's murder on Alan and vice versa. But no one ever came forward with a single shred of evidence to place Alan at the scene. Then Helen claimed that Will shot Lila. Changing her story so many times, Helen diminished her credibility significantly. Besides, there was the matter of the unregistered revolver Helen held on me in the attic—the same caliber as the gun that killed Lila. The likelihood that a jury of Helen's peers would believe her latest version appeared doubtful. Her attorney advised her to admit her culpability.

At the end of a week in jail, Helen conceded to the evidence stacked against her and confessed to Lila's murder. After her sentencing, the newspaper ran excerpts from her taped confession, in which she acknowledged that she had made the plan, shot Lila, and convinced Will to burn the body. She steadfastly refused to accept blame for the hit-and-run of little Marcus Whitney, though. That, she maintained, didn't count—being purely accidental.

We visited Will Payne at the hospital nearly every day. Ed and Zora Jane came with us. Will's progress was slow. Sometimes we assisted with his treatments, but mostly we stood helplessly by, watching him struggle. They kept him sedated as much as possible. The stroke had paralyzed his right side, so he couldn't talk. After a week, they moved him out of ICU, but he slept through most of our visits.

During one of our walks in the hall to stretch our legs, Jesse and I happened on the lady we had observed in Rosita's—the one with the huge red purse full of food. I tugged Jesse's sleeve. "Don't look. It's her."

Jesse looked anyway and his eyes widened.

My imagination revved into high gear. "She's wearing a hospital gown, so she's a patient here. She got caught stealing food from the cafeteria but had a heart attack when they tried to arrest her."

Jesse reprimanded me with a glare over his glasses. "You never quit, do you?"

"Okay. How about this one? She's freeloading off the hospital. Lives here and steals their food."

Jesse chuckled. "That one's wild, even for you."

By that time, we'd ambled several yards past her. Without warning, Jesse spun on his heel and marched back to where she leaned against the wall. I couldn't believe my eyes. Too mortified to follow, I shuffled from one foot to the other, waiting without openly peeking at them.

While I stewed, they conducted a short conversation. The woman pointed. Jesse nodded and returned to where I paced. He took my arm and guided me down the hall.

I couldn't stand it another second. "Did you ask what she's doing here?"

He grinned.

"I know you did. What did she say?"

"She said," he faced me, expression serious. "You must quit snooping into everyone's affairs or she's going to sue you for harassment."

I punched Jesse's arm. "She did not! Come on."

Jesse rubbed his arm, a smile playing on his lips. "What she actually said was, 'The cafeteria is just down the hall.' Gotcha!"

❧

One afternoon, with all four of us gathered around Will's bed, Jesse said, "It's amazing how the story of Lila and Will turned out, isn't it?"

The way the two disappearances intertwined amazed me. "If Molly hadn't gone missing, I doubt we'd have stayed interested enough to hang in there until they found Lila."

Zora Jane sighed. "Such a sad story."

For a second, I feared they might blame me for not rescuing Lila. My failure in that department still stung. Would I ever fully forgive myself for not getting to her before it was too late?

Will didn't usually acknowledge our presence. At that moment, his steely eyes were closed, and he appeared to be sleeping. Jesse watched our nearest neighbor with a thoughtful expression. "They made some rotten choices, didn't they?"

I nodded, considering the pain inherent in everyone's life.

Ed stared at Will. "Some people get all tangled up in their misery, though, and they never get out."

Russell Silverthorne's entrance interrupted our analysis. "Came to say good-bye. Time to head back to Iowa." Jesse dragged a chair from the hall. When Silverthorne had settled in it, he laced his fingers in his lap and stared downward, chin quivering slightly.

I patted his arm. "I bet your wife will be glad to see you."

When he glanced up, tears had pooled in his eyes. "Especially since I'm coming back free. Now that I know what happened to Baby Blue, we can get on with our lives."

Jesse extended his hand. "We sure appreciate what you did. Wouldn't have happened without you."

Silverthorne gripped Jesse's hand. "Nor you four."

Ed slapped Silverthorne's shoulder and left his hand resting there. The three men seemed reluctant to disconnect.

I sensed a group hug coming. "You're going to make me cry too."

"Oh." Silverthorne chuckled. "Don't want that. Anyway, the DNA results finally came back."

Jesse arched his eyebrows. "DNA?"

I'd forgotten about that.

Ed leaned forward. "I wondered about the DNA."

Silverthorne's blue eyes twinkled. "They matched Baby Blue with Lila."

"Sure," Jesse said.

That was a no-brainer. "Of course."

Zora Jane nodded.

Silverthorne grinned. "We all expected that part."

What was he saying? "Is there more?"

He paused.

We collectively tensed.

"Also, Will Payne's DNA came back as a positive match to Lila's." He looked at each of us, turning last to Will's quiet form resting between the white sheets. "Pretty sure that means Lila Kliner was Will's daughter."

Will's delicate eyelids fluttered.

I bent over him. "Did you hear what Mr. Silverthorne just said? Lila was your daughter."

Will didn't open his eyes, but he bobbed his head up and down a couple of times. Then gravelly words tumbled out, low and slow. "Thought so."

A soft murmur rippled around the bed.

"You thought so?" I leaned closer. "Is that what you said?"

He blinked his steely eyes open, looking from one face to the next. "Met Lila's ma at a farm show in Des Moines one summer." He closed his eyes again and shook his head. "Never should've gone without the wife."

All eyes in the room registered shock.

I could hardly believe my ears. "Did you and Lila discuss that?"

William Payne opened his eyes a slit—just enough so I could see the familiar glint. "Didn't need to. She looked just like her ma."

The highlights and lowlights of the Payne tragedy flickered across my mental movie screen. All that misery could have been avoided if they had been able to communicate.

I shook my head. Relationships. Was anything in all creation more difficult to do the way God intended?

I met Jesse's gaze across the bed and our hearts connected.

Waiting for Jesse to return on the day Molly went missing, I whipped up a batch of his favorite chicken lasagna. I inherited this recipe from my mother, an outstanding cook.

2 Tbsp. butter or margarine

3 Tbsp. unbleached flour

1 can chicken broth (no fat)

2 C. nonfat milk

1 large clove garlic (minced)

½ tsp. salt

1/8 tsp. pepper

2 tsp. nutmeg

½ C. fresh mushrooms (sliced and sautéed)

½ C. chopped green onion

½ C. non-fat sour cream

½ C. low-fat mayonnaise

12 lasagna noodles (cooked)

3 lb. chicken (boiled, skinned, boned) fat removed and shredded (3 C)

8 oz. Reduced fat sharp cheddar cheese shredded (2 C)

8 oz. Reduced fat jack cheese, shredded (2 C)

Parmesan cheese, grated

Preheat oven to 350 degrees. Melt butter or margarine in saucepan. Add flour and stir over medium heat 1 minute. Do not brown. Add broth and milk and stir over medium heat with wire whisk until mixture comes to a boil. Add garlic, salt, pepper and mushrooms. Cook 1 minute. Remove from heat and stir in sour cream and mayonnaise. Spray 13" x 9" lasagna pan with PAM. Layer one-third noodles, one-third chicken, one-third sauce, and one-third cheese. Sprinkle with one-third green onions and nutmeg. Repeat two more layers. Sprinkle Parmesan cheese on top and bake for 30 minutes until bubbly. Let rest for 5 minutes before serving. Makes 8 servings.

**I modify this recipe depending on what I have on hand. Sometimes I add grated carrots, or layer in well-drained cooked spinach. I may also use uncooked lasagna noodles, increasing the liquid so the noodles soften in the oven.

ACKNOWLEDGMENTS

Until I slugged through six years of writing and rewriting this book, I never understood the collaborative aspect of authorship. Creating a novel requires a large, fluid team. The writer merely strings words together to make a story. God sends ideas, encouragement, training, and sometimes inspiration through various channels at the appropriate times. I appreciate your contributions, so I have tried to remember all your names.

God's wise design of family functions best as fertile ground to nurture the dreams we don't speak of in public. But for their support, I never would have taken the necessary baby steps to get started. My husband, Bob Leggitt, never said *no* to the needs of my writing obsession, even when it meant no dinner on the table or folding his own laundry. My faithful cheerleader and firstborn child, Jule Wright, read each revision with enthusiasm and even sponsored one of my visits to a writer's conference. Son, Jason Leggitt and his wife Angie, provided a real writer's iMac—a dream machine. My father-in-law, Dale Harman, never let me off the hook. If I wanted to be a writer, then why didn't I write? Sister-in-law, Merrilee Leggitt, trusted me with a *Thesaurus for the Extraordinarily Literate* bearing her inscription to the family author and critiqued one or two drafts. My fabulous sisters—Toni Deaville and Patty Little—begged for more after reading one draft of this book. My sweetheart Pop, Gene Rogers—formerly employed by the San Bernardino County Sheriff's Office—explained just enough about the complex world of the sheriff's department to keep me on the right track. I also thank Gary Wright and Jerry Leggitt for supplying just-right words of support.

Friends and acquaintances played important roles, as well. God answered the prayers of Virginia and Ben Coats, Dan and Kathleen Prout, Sandy Balaam and Maxine Arvidson, helping me understand that God's story must be part of every story. My sweet friend, Vickie Quiarte, suggested I take the manuscript to the writer's conference at Mount Hermon. Neighbors Sarah and Mike Wynn boosted my morale and imparted information regarding local law enforcement. Donna Nelson at the Nevada County Sheriff's Office and Debbie Harris, Crime Scene Investigator from the San Bernardino County Sheriff's Office supplied technical details.

At the 2006 Mount Hermon Christian Writers Conference, I was introduced to writing as a craft. The wonderful network of Christian authors I discovered there planted the desire-for-excellence seed in my heart. In that fertile mountain soil, it sprouted immediately. I offer much gratitude to the beautiful and talented author Brandilyn Collins for being truthful without breaking my spirit in my first critique. She saw a story " hiding behind too many words." Author Nancy Farrier, my Mount Hermon first-timer buddy, consoled me afterward. Sherry Kyle, my first writer friend, became a sounding board for my walk through this process.

Head bulging with new ideas, I rewrote the manuscript and tentatively submitted the first three chapters at the 2006 Mount Hermon Writers Clinic in the fall. Oceans of thanks to our critique group leader, the astute and tactful author/editor/publisher Karen Ball. Her interest in my work and accessibility as a mentor spurred me onward. To our fabulous critique group—Jackie Strange, Beth Self, Sandra Lee Smith, Lizette Vega, John Clarke, Nancy Ellen Hird, and the unbelievable nice guy, Techno-Thriller author Austin Boyd—who contributed interesting new insights, a giant thank you.

I rewrote the manuscript again along with the first three chapters of *The Dunn Deal,* and attended the 2007 Mount Hermon Christian Writers Conference. There I met the marvelous and creative author, Susanne Lakin—winner of the 2009 Zondervan Writing Contest for

Someone to Blame. After the conference, she read the fourth version of *Payne & Misery*. Her right-on suggestions jumpstarted my fervor for writing at a time I felt overwhelmed by the massive remedial work my manuscript still required. Two more visits to writer's conferences, professional editing, and several online writing courses led to six more rewrites. Through it all, Susanne has relentlessly spurred me forward and challenged me to reach ever higher. She continues to bless my life with ready wisdom, a perpetual fountain of knowledge and experience. The idea for the *new* first chapter came from her. I cherish her friendship as a precious treasure.

Another author in our Mount Hermon critique group, the witty Renae Brumbaugh, also faithfully read and critiqued my manuscript.

My incredible content editor at Glass Road Public Relations, Jessica Doty, contributed sparkly suggestions; line editor, John Leatherman, polished the grammar; and Rebeca Seitz of Glass Road gave good counsel.

The Valley Springs Book Club called me *author* before I dared refer to myself by that esteemed moniker and contributed a generous financial gift. Thank you to Janna Schumacher, Sandy Pendley, Michelle Erbeck, Lonnie Reid, Laurel Jolliff, Gael Mitchell, Susie Gossett, Danielle Byerly, Laurie Johnson, Carla Zermeno, and Kim Campos.

The sweet ladies in the Stockton Day Women's Bible Study Fellowship leaders' circle, led by the inimitable Pam Regan, were a constant inspiration and example. You have taught me much about patience and perseverance. Thank you for your faithful prayers and encouragement.

To the gracious judges of the Westbow Press Writing Contest where *Payne & Misery* came in second place—particularly to the wonderful author and mentor Kathi Macias—may I say what an honor to be singled out and encouraged by your praise. I am grateful for the able assistance of the editors and production staff at WestBow Press who first published this manuscript.

To Rochelle Carter of Ellechor Publishing House, who fulfilled my dream of having all three of Christine Sterling's adventures published together, I offer much gratitude. May God bless the work of your hands.

To my generous benefactors who wish to remain anonymous, your reward will surely be in heaven. Thank you for believing in me and in this project enough to invest in it.

Most thanks of all to my Lord and Savior Jesus Christ. You who hung the stars in space, your creativity knows no bounds. Thank you for sharing this tiny bit with me and for letting me have such fun discovering it.

DISCUSSION QUESTIONS

1. Christine Sterling learned that pain is an inevitable part of life, but misery is a choice. How did Will Payne's choices lead him down the path of misery? How about Lila Kliner's choices? Helen's? Alan's?
2. When Christine focused on what was missing from her relationship with Jesse, she considered her marriage convoluted and troubled. With God's help, she let go of complaining and saw a change in her relationship. Where are you complaining about what you don't have—choosing misery—instead of being thankful for what God provides?
3. Christine discovered that God had been answering her prayers all along. She simply hadn't acknowledged his presence or given him credit. Does God care about the details of your daily life? Does he listen to your prayers? How do you know? Can you think of a time God answered your prayer?
4. Christine's impulsive nature landed her in trouble more than once. Have you ever jumped into a situation without planning or praying beforehand? What happened?
5. Christine's motives for wanting to help Lila Kliner were noble and good, but what do you think about her methods? Were you bothered by the predicaments that resulted from her snoopiness? Does the end justify the means?
6. God seems to have built waiting into his world. Christine struggled with waiting, often allowing her impatience to prod her into action. How do you handle waiting? What's your attitude toward waiting?
7. Zora Jane Callahan wanted everyone to know about Jesus. Would boldness like hers draw people to God or

push them away? What kind of witness does God call us to be in the world?

8. Whether you agree with her methods or not, when faced with someone who needed help, Christine did move toward serving someone in need, regardless of the personal cost. What do you do when you meet people in need? What about the people who beg on the streets? Do you offer them assistance? Why or why not? Bessie Parrish, the older woman who spoke at Christine's church, took food to the homeless teens living in the local park. What can you do about the homelessness problem?
9. Christine struggled with finding meaning and purpose in her retirement years. Do you wonder what your purpose is? How can you discover what God would have you do in whatever stage of life you find yourself?
10. Did you see yourself in any of the characters in this book? Which character did you identify with the most?

ENJOY A SAMPLE FROM BOOK 2 IN THE CHRISTINE STERLING MYSTERY SERIES

THE DUNN DEAL

The sketchy details of Baxter Dunn's death dribbled into my brain as I struggled to organize them. Across my mental movie screen flashed a hideous image of his mangled body strapped onto a stretcher being dragged from a remote ravine. Shivers rocketed down my spine and the bottom dropped out of my stomach. None of it made sense.

Shaking my head to clear the haze, I forced myself back to the present. Socially appropriate words passed my lips. "I'm so sorry." How inadequate they must sound. "So very, very sorry." Would repetition make them more effective?

Zora Jane Callahan blew her nose on a soggy tissue, honking a bit louder than normal for a classy woman. No one would hold that against her—not with her beloved son-in-law lying dead on a slab in the morgue.

Words alternating with sobs rolled out of her like stormy waves. "What about the children? They need him. He's so good with them and they love him so much. What will they do without him?"

I'd never heard the name Baxter Dunn drop from my best friend's lips without words of praise or thanks to God attached. I mumbled another string of powerless words. "He was an extraordinary man." When I reached toward her, she dissolved into my arms.

As this latest wave of sorrow trickled away, she pulled back to grab another tissue. "I started praying for him when I rocked Kathleen to sleep as a baby. I asked God to prepare a man for my daughter—a God-fearing man to cherish her and bring out the best in her—a man to be the spiritual leader in their home, generous and compassionate. God answered every one of my prayers when he gave us Baxter."

I nodded, feeling older and more useless than my fifty-six years warranted.

Fresh tears flowed when she wailed, "What will Kathleen do now?"

At stressful times, I usually babble. But right now, I could only wield a Kleenex box. What words would be comforting? I'd never be able to cope if this happened to one of my children. I held her and prayed she would soon remember God's sovereignty and ultimate goodness, although I couldn't see how even God could bring good from this tragedy.

As each new detail reached us, I wrestled all over again to reconcile the reality, unable to grasp the finality of such devastating news. The high-speed car chase. A fall from a high cliff. Impaled on a rusty spike. The terrible scene of Baxter's untimely death lurked behind my eyelids, making me afraid to close my eyes. I might never sleep again. Maybe it wasn't true. Maybe someone else's body had been discovered in that ravine. Please, God. Make it all go away.

Once I reached home, I pummeled my husband Jesse with my questions. "Where was God? What kind of God separates a father from his little children? From his family?"

Jesse held me, rocking from side to side. "These foothills should have been heaven on earth. That was the plan." Yet two murders had intruded on our lives in less than four short years. Who could have predicted such atrocities? Our nearest neighbor, Lila Payne, was murdered under bizarre circumstances and now the son-in-law of our best friends.

Someone was to blame. It must be Jesse's fault. He convinced me that this quiet place in the country—fourteen wooded acres in California's Sierra Nevada foothills—would buffet us from the world's craziness. Retirement offered the opportunity to leave the noise and pollution behind in Southern California and look what happened. We'd moved to a place where neighbors got murdered. Railing against Jesse, screaming and pounding my fists on his chest might make me feel better. But deep down I knew it couldn't be Jesse's fault. "Guess we wouldn't be safe anywhere these days."

Jesse answered with a slow shake of his head.

I scanned his face. The sparkle had drained from his hazel eyes. This horrible event had aged him in mere hours. A solitary tear squeezed out the corner of one eye and trickled down his cheek. I reached up to wipe it away. My emotions dissolved with the tear. How could I stay angry with such a tenderhearted man?

The dreadful reality of Baxter's death settled on our community like a dense paralyzing fog. No one could believe such a thing could happen to this dedicated young deputy. Soft spoken, caring, exactly the sort every mother hopes her son will grow up to become.

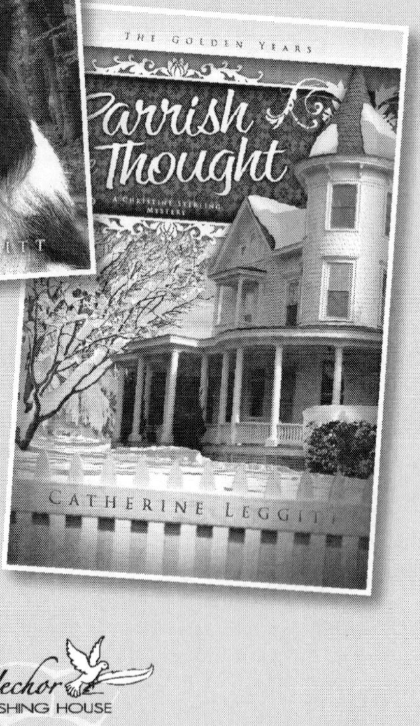

Catherine Leggitt welcomes comments, ideas, impressions, and questions at: www.catherineleggitt.com or c.leggitt@aol.com